The Odyssey of Zalaman Aszer

Life and Death Under the Tsar

A Novel by

Jim Belson

This is a work of fiction. All characters, organizations, and events portrayed in this novel are either products of the author's imagination or are used fictitiously.

For information regarding permission, please write to:
info@barringerpublishing.com
Barringer Publishing, Naples, Florida
www.barringerpublishing.com

Cover, graphics, and layout by Linda S. Duider
Cape Coral, Florida

Author photograph by Sara Risher

ISBN: 978-1-954396-52-4
Library of Congress Cataloging-in-Publication Data
The Odyssey of Zalaman Aszer / Jim Belson

Printed in U.S.A.

For my mother, Florence Belson,
bringer of love and books.

TABLE OF CONTENTS

Foreword

Aside from a few low hills to the east, the world surrounding 19th century Lahkvna is relatively flat with vast forests and small woodlands interrupted by plains and meadows, punctuated by the occasional swamp. It's a patchwork land, sectioned off into rows conforming to the human geometry of plowing—centuries of it. The rows are sometimes straight, sometimes meandering, tracing rivers and streams, flexing around protrusions of the rocky deposits of ancient seismic activity. In the fields, spring and on into summer, when the rivers flowing to the Gulf of Riga are high with rain from the Baltic heavens, potatoes, onions, turnips, carrots, and cabbages are watered through irrigation ditches. Silver birches and grey willows line these streams and rivers, too. One of them, the Abava, wanders right through Lahkvna before emptying into the Baltic Sea.

In Lahkvna, a *shtetl* in the Courland region of what is Latvia today, everything points to the west—the fields and trees and, eventually, the sea. To the east, north and south, Lahkvna, a settlement in the Pale of Settlements, is encircled, not to say embraced, by the larger, Christian town, Navharadak.

The houses, shops, and stables in Lahkvna have a ramshackle look, crumbling here, patched there, because the Tsar has decreed there shall be no new building in the *shtetls*. The streets are a maze of narrow, bumpy alleys with stone gutters and plank sidewalks that go right up to the hutments and lean-tos; buildings that seem to kneel in submission to the cold north wind from the Bay. The lanes radiate out from the *kvadrat*.

As in other *shtetls*, Lahkvna is dominated by its *kvadrat*, a central market and square. From dawn to dusk, it is bustling with life—vibrant despite, or because of, the Tsar's decrees, depending on your allegiances. Six days a week the *kvadrat* is the stage for farmers and peddlers with their wagons and dray animals and their customers seeking turnips and wisdom. There are newly liberated serfs and there are Christians from Navharadak whose business the Jews cherish, though they complain about how the Christians are not interested in quality, only a bargain.

From dusk to dawn, there is pre-industrial darkness and a quiet broken only by lowing, whinnying or the cry of a wild animal.

Under all the activity, the surface of the *kvadrat* is a confusion of warped wooden planks, stones, and hard-packed earth. When the Baltic breezes fade, Lahkvna reverts to its normal state: damp. At its soggiest, the rain and fog mix with a wealth of deposits from the many beasts of burden—horses, oxen, donkeys—pulling their produce, craftwork, and tools, even manufactured goods from distant cities. But looking closely, when cleared of the muck, you would see that the floor of the *kvadrat* was dirt compacted between stones of various sizes, flattened and smoothed by centuries of grinding, load-bearing wheels, shod hooves and the shod feet of men and women walking, children playing, some occasionally stopping to hear stories from neighbors, especially Osher and Henzel, the sages of Lahkvna—stories that mix the newsworthy with teachings of the *rebbes*, gossip that weaves life into parable.

CHAPTER ONE

The Chapper

That summer day, in 1866, when the chapper came for Zalaman, he hadn't had a sip. He'd considered it. From time to time, over the course of the previous winter and spring, he'd developed a habit of taking little sips. *Krupnik*, mostly. And from time to time, his father would think he smelled it on his breath and scold him, warning him he would become an *alkoholiker*. Zalaman feigned innocence, assuring his father it was simply the fragrance of the shop—a residue that saturated everything. Perhaps Jossel wasn't convinced. He couldn't be sure. He just said his youngest son was too young to drink alcohol. But he was old enough to help in his dispensary, where he tried to act like his father pouring out *krupnik* and other intoxicating liquids for Christians (and the random Jew) on Sundays and now, even on some weekdays when Christians operated their own shops. Last year, Zalaman's father had received a special permit from the Trade Commissioner of Navharadak, the Christian city surrounding the *shtetl* of Lahkvna, allowing him to open this business. All under the protection of the Tsar, which was an unusual situation for a *shtetl* Jew of the Pale but not out of keeping with other decrees of Alexander II and his law that made possible Jossel's elevation from peddler to shopkeeper.

Big for his thirteen years, Zalaman swept the floor and rolled heavy, wooden barrels and tried to be endearing to Papa's customers. A sip or, at most, two of *krupnik* made the work more amusing. Three sips would make the work more difficult, especially the rolling of barrels without their toppling over or the handling of jars without breaking them.

But this day, when his older, more pious, and studious brother, Davin, had been excused for the day, Zalaman hadn't had a sip. There were no customers, just him and Papa, when the two holy men entered Jossel's shop, sporting beards and with robes down to their sandaled feet. Introducing themselves as Brothers Ginter and Natan, they asked him to fill their flasks with *krupnik*, claiming *krupnik* was a drink the Benedictines had themselves invented centuries ago, mixing honey in their vodka. Jossel thought the monks looked like members of *some* Christian order, but Benedictines?

Zalaman translated his father's puzzled look to mean, "Aren't Benedictines a wealthy order? Don't they wear nicer robes?" Zalaman studied the monks' rough-sewn garments, but this was neither the first time he'd seen monks looking the worse for wear, nor was it the first time Christian brothers had come to Jossel looking for something stronger than sacramental wine.

It was the monks' coins that did the trick. Once they jiggled the bags of copper, it was all caution to the wind. Their personal story was no concern of his. Jossel said it would be an honor if the holy brothers would like a taste to test the quality. The 'free sip' from time immemorial was the universal come-on that encourages return buyers as Jossel had explained to his son. And Zalaman had witnessed how the practice encouraged first-time sales, as well. The monks thanked Jossel. Brother Natan claimed he had heard of the quality of Jossel's alcohol and said Jossel was well-regarded, a trusted purveyor of that drink that was the order's very own creation. The way Brother Natan said so reminded Zalaman of Davin when Davin would excuse himself from work to study, telling Papa he had to talk to the *rebbe*, when Zalaman knew his brother was going to meet Ev in the *kvadrat* so they could watch girls and talk about the Holy Land. If Zalaman had wondered whether his Papa would offer these bedraggled holy men a free sip, once Brother Natan jiggled the ban of coins, the son knew his father would not only offer the free sip, but that he would do so with enthusiasm.

Jossel led the monks to the rear of the shop, while Zalaman stayed up front, supposedly sweeping the floor and where he thought he might take advantage of being alone and have a little sip of the Benedictines' creation from the jar he kept hidden away for just such opportunities. His father and the monks were talking loudly and laughing in the back of the shop as he fumbled for the hidden jar when he was seized from behind without warning, a gag stuffed in his mouth before he had a chance to scream. He was held in a viselike grip by someone with strong arms and nimble hands who dragged him out the door and onto the street.

It was broad daylight, but Jossel's shop was in a little-used back alley, so the abduction went unnoticed. Even if it had been noticed, there would have been a good chance that any passersby would have looked the other way, pretending not to see. This dissembling was not due to lack of fellow feeling—the good people of Lahkvna cared about and for one another—so much as a healthy interest in self-preservation. Such a flagrant kidnapping was likely the work of a *chapper* and, thus, had probably been sanctioned by the *kahal*, the town council of Lahkvna. The *chapper* might even have been council-appointed. There was a quota system laid out in The Liberator's edict regarding conscriptions—a system that contributed to uneasy relations between neighbors, people who might think to protect their own young sons at the expense of others. The *kahal* was really nothing more than a government-sponsored community council charged with interpreting the Tsar's rules, in this case, the rules concerning quotas for human sacrifice.

So Zalaman was the victim of a flawlessly executed kidnapping—audacious, in bright daylight, very professional, accomplished in seconds. The *chapper* knew his business, quickly wrapping Zalaman up tightly in a smelly blanket that he dumped into the back of his horse-drawn cart.

As the cart rumbled away, Zalaman was too tightly bound and gagged to muster any protest. He couldn't see a thing; it was dark as night inside the rolled-up carpet. The gag in his mouth was the worst part. He couldn't struggle against his bonds because he had to devote all his efforts to avoid suffocation. While the cart bounced down the road, out of Lahkvna, the primary struggle was the effort to breathe.

Then there were no more thoughts. He passed out of awareness and was asleep for an hour or perhaps only a few seconds; he wasn't sure when the bumping woke him.

Despite being rolled up in the rug like wurst in a bun, his body was not well-cushioned. In addition to the bouncing and thumping, the wheels of the chapper's cart slid around on whatever sort of track they were on and the rug that encased him would roll from side to side making him feel dizzy and, at the same time, like he was being strangled.

The cart slowed and he was able to work his head into a better position. It was a painful process, but now he could see light through the tunnel of rug. It wasn't much but it was the world and it allowed him to try to calm himself. He thought about his parents. They would panic and they would rescue him, he told himself, though he knew better. It had to be a *chapper*, someone he'd been warned about his whole life. *Chappers* had been one of the reasons most frequently cited by his parents—second only to creditors—for the semi-nomadic existence they'd led up until not that many years ago. Now they were permanently settled in Lahkvna and maybe they'd grown too complacent. He was close to the age the Tsar preferred. He passed out again, still trying to convince himself that Jossel and Lael, Mama, would know what to do.

The *chapper* reined in his horse to a slower gait, giving the animal a blow. He was convinced they were far enough from Lahkvna now that he could relax a bit. The rules of the *chappering* profession had been ordained by the Russian Tsar,

Alexander II, "The Liberator." As he had been told many times by parents and more than once by friends about the disappearance of an acquaintance, the rule said that every year every *shtetl* owed the Tsar a minimum number of young male recruits for service in the Russian army. Serving in that army, at least for raw and expendable recruits, was a death sentence. Even Polish volunteers rarely returned. And no one had ever heard of anyone returning after having been taken by a *chapper*. Parents in every *shtetl* lived with the completely rational fear of their children disappearing. Boys even younger than Zalaman were snatched.

The routes of Zalaman's nomadic life as a child had been largely determined by reports of *chapper* activity. For the last three years, his family had settled down in Lahkvna, where Osher and Henzel, the two gossip-sages of the *kvadrat*, talked about a nine-year-old who had been taken. Zalaman's friends seemed to agree that these abductions were, more or less, death warrants. If you didn't die in battle, you just died a bit later from an infection you'd acquired in battle. Or, if a bullet or a festering wound didn't do the trick, there was always starvation and freezing cold. So, there were many stories the children shared about opportunities to die in the Tsar's army, the kind that find their way into your nightmare.

Zalaman thought perhaps this was just a nightmare, but the pain from being so tightly, suffocatingly bound destroyed that hope. There were stories shared by Osher and Henzel about abducted boys who managed—miraculously—to live for many years. When Zalaman had heard such stories, he hadn't been able to avoid noticing how older and wiser people wrinkled their brows in disbelief. There was one constant in these stories (and 'stories' he knew they were): the boy who returned had been away from home for so many years that he neither remembered where he had come from nor even who he truly was. That's the part that made Zalaman question those stories, not the frowns of the adults, for how could you ever forget where you came from or who you were?

The fact that neither Papa nor Mama would be able to rescue him, did not seem possible. This couldn't be real. He was dying of thirst, gasping for air which, when he managed to take a reasonable gulp, filled his mouth with dirt and who-knows-what debris from the fabric of his cocoon. He tried taking quick shallow breaths and he felt a little better. He repeated a story Mama had once told him about an abducted child who was eventually raised by a king and given fabulous riches. The story was from one of Mama's romances, but it provided a welcome fantasy. Coming from Mama, it had a temporary, if strained believability. Zalaman's thoughts turned to dying and he became frantic then burst into tears. He cried for himself, his family, for his friends, Aron and Ev, who were likely right now studying in the *shul*. Zalaman wasn't happy there, wasn't able to have any fun there, but, at the moment, it seemed a splendid oasis of safety. Papa wanted to know what 'fun' had to do with the price of potatoes. The memory helped Zalaman stop his tears. Snot was exacerbating his breathing problem. He reminded himself that he was thirteen years old now and he shouldn't be crying like a baby. He would look for a chance to escape and take it, if one came, though there were no current prospects.

As the cart slowed, it turned onto a more uneven trail, where the jolts came less frequently but were sharper when they did. The vehicle would lean this way and then that, yanking him about on the wooden floor. The rug in which he was wrapped softened the jabs from the studded iron nails he kept rolling over, but with each lurch they bit deeper. He figured the *chapper* had left the main road, which would make it tricky for anyone giving chase. Davin! Zalaman thought his brother would probably try to track him down. Not Papa. Papa was brave, but he referred to himself as a realist and then it struck Zalaman that in an unforeseeable way, his Papa may have been responsible for this—for his own son's death! When Jossel had assumed his new position—thanks to his friend the Trade Commissioner, a valuable relationship which Zalaman and his mother had played a big role in forging—they all hoped it might offer the Aszers extra protection from threats like chappers. The Aszers were respected. But maybe this hope had made him careless. The local authorities exercised some degree of power over the *chappers,* but they rarely interfered with their awful, lawful work.

Many on the *kahal* profited, including some of the elders. The fact that his papa had become well-known had put them in greater jeopardy, exposing them in a brighter light. Envy might have played a part.

Zalaman didn't know how many times he'd passed out and slept, but when he eventually came back into his own head, the pain in his wrists and arms and neck and throat were still there, but the initial panic had subsided. He tried hard to think about his situation, tried it as a tactic to avoid thinking about his painful thirst. He supposed the *chapper* who had abducted him was likely the same man who was driving the cart. Judging by the ease with which he'd bound and gagged and dragged him, he must be large and dangerous. He was likely to stay off the main road to avoid anyone who might be giving chase. Zalaman's only hope of not dying of thirst was that the *chapper* would not want to deliver the Cossacks a dead body. He imagined his mama and little sister, Keila, shedding tears over him. Would they be angry with him for his carelessness? He could imagine Mama berating Papa for falling for the *chapper's* tricks and certainly the bearded priests were there to distract Papa. Unless he left to find him, Davin would do his best to console them. They would try to reassure one another, perhaps find some hope in discredited stories about child conscripts returning home.

><

In fact, Jossel and Lael and Keila were at home in their house in Lahkvna. Jossel was trying to comfort his wife and daughter with precisely such a hopeful story, but Lael was distraught to the point of hysteria. She would not deceive herself with stupid fables. "Such things happen only in romances," she said to him. "You know better. Hope has to come from elsewhere. Perhaps Davin . . ."

Davin had been walking toward his father's alcohol dispensary when he noticed the man. It was the man's size and quickness that drew his attention—that and the way he deposited a very heavy rug into a horse-drawn cart and then drove off. He paid it little mind until he got to the shop and found his father wondering aloud about Zalaman having disappeared. What did he mean 'disappeared?'

"He was right here!" Jossel swore.

"A *chapper*," Davin said, realizing at once what he had just witnessed. His little brother was rolled up in that rug. "I'm going to get him," he said. And that was all he said before he was off and running to the stable around the corner where the Aszers kept Marengo, their one healthy horse.

Jossel didn't know how Davin thought he was going to be able to rescue his little brother, but he knew in his sinking heart that Davin was right. It seemed so obvious now. Those fake monks. He locked up the shop and went home.

"They were supposed to be clerics of some sort," he sobbed to Lael. They cried for a while and were joined by Keila who had confidence Davin would bring him home.

"They were too friendly. I should have known," Jossel reproached himself as Lael moaned and held her head. "Their jokes made me suspicious. I started feeling like they were not really there to make a purchase at all. And so, they've disappeared as has Zalaman, although it was not the monks who did the actual *chappering*. They were there as a distraction, working with the *chapper*, and they were damned good at it! Of course, we don't know for sure what has happened," he said, but Lael would not be comforted.

"Yes, but Davin ran off without knowing about the fake monks. It might have helped," she said. Jossel hugged her closely.

Davin didn't bother with a saddle. He rode off in the direction from Lahkvna and skirted the small, Christian city of Navharadak that held Lahkvna in its friendly but firm grasp.

The fake monks were driving their rickety old carriage on the route agreed upon, toward a spot where they would meet the *chapper* business partner, who would be carting the boy off to the Russians and collect their due. Ginter, the younger one, was laughing and praising his partner's work and congratulating the two of them on having fulfilled their mission, their part of the bargain, creating the diversion that would allow Georg to do his dirty work: grab the little Jewish recruit in full daylight without creating a commotion. Once they got to the designated spot, a wooded area outside Navharadak, they would collect the second half of their fee.

"Successful performance?" Natan said to Ginter. "It was more than that—it was *brilliant*."

"Did you hear how the old Hebrew would laugh as loud as we did? He created more noise than we did. He couldn't have been more patronizing."

"Well, that's what he's supposed to be. But yes, it was like having an accomplice."

Natan and Ginter approached the designated spot and were disappointed to find that Georg, who should have been there before them, had not yet arrived. They sat in their carriage, still in their monkish costumes, but they didn't wait long before Ginter asked the question. Was there a chance Georg had simply kept going, anxious to get wherever he had to go with his human cargo? Might he just have driven on without stopping and try to avoid paying them what was their due?

"He's come through for us in the past," Natan reminded him. So, they waited. "But do you think he's fucked us?" Ginter asked after they'd been waiting too long.

"So, it appears," Natan answered grudgingly, angrily, turning their rickety old carriage back toward Navharadak. "He should have been here by now. There's no need to wait any longer. We'll collect . . . somehow, sometime."

"I don't know about that," said the younger and needier. "I say we chase him. Once we catch him, we'll make him pay on the spot or we'll take the boy ourselves. We could probably get more from the Cossacks than Georg would pay us—*if* he pays."

"It doesn't work that way," Natan said. "You've never dealt with the Cossacks. Besides, we'd never catch him with this nag and in this carriage. And Georg is big. He's dangerous."

"But there are two of us."

"And he's devious. We're no match for him," Ginter spat. He could take Georg in a fight. And he could be just as devious.

But, then, right in front of Natan and Ginter appeared a young man crouching alongside a horse. Natan slowed the creaking vehicle right up to the youngster there by the side of the road, holding the reins of a nice-looking horse. The young man was sobbing. Very unusual. A sign from the Heavenly Father? The Brothers looked at one another in wonder—calculation. Was it some kind of trick? They got out of their carriage to ask if the lad was well, perhaps in need of assistance—and lucky for him, compassion was their mission.

Davin told the monks what had just happened to his little brother. The telling practically included Ginter and Natan as characters. "My father was distracted by customers . . ." Ginter had to cover his mouth to suppress a cough. This was their victim's brother! "I'm not much of a tracker. I can't find them. I'm beginning to feel hopeless. I can't decide what to do or which way to go."

"Maybe we can be of help," Natan said, introducing himself and Ginter. "Just give us a minute for some church business." But before he could move them off a distance to talk to his fellow monk in private, Davin thanked them and introduced himself and told them how grateful he was. He told them his father was the official alcohol provisioner of Lahkvna and would reward them, if they would help him.

"Our Father in heaven will provide the award," Natan said, 'but thank you for the thought."

Noting the rag-tag quality of the monks' robes, Davin, even in his grief, thought maybe their Father in heaven could provide these brothers with better costumes, while his, Davin's father certainly could reward them in some way more commensurate with Zalaman's worth.

"It's our privilege, in fact it's our calling, to help—even a son of Abraham," Natan added. "And aren't we all sons of Abraham? Saving your brother would be reward enough."

He asked Davin again to excuse the two of them for just a minute. He and the other monk had to confer among themselves about the ecclesiastical implications of this service.

Well away from Davin's hearing, Ginter tells his older companion that they need this young man on their team. "The three of us against Georg. The boy is undernourished but tall. He could help us overcome Georg thinking to free his little brother—and then we will take both brothers to the Russians."

Marengo started to wander over to sniff the monks' horse, but Davin held the reins to stop his movement, trying to hear what the monks were saying. He didn't want clip-clopping or neighing to interfere. He could see Natan shaking his head in disagreement with something. He made out the word "genius" before they lowered their voices.

"*Genius!*" Natan made fun of Ginter. "You don't know how these things work. I've said that more than once today. Our fortune is more likely to be made with this Davin alone.

"He's here, delivering himself to us."

Ginter looked over at Davin. "'A bird in the hand,' my mother used to say," Ginter admitted. "Well then," he grunted, "we mustn't reject the Lord's bounty."

As the monks approached, Davin didn't like what he saw in their eyes. He didn't have time to mount up, so he slapped Marengo on the rear, knowing he would gallop back to the stable in Lahkvna by the shortest route possible. The monks saw this as a slap in their faces, the loss of an asset, and they reacted with hostility. The fight was brief: Ginter and Natan were bloodied, but so was Davin, who was roped and tied to the back of the little carriage, bound as tightly as Zalaman.

In Georg's wagon, with Zalaman rolling about in the back, the *chapper* was more concerned about the possibility of pursuit by some independent authority like the boy's family than he was about cheating his accomplices. He wasn't going to cheat them, not necessarily. He might need their services again, if he kept up this line of work. But there was no need to concern himself with that. He would pay them sometime in the future and didn't worry about their having the temerity to come after him. Military conscription at this level was a dirty business. Ginter and Natan recognized that.

Georg just kept going.

Zalaman, still rolled up in the carpet, wondered how long he could hold out before he died of thirst. He was dizzy, but not dizzy enough—he was all too aware of the lethal result of being *chappered*, how joining the Tsar's army was going to your execution. The tears came again. He tried to calm himself and found he could stop the tears.

When he got breathless, he tried practicing slower breaths, reminding himself that he wasn't dead yet and wanted to stay that way. As he exhaled through his teeth he bit on his gag and after what seemed like an awfully long time of this intermittent nibbling—an exercise interrupted by the jostling of the cart and painful bites on his tongue or inner cheek—he chewed his way through the gag.

There was no point in screaming, muffled as he was and with the squeaking of the cart; the more methodical breathing calmed him and made it easier to think. The *chapper* didn't really want to kill him but would or should want to deliver his conscript in reasonably good shape, probably a condition of whatever reward he was to receive.

Zalaman had no idea how far away the Russian Army outposts were. Even in his nomadic childhood, he'd never encountered one, so he assumed they were far away. He pictured himself in a Russian uniform taking his place in a perfect line of uniformed soldiers. This was a picture Mama had shown him in one of her illustrated journals. He pictured himself carrying a bayonet-equipped rifle over his shoulder. But *chappered* Jews were probably never awarded medals for bravery, probably never even provided with a uniform, since it would soon be ruined by blades or bullets.

Georg was reconsidering how far he was going to have to go to reach the nearest Cossack outpost where he could deliver Zalaman. Being a *chapper* was lucrative but dangerous and he wasn't getting any younger.

He looked at the lumpy rug in back and wondered if he ought to check on his prize. First, he should put a bit more distance between himself and Navharadak. He drove the horse a little harder, not too fast, but relentlessly, tossing Zalaman about in the back like expendable cargo—which, Georg recognized, Zalaman was not. He soon slowed his vehicle. He should be more careful with this recruit. The Cossack's money could feed Georg's family for months, maybe he could even buy something for his girls. It didn't pay for Georg to think too often about his children when he went about his business.

He couldn't completely ignore the fact that his victim was someone's child. It seemed to him that most *chappers* had that ability to rationalize their work. He used to be able to do that, but he still wasn't completely inured to it. He was maybe beginning to feel remorse.

The kid in the rug in back was a Hebrew's child, it was true, but still a child. The fact that the kid was a Hebrew did make it easier for Georg to dismiss undesirable moral considerations. He'd spent much of his life as a *chapper*. The work offered excellent rewards. He would worry about this Israelite only in the sense that he had to be delivered alive and unbroken. Had he wrapped the kid too tight? He didn't want the boy to suffocate. He'd been silent back there, as far as Georg could tell over the rattle of wheels and clomping of hooves. Oh yes, he remembered—he'd gagged the boy.

He finally stopped and watered himself and his horse, before he looked down into the rug and saw that the kid had chewed right through the gag. Looking up through the peephole, Zalaman got a first view of his captor—one bloodshot eyeball and bulbous nose. He coughed, gasping "*bitte . . . pozhulsta . . . wasser . . . uhh voda . . . woda . . .*" and was grateful when the chapper responded with "*Tak*." Polish was practically a second, at very least third, language for Zalaman.

"I need water. My arms and legs are asleep. You've cut off the flow of blood. If I can't use my limbs, I'll be of no value to the Tsar."

Georg grunted in response to Zalaman's pleas, his list of pains and grievances. He wondered if the kid would ever shut his trap as he set about loosening the leather straps around the rug. He was not giving away any secrets when he admitted, "You're worth more to me alive."

Still wrapped up in the rug, but no longer tightly bound, Zalaman could feel the blood prickling back to his arms and legs. Georg poured the remainder of his horse's water down the center of the rug, right on top of Zalaman, who spluttered and tried to catch some of liquid in his mouth.

"You'll be able to stretch your legs soon enough," Georg said. "We'll have to stop for the night. There's no way to get to the outpost today." Zalaman pleaded that he be allowed to stretch his body now. He was in pain and was afraid something might be sprained and a limping recruit wouldn't provide a good payday for Georg. While Zalaman argued for leniency, Georg re-tightened Zalaman's bonds—but not quite so taut as before. He got back on his driver's bench and snapped Krysa's reins and the cart rolled and bounced down the road. Zalaman, more loosely muffled in the rug in back, gratefully passed out once again.

><

Davin watched and listened as Natan and Ginter stopped to water their nag. They were arguing about where the nearest Russian outpost might be. Natan worried that you couldn't just show up any time with any Jew you'd like to sacrifice. Didn't the deal have to be approved in advance by the *kahal*? Ginter pooh-poohed these concerns.

He was sure the Russians would pay even more for a grown man like their captive, than they would for the little brother.

"It's not like you think," Natan said, trying to reassure Davin, who would moan at every suggestion they made about his future. "You always hear that the reward for joining the Tsar's army is an early grave, but that's not always the case. You probably haven't heard—"

"—Horse shit!" Ginter interrupted. "Don't believe it," he cautioned Davin. "I've heard the story before. It's just wishful thinking."

"I've heard it, too," Davin said.

"None of you conscripts ever get honored with a grave. They just leave you out to rot," Ginter laughed.

"Don't mind him," Natan said. "I've heard of recruits surviving for months—even years. Eventually yes, of course, things happen—"

"—like catching a bullet—or starving," Ginter said.

"—but in the meantime," Natan continued, it only made things more difficult—"it can have its compensations—"

"Women, for example."

"Ginter! Shut up. You're starting to bother me."

It seemed to Davin that Ginter was purposely trying to provoke the older man. Hearing their unapologetic and outspoken agenda, he'd learned what their role had been with Zalaman's *chapper*. Was this another performance? It was possibly all in jest, a way of making their work lighter, to seem of less consequence. They both looked extremely uncomfortable in their dust- and sweat-streaked robes.

"Where are you taking me? What about my brother? Aren't you going to catch up to him and get your money?"

Natan turned and leaned back as if to take Davin into his confidence, talking loudly enough that Ginter could also hear. "Who got your brother? His name is Georg and he's a *chapper* among *chappers*. Been doing it successfully for many years, which is something not many can say, not many can last that long. It's an occupation that has its dangers. One can make many enemies—as even Ginter would have to agree.

"Here is a true story: one of the kids Georg abducted"—Natan glowered at Ginter and told him to shut up when he tried to protest—"A true story. It was about ten years ago. This little Israelite, smaller than your brother, worked his way up to become an officer in a Cossack regiment. A Jew leading Cossacks! And then, on his own initiative, this Jewish officer travelled to America with Blandowski, where he is fighting now—for the Union army."

"I thought the North won the war," Ginter said to his partner, then turned to Davin, "But Brother Natan here is right about Blandowski bringing considerable military skills to the side of the North. He fought, or he's still *fighting* for the Union, according to Natan. I heard it was all over and the North won. Who knows?"

"You think I could become an officer in the Tsar's army?" Davin asked. He wasn't quite as naive as the question sounded, but he thought it was a good idea to get them to keep talking, foster a relationship that might lead somewhere other than to the Russians, like a character in one of Mama's books.

"You?" Ginter laughed. "You might live a few months, if you're lucky, but it doesn't seem like you're all that lucky to me."

"So, just kill me now." Davin moaned with all the sincerity of a bound and condemned man. "I'd rather just die here than in the frozen lands where the Tsar rules." Davin had long dreamed of emigrating to the Holy Land. Now he never would. He would try something heroic. He was going to die anyway.

"Yes," Natan said, "but how would we profit from that? And don't talk to us about your father paying handsomely for your return. Those arrangements never work out. Too risky. We know. Don't waste your breath."

The three were quiet, contemplating Natan's remarks. The monks seemed to be remembering what "We know" referred to. Davin could see how the ransoming process could be difficult. The carriage came to a stop and the silence, the end of the constant squeaking, was a pleasure to all three. Ginter adjusted the harness for the continuation of the mission. Whatever that was.

Natan held a bowl of water so Davin could duck his head in it and drink, but he was much more thoughtful than Georg had been with Zalaman. "You should behave yourself now," he warned Davin. "We are your best chance of ever seeing your brother again."

Davin sobbed something about going to Jerusalem—his obsession.

"Jerusalem is a long way from here," sighed Natan.

"I'm going to take a voyage to Jerusalem where it's warm and sunny," Davin said as he lay back and closed his eyes. Maybe this was all just a dream.

"It's a holy land for us Catholics, too, you know."

"You're really Catholics?" Davin asked, unbelieving.

"We aren't *officially* holy men," Ginter scowled, "but we do believe in the Virgin Mary and the Catholic Church, and I will tolerate no criticism of my religion from a dirty Jew." He tried to deliver a kick to Davin's head, but Natan restrained him, reminding Ginter that they needed to keep Davin in good health. Ginter growled and flicked the reins. When the nag finally took notice, they continued in the direction they felt Georg would be most likely to have taken—a process of hit and miss. "Maybe the Tsar's army is close," Natan offered in a voice both hopeful and anxious at the same time. Ginter sighed in agreement.

Wrapped in the rug and dreaming through physical discomforts, Zalaman dreamed of Lahkvna—the *kvadrat,* the public market, where he played the game of Cossacks and Cowboys or Chappers and Jews with his friends, and where Osher and Henzel, the sages of Lahkvna, told their stories and delivered the 'news'—most of it old, but some of it new, even some of it true.

When Zalaman woke the dream evaporated. The dream had something to do with Heri Benowitz' mysterious disappearance from Lahkvna, an event endlessly discussed—in this case by Osher and Henzel. Heri had been the town butcher (a highly respected position in Lahkvna) and was the father of Zalaman's best friend, Aron Benowitz. But thrust from his dream of Lahkvna by a violent cough, then pain in his limbs, Zalaman's current situation seeped slowly back into his brain. He realized the pattern and creatures around the dim, round glow he'd been staring at were the visible edges of a turkic carpet. He tilted his head back to study the cone of light blinking at him. Despite his aching bones, the conditions were more comfortable than they had been before the *chapper* had loosened his tightest bonds. Dizzy from thirst, the tunnel of light became a kaleidoscopic peephole through which appeared a tumbling green landscape, then blue sky, then grey clouds as he rolled back and forth in the wagon. His delirium diminished as the shining, colored coins became an eye on a countryside he'd never seen but one that recalled the green forests and fields of home. Intermittent spurts showed tree-lined rows defining farms, darkening hollows where men worked the earth and children were even dirtier than he was. As the wagon again slowed, its movement rocked him back to sleep.

Perhaps because he was in the same unusual sleeping arrangement or maybe it was the natural desire to turn to what was comfortable and known as a means of deflecting the frightening and unknown, but he retreated again into the dream of Osher and Henzel and their explanation of the disappearance of the butcher: "He ran away to America." But Zalaman did not dream he was in the *kvadrat*. Now he was in the butcher shop itself. It was one of his favorite places to be. Was that because he liked watching Heri and then Adnon, who replaced Heri when the latter disappeared, expert carvers both, perform their art as Zalaman told everyone? Or was it because he liked watching Heri's beautiful wife, Minya?

Georg slowed the pace, and the change woke Zalaman. He wondered if someone would replace him back in Lahkvna? But what was there to replace? Only his family and a few friends will miss him. He decided he'd better start thinking like Papa. He had to figure a way out of this. He might bargain with the *chapper,* who was big and strong, but didn't look to be all that intelligent. "Stop! Water! I'm dying back here!" Zalaman roared as best he could.

Georg, who had been lost in a reverie that involved quitting the *chapper* business for easier work, heard but couldn't quite understand his muffled cries. He snapped the reins at Krysa to pick up speed and maybe shut the kid up. He had obligations to his employers and his family and couldn't afford to let sympathy toward his young Jew lead to the detriment of his work. He wanted to make it to a little wooded area he knew, where it would be safe to spend the night.

It was not quite dark when they stopped for the night. Zalaman could see well enough through his peephole to tell they were in hills, a grove of oaks, no familiar landmarks. The *chapper* crawled into the back of the wagon and loosened Zalaman's bonds, then helped him stand and Zalaman saw they were in a small clearing surrounded by trees. He was shaky and it took a while for Georg to steady him—one hand on Zalaman, the other on his revolver. Sticking the revolver in his ribs seemed unnecessary to Zalaman, who could barely stand, let alone run.

The *chapper* was a big man, but not a giant. He used his revolver to prod Zalaman to sit down against a wagon wheel, then roped him securely onto the iron spokes. "Call me Georg," he said, interrupting Zalaman's complaints and pleas and he poured Zalaman a mug of water from a jug. Zalaman took a long drink and introduced himself to the *chapper*. "I know your name," Georg said with a sigh, suggesting he knew much more than that. It was getting too dark to see, but a partial moon intermittently revealed wooded countryside. Georg stuck a piece of black bread in Zalaman's mouth. It was tough to chew, as bitter as the water was sweet, and yet he managed to devour it in under a minute. Georg refilled his mug. And Zalaman drained it again. "Where are you taking me?" Zalaman asked after draining the mug again in one long swig. Georg was too busy chewing to respond. "I can offer you something that might make it worthwhile to take me home."

Georg just laughed. "How old are you?" he asked then answered his own question, telling Zalaman he knew he was thirteen and shouldn't try to pretend he was so innocent. George swallowed his bread, then got up to care for Krysa as Zalaman watched, marveling that Georg was certainly the worst person he'd ever met, worse than Linards, the Navharadak policeman who liked to terrorize the Jews, yet there Georg was caring for Krysa like someone who loved his horse. Feeling was slowly returning to Zalaman's limbs; the bread had restored some sense of life. While Georg was preoccupied with his horse, Zalaman tested the strength of his bonds. He tried to do it discretely but managed to alert some sixth sense in Georg, who simply looked up and frowned, shaking his head 'no.' Zalaman rucked up his shoulders as if he had no idea what Georg was talking about, as if he had just been trying to stretch his aching muscles and joints.

Georg sat down near Zalaman and started cleaning his revolver. He was meticulous in the way he did it and it had a calming effect on Zalaman who recognized something akin to Heri Benowitz sharpening his knives. Zalaman knew very little about guns, despite having fired his father's shotgun one or two times. He thought, 'this will be the first night I have ever spent without other Aszers nearby' and that thought brought a fresh wave of anguish and well-deserved self-pity.

He stopped himself from tearing up and asked Georg how he could live with himself, live with the cruelty he was inflicting.

"Think of my parents," he pleaded. "What they must be suffering. You must have had parents yourself . . ."

Georg laughed, stopped his cleaning, and looked at Zalaman. "I *am* a parent," he said. "I have mouths to feed. Why else would I do this?"

"What? You have children—and yet you steal children?"

"I take them to pay the debt I owe—as a parent—to the Tsar, the service everyone owes the Tsar. I have been doing this for many years. Don't think this is easy for me. You think it's easy on my family all this traveling I must do? It's dangerous work. And the worst of it is all the negotiating between the Jews and the Poles and the Russians. Not that they care much about my opinion of anything, of course."

It must have been Georg's completely ignoring Zalaman's question that finally got him sobbing. The *chapper* sounded like he was seeking sympathy from Zalaman for his own plight, rather than sympathize with Zalaman's.

"Oh, come on. You might well survive." Georg tried, but it was less than encouraging to Zalaman. "You're big for your age. Are you truly only thirteen?" Georg's pretend pity couldn't stop Zalaman's tears. "I've lost count of how many kids I've delivered to the Russians," Georg said. "Kids like you. This is where I get the pleading speeches. How you can offer me money. But don't waste your breath. I know the Jews are as stingy as the Russians—almost. *But* I have more respect for the Russians—they don't sell out their own kind."

Zalaman wanted to ask for clarification, but he didn't. He already knew the Lahkvna *kahal* was complicit in the *chappering*, but he wouldn't give Georg the satisfaction of talking about it. He remembered his father telling him that ever since he, Jossel, had been appointed the *shtetl's* official purveyor of alcohol, he didn't think the *kahal* would dare agree to Davin or Zalaman getting *chappered*.

Georg had been given information—not too much; there was not much that he had to know or wanted to know—about Zalaman's father. "It only takes one member of the *kahal* to submit your name for it to be considered. Maybe some member of the *kahal* was jealous of your father's business success. Or, maybe not. Maybe it's all about the quota—which is really up to the Russians. They don't care who is taken. You never know."

Georg said they had a long way to go tomorrow, so he took the blanket Zalaman had been wrapped up in earlier and lay down on it, turning his back on his captive and almost instantly breaking into a snore that startled even the horse.

"Georg!" Zalaman yelled at the top of his voice. "I have to go to the bathroom." He had to yell it twice to wake him.

"Do it in your pants. You're too delicate."

"The Russians won't like the way I smell." There was no response. Georg had gone back to sleep. "I have to shit!"

Georg sighed. It was likely a trick. But they did have a good distance to travel tomorrow to get to the Russian outpost and he really didn't want to suffer from the stench all day. He got up slowly, upset that he had to do this, already suspicious because of other escape attempts made by those who had come before.

Even by the dim flickers from the campfire, Zalaman could see Georg's displeasure. He held his gun in one hand while he loosened the ropes that tied Zalaman to the wagon wheel, then played out a bit more of the tether so that the two had enough distance between them to walk into the underbrush, Georg using the rope to steer the boy like he would with the reins on his horse. They reached the underbrush that bordered the woods. Georg told Zalaman to be quick about his business and warned him not to try any funny business. "And hurry up!"

"I can't undo my trousers," Zalaman cried.

"Don't think that I'm going to come over there and help you shit."

Zalaman's hands were bound tightly at the wrists. He struggled with his pants. He didn't think Georg couldn't see his hands, but they were bound so tightly, what did it matter? What could he do? If he could undo the rope around his wrists . . . But he couldn't make the knots budge; he was ripping his skin.

There seemed to be no other choice. It would never work, but he had to try. He took a deep breath. He had to believe it was possible. He took another breath. Give it everything. He grabbed the tether in both hands and jerked with all his strength. Georg, despite all his suspicions, lost his balance and his grip on the rope. He fell. Zalaman took off, hopping more than running because of the thickness of the underbrush. If he could just make it into the woods. The rope, slapping against wrist and legs, caught on the brambles and pulled him off his feet. He was immediately up and running, the underbrush slashing at him, grabbing at his clothes, poking him like little daggers, snatching at the dangling rope. Yet, he was still free and filled with hope.

Unfortunately, Georg was not only big and blessed with dexterous hands that enabled him to tie unbreakable knots; he was faster than Zalaman and unencumbered. His bulk and thicker clothing allowed him to crash right through the underbrush. You have to have physical strength to be a successful *chapper*, as Georg had demonstrated when he had so cleanly snatched Zalaman in Lahkvna.

Zalaman didn't look back, but he could hear Georg puffing and swearing and getting closer. All clarity vanished when Georg brought his heavy fist down on Zalaman's head.

Zalaman dreamed of Heri and Minya Benowitz' butcher shop, and Officer Linards entered, leering at Minya. He was as attracted to her as Zalaman was. But Zalaman was a little boy. Officer Linards of the Navharadak Department for the Protection of Public Order was the scourge of the *shtetl,* feared and hated in equal parts. For his part, he tried to tolerate the Jews—they were his bread and butter—but was unable to approach anything that could be mistaken for open-mindedness. Like the other officers of the DPPO officials of Navharadak, the Christian city surrounding Lahkvna, Linards reported to the Russians, and he knew the Russians prized normalcy above all else in the *shtetls* of the Pale. This required acting swiftly and uncompromisingly before any issues among the Jews got out of hand, and so he should act swiftly and directly now with Minya. Her husband

Henri had disappeared and she'd come to him for help. He could have her . . .

And Zalaman awoke, annoyed, stunned to realize he'd been dreaming of Linards more than he was shocked to realize he was back entombed in his rug cocoon. His head was pounding. There was also pounding coming from beneath him. Georg or someone was pounding the bottom of the wagon. That pounding stopped, but the pounding in his head continued; it was a throbbing from the spot Georg had struck him. It all came rushing back into his aching head: how he'd tried escape. He'd failed but he was proud he'd at least tried. He hadn't been sure he'd have the nerve. He'd taken the chance.

He could hear Georg snoring even through the rug. He tried to wiggle his arms and found they were sticky with blood. He remembered the branches tearing his flesh. The bottom half of his body was prickly. Only the rug was covering him there. He had no trousers or underclothes. No shoes. This was the price of his escape attempt. The rug was very rough on his exposed lower body parts. He wished to go back to sleep, but the pounding in his head made that impossible.

The weak dawn of light crept all the way into the rug. He listened to Georg moving about, feeding Krysa, perhaps. Zalaman thought how his being *chappered* would make it less likely for Davin to follow his dream of going to the Holy Land as he was now the only remaining son.

He was sure the new day would be a terrible one, so Zalaman was in no hurry for the sun to rise. But it rose quickly anyway. In short order, he and Georg were once again headed down the road toward the Russian outpost, to Zalaman's doom. Georg would not respond to Zalaman when he cried and pleaded or demanded his pants back. After many twists and turns, though only one stop for water, it felt like they'd been traveling forever.

Georg drove in dimming daylight, watched the gathering clouds. For all his experience, it was impossible to know whether he was in friendly country. They were not necessarily under the protection of the Tsar. But he decided he wasn't really concerned about the Tsar; he wasn't worried about Natan and Ginter, either. They knew he'd be good for it when he came back with more money and more work for them to do after delivering Zalaman Aszer.

The not-so-little Hebrew had surprised him. He didn't seem like the type. He admired Zalaman's escape attempt. It just made him question again whether he really wanted to continue in this business. He'd saved. He'd established contacts. Through no fault of his own since we can't determine the destiny of our birth, this boy now finds himself rolled up in the back of the wagon—without pants or shoes. Georg has found that removing a would-be escape artist's pants and shoes is an effective means of inhibiting his desire to run. Georg was getting older and he wanted to find a different trade. He'd always had a good head for sums. But could he tolerate a sedentary life? Being a *chapper* was all he knew. He was good at it.

The darkening sky reached further west to hover over Davin and his two abductors. Davin welcomed the cooler air. Ginter and Natan believed they were tracking Georg and that they might overtake him before long. There were two of them and they could spell one another at the reins while Georg had to do all the driving by himself and would need to sleep at some point.

This was the same conclusion Georg reached and he knew them much better than Davin. Still, he wouldn't put his guard down. He could smell the rubles already. He used to make more when he was younger and able to handle two or three boys at once. Now he had trouble with one. He couldn't believe he'd fallen for the kid's game. It was proof he was getting too old.

After going uphill for hours, it was mid-afternoon, they were high on a hillside and it looked like rain. Georg wanted to take a break, a last stop before the Russians. He would water Krysa and see to Zalaman before the rain started. As soon as he thought it, the first drops started to fall.

The upward tilt of the wagon kept Zalaman pinned to the back to the wagon until Georg finally pulled off the road, stopping under a stand of trees that might provide a degree of shelter from the rain. Zalaman was subdued, not the same hopeful fool who'd attempted escape, but, still, he had to be careful. As he unwound Zalaman from the carpet, he didn't put his guard down. The trees were porous, but for both Georg and Zalaman the rain was a pleasant respite from the heat, as restorative as the mug of water Georg passed to Zalaman, who had been trying, unsuccessfully, to get his limbs to come back to life. The water cleaned the dirt from Zalaman's mouth and the rain washed it from his half-naked body along with the blood from his head wound. He shivered despite the summer warmth.

"Drink slowly," Georg said as passed Zalaman the water. "I'm sorry I hit you so hard, but you should never have tried such foolishness. If I injured you, it's your own fault."

"I want my pants." Zalaman sat down, tethered fast, on the edge of the wagon.

"Hah-hah! That's the least of your problems. You'll just stay as is for now. Believe me, I'd just as soon not have to see you like this, but we're close to our destination. You shouldn't worry so much about your appearance. The Cossacks won't care." But Georg threw the rug over Zalaman's lap. After making a show of the revolver in his jacket, he tightened the ropes binding Zalaman's hands and walked away to care for the horse.

The rain was light. It cooled the air but allowed Zalaman a decent view of his surroundings: high ground enveloped by fir and oak, the needles and leaves sparkling in the afternoon's sporadic light.

He'd never seen hills this size around Lahkvna or anywhere else the Aszers' travels had taken them. In the distance, there were even higher hills and then, barely discernible on the horizon, grey mountains of indeterminate height. Where they already in Russian territory? He shivered. If they were, it could mean his immanent end. As Georg fed his horse, Zalaman asked about that and Georg said, "It's all Russian territory, isn't it? We're always in 'Russian Territory.'"

Zalaman imagined he saw an improbably blue flash in the middle distance as Georg continued about how he might find the right Russian procurement officer. Zalaman encouraged him to go on, but he watched that space. It had been too big a splash of color for a bluebird, but it was clearly a color not of the natural world. He must have been dreaming. But then there it was again, in a slightly different spot. Closer. An angel in blue come to rescue him. Zalaman caught his breath but kept Georg talking. He didn't want Georg to hear the angel, but angel, Cossack, or phantom, it made no sound, nothing could be heard over the light rain and Georg's voice. Georg had waxed enthusiastic about collecting his money, prattling on about the ignorance of the Russians. If there had been any rustling from the trees, he wouldn't have heard it anyway—until he suddenly stopped talking. He sensed something in Zalaman's voice. He was talking too loudly.

"You're a fool not to take me home," Zalaman was shouting. "My father will give you twice as much as the Russians!"

"We've been through that. And don't exaggerate. And keep your voice down. You never know who you might run into in these woods."

Zalaman grinned and watched the bottom of a pair of ragged trousers sidestepping alongside the trunk of a nearby oak. He looked away so Georg wouldn't catch him staring. But the *chapper* was alerted. Zalaman seemed overexcited. He walked over to check Zalaman's bonds.

What if it's a brigand? Zalaman wondered. No, now he could see snatches of two figures. Both heavily armed and perhaps bringing an even more immediate death than what he might face with the Russians? The two men moved out from behind the oak and approached, quieter than Zalaman would have thought possible. Georg, his back to the intruders, was a known and unacceptable quantity and these two in blue were simply an unknown. Zalaman strained and squirmed against the ropes and made more noise. "Let me loose. I want to go home!"

"Shut up," Georg said, cinching Zalaman's knots tighter, oblivious to the activity behind him. "I've explained it to you. It's nothing personal, but I am a parent too. I have a child to feed. Life is unfair, yes—not just to you, but to me, too—"

"—And me!" grunted one of the blue men as he pushed his pike trench into Georg's back and then all the way through his chest, the emerging tip releasing a spray of blood on Zalaman.

Georg's mouth was open, gurgling and spouting additional blood. It reminded a stunned Zalaman of a bloodletting he'd witnessed in Benowitz' butcher shop, including the pulsing, flopping organs clinging to the hook. Georg collapsed onto Zalaman's lap.

The smaller but stockier of his two liberators—'liberators' he hoped—placed a well-worn boot on Georg's butt for leverage and slowly, screwing it back and forth, pulled out the bloody pike. He shoved Georg off Zalaman and onto the ground, where he flopped twice and then was still.

CHAPTER TWO

The Uprising

His two saviors demonstrated no ill intentions toward Zalaman. Quite the contrary, they turned out to practically be neighbors—Poles from Navharadak. The shorter and more powerfully built, who was also the older and quieter of the two, was called Rodak by the tall, younger man who introduced himself as Stanko. Stanko said Rodak—who, by skewering Georg had saved Zalaman's life—was his cousin. In addition to the pike, he'd used to dispatch the chapper, Rodak carried a large hunting knife. He showed it to Zalaman, then gripped it ominously before emitting a grim laugh and deftly slicing Zalaman's tethers.

Zalaman thanked them for saving his life, but getting up to introduce himself, the rug slipped off his lap and exposed his naked bottom half.

"Oh, Rodak," Stanko laughed, "we must have interrupted something!"

Zalaman tried to explain that he'd be the victim of *chappering*, but the Bartos cousins needed no explanations.

"You're a victim of this *chapper*," Stanko said. "We know all about it. Not so much about you, but we've been following you two since you were taken."

Rodak pointed his pike at Zalaman's penis and spoke for the first time. "Maybe that was more impressive before the circumcision."

Zalaman tried to cover himself. His trousers, when he finally located them, were soaked from the rain. He shivered and pulled them on with difficulty. He was suddenly overcome by a rush of emotions—horror and then relief; anger and then fear. But, finally, gratitude. He might not be going to his death after all, and the realization that this was true made him feel lightheaded—lightheaded, but alert enough to understand that Rodak and Stanko were two derelict soldiers. They claimed their allegiance to Poland was unflinching, but it was impossible to determine in the faded and patched blue uniforms—the blue caps he'd seen moving in the woods, the identical, tattered trousers, and their long-backed, yellow-grey military style coats.

"Don't worry about the outfits, Stanko smiled when he saw Zalaman looking them over. "Use your imagination. Once they were white, before they were dyed. But that was a different war and a different side . . ."

"What war are you fighting?"

"The Polish Uprising."

"I was told that was over years ago."

"You were told wrong," Rodak said, in a tone that announced there was to be no debate on the subject.

"The November Insurrection of 1830?" Stanko asked. "That didn't last a month. But people who tell you the January Uprising of 1863 is over? They don't know what they're talking about. As you can see," he said, spreading his arms to indicate the cousins were all the proof that was needed. "Rodak here is so old he fought in both uprisings. Me, I just started in with the new one. It's been three years, but there are still Cossacks need killing."

Zalaman was grateful to both men, of course, but he found Stanko's manner and speech original and entertaining.

"The battle isn't over. There are many people still fighting for Polish sovereignty," Rodak said, sounding more grim than hopeful.

Zalaman didn't like feeling that he was being evaluated. He didn't want to be a part of any army, certainly not one with such ragged wardrobes. Georg's death (Zalaman's freedom!) was the first time he'd witnessed the violent death of a man, but these cousins seemed to take it in stride. This was nothing new for them.

"We've seen a lot of death," Stanko said, reading Zalaman's thoughts as the youngster stared at Georg, "but it always affects you deeply, no matter."

Rodak snorted, but admitted it was best not to let yourself grow indifferent to the death of others. "Even those who tried to kill *you*, because it could cause carelessness and one's own death."

In the romances his mama had read to him, Zalaman heard heroes and heroines bewail their fate, but ultimately, welcome their end. How ridiculous it all sounded now. The moment Georg's face had slackened—directly in Zalaman's own face—Zalaman watched the man cease to be. There had been a Georg, a man with children, and now no Georg. Ceasing to be. It was the initiation into a mystery in which Rodak and Stanko were well-versed.

"We don't mind that people think the Uprising is over," Rodak said. "It tends to make the Cossacks less vigilant. I don't know about the Jews, but the truth of the matter is the Polish people share the ideals of the Uprising."

"We wouldn't be successful otherwise," Stanko added.

The way he said it, made Zalaman want to ask what success meant exactly—what they did—because it hinted at something more than killing Cossacks, but he kept his mouth shut. Rodak walked back into the woods to retrieve Beth, the horse he and Stanko had been sharing since they'd ridden out of Navharadak. They'd been on a lengthy furlough from service, when they were just getting started on their way back to headquarters, they heard about Zalaman's chappering.

Stanko lowered his voice when Rodak was out of earshot anyway. "Rodak isn't interested in saving Hebrews. Doesn't care for them much. It was for the opportunity to kill a *chapper* and liberate the *chapper's* purse. Liberating *you* is a side benefit."

Rodak and Stanko took possession of Georg's horse and wagon, but after searching high and low, couldn't find the *chapper's* purse.

"Give me a knife," Zalaman said and scooted under the wagon. There was a ripping sound and then the cousins watched a muddy Zalaman emerge from under the wagon. "I wasn't sure if I'd dreamt of Georg working at something under the floorboards. I had not," he said, presenting them with a considerable purse.

It was delightfully stuffed with coins and banknotes. The cousins thanked Zalaman and congratulated him for his cleverness.

"My thanks for saving—me. But . . . if you want to share, I wouldn't say no . . ."

Rodak shook his head. "Jews! This must go to help support the Uprising."

"Which is us," Stanko grinned.

"You are big for thirteen," Rodak said, regarding his new charge. "For a Hebrew." Rodak was well over thirty, and about the same height as Zalaman.

"The old man here," Stanko said, motioning to his cousin, "is in his thirties. I'm only seventeen, myself. I was only a year older than you are now when I joined Rodak to fight the Cossacks. You are big enough to fight, even if you're still a boy. Do you know how to fire a rifle?"

"No." He couldn't be sure what the 'right' answer might be, so he'd opted for the truth.

"You'll learn," Stanko assured him, though the idea was not all that reassuring to Zalaman.

"I will?" he asked.

"We just saved your life," Rodak said. "A life for a life."

Zalaman didn't think he liked the statement's implications.

"He simply means that having saved your life, you owe us," Stanko explained. "It's a well-known principle." But Zalaman looked distressed. Stanko patted him on the back.

"Jews don't understand that principle," Rodak said, looking over their new bounty and pocketing Georg's fancy revolver, then stacking their gear in Georg's wagon. The cousins now owned an arsenal of two revolvers, two old muskets, and the antique but deadly pike, rinsed clean by the rain of blood and organs.

Stanko opened the purse and dumped its contents—coins, currency, and one dazzling piece of jewelry, a necklace—on the wagon bench. "You'd be in great luck to join us, you know. Fight the Russians who have been so terrible to your people and earn a pile of gold at the same time," Stanko said, though Zalaman, looking closely, could see no gold in the pile.

"All you had to do was mention a pile of gold and you got the Jew's attention," Rodak laughed.

Zalaman assured them he was grateful for their freeing him from the *chapper* but assured them they'd be better off in battle without him. He had no experience with guns or swords. He'd only get in their way.

Rodak shrugged as if it was of little importance to him, one way or the other. "Leave the Jew here and let him fend for himself."

"Is that why you saved me? To recruit me for a different army?"

"We hate *chappers* too," Stanko said. "Rodak won't admit it, but the Poles are like the Jews that way. We're from the same place as you, the same town."

"Even though they touch at the Outer Circle, Navharadak's not the same town as Lahkvna," Zalaman said and smiled, "your buildings are much less crooked." He recalled how he'd been awestruck years before when his mother took him to the stately, imposing, symmetrical house of the Trade Commissioner.

Stanko said they'd been in Navharadak, visiting Stanko's mother—who was Rodak's Aunt Elizavetta, though she was more like a mother to him—when, just two days ago, their furlough had run out. "We were leaving Navharadak, ready to load up

Beth and ride back to HQ, when we heard about the *chapper.* It felt like a lucky omen—lucky for us, but for you, too. We were pretty sure the direction Georg would take because we're familiar with most of the Russian army outposts in the region." Even if it had not already disappeared from Stanko's memory of the recent chase, Stanko would have seen no reason to mention how they'd passed a rickety old carriage driven by two ugly monks, who, from the way the avoided eye contact, might have been carrying some quite unholy cargo, but they had not seen Davin.

"Just two days ago?" Zalaman asked. "Seems like much longer."

"By the size of that knot on your noggin, you're lucky to be with us at all."

Zalaman wanted to see, but it was still too sore to touch so Rodak handed him a piece of mirror from his pack. He laughed when at first he didn't recognize the grime-streaked face, but when he saw the size of his head wound, he was afraid. How could he laugh? He inventoried his memory to confirm his brain was still working. He realized he wouldn't be able to tell if his brain was damaged, because his brain was damaged, but decided this insight proved it was working just fine, so he told Rodak he could help them bury Georg when Rodak said they had to clean up "the mess."

They pulled Georg into the trees and dug his grave, taking turns with the short spade from his own wagon. The sun had come out, but it was low and their shadows were elongated. The soil was wet and heavy and thick with tree roots and so they readily accepted failure. They didn't have enough time, Rodak said—it was obvious who the leader was in this little group. They used leaves and branches to cover the parts of Georg that were still protruding from the narrow grave.

Back at the cart by the roadside, Stanko went to retrieve Georg's cap. It had been left in the road. But Rodak told his cousin to leave it alone. Stanko and Zalaman should come see something.

"This is the best gift from Georg," Rodak said, removing a gleaming pistol out of the leather case he'd found in the Hessian bag Georg had kept under the driver's seat.

"Lefaucheux," Rodak called it, using the name of the famous French arms manufacturer. "I wondered who he'd stolen it from."

Rodak showed them his 'old revolver.' "This old thing has been a trusted life saver and I love it dearly, but I'm going to give it to whoever is the best shot."

Zalaman insisted that would be Stanko. He, Zalaman had no need for a revolver. He wouldn't know what to do with it. Rodak insisted right back. They would have a shooting contest. Rodak wanted to see if taking Zalaman with them was worth the bother. "I know you aren't committed to our enterprise," Rodak said to Zalaman. "If you don't join us, the weapon will naturally go to Stanko."

Joining them, whatever that meant, was not of interest to Zalaman. Still would it be an affront to Rodak if he said he didn't want his treasured old weapon?

"Thanks for including me," he said, "but there is no chance I could win a shooting contest. I've never fired a revolver."

"You have a decent chance," Stanko assured him. "I'm a lousy shot."

Rodak pointed at Georg's cap, lying in the mud some fifty meters away. Stanko and Zalaman watched Rodak take six metal cartridges from Georg's ammunition box and load them into Lefaucheux' chamber. Stanko held Beth's muzzle and asked Zalaman to do the same with Georg's nag.

"Krysta, Beth," Zalaman said, introducing them to one another.

With a rigid right arm, Rodak slowly raised the revolver, tilted his head, closed one eye, and slowly squeezed the trigger. The shot kicked up a deep wedge of mud very close to the cap. Rodak scolded the revolver like it was a naughty boy—"So that's how you are!"—and took aim again, squeezed the trigger and sent the cap flying out of the mud with a brand-new bullet hole.

They congratulated him. "See? That's what years of killing Cossacks can do for you," Stanko told Zalaman. He wasn't sure the reward was worth the risk. Stanko assured him he had a lot to learn. Rodak said he wasn't sure a Hebrew could be trained to shoot well, but Zalaman ignored his taunt.

Rodak handed the weapon to Stanko. Stanko weighed the Lefaucheux in his hand. "This isn't really fair," he complained. "The *chapper's* cap's now ten meters further away."

Zalaman couldn't believe they were playing a game. He'd just been rescued! Georg was still lying in the mud, just like the cap. At least, they weren't using the body as a target. "Didn't you say something about us not having a lot of time?" he asked Rodak.

"Never mind." Stanko said. They could leave the cap where it was—he didn't care. He squeezed off one shot, then another, then a third—each shot getting a little closer to the target, but none of them hitting it.

"That's alright," Rodak consoled him as he handed Zalaman the weapon. "The important thing is that each time you took another shot, you got closer. Zalaman here won't have that chance because you only left him with one last cartridge."

Zalaman took the revolver. Its weight confirmed the reality of the weapon. He felt that he was entering another life. He had no experience with firearms beyond the one time he was given a lesson by his papa on the use of his ancient blunderbuss. He tried to emulate the cousins' technique for taking aim, but he was on the verge of rushing it when Rodak advised him to slow down.

And so, he did, making the worst of Stanko's three shots look good. And that's all they really wanted—for him to pull the trigger. They didn't care how bad a shot he was, in fact, they enjoyed his ineptitude. It validated Rodak's attitude about Jews, so Rodak got a kick out of Zalaman's concern. Stanko laughed at Zalaman, too, but with goodwill.

Zalaman had no intention of giving in to this "life for a life" proposal. He just wanted to go home, see his parents, brother, and sister. He made no pact with the two partisans, but he didn't want them to just leave him there.

Rodak asked if Georg had talked about the location of the Russian outpost.

All Zalaman could tell them was that Georg had said it was close. "He was counting on getting there before nightfall."

"It doesn't really matter," Stanko said. "The front lines change all the time." After many months in Navharadak, away from the fighting and with no news from HQ, the cousins had no idea where the Cossacks might be. They knew where their own HQ was, or had been, but could not be sure where the Russians were actively patrolling. They only knew they should leave this area quickly. It wouldn't be safe if the Cossacks were that close.

"We're lucky there aren't soldiers already here after those six shots we fired," Rodak said, mounting up, Lefaucheux in his belt. Commandeering Georg's wagon and Krysta, Stanko motioned for Zalaman to get up on the bench with him.

Rodak rode ahead on Beth. Stanko turned the wagon to follow, all casting long shadows that were stretching in the fading light, heading back the direction Zalaman had come with Georg. Then there was no more speaking—only occasional shouting—over the creaks and rattles of the wagon. Despite the predicament he may have gotten himself into, Zalaman was happy beyond words. He'd been saved from the Tsar's army!

They rode through the night and the next day, through woodlands and open fields, until the sun was close to setting. Zalaman and Stanko traded places a few times, alternating between driving Georg's wagon and resting in the back, Rodak riding ahead. The wagon entered some low hills thick with trees, then emerged into an open space where they caught up with Rodak. He was sitting on Beth looking out on a broad valley below, bisected by a winding river, small farms on both sides.

Beyond the farms on the other side of the river was an endless forest fronting distant high hills. In the setting sun, the shadows of horse and wagon moved over the rocks and brush, the men stretched like dark giants. They stopped and the only sound was wind and the heavy breathing of the horses.

"The river is called Aryot," Rodak said, "a tributary of the Shchar. Down just a bit there's a stand of beech, well off the road, where we can sleep well-hidden. We'll cross the Aryot tomorrow." Stanko didn't question Rodak's decision and Zalaman knew he certainly had no say in such matters. He wouldn't know what to say, if he did.

They descended slowly along a rocky path that led them to the beech woods where a little creek rushed down toward the big river. It was getting difficult to see, but Zalaman noted a bridge across the Aryot, a bridge which should make crossing tomorrow a simple task. But Rodak and Stanko dashed that hope. The bridge wasn't complete and even if it was, it would be too dangerous. They didn't elaborate. But they were both amazed at how the bridge had grown in the few months since they'd last seen it.

They made a little camp in the woods after they had taken care of Beth and Krysta. The cousins laid out all the little food they had been carrying, supplemented by what they had taken from Georg and a varmint that Rodak had shot along the way. A wild pig.

Zalaman butchered the pig—an animal he'd never dealt with, nor seen Heri or Adnon deal with, in the Benowitz' kosher butcher shop. Even Rodak was impressed with Zalaman's butchering skills. They started a small fire and watched the meat roast; the aroma caused mouths to water. The cousins watched Zalaman eat his share.

"Some Jew you are," Rodak said with a sneer.

"I'm a hungry Jew," Zalaman said.

Zalaman was exhausted and invigorated at the same time. He hoped God wouldn't punish him for eating the pig, but he wasn't overly concerned, having absorbed the religious skepticism of his father. He was living a page out of one of Mama's novels. What adventures lay ahead?

He wondered it out loud what lay ahead and triggered a long and wide-ranging discussion of the immediate future: how they would get to their headquarters on the other side of the Aryot and how, on the way there, they would stop at the safe house Rodak and Stanko had 'established' ("appropriated," Stanko corrected his cousin) before they'd gone on their self-declared furlough and how they hoped that farmhouse would still be 'suitable,' but they would have to be alert to make sure conditions there were amendable. It was easy to imagine the conditions might have changed—might have become dangerous.

The HQ to which they were headed was an unimpressive remnant of the Uprising of 1863. But they told Zalaman, to prove their point that the Uprising was not dead, at HQ he would see hundreds of partisans training and going out on exercises. Rodak, who had been fighting for more than twenty years, as one uprising collapsed and another grew from its detritus, was not only ridding Poland of Russians, but also making a good living in the process.

"We are not the only people who want the Cossacks to leave," Rodak continued, poking the embers of their small campfire with his pike. "There are many keeping the hope for Polish freedom alive. You're a Jew, but can you understand?" Zalaman nodded and Rodak explained their 'modus operandi,' how he and Stanko would make surprise attacks on small groups or individual

Cossacks. "Surprise and good luck are the keys to success," he said.

"The same thing can be said of chappering," Zalaman said. He was eyeing Rodak's ragged trousers and the toe sticking out of Rodak's boot. He didn't want to come right out and contradict him, but asked, "What kind of success do you mean?"

Stanko laughed and held up Georg's purse. "This kind," Stanko laughed. "It's not easy doing what we do. It's hard work. Cossacks tend to group together. We could do much better with a good third man—"

"The reward is the fight itself," Rodak interrupted. "We had a third partner, but he's no longer with us."

Zalaman wasn't sure he wanted to know what had happened to their third man, and before he had a chance to ask, Rodak added, "But considering your aim with the pistol, you just might just be an added complication."

"I could learn," Zalaman said, attempting to speak with conviction, but it didn't quite come out that way. "If I wanted to," he said, qualifying his statement although Rodak found it unconvincing and unjustified, but promising. But he and Stanko smiled in acknowledgement.

Zalaman naturally had misgivings, but he did want to please his rescuers. He was feeling safer with these two *goyim* and starting to experience a thirteen-year-old's yearning for adventure. He was a thirteen-year-old raised on the novels his mother read to him and taught him to read—in the languages that were available. On the other hand, Zalaman didn't want to die. He wanted to go home. Eventually. It was exactly what Rodak and Stanko wanted to hear.

"The upheaval that was called 'The Uprising' is now just a series of little Polish *fartsn*," Stanko said. "The Cossacks have gold they have stolen from Poles—just like you were stolen—and it's no sin to try to get it back into Polish hands."

"Yours," Zalaman said.

"Ours," Stanko corrected him, including him.

"But there is a bigger reward," Rodak added, "a reward beyond the money and not in heaven but in the feeling of freedom you experience when fighting for an honorable cause."

"Even if it's a lost cause?" Zalaman asked as politely as possible.

"Especially if it's a lost cause," Rodak said. This sounded consistent with Mama's stories.

"You said you could learn," Stanko said. "That's what's important. You're willing."

"I didn't say I wanted to be a partisan. Probably, Jews shouldn't be partisans."

"No, there *are* Jewish-Polish partisans," Stanko assured him. "Although they are usually Jewish first and partisans second," Rodak said, passing Zalaman a flask. The *krupnik* made Zalaman feel at home.

"What about King David?" Stanko asked. "There was a great Jewish fighter."

Zalaman, who always associated Davin with King David, felt a wave of homesickness, and wondered how his brother was. "I'm no David," he said. "I really have to get home. My family—my parents and brother, Davin, and little sister—they think I'm dead. I can't let them believe that."

"Couldn't he send them a telegram from Syp?" Stanko asked Rodak, referring to the town where the partisans had their headquarters. Rodak answered that it would be up to the commandant, but that it would be more likely if Zalaman was a partisan. Then Rodak lay back and was soon asleep.

Stanko and Zalaman talked about their parents. Rodak's were dead, Stanko said, but his mother had been like a mother to Rodak. "My mother has Jewish friends. She's not like Rodak and his side of the family. She tried to educate Rodak, but it didn't sink in. You'll educate him. Yeah, I think you will."

They had to speak louder to hear one another over Rodak's snoring. "My mother is an educated woman," Zalaman said. "She read us big books when she could find them. Not children's books. Russians. Pushkin. Gogol. Germans, Goethe, and Heinrich Heine. Some she read to us in translation, some were really just language lessons. Then there were adventures. The adventures of Randall the fur trader in the Wild West of America."

Zalaman was warming to the topic and would have continued, but heard Stanko now snoring, too, so he lay back on the bed of soft green twigs and leaves—some not too dead but springy and forgiving, a welcome relief for his body with its many rug-induced aches and scrapes. He felt the lump on his head. The lump was still there, but it was somewhat diminished and he could touch it without great pain. He pulled up Georg's rug, the same one he'd been rolled in. He could hear the murmur of the little blackwater creek, just a trickle this late in the summer, but speeding on its way to the broad Aryot. There was a slice of starry sky staring at him beyond the beeches.

On the road, a full day behind Zalaman, Davin was not finding it so easy to sleep. He was still bound by the leather straps; cargo hauled by the two would-be chappers.

Earlier that day the threesome rolled by the site of Georg's recent piking. Something red in the mud caught Ginter's eye. He reined in the horse, jumped off the carriage and picked up a cap. It was muddied and torn, but he recognized it as Georg's.

Natan took it from Ginter and stuck his fingers through two holes on either side. "It looks like Georg got shot right through the head. Bullet came out the other side."

"Or he was shot from two sides at once," Ginter said, grabbing the *capo* back.

Davin was craning his neck to get a look. "Maybe it was just his cap, that got shot, not Georg. There's no blood on it."

Ginter discovered what looked like a fresh trail leading into the woods, so he followed it, Natan and Davin in the carriage behind. In the woods they encountered a stench, and the two would-be monks knew what they were going to find even before they saw the partially buried body of their erstwhile partner-in-crime. “Georg the *chapper* finally met his match,” Natan said, throwing aside the branches. Georg hadn’t been shot through the head—he’d been disemboweled. Maggots were already gorging. Perhaps it had been a competitor *chapper*? Not Cossacks, they wouldn’t have wanted to kill their source for so many recruits. Certainly not Zalaman. But where was Zalaman? Davin rejoiced in the hope that his brother had somehow escaped. One thing was clear to Natan and Ginter: now they would have to take Davin to the Tsar’s officers.

Otherwise, there would be absolutely no profit whatsoever from this time-consuming adventure.

Chapter Three

The Bridge Over the Aryot

Rodak was already at the bank of the Aryot early in the morning when the wagon carrying Zalaman and Stanko caught up. Rodak had been trying to figure out the best place to cross. They wouldn't be using the bridge. They were a good thousand meters away from it, but the bridge loomed large in the distance. What Zalaman had not been able to see yesterday when he was further from it, was that what he'd thought was one massive bridge, was, in fact, two bridges: a small ancient bridge of wood and iron bolts and a much larger bridge, brand new, made of steel, running parallel alongside the old one. But the new bridge was incomplete, in the final stages of construction. There were men on the new bridge all the way to the far shore of the Aryot. Zalaman pointed out the giant carriage sitting on that side.

"The new bridge is a railroad bridge—and that giant carriage is a train engine," Stanko said.

Zalaman pretended that, of course, that's what he'd meant. He had once seen a train in Kuldiga, but never a locomotive so powerful looking. It looked like a machine that belonged in the city. Here in the countryside, it looked so out of place.

They would ford the river upstream from the bridge workers—far enough away to avoid detection. "It would be easier to do it downstream, but we would be sure to encounter Cossacks," Rodak said. "Upstream we face the danger of the current carrying us too close to firing range, in case there are any Russians with those workers. I'm counting on the workers being too engaged in their work to notice us. It's alright, the current's not too bad up just a bit further, though it widens there. The trees on the other side will provide some cover when we've crossed. We'll be out of the range of their guns by then anyway."

"You think they are unfriendly?" Zalaman asked. To which Stanko replied, "You always assume they are not friendly." Rodak nodded his approval. His big little cousin was learning. "That's right. And even more so because the railroad is partially funded by the Romanovs."

Where they stopped to make their crossing, the Aryot was lined with trees and there was a gentle incline from the rocks to the water where it would be easy for the wagon to enter.

"I'm less worried about Cossacks on the bridge than I am about just getting across without capsizing the wagon. Can you swim?" Rodak asked. Zalaman said he could—"somewhat."

"Don't worry," Stanko said. "The current isn't bad here. I don't think we'll be in anything deeper than shoulder height. You won't have to swim—or at least not much."

Zalaman was not calmed by this. The top of his head barely reached Stanko's shoulder. "What if I float away? Will the Aryot take me home to Lahkvna?"

They smiled at his joke. "Eventually, they all do, all the rivers," Rodak said. "Look, If the current takes you a little, don't worry. You'll be with Beth and she'll keep you safe. You use her like a floating log."

They tied down everything they could in the wagon, wrapped the firearms and bullets as best they could, lightening the load on Beth as much as possible. They would drive the wagon across the river; it couldn't be helped that the current would pull them downstream somewhat, but they would try to cross in as straight a line as possible.

Zalaman pointed out some fishermen along the riverbanks, but Stanko said they were of no concern.

Krysa pulled the wagon into the water without hesitation, Rodak walking alongside, holding her. Stanko stayed by the wagon's tailgate. Zalaman entered the water with Beth, on the right side, away from the bridge. He was used to the cold water of the Baltic Sea but preferred the summertime lakes like the Rekyvos. The Aryot was even colder than the sea. He was not much of a swimmer, and he was more worried when the cousins admitted they weren't much either. For the first 100 meters, about halfway across, they were fording the Aryot without incident, aside from Zalaman complaining through chattering teeth about the cold.

"This is nothing," Stanko said when his shoulders were still well above the water and Zalaman's and Rodak's were barely so. "In the German Confederation, we once had to cross a much bigger river in early winter. It was already icing up. And we didn't only have to look out for Russians. There were Germans, too, who we had to fight where they were—right on Mother Poland's other flank. As you can see, we made it across."

About midway, the current picked up speed and the water deepened. Struggling as they might toward the other shore, they were making progress, but the current was pulling them downstream even faster and they were soon helplessly floating at the mercy of the current. But for the strong swimming of Krysa, Zalaman, kicking madly but ineffectually, along with the wagon and Stanko, would have surely floated under the bridge. The tiny figures on the big bridge grew larger, but then Krysa pulled them beyond the swift midstream current, into something gentler for the final third of the crossing, although by then they were uncomfortably close to the two bridges.

The steel bridge, incomplete as it was, was already a towering structure, dwarfing the old bridge that stood between the construction workers and the three men and two horses in the water. The old bridge was still used by beasts of burden and their loads. From time to time, the old bridge and its traffic helped block the river-crossers from the view of any men who might be looking their way. At times, the three were close enough that, should the men—workers or inspectors—look toward them at the wrong time, they would be able to see their faces as they forded the river. And one of the workers did notice them just as they neared the other bank. The three saw him staring. They tried to hide their faces, but they could not help but try to see what the man would do. He was leaning over the railing, staring right at them. There were other workers milling around this man, but they remained focused on their labors. There was nothing the three could do but keep going. They were exhausted, but still kicking as best they could, sticking close as possible to the horses and wagon vehicle, and finally made it to the far bank, where they turned to look back and saw the man on the bridge still staring. As horses and men scrambled for purchase on dry ground, the sentinel stayed there, watching impassively.

Georg's wagon was less than waterproof. It had come close to sinking, but once they got it back on land, the waters of the Aryot drained quickly out through all the cracks. After that swim, the horses strained to ascend the riverbank to drier earth. The bridge was still there and so was the sentinel. As long as they could see him, he had continued to stare in their direction, but he made no move to raise an alarm. He was an unknown ally, certainly no sentinel. They disappeared into a wooded area, and soon penetrated the edge of that vast forest Zalaman had marveled at yesterday evening from the other side of the river.

They didn't stop to dry their clothes or other belongings but made sure their guns and Georg's bank notes had remained dry in their wrappings. Then they had to move on. There was a chance that a party of Cossacks, perhaps alerted by the man on the bridge, would be looking for them.

They took a little-travelled road northeast, not much more than a trail, but a trail Rodak and Stanko knew well. Up toward the forested hills and into greener woods on the northeast side of the Aryot and to the farmhouse where they had stored provisions, including weapons and ammunition.

They didn't stop until they were high above the river. They were exhausted—the Aryot crossing had taken a toll—and it was too dark to travel any further safely. They made camp in a meadow bordered by birch and towering oaks, fed the horses from the abundant grasses, long and bowed in the fading summer. Stanko showed Zalaman how to use the long grasses to fashion mattresses, while Rodak started a small campfire and they talked and roasted a couple more varmints supplied by Rodak's gun and prepared by Zalaman.

It was cooler at the higher altitude, but the temperature change felt like a harbinger of fall. They were exhausted but invigorated at the same time and cleaner than they had been before their frigid and frightening baptism in the Aryot, a cleansing away of much mud and blood. Zalaman wanted to know if they weren't surprised, like he was, that the man on the bridge hadn't given them away. "Maybe that means we're in friendly territory?"

"The people, yes," Rodak said. "But I was afraid there might be a Cossack with them."

"It's a good sign," Stanko said. "An omen." Rodak said he didn't believe in omens, just a good night's sleep.

The sun was up when Zalaman opened his eyes the next morning. Squinting into the light, he saw Rodak silhouetted against the sky. Stanko was still snoring peacefully.

Zalaman didn't get up. He watched Rodak as he knelt by the little stream, a modest confluent of the Aryot that ran through the meadow. The 3-inch, cracked pocket mirror, the one Zalaman had used to observe the knot on his head he'd received from Georg's blow, was propped up on a tree branch so Rodak could shave, working to improve the shape of his sideburns, goatee, and mustache. He took much care in this operation, a trait of the focused attention Rodak brought to other endeavors, like cleaning his guns—and shooting them. Zalaman often felt animosity from Rodak, yet in some ways he wanted to be more like him. He rubbed his own face and thought he felt something there. Had he grown facial hair since the chappering?

Rodak saw him and laughed. "Don't worry, kid. You'll become a man some day and you'll see—hair all over. Jews are famous for their luxuriant beards."

"You're always talking about *Jews.*"

Awakened by Rodak's ribbing, Stanko stretched his limbs and scratched his own beard. "It's not Rodak's fault," he said. "Rodak is the victim of a bad education—a bad upbringing, until he came to live with us—my mother and me."

"What did I say?" Rodak complained. "I was paying the Jews a compliment."

Stanko got up to relieve himself but kept talking. "Rodak's father is to blame for Rodak's bad attitudes. He hated everyone who wasn't a Pole, and you couldn't be an authentic Pole unless you were an Orthodox Pole. But he reserved a special place in his heart for Hebrews. A very bad place."

Rodak just chuckled and shook his head, looking at himself in the ruined mirror. There were a few nicks, the result of a poor blade rather than an unsteady hand, he told himself. He made strong tea, boiling water in a small iron samovar held over the fire by an iron tripod. He poured some for Stanko and Zalaman.

The sun hadn't yet had a chance to warm the air, so Zalaman wrapped Georg's ample old muslin shirt around him. It was coarse and big enough to fit like a greatcoat. It would have fit Stanko, but Stanko didn't want anything of Georg's that wasn't instantly redeemable for gold or silver. He held up Georg's river-washed trousers and said he could make them fit Zalaman, "If you want, and I'll still have enough material left over to make you a wool vest. I was a tailor's apprentice before I was hijacked into the Uprising. Not physically hijacked, like you. Seduced. But I can cut and sew and you'll have a wool vest like an American cowboy."

Zalaman had seen an engraving of such a cowboy vest in one of Mama's books about the American West. He was touched by Stanko's offer and said thank you, but he wondered why Stanko was being so nice to him. He suspected it was part of an attempt to seduce *him* into joining the Uprising. He told himself wasn't going to fight Cossacks, but he saw no problem and perhaps no choice as far as accompanying the cousins to their HQ where he might be able to send a message to his parents. Rodak had said the Aryot could take him home, though he had never heard of that river. Maybe it was just a saying, 'All rivers lead home,' something Zalaman might hear from Osher and Henzel in the Lahkvna *kvadrat*. Or "Aryot" might be only one of its names. Rivers had different names in different tongues, in different regions. Traveling alone on a barge, if he had a few of Georg's coins, would be exciting and probably safer than throwing in with Polish partisans who say they have been fighting the Tsar for three years—Rodak much longer than that—but were obviously not profiting much for their trouble. Killing Cossacks was not only unimaginable, but it would also be dangerous work and it provided these cousins from Navharadak with badly worn boots and patched trousers, faded and mismatched uniforms.

The next morning, they descended to the other side of the hill, fording a minor branch of the Aryot, then continued up into the high hills that reared up before the mountain range. Going up was a struggle. When they stopped to feed the horses and rest them for the next hill, Zalaman asked about the farmhouse they were headed toward. You'll see tomorrow, they promised him. It was off the main path, the house itself backed up nearly to the base of a steep, protective cliff and a good spot to mount quick raids and ambushes on Cossacks. The partisan-friendly farmer, Bazily, who owned the place, was looking after their weapons and provisions.

"We've stashed quite an arsenal at the farmhouse, for one thing," Stanko said. "Most of the other rewards we'd accumulated we left with my mother in Navharadak." When questioned by Zalaman, Stanko admitted that their 'furlough' was not actually an official one sanctioned by the Uprising, it was more a case of two war-weary veterans taking some necessary time out—a time to rest and put on some weight eating his mom's cooking.

They made good progress that day, stopping for the night when it got dark and dangerous for horses and men. They found flat, level ground near a hillside, positioning their campsite so they had a view of their surroundings. Somewhere in the valley below was the farmhouse. Stanko and Rodak said they could get there the next day, if they started before daybreak.

Before lying down, Rodak asked Zalaman how his father had been lucky enough to be rewarded special dispensation from the Tsar allowing him to sell alcohol to Christians on Sundays. "Was he some kind of friend to the Russians?"

"Maybe it wasn't luck," Zalaman said defensively. He felt he and his mother had played a big role in the honor the Trade Commissioner of Navharadak had bestowed on his father: his mother's friendship with the Commissioner's wife through her literary interests, and his own with Hadar, the Commissioner's daughter, but that would be a long story and he was tired.

"It's odd. That's all," Rodak said. "I don't know how much *shtetl* Jews know about the Christian world. About what's going on outside your *shtetl.*"

"I do know there was an Uprising. All I've heard spoken about it though, before now, was that it was over—and that was from our sages, Osher and Henzel, so I'm not surprised if I've been misled. My father always said they made up facts to support their message. My father also said the Uprising accomplished nothing but a lot of Polish deaths. He said this was bad for the Poles, but for us, too." Zalaman did not add his father's reasoning that this was because when the Poles were angry, they were likely to take it out on the Jews. "He also said that it was the peasants who suffered the most."

"You are talking about the Uprising in 1830," Rodak said. "'The November Revolt.' I was in that one, too, and it did include the peasants. Out intention was to liberate the serfs, but the Tsar got wind of it and beat us to it."

Stanko groaned at this interpretation of history and Rodak said, "Whether or not the serfs are truly 'liberated' is another question. The Tsar's actions took away the serfs' incentive to join the fight. Now, leap ahead thirty years to our new Uprising—our only *significant* uprising since 1830, and I know because I participated in some of the other, lesser ones, too. Three years ago when we began our new fight, when Stanko joined up, it looked like we might really challenge the Tsar . . ."

". . . But it ran into some problems since then," Stanko said. "It didn't take me more than a couple of months to figure out we were never going to get rid of the Tsar. Our patriots, our 'rebels,' most went home early. So, Rodak and I have to fight these pitiful, little skirmishes with the Russians. We're just harassing them—and sometimes their Polish sympathizers as well . . ."

". . . It's patriotic work that's got to be done," Rodak interjected.

"And we make a living at it," Stanko continued. "We are responsible only for ourselves. There is no or very little pay coming from our command."

"So why are we going to the HQ?"

"They provide useful information," Rodak said. "And hope."

They broke camp before sunup and headed for the farmhouse. The cool night air quickly warmed to something more like August. They took their one water break before approaching the farmhouse and Rodak returned to the evening's discussion.

"The truth about these uprisings . . . what you start to see . . . is that our history is all one big uprising. There's never been a shortage of oppressors. The Orthodox Church has been one of the worst. But that's history. Today we have to keep our minds on the business at hand—on this world, where the Tsar is busy turning Polish lands into what he is calling the 'Western Region' of *his* Empire. That's why we must stop him. If we don't, he'll keep turning Poles into servants in their own country. He's not only stealing Polish land, but he's also killing young Poles when he conscripts them into his army."

"Jews, too," Zalaman said.

"Jews, too," Rodak agreed.

CHAPTER FOUR

Battle at the Farmhouse

They would approach quietly, making sure everything was as it should be, as they had left it months earlier. Rodak scouted ahead and when he reappeared, riding Beth at a healthy trot, he was pointing up at the sky. Zalaman and Stanko looked up and saw the wisp of smoke.

"That's it," Stanko said.

Rodak rode up with his finger now across his lips. "No shouting," he said. There was no way Bazily would be wasting firewood on such a fine day. "About 100 meters from the farmhouse, I started to catch snatches of voices in the wind."

"Bazily? Russian voices?"

"I couldn't be sure, but it's more than one voice." Watching for sentinels, they would sneak up to get closer to the farmhouse without showing themselves. Just in case. From the cliff, they could be hidden while looking down on the farmhouse, practically beneath them.

They maneuvered wagon and horses to the base of a hill, hid the wagon, muzzled the horses, and then tied them to birches and walked slowly up the hill, Rodak and Stanko carrying weapons and communicating by gesture. There was no talking. For Bazily to have visitors would not necessarily be a bad sign, but for Rodak, burning winter fuel in the fireplace was a sign that Bazily was not there—or not in charge. It would be stupid not to assume the worst. Always assume the unknown is unfriendly.

Several meandering trails lead to the summit through brush and over rock soil. Rodak led the way, taking the path where they would be least likely to be seen or fall and make noise.

They stayed close together, stopping once for everyone to catch their breath. It was hot and rocky but this was no time to rest. Zalaman accidentally started a minor rock slide, tempting Rodak to send him back down to stay with the horses. But after that, they reached the summit without incident and without seeing any sentry as the trees and underbrush gave way to an open space, with a garden of boulders and scattered stone. The three, scratched from the rocks and underbrush, were relieved to reach the top.

Stanko poked Zalaman in the shoulder and pointed behind them. The height they'd attained allowed him to look back at the land they had travelled the past two days. The Aryot was hidden below many hills, but to the south, faintly, he thought he could discern the immense woodland where Rodak had dispatched Georg. He suddenly felt very distant from everything he'd known. The towering slab of rock which was the cliff edge gave them cover, allowing them to look down on the back of the farmhouse. They could hear snatches of voices—there were several male voices—but crouched behind a boulder they still couldn't tell what language was being spoken. To see what was going on and to hear better, they would have to expose their heads.

Rodak inched his head beyond the boulder to peek, then quickly pulled back. Stanko peeked and then they let Zalaman look, Stanko holding him back so he wouldn't lean out too far and expose their whereabouts. It was a breath-taking view of the hills beyond and the fields and woods and fifty meters below them the farmhouse itself—sprawling, wood shingled and looked to be accommodating a number of Cossacks who were loitering about. Some carried holstered revolvers. Restrained by Stanko, he still managed to stick his head out another inch and saw right below them a stack of muskets leaning against a big wagon parked half-way into the farm's stables at the rear of the farmhouse.

Without a word, taking their time, they walked softly back down the hill until they were back in the copse of birches with the wagon and horses and out of earshot.

Rodak counted at least six Russians, although there could, of course, be more inside the house. Zalaman assumed they'd go straight to HQ. Maybe get some reinforcements. That's what he would do if they encountered a similar situation in the *kvadrat* while playing cowboys and Indians with his friends.

"Bazily wouldn't betray us," Stanko said to Rodak. "He's either in the farmhouse or dead," Rodak said. "They've taken our weapons. We must get them back."

"Shouldn't you at least get reinforcements?" Zalaman said 'you' instead of 'we' and the cousins took note.

"So, you aren't going to fight?" Rodak asked. "After we saved your life?"

"I can't kill anyone. It's quite a sin for us Jews."

"I didn't think you were religious," Stanko said.

"He'd only get in the way," Rodak said dismissively. "He'd give us away. And he can't shoot."

"You're badly outnumbered—with or without me."

"But we will have the element of surprise," Rodak said to Zalaman, then turned his attention to his cousin. "They've been here awhile and grown complacent. The smoky fire. No sentries." Zalaman should have been happy to be dismissed, but he wasn't, because it did feel cowardly to abandon them now. There was going to be bloodshed and he'd had enough of that already.

Georg's and his own.

"You should come with us," Stanko said, disappointed to think he may have misjudged Zalaman. "It's time for you to grow up. See what it's like to be brothers in a fight. We are all of us, Poles, and Jews, hurt by this Tsar."

"How is it even possible?" he asked. "They're well armed and there are many more of them."

"Go home," Rodak said. "I've had enough of you."

Stanko was not so harsh, but not wanting to be responsible for Zalaman getting killed, especially after having saved him, he suggested Zalaman walk back the way they'd come and sneak home on some river barge to at least get started in the right direction.

"You'll likely be picked up by another *chapper* before you make it home," Rodak said.

Zalaman refused to be so easily dismissed. "Bazily knew you were coming back, so the Cossacks probably do, too. The Cossacks would know that a farmer isn't going to have all those weapons—that you'll be coming back for them sometime."

"So?" Rodak demanded.

"Maybe he has a point," Stanko said. "They look relaxed, but that doesn't mean they aren't waiting for us."

"Did you notice the uniforms?" Rodak asked. "There are no officers enforcing regulations. Have we seen any sentries?"

"Cossacks don't always follow regulations."

"We know Cossacks can be dangerous, but the way these ones are lolling about, midday, no lookouts—that shows a big lack of discipline and that's to our advantage."

"So, we strike now," Stanko said. It was half-confirmation, half question.

"We strike now," Rodak said, "before the situation changes, before they get wind that we are here."

Zalaman not only felt he was too young to die, but that killing was forbidden. He was sure it was forbidden to kill someone who had done nothing to you. Like the Cossacks. They were no threat to him—no immediate threat.

Stanko was disappointed in him. Rodak contemptuous. And Zalaman wanted their approval almost as much as he wanted to preserve his life and go home. Almost. The cousins gathered their weapons, the old musket, two revolvers, the pike, and knives.

When Zalaman tried to ask what their plan was, they didn't seem to have any plan at all. Either that or they didn't want to talk to him about it. When they had their weapons and were ready to go, Stanko told Zalaman he didn't have to go home. He'd get lost. Rodak had gone ahead and didn't hear Stanko tell Zalaman to stay with the horses.

"You don't have to leave. Keep our earnings safe. We'll be back. We are good shots, as you've seen. Rodak will take three Cossacks before any of them gets off a shot. The trick with a musket is you must get close to your target. If we can get within seventy meters, they'll be dead men, you'll see."

"You don't even know how many of them there are."

"Go, then," Stanko said. "I don't care." He disappeared into the trees after his cousin. It would be a struggle to get to the positions they needed, especially to do it silently with heavy weapons. They would approach from two sides at once.

Zalaman sat alone in the wagon, struggling with nerves and indecision. He ate a remnant of Georg's bread. Once the Cossack's had killed Rodak and Stanko, the risk of his being found was high. Best to go home like Stanko said. Reverse course and walk down the road they'd come down, make his way to the Aryot and take it from there. He chewed but his mouth was dry and he had little hunger. He thought about the man on the bridge. Perhaps he had been a messenger, a sign for him to come home, get away from the partisans. He felt bad about leaving his new friends after all they'd done for him. But a life for a life? He didn't know. Could he even find his way home? He pictured them all—Mama, Papa, Davin, Keila, his friends, Ev and Aron. Their mother, Minya. The memories made him sad, not just missing them, but knowing Lahkvna wasn't ever going to be the same because he wasn't the same. He'd been snatched away from all he knew, then snatched from death, and now here he was, in some woods at the bottom of a hill, who knows where, guarding the cousins' precious cargo. Waiting for what? He laughed at himself. Despite everything, he didn't really want to go home yet. He could not make up his mind what to do. His body ached but was slowly healing, and his head was still sore from Georg's blow, but he felt stronger. He'd kept up with two rough men—and had learned a lot. If he stayed, what might be in store for him? A bullet. Or a treasure. If he could get a message to his parents, he'd feel better. They would be thinking he was dead or as good as. Perhaps they had held some kind of service to pray for him, like there had been for Heri Benowitz, when he disappeared.

He swallowed the last of the bread and there was a silence broken only by the birds' singing overhead and the horses chewing the grass. Or did he hear something like a shout in the distance, from the direction of the farmhouse? He decided it was time to go. He gathered up some of his things. He would have no one to guide him. He would have to stay off the main roads to avoid *chappers* and just about anybody else. If he left now, it might not be too late. He could leave the horses and wagon, just help himself to a bit of Georg's purse. Or he'd never get a barge ride.

And then a shot rang out. The horses flinched and Zalaman jumped and grabbed the reins. The shot's echo reverberated in the hills. Then there was one more shot, followed by its echo and then silence. No more shots nor birdsong. Was it already over?

But then there was a third shot, and something snapped in him. He grabbed an old hunting knife—the only weapon Rodak and Stanko hadn't taken with them—and scrambled back up the hill where he would be able to see what was going on from the rocky outcropping over the farmhouse. As he ran, scratched by branches he didn't notice, trying not to make too much noise hurrying across loose stones, three more shots echoed. Then shouting. Then two more shots. Then when he got to the top, nothing.

The shots sounded more like an exercise in target practice, than what he thought a battle would sound like. Maybe that was a good sign. Maybe the cousins, facing impossible odds, were holding their own.

There had been several minutes of silence by the time Zalaman situated himself behind the boulder overlook. Forty meters down, almost directly below him, he saw the heads of two armed Cossacks. They felt so close, he pulled back behind the boulder before exhaling and then took another look. The two were pinned behind the big military wagon, parked halfway into the stables. The two Cossacks were trying to avoid being picked off by Rodak or Stanko who were shooting at them from across the road in front of the farmhouse. They were largely hidden from view behind trees, but from his vantage point he could make out Rodak, sprawled out on his stomach with his musket in one hand and Lafaucheux in the other, and, deeper in the woods, a glint from the bayonet on Stanko's musket. There were three figures in the middle distance, but then Zalaman quickly withdrew behind the boulder as Rodak and Stanko both fired.

After an interval of Russian shouting but no shooting, Zalaman hazarded another look. The three figures were three Cossacks on the ground. Neither was moving, but at least one could be heard moaning. A shouting of orders in Russian—to "Sandor" and "Petya" and "Mika." Whoever the two Cossacks directly below him were, he could see how desperately they wanted to get to the rifles and muskets that were stacked in front of the wagon but couldn't because they were pinned down by Rodak and Stanko's bullets. When they weren't shooting at the soldiers behind the wagon, the cousins aimed a few shots directly at the farmhouse, indicating to Zalaman that there were probably more Cossacks inside.

Zalaman stuck his head out again to get a longer look at the three Cossacks sprawled out in the farmhouse's yard. Two were in the awkward, contorted postures often assumed by those slowly dying painful deaths. Zalaman had witnessed something similar when Georg was writhing in the mud. The body's final grasp at life. The nearest of the three downed Cossacks, only thirty meters away from the military wagon, was not yet dead, but was lying in a river of his own blood and given the nature of his cries, it didn't seem that he was going to pose any further problems. Ten meters further on, closer to the road—Stanko and Rodak were firing from the other side of the road—was another man, not yet dead either, but also close to it. He sat quietly, slumped, and unmoving against a tree and surrounded by another impressive pool of blood. The third man was very dead, limbs, too, at odd angles. He wore a Russian army tunic like the others, but this one had a familiar, organ-festooned pike sticking out through the fabric.

Zalaman became so riveted by the scene playing out before him, he forgot all about hiding. He got a better view of Rodak, who was sprawled on his stomach but didn't seem to be hurt. He was using his elbows to prop up his musket and hold it steady, now occasionally shooting toward the farmhouse, not at the Cossacks below. Stanko, barely visible from Zalaman's perspective, was hidden in the trees, but he was exasperated by the situation he'd put himself in. To finish what he'd started, he fired at the nearly dead Cossack slumped against the tree and the shot blew the man back into the dirt—a piece of his head missing. This made Stanko feel a little better. It was as if his aim had improved in the heat of battle.

On their way to the farmhouse, he and Rodak had formulated a plan of sorts, which had consisted of one idea: approach the farmhouse from two sides. Stanko had a much longer walk to skirt the farmhouse to become the eastern half of their pincer, but they found their blinds for shooting, after Rodak had already dispatched the nearest Cossack with his pike and then run for the cover of the evergreens. He and Stanko fired the first two shots, both successful, and pinning two other Cossacks behind a supply wagon. On the cliff behind them, above the wagon, where they'd earlier gotten their glimpse of the new order at Bazily's, Rodak thought he saw a head peek out. Then it disappeared. He thought he must have been mistaken, but then the head reappeared. Rodak shook his own head in disbelief. The Jew! Rodak started firing at the two Cossacks but they were well-protected behind the heavy military cart, and his bullets lodged harmlessly in the cart's heavy timber or zinged off an iron-clad wagon wheel.

Zalaman, crouched down behind a bolder the size of a small house, thought how Samson could push one of the boulders—for this one he'd need black powder as well as God's hand—over the cliff and smash the farmhouse below. Stones were plentiful, but useless. He tried a few of the bigger stones and, digging one out, found it to be much bigger than it had looked, most of it hidden in the dirt. It was almost as big as his head, big enough to do some damage. If he could lift it, he could send it crashing down on the two Cossacks behind the wagon, hopefully without getting killed himself in the process.

It was, in fact, too heavy to pick up. It was oddly shaped, but he managed to roll it awkwardly toward the cliff edge. Intermittent shots rang out. He was sweating by the time he rolled it to the edge. Looking down from his protected spot behind the boulder, he could see that his chances were slim that he would hit either of the Cossacks or do any real damage by just rolling the rock over. He would need to lift the rock and heave it out as far as he could. God was going to have to help him. He had to believe he could do it, so he did his best to convince himself. He took a breath and steadied himself, then bent down over the rock and struggled to get an arm under. He was slippery with sweat, and it slid off his arms. He wiped them on his trousers and tried again, finally managing to get both arms under the rock. He strained to straighten his knees, which were shaking when he lifted the rock about one meter off the ground then, immediately, before he lost his grip, and with an uncontrollable groan, launched it underhand at the head of the Cossack most directly below.

The moment it dropped, the Cossack, hearing the groan if not the plummeting rock, turned slightly, enough that the rock missed his head by a centimeter and smashed into his thigh instead. The sound of his thigh bone snapping could be heard through the soldier's scream. He dropped his rifle, grabbed his leg and fell over. His fellow Cossack looked up at Zalaman and swung his rifle around to shoot. Zalaman ducked behind the boulder just in time and the Cossack missed, but then crumpled to the ground. Straightening up to shoot Zalaman, he'd exposed himself to Rodak's line of fire.

Shuddering from fear and exhilaration behind the boulder, Zalaman heard the injured Cossack below crying from pain. Zalaman peeked out to take a look and saw the Cossack Rodak had shot make a vain attempt to grab a weapon from the pile of rifles and muskets leaning against the supply wagon. He was rewarded for his effort with a bullet from Stanko and he collapsed one last time.

Except for the whimpering of the Cossack whose leg Zalaman had shattered, it was momentarily quiet. And then a shot rang out from a side door of the farmhouse.

The bullet zinged off the boulder, taking a chunk out of it, but missed Zalaman. The shooter emerged from a side door of the farmhouse, firing now at Stanko but failing to see Rodak, who leveled the Lefaucheux at the man and shot him in the chest. His knees buckled and he fell in a heap, arms, and legs akimbo, like the two sprawled on Bazily's yard.

"You were like David and Goliath all in one," Stanko laughed when the three had reunited and were huddling behind the Cossacks' supply wagon. Next to them, the man whose leg Zalaman had crushed, was moaning softly. Rodak had killed the Cossack who'd come out of the house firing at Zalaman on the cliff, but the farmhouse still wasn't emptied out, as proved by the shot from inside that had convinced Rodak to get behind the wagon. He'd looked up and motioned Zalaman to come.

Making his way carefully down, then around the hill, sometimes crawling, running from tree to shed, Zalaman joined Rodak and Stanko hunkered down with the wagon between them and the farmhouse.

"No, not David plus Goliath—Samson at the pillars of the temple," Rodak said, clapping Zalaman on the shoulder. Zalaman could remember only one other time Rodak had bestowed such a smile on him. The other time it had been for his prowess butchering a pig.

"David needed five stones to bring down Goliath," Stanko said. "It took you only one!"

"It was supposed to hit him on the head," Zalaman said, "but he moved. I could barely lift that. I was lucky I hit anything. You two were much more successful!"

"But you're here! You came!" Stanko marveled.

"You did fine," Rodak smiled again "I have to admit, I'm surprised."

"Samson was a Jew," Stanko pointed out. They heard Russian curses coming from the farmhouse.

"There is still someone there and it's not Bazily," Rodak said. "We can't move, not knowing what room he's in." They tried to think, but the Cossack with the crushed leg, who had been bawling, distracted them as he whimpered very softly and then died, saving them the task of putting him out of his misery.

"There may be some Cossacks out on patrol," Rodak said, "but, if there are, they're not many. This little farmhouse couldn't accommodate many more than who we see lying on the ground right now. My guess is that we have only the one remaining Cossack to clean out."

"Your 'guess?'" Zalaman asked. Rodak shrugged. He told them he had to think. He'd come up with something. That was the best he had to offer and the other two had nothing better. In the meantime, taking care not to put themselves in the farmhouse's line of fire, they inspected the weapons that were stacked around the military wagon, a combination of the Cossacks' arms and those the cousins had stashed before the Cossacks had come.

In the supply wagon, Zalaman found a fine leather bag. Inside it he discovered a beautiful spyglass. Stanko, pointing out the sliding lens protector and the beauty of the brass lens cover, said it was a great find and Zalaman should keep it. Along its length were finely etched Cyrillic letters with the name of the manufacturer and, in the most ornate flourishes, "Opticians to the Romanovs."

Rodak held up a real rifle, one that used the rounded bullets he now had in his other hand. "Ten times the accuracy of our muskets," he claimed, "of which we now possess nine—the arsenal we left here with what we've gained from the Tsar today. *Will* gain." He yelled something in Russian at the farmhouse, basically: "Come out and spare your life." Whatever he said, it drew curses and a threat from inside, precisely: "All of us here inside, my comrades and me, we have food and ammunition to hold out for days, but we won't need to do so because our replacements arrive today. If all three of you throw down your arms and stand where you can be seen, I will make sure they spare your lives."

"Now, I'm sure he's alone," Rodak laughed.

"So, what should we do—storm the place?" Stanko asked.

"There's a stack of straw in the back of the stable," Zalaman said. "You can see it from the cliff. Maybe we could burn him out?"

"No," Stanko said. "It would be a smoke signal to any regiments that might be around. Not to mention," he winked at Zalaman, "where would we sleep tonight?"

"Not here," Rodak said. "We need to take this great arsenal and wagon and horses and get out of here. Too risky to stay." He looked at Zalaman. "If we burn him out, we need to do it now, before it gets dark when a big fire is really going to stand out—a lot more visible than smoke will be now. The Cossack inside may be lying about reinforcements or supplies on the way, but we are going to assume it's true, that there are at least patrols in the area. The smart thing would be to get out. We've got the arsenal we came for," Rodak said to Stanko and then to Zalaman—"and much more."

"And eliminated some of the Tsar's army," Zalaman said. Rodak looked at him and nodded in agreement because the kid was just stating a fact. He wasn't gloating.

"Unfortunately," Stanko pointed out, "the bastard inside is trying to kill us."

"Let's make it a very hot fire," Rodak said, "so it will burn fast and be less of an alarm to any Cossacks."

The straw was dry as dirt and it didn't take more than the second scratch of Stanko's flint to light what they'd managed to pile under one rear corner of the roof. The flames rushed up and across the thatched roof and in just a few moments the whole place was engulfed in flame. While it burned, they kept an eye on the progress of the fire, the doors for an escapee, and they gathered the Cossack horses, lashing them together in a line strung from their new military wagon. They filled the vehicle with enough weaponry for a small army.

And then it was over, the farmhouse reduced to little more than glowing charcoal with a stone chimney and stone walls. No escape attempt had been made, but inside, close to the front door, they found a rifle butt in a large lump of charcoal. Stanko poked at the lump with his bayonet, dislodging ash in the process and revealing a blackened foot on a charred leg.

"He tried to get out," Rodak said, "but he waited too long. He was overcome by smoke."

The three rode off with their booty.

><

They headed toward the partisan headquarters outside the town of Syp where they hoped to be greeted as conquering heroes, driving two vehicles pulled by three horses, with four more trailing, and carrying the arsenal along with a bit of silver Stanko had found in a charred satchel in the farmhouse, much of it, not all, to be shared with the partisans at Syp. They rode through the night and well into the next day.

To Zalaman they looked like one of those wagon trains of the American West depicted in Mama's illustrated journals. He drove Georg's cart. Inside it and in the much larger Cossack wagon, they carried an extensive and odd assortment of weaponry—the Russian rifle, nine muskets and several revolvers, ammunition for each, and other favorites like the pike and various blades—and considerably more silver and coins.

Ahead of him, Stanko was in the middle position, driving the large, military wagon which required a team of two horses. The weaponry was as heavy as both the silver and the wagon itself. Rodak was up front on horseback thinking how the commandant was going to be thrilled with what they got. They traveled through woods and skirted any farmland, staying off the main roads whenever possible, avoiding anything that might even be considered a village, any grouping of more than three residences. The wagon train would take several days to reach Syp.

At one campfire, Zalaman asked about the "HQ' and Stanko told him they personally didn't refer to Syp as "the Command Post" as other partisans did, because they didn't take commands from HQ, they took information. HQ was a good source of information on the current state of operations and the state of the people's sympathies.

"Our mission is only possible with the support of the people." Zalaman didn't ask for specifics of the mission.

Rodak said their duty was "to harass the Tsar. We accomplish this by killing Cossacks and taking from them the riches they've taken from our people—from our land."

Stanko passed around a bottle of Polish Vodka he'd rescued from the farmhouse. Stanko was very fond of alcohol. He claimed there was nothing better to relieve the soreness of a long drive.

"And to prepare us for the road ahead. To Syp!" He took another long drink. Rodak looked at this with disapproval and put the bottle away once he and Zalaman had each had one more sip.

"Over the years, we have contributed much more than we've received from HQ," Stanko complained.

"And now we'll be contributing all this?" Zalaman asked.

Rodak said they would hide some of it away. "It's our due. The commandant is a friend, but he'll be thrilled with the guns and the big Cossack wagon we're giving him. He would expect us to hide some away for ourselves. He'd do the same if he wasn't the commandant."

Zalaman wondered what his cut would be.

The journey to Syp took several days. They were peaceful ones. With Rodak's assistance, Zalaman worked on his abilities with musket and revolver. He was making progress, Rodak said. Rodak shot a hare and Zalaman impressed the other two once again with his talent as a butcher, explaining as he sliced how he came to learn the art, about Heri Benowitz, his friends' father, a butcher who emigrated to America and got rich in Chicago and wrote back a letter to his father telling him all about it. "They eat so much beef there, you wouldn't believe it. Ham, turkey and hung beef for teatime!" He'd boasted.

The cousins liked the idea. Stanko was enthusiastic about such a diet. "That's a very smart place to open a butcher shop," he said. "Probably more profitable than Lahkvna, which sounds like a crumbling mess."

Knowing Syp was close, they picked up as much speed as their new encumbrances would allow, avoiding civilization and potential encounters with Cossacks. Avoiding the latter proved to be easy. They interpreted this as a good sign. HQ would still be where it was the last time they'd stayed there.

Zalaman hoped that a real headquarters would make him feel better about getting involved in any 'uprising.' It went against everything he'd believed in to think he might become a partisan and fight Cossacks, but then, aside from Mama's love, maybe he hadn't really believed in anything all that much. He wanted to reassure himself that these cousins weren't simply crazy and that there was still an actual Uprising underway. Most of all, he hoped he would be able to send a message home.

One day, the evening before the day they planned to arrive in Syp, they stopped early. While they would eat with the other partisans when they were at HQ and would share their weaponry, they had no desire to share their remaining food stocks—five doves they'd shot that day and vegetables they'd picked out of dry fields ready for harvesting. The silver from Georg and some of the ammunition they would hide, but the provisions wouldn't keep. They wrapped in burlap what they wanted to keep for themselves—Zalaman's spyglass along with silver and weapons—and walked deep into the woods to bury it. Then they ate the doves. Afterward, Stanko leaned against a tree trunk and wielded scissors, needle, and thread to alter Georg's trousers for Zalaman. He would save the scraps of wool left over for a woolen cowboy vest. Rodak talked to Zalaman about their dependence on making alliances with the local pro-partisan, anti-Tsar civilian population wherever they went. "The trick is you never know a civilian's—anyone's—true allegiance unless you've known them a long time. We sometimes need to make unholy alliances just to make sure we can eat."

Syp was the shortened name of a town whose full name was unpronounceable even for Poles. There was no visible Cossack presence in the town. On the short road from Syp to the HQ, everywhere there were partisans of the Uprising serving as sentries. A pair of these sentries would materialize out of the woods along the route, ask Rodak a few questions and he knew all the right answers and passwords. He even waved a piece of paper with an official seal. After their inquiries, the sentries would dissolve back into the woods, and everything would return to normal.

HQ consisted of two parallel rows of small tents with one big tent at one end attached to an old stone farmhouse. The camp had been extending further from the farmhouse, growing, then receding over the years in synchronicity with the ebb and flow of the Uprising. Headquarters had its own stables, cleared and fenced yards, and shooting range. Three years earlier, shortly after the insurrection in Vilna, this was where the Uprising launched its initial operations against the occupying Russian army. There had been only two major operations launched directly from this camp and both had ended in catastrophic losses for the partisans. Their Syp location was never discovered. It had become a useful place for weapons training and sharing useful information and material with others.

Rodak, Stanko and Zalaman and their vehicles and horses kicked up a lot of dust and raised a lot of interest when they rode in, passing by the rows of tents and up to the stone farmhouse where the commandant and other partisans congratulated them on their success. They welcomed the recruit, Jewish or not. They also accepted the booty the three had brought. The coins, weapons and horses could be put to good use. The HQ was partly compensated by mysterious Polish loyalists in Warsaw, but their generosity was never sufficient. Operations were mostly carried out by little groups like Rodak's three, but there were as many as a dozen or more soldiers in some patrols.

They would come and go, returning with booty or injuries or dead comrades. During their time there, Zalaman noted that some patrols didn't return at all.

Rodak, Stanko and Zalaman were in an assigned tent. They practiced with their muskets and a rifle supplied by the commandant (they'd hidden theirs with the other valuables). They were provided with information about the movement of Cossacks who were busy enforcing the Tsar's edicts in various parts of the region. There were shown maps detailing the movements of the Russians and partisans, revealing places where partisans had recently been effective and others where they had suffered defeats.

The three would be granted an area of land where the prospects of engagement and reward were promising. They would stay at HQ for at least two weeks, eating, resting, and training with experts in combat, including guns that used metal-encased bullets. Then, their way would be open to the potentially lucrative, relatively unscathed, but always disputed Polish-Russian border area of Kietlanka-Stok-Kleczkow, between the Narew and Bug rivers.

Rodak took Zalaman to the commandant to see about getting a message to his family. Zalaman's request was a civilian matter, but Rodak explained his feelings that "in view of Pan Aszer's heroism at The Battle of the Seven Cossacks" (as it was being referred to in HQ), "he should receive some consideration." Unfortunately, the telegraph lines were down again. Zalaman would have to entrust a brief note to their courier. The only problem was that there were currently no couriers available. Once they found one, the commandant said that Zalaman should understand that it was a long way to Navharadak or Lahkvna so the letter might not arrive right away. But thanks to a bribe of additional ammunition from Rodak, Zalaman's letter went out the next week. It was restricted to a brief note, simply letting his family know he was alive and well and that he loved them and would see them soon and explain everything. He was sorry he had to keep this note so brief, because he had so much to tell them. It wasn't strictly true that he had to keep the note so brief. He could have written something a bit longer, but when he had started to do so, he realized he didn't know how to tell them what he'd done. He didn't want to frighten them. He didn't want to write to them about killing people. Even if they were Cossacks. The commandant explained that the courier would be one of several men who would be responsible for the letter, transferring it to others, over the course of its journey to Lahkvna. When his letter left for Lahkvna, Zalaman was relieved. He would no longer be torturing his parents and brother and sister with the assumption he was dead, that his young life had drained away in a far-off battlefield. With this worry removed, Zalaman could now consider his options. It would have its hazards, but if he stayed with Rodak and Stanko—say for the winter, since travel might be as hazardous as fighting—he might bring home some real plunder.

Zalaman enjoyed target practice, Rodak showing him how to pull the trigger without moving the pistol. Zalaman worked his way up from awful to mediocre. He winged the target practice dummy. Using a bayonet, he managed to stab the practice dummy's heart and thought *bayoneting a dummy is one thing, I'm not sure I could do it to a man.* He practiced shooting from horseback. It was hard, but he improved.

"I try to imagine I'm home on Marengo," he said and Rodak laughed at the audacity of a Jew to use the name of Napoleon's horse.

One day shortly before the three left the HQ, Zalaman had just finished a target practice session when he ran into the commandant and took the opportunity to ask him about the Uprising. He could see now that it was something real, just hidden, but he wanted to know the commandant's understanding of it.

"The Poles will always remember the Uprising of 1831, not the current one, the 1863 chapter. It wasn't the disaster this one has been. It didn't need to be so. Things went well for a few years, but the Tsar had more and better arms, and he was aided by our own bad timing, the bad timing of the leaders of the Uprising. So long as the Russians are here, there will always be uprisings. It wasn't quiet in the years between uprisings. It wasn't as if the ideals of the Uprising had disappeared. There were underground groups, mostly landed gentry who still, by the way, support the idea of a Polish National Government. That hope won't go away. You may not be aware of it, but it's the objective of *many* secret societies. They're all closed to Jews, of course. But all along, they've funded forays against the Cossacks. Some are successful but accomplish little toward ridding us of the Russians. Three years ago, at the start of this Uprising, I—we, that is, Stanko and me and others—we found ourselves here in Syp at the right moment. The secret societies decided it was time to strike the Tsar's occupying forces and we all banded together. It was January, a bad month for soldiering, but we were able to move freely and quickly, and we had popular support. Still do. We couldn't be here without it."

CHAPTER FIVE
The Gmerks

Having said their goodbyes to the commandant and other partisans, the three rode out to collect what they had stashed away. It felt like the summer was coming to an end.

The nights had grown cooler, but the leaves had not yet turned. They were a leaner, more mobile trio, having donated the big military wagon to the cause. It would be too big and unwieldy and might draw unwanted attention. At HQ they would be able to fix it up so you could no longer identify it as having had anything to do with the Tsar. They kept Georg's *chapper* wagon, filling it with the provisions they received from HQ—thanks for their generosity with the wagon they contributed, along with muskets and horses.

They were down to Krysa and a Cossack horse pulling the wagon and Rodak's mount, Beth. Zalaman was told that their work might require the ability to move quickly. They didn't want to be weighed down by extraneous gear or vehicles. Their arsenal now consisted of two rifles with bayonets and two revolvers along with a small crate of metal-cased bullets. They also possessed three muskets, three sabers and the ancient pike. All this barely fit into the cart, which had room for little other than clothing food and utensils.

Rodak and Stanko carried revolvers in their jacket pockets and Rodak's saddle bag was stuffed with maps from the commandant. In the back of the cart, they had salted meat and bags of flour and vegetables—all tucked away under woolen blankets—enough to feed them for weeks if need be. They were on their way to a region beyond Kleczko—the area circled in bold strokes on Rodak's map.

On the second day of their travels, Rodak rode back from his forward position to tell Zalaman he wanted him to ride ahead and scout. "Take Beth and the spyglass, and Stanko's rifle, and then, then *pay attention* and don't stay away too long." Stanko added with a laugh that he should be sure not to expose himself. Zalaman's new role as scout started, alternating with Rodak—who'd shown some trust in him—and even if at first he wasn't sure what to do, riding ahead, wearing the new cowboy vest from Stanko, and enjoying the use of his spyglass, the way it made unseen things appear, it didn't take long before he started to pay more attention to his surroundings and less to his thoughts.

The three bypassed all military activity thanks to the careful advance scouting, and Cossack patrols were appearing more and more as they traveled to Kleczko and beyond. One day, they would be in open country dotted with fields and woods; the next day, skirting small towns and villages in what was called disputed territory. They crossed the Bug without getting wet as the bridge was in neutral hands that were eager to accept anyone's toll, then decided to get wet anyway, taking badly needed baths in the Bug's cool waters. They entered a border area that stretched all the way to the Narew, avoiding the larger towns like Kietlanka where there was a railroad line and Stok where there were many Cossacks. The Cossacks rode mostly in patrols of ten or twenty, but in one instance they watched from a distance as a platoon of sixty kicked up a veil of dust in a blue August sky.

One day, after skirting the town of Kleczkow, they found themselves back in heavily wooded country. They couldn't see very far ahead and Rodak's maps were proving less reliable the further they got from HQ. But somewhere ahead was a valley inhabited by honest farmers who were regularly tyrannized by Russians.

Zalaman scouted ahead on Beth until the woods grew so thick he had to dismount and proceed on foot, following whatever paths he thought might lead to higher ground.

When he found an elevation that revealed a vast clearing to the east, he saw a patchwork of family farms stretched below, their fields looking ready for harvest, the boundaries of each farm etched by lines of mature birch or conifers. Each field was dotted with a house or two. The openness of the valley provided an ideal space for use of the Romanov spyglass and Zalaman's close attention. Zalaman removed the spyglass from its sheath, slid off the lens protector and brought it up to his eye. He moved it in a slow sweep from farmhouse to farmhouse, checking for Cossacks or any other signs of official authority but seeing none. There were farms with fields of rye and onions, potatoes, and beets, some of them already under harvest. It was a peaceful scene, rounded in his lens: dairy cows, cherry trees, sheds, barns, and occasionally farmers and their families. He had fleeting misgivings about his friends' potential for disturbing the bucolic hush. Easier to think that it was merely the physical distance that made it seem so peaceful. Maybe if you got closer, you would see something different. The spyglass couldn't bring them close enough to determine anything beyond the fact that they were not Cossacks. They were farmers being farmers.

Rodak said this valley would be ideal for their purposes.

Zalaman went back the next day to locate a place somewhat off the beaten path from which they could launch their forays against Cossacks. Now, more familiar with the lay of the land, he rode within the camouflage of trees, less concerned about Russians than the naturally curious and naturally suspicious farm people. Every farmhouse appeared to be too exposed for what

Rodak wanted, too close to the main road through the valley, even if it was little more than a dusty path, meandering alongside a tributary of the BUG. Using his glass, he thought he might finally have found what he was looking for, or so it appeared from a distance. The candidate was on the far eastern end of the east-west valley. Row upon row heavy with the tangled vines of yet-to-be-harvested potatoes, the field came right up to the edge of the woods. 100 meters away was a stone farmhouse with a grove of shade trees, bigger than a peasant's cottage, with a nice barn and sheds close by, and all of it far off the main road. It was well-tended, a look of prosperity and success about it.

Eventually, several people, members of the family (presumably) emerged from the house. Two men headed for the barn, and three women sat down in cane chairs and proceeded to bask in the late afternoon sun. There were two dog—one sleeping, the other sniffing the air. Zalaman was sure the dogs were smelling him and he froze, but realized he was too far downwind to be concerned. Dogs, he knew, were the best sentries and could present a problem if you were trying to sneak up. Both dogs stretched and walked over to watch the two men now absorbed in caring for an ox and a mule.

The leaves, still clinging to the trees, still full of summer, though some were displaying the first tints of autumn, provided Zalaman with excellent cover. But he was going to have to leave Beth and the woods if he was going to get a better view, perhaps try to get within hearing range and maybe hear something that would reveal the type of people these were—where their sympathies lay.

Once he emerged from the woods, he was exposing himself, so he stayed downwind, which meant crawling around to the back of the house, using whatever bushes or vines he could for cover and get close enough to eavesdrop. He got as flat on the earth as he could and started swimming against the current of a dense sea of vines. He'd left everything on Beth except for the spyglass slung on his back.

He stopped crawling fifty meters from the three women. Any closer and he'd be in danger of giving himself away. The last rays of the sun made the women shade their eyes. It would make it more difficult for them to see Zalaman. He drew out his spyglass and focused on the women, who now turned to greet a fourth woman as she emerged from the house carrying a green plant whose leaves she distributed to the others. They all began plucking them and dropping them into a big bowl.

He crawled a bit closer where he was able to catch and understood just enough words to think he was hearing an unfamiliar dialect of Polish. Each woman wore a long dress of hand-sewn muslin and wool. The bent old woman was grumbling about something, maybe offering unsolicited advice to the three other women, who did not seem to be paying any attention. Beside the crone, was her daughter or, no, more likely, Zalaman decided, the crone's *daughter-in-law*, based on the way they interacted, the younger woman lolling about while being lectured to by the old biddy. There was also a younger daughter or in-law he watched closely through the glass as she moved here and there, picking up this and carrying that, full of energy and purpose though she hobbled about on a crutch. The middle-aged woman who had emerged with the greens, Zalaman decided, was the mother. He committed the picture and his story to memory—the people and their strange dialect with only snatches of words: "firewood" and "laundry." The sister with the limp carried the firewood, while her older sister, who seemed to have two perfectly good legs and nothing particular to do, made fun of her, laughing while mimicking her gait when she was out of sight. But a word from mother and she got up to help with the firewood.

Zalaman was further away from the men and their animals, but his spyglass did reveal a man about his father's age and someone much younger, a boy younger than Zalaman, perhaps the man's son. The two were dressed in similar jackets with long pants over leather boots and they patted the ox and mule and the boy shoveled feed to the ox. He had real biceps despite being so young. Zalaman caught only one familiar word from the father, "Alexandrovich."

He couldn't get any closer and the light was fading. He turned in the furrow and crawled back toward the woods and Beth, but he hadn't gotten very far when he heard an outburst from the father. "Alexandrovich" again. Zalaman turned to look and saw the father and the son were laughing and patting the bull. Who would name a bull after a tsar? Were they making fun of the Tsar? Whatever their loyalties, would they have a comfortable bed for him?

> <

"Just peaceful farmers?" Rodak said when Zalaman returned with his news. Rodak was upset that Zalaman hadn't gotten more information.

"Maybe he should have introduced himself and asked them if they were enemies of the Tsar and, if so, would they be willing to share their big house with us for the winter," Stanko said.

Rodak ignored Stanko's sarcasm. "They are not likely to be friends of the Tsar, given the abuses we know they suffer from the Cossacks. That's true, but we should always assume the worst and prepare for it. We'll subdue and test these farmers. They'll have to earn our trust. And we'll have to prepare a distraction for those dogs." Zalaman found it reassuring somehow that Stanko and Rodak could kill Cossacks but wouldn't hurt dogs. They said they would not harm any animals unless they were going to eat them. They would lace the meat with some 'marching powder' they'd taken from the Cossacks at Bazily's. Marching powder was a potion used by soldiers to stay awake, but it had the opposite effect on dogs. Zalaman asked if he could try some and they laughed and told him to wait. If he took some now, he wouldn't be able to sleep tonight.

By the time they arrived at the edge of the forest, the family was out and busy with their farm work. Stanko laid out the fresh meat laced with marching powder—and they all moved downwind of it. The dogs' highly praised sense of smell didn't do the trick immediately, so Stanko threw a stick in the direction of the rabbit meat and instantly, the dogs' ears perked up, calling into question Rodak's theory about a dog's sense of smell being better than its hearing. Both dogs took off at the sound of the stick and were in no time tearing at the rabbit. The three partisans waited and watched the dogs eat. They ate it all, but they did not fall asleep. They barked and leaped like Russian soldiers on marching powder and then ran to join the farmer and another man—a new character in the family story Zalaman had concocted—a fully grown one, not the boy Zalaman had seen the day before. He would turn out to be a hired hand, and, according to Zalaman's calculations, he brought the farmhouse population to seven.

"Soon to be ten," Stanko said.

"Remember, we are the partisans," Rodak said. "We can make threats, we but should do so only when forced to. We are fighting *for* these people."

In response to the barking, the mule was now braying, but the commotion didn't distress the farmer or his man. They were accustomed to the randomness of the mule's outbursts. The noise, including all the clucking and mooing, created the best possible distraction for anyone sneaking up from behind, as the cousins were, but they sent Zalaman around to approach the farmhouse from the front just to insure they maintained the element of surprise.

><

"Hello!" Zalaman yelled, serenely walking down the path from the road to the farmhouse. He hoped he looked like a harmless thirteen-year-old boy, to the mother and daughter who were watching him, both women cradling muskets. "Forgive me," Zalaman pleaded, "just in need of a little Christian kindness. Violence is unnecessary," he assured them, though they only raised their muskets more menacingly. When he said he'd been separated from his family, something he could say with convincing emotional intensity, they relaxed the grips on their weapons enough that Zalaman was able to grab both muskets from the startled women, at the very time the farmer and his helper appeared, their hands trussed up behind them, Stanko and Rodak, who had jumped and bound them in the field without firing a shot, were prodding them along with their bayonets.

After ferreting out Granny and a twelve-year-old named Karl, the cousins tied the whole group together, each family member along with the hired hand, Bern, and then tethered the lot to the legs of a heavy oak dining table that dominated the farmhouse's big room which included the hearth, kitchen, dining room and space for the many activities of daily life. The three partisans held weapons which they reassured the family—the family's name was Gmerk—they had no wish to use. They meant no harm. That got a laugh out Granny. No, the partisans insisted, they were trying to avoid hurting them, but the more they twisted their restraints in resistance, the more it would hurt. Once they understood one another, Stanko promised, there would be no reason for pain or bloodshed.

The Gmerks, as a body—and in their current condition they resembled a single body with many arms and legs—swore that they were not opposed to the partisans. They were simple farmers, trying to get along peacefully. They yelped overly loud, exaggerating, Zalaman thought when he cinched the knots a bit tighter. Pane and Pan Gmerk, Lena and Karl, Sr., both professed to be enemies of the Tsar.

Zalaman was feeling that something wasn't right, that someone was missing, when the girl with the limp rushed out of a side room and bashed him on the head with the heavy end of her crutch. Thankfully, it was not the same spot Georg had bashed only weeks before, but he blacked out from the blow, which brought pain, stars, then nothing.

This Gmerk, Anna, the best-looking of the Gmerks, perhaps next to Lena, was to become Zalaman's first love—and he hers—even if it didn't get off to a very promising start. "She knocked me off my feet," Zalaman would say, then shake his head when people would insist "You mean 'swept' you off your feet."

After blacking out, he woke to the sound of sobbing and saw it was coming from that girl. She had been easily subdued by Rodak and Stanko and was now tied up with the rest of her family. Zalaman remembered watching her the day before through the spyglass. Had he not paid attention, discounted her because of her limp? She'd impressed him with the way she worked. His head was pounding, but he understood she was trying to apologize for hitting him. She professed she was like the rest of her family—they were traditional Poles and were inactive believers in the Catholic Church of Poland and naturally hated the Cossacks—bullies and tax—and considered them invaders and said they would help the partisans in any way they could.

She tried to rub away Zalaman's blood from the head of her crutch. The blood had stained the heavy end, a diverging branch of the birch from which it was cut and the end that fit under her armpit when she was using the way it was intended and not as a weapon. Of course, the Gmerk family would say anything to be free to go on about their busy, pre-harvest lives untethered.

Pane Gmerk, Lena, was the family's main spokesperson, after Anna, and she spoke directly to Zalaman's fears, stroking his brow, his head in her lap. "You have no reason to believe us when we tell you we are with you," Mrs. Gmerk said, "because we know what you want to hear and we know you know it. But untie us and treat us fairly, and you're welcome to stay for a few days and refresh yourselves." The Gmerks mumbled their various degrees of agreement—from Anna's enthusiasm for revenge against the Cossacks to Granny's enigmatic: "Glory to God!"—which could be interpreted as celebration or lament.

The partisans looked at one another. 'A few *days*'? Was she joking?—but said nothing. Zalaman saw the look Anna and her mother exchanged. It was a look that told him he and the cousins weren't the only ones dissembling. He sensed Anna and her mother were holding something back and later, Rodak and Stanko agreed with his assessment. So, they instituted a period of indeterminant length during which the Gmerks would remain tied up—to one another or to one of the partisans, if not guarded with a weapon, until they were convinced such measures were unnecessary.

Lena had noted their look when she said, "a few days," so she corrected herself, "Or longer, if you need. We're having a plentiful harvest and are not stingy to people of the faith." She was applying a wet cloth to Zalaman's head. It was sore and pounding and he was groggy as he stared up at Anna's pretty face as she held forth on Cossacks. He admired her passion for the subject and had to admit she had good aim and a strong arm. He was lying on his back and just now realizing the gratefully soft pillow he was resting his head on was Mrs. Gmerk's lap. She cradled his head there, staunching the blood, professing to be on their side and asking what they could do to show their friendship, their support for the partisans—and get themselves untied. He could feel her movements, the curve of her thighs and their warmth permeating her lightweight muslin summer skirts, though the pounding in his skull precluded desire—a feeling no longer dormant in Zalaman's own loins.

Mrs. Gmerk knew it would not be easy to convince this ragged trio of intruders that her family was on their side. She was less than completely convinced of it herself, probably less than the other members of her family. Yes, she maintained a generational hatred for the Russians, but who were these ragtag intruders, anyway?

Mercenaries. Although the dark-haired one whose head was in her lap while she applied the compress, was an attractive young thing. Too young for her, but not too young to worry about should there be a prolonged stay. She saw how he was studying Anna. Less concerned, she noted how the young giant's gaze, the one they called Stanko, lingered on her older daughter, Flora.

Lena trusted Flora more than Anna, trusted Flora's recognized commitment to Bern, the Gmerk's hired hand. She, Lena, was as outraged as the rest of her family over the Cossack's annual raid, but she considered herself a realist. It was a tax and it was perhaps the best way to get the Russians to leave them with at least enough for their own well-being. Only by maintaining the health of the farmers could the Russian troops continue to be fed. She was fortunate to have two good-looking girls who did their best to conceal their fear and disgust, if not their contempt for the Russians. Contempt they no longer feared to express directly, having discovered the Cossacks didn't understand their expressions. Flora and Anna considered them animals. Pane Gmerk just considered them uneducated brutes. She knew her girls were beautiful and appreciated the role they played in the Cossacks' decision not to come down too hard with the official looting of their harvest. When the Russians weren't around—in other words, 99% of the time—the Gmerks and Mrs. Gmerk were not shy about complaining. They would have been considered untrustworthy by their neighbors if they didn't go along with excoriating Cossacks.

The beliefs they expressed to Rodak, Stanko and Zalaman—that the Cossacks were primitive Eastern Orthodox sinners who would one day rape or murder them all—were honestly held.

Granny sat pulling sullenly on her restraints, considering her misfortune. Even if Karl was the only one who still obeyed her orders, she was the one used to ordering about and now here were these partisans ordering *them* all about. But worst of all were the Cossacks with their thieving and degeneracy. Sinners thanks to their Eastern Orthodox religion, she was thankful they had only been plundered and not raped.

The boy, Karl, kept his mouth shut and stared defiant, angry, and apparently without fear at Zalaman whose bloody head was receiving such loving treatment in his mother's lap. And why did he have to be shackled to Bern, the hired hand, who was always all over his sister Flora.

Bern, tied up nicely between the two of them, didn't mind the part about being cinched up against Flora. He was looking forward to soon being a part of the family. He was convinced the partisans needed them and they would have to release them. He had knowledge to share with them once he decided he trusted them and believed they truly were what they said they were.

Flora was the aptly named older sister—aptly named because it was her wizardry with plants that kept the whole family healthy—who might be guilty of making fun of her little sister occasionally, but loved her, too. As she did Bern, although the huge blond man, Stanko, fascinated her. Something about him made him seem the antithesis of Bern, whom she loved. Yet there it was—Stanko was colossal. Compared to him, her father was a small man. Physically. But her father, like Bern, was also too deferential to her mother. They both let her make all the decisions. Whereas Stanko, when he got orders from his older cousin, Rodak, was not so compliant.

While the others whined about being bound, Zalaman watched Anna, his assailant. She started crying for no apparent reason, then stopped and dried her eyes which were as dark as her hair; eyes and hair in dramatic contrast with skin and teeth which were as white as milk.

"We want to trust you," Stanko assured them, directing his wish at Flora.

"We fight for Poland," Rodak said, "and want to use your house as our base while we look for opportunities to do our part in helping rid the land of Russians. We hear there is plenty of Russian activity in the area. We will do them some damage—"

His mention of "opportunities" occasioned an exchange of enigmatic looks, not only between Mrs. Gmerk and Anna, but Mr. Gmerk and Bern as well. "—all at our expense," Mrs. Gmerk interrupted. "Because, of course, you'll be damaging us, as well."

"We won't take up much room," Zalaman said, eager to please the lady caring for his wound. "We can help you with the harvest." This was a commitment for something he had not discussed with his partners, but they understood what he was doing, mollifying the Gmerks, so they didn't immediately deny it.

"You're not fooling me a bit," Granny said. "Stick to killing these Cossacks, I'm fine. You're going to be eating our food, so you'll pay for that. Just let us get in this crop. Leave the farming to us who know what we're doing. We're good at it, Glory to God. Are you any good at it?"

"We're not farmers," Zalaman admitted, "but I've had some experience."

"Rodak, here, is one of the best when it comes to killing Cossacks," Stanko said. "He's been the Tsar's scourge for decades. And our little friend here," looking down at Zalaman, his head on Mrs. Gmerks' lap, "he may look young to you, but to the Cossacks he is King David and Samson rolled into one."

"Trust is earned," Rodak said, "but we won't let the harvest suffer. When I'm off scouting, or Zalaman is, there will still be two of us here with you. Always. One inside and one out, depending on where you all have to be. No one will be leaving the farm. Including you, Bern."

It was Bern's practice to walk the short few miles home every night and return early the next morning. This new arrangement was quite alright with him. He had no one to report to in the village where he kept a room, and he had been planning to move in with the Gmerk's anyway once he and Flora were married. Now he had to stay overnight and that was a very good thing seeing how Stanko looked at Flora.

"You understand that if one of you disappears, or, for the present, even tries to leave the farm, things could get very difficult for the rest of the family," Rodak warned them.

"Treat us like your friends and we can all succeed," Lena said. "Treat us like your enemy, and you send us into the arms of the Cossacks." Rodak had Stanko go through the house with Mr. Gmerk and gather up all the weapons.

Rodak spent the next few weeks scouting, Stanko kept an eye on the men, now busy with the harvest. Sometimes he lent a hand. Zalaman watched the women, mostly indoors, cooking and cleaning, but then, as the harvest began to pick up, the women, apart from Granny, often worked in the fields with the men. Zalaman's head cleared and, like Stanko tried to make himself useful to the Gmerks.

Zalaman liked the physical labor outdoors. Fall had always been an exciting time to Zalaman principally because it meant winter was not far behind. And he loved snow. But this was different. It was like he was an adult—working as farmhand and guard.

While Rodak was out scouting, Stanko watched over Karl Sr. and Bern who did the bulk of the potato picking and the mowing of wheat and rye, but his rifle lay abandoned, leaning on a basket of potatoes, when he helped.

When they weren't helping with the harvest, or collecting eggs and milking Mitti, the cow, the women, Lena and Anna, worked inside—cooking and cleaning. Zalaman liked the cooking part best. He marveled at the Gmerks' cast iron stove with all its dampers and burners. It had a side roaster and big hot water reservoir. Anna and Lena appreciated his enthusiasm for its wonders. Lena and Pan Gmerk had hauled the enormously heavy object all the way from Vitebsk. The threesome—Zalaman, Lena and Anna—became a team around the stove and the chopping table, itself an enormous, single block of ancient oak as impressive in its bulk as the stove. Mother and daughter were favorably impressed with Zalaman's skills—butchering and social. Like Stanko with the men outdoors, Zalaman left a revolver nearby, but had stopped worrying about anyone making a break for it.

Flora preferred working outdoors with her plants—herbs, spices, medicinals—but now, even more, with the men, where she now enjoyed the attention of both her intended and the powerfully built newcomer. Granny and young Karl liked it outdoors, too. Who didn't? Winter would be here soon enough. Granny felt compelled to dole out advice regarding the harvest—"Let's not be like last year," she said, "you went too fast and missed too many potatoes. Glory to God!"

Zalaman had no experience with women or girls, but he was thirteen now and more than willing to gain some understanding, some satisfaction of his new, powerful urges.

The big iron stove was a nice diversion, but the object of his attention was always one or both women, the middle-aged mother and her youngest daughter, entertaining erotic fantasies which were hampered by his complete lack of experience. He was interested in cooking, but his sexual longing was of a different order, yet he was afraid of doing something that would spoil any chances he had with either Lena or Anna.

It was Anna to whom he was most attracted. Mrs. Gmerk was in her thirties and while he couldn't help but feel a surge of heat when she inadvertently exposed a little extra flesh, he didn't feel having sex with her was a possibility. Anna was just a year or two older than him. To Anna, their difference in ages felt like a chasm, but she couldn't deny she was attracted.

Zalaman was sitting on the big stove—a nice warm place to be early in the morning—cleaning his gun when not sneaking peeks at Lena. She was adjusting her clothing when she exposed, inadvertently perhaps, more leg than Zalaman had ever seen outside his own family. Lena was thinking that maybe it was just the oven, but she could feel the heat of his gaze. She gave him a quizzical look he could not interpret but did anyway: the slash of thigh had not been inadvertent. She smoothed her skirts and walked past him, grazing his skin, and in the process infused him with the scent of the rosewater that she sprinkled herself with daily and which for the rest of his life would inspire an erection.

And then, Anna was there, hobbling just the slightest bit on her crutch, but moving with great assurance. Zalaman marveled at how smoothly she moved with this aid. He wondered if she even needed it and rubbed his now healed head recalling how effective a weapon it had been.

"The way you move," he told her, "you don't seem like you need that crutch."

"I don't. I just keep it handy in case someone needs a head-bashing."

"Why did you pick *me* to hit over the head?"

"Convenience." She smiled and he smiled back. She liked the openness, perhaps the naiveté of the young man. That and he was cuter than any of the farm boys in the valley—not that that was saying much. "You were pointing a gun at my family. What would you have done?"

He thought he would have the courage to do what she did. He went with her to watch her milk Mitti. It was a warm, early September sun, but in the barn it was cooler and quite dark in places. Watching Anna hitch up her skirts and go to work on Mitti or a goat would have been more enjoyable where there was more light.

While Stanko and Zalaman are doing their 'guarding,' Rodak is away doing the all-important scouting, exploring territory that was described on the commandant's maps as "disputed," but according to the Gmerks and from what Rodak witnessed on his expeditions, there was no question as to who was in control. There were two villages within a day's ride, both crawling with Cossacks and controlled by their Polish enablers. It would be out of the question for just three partisans to do any successful marauding in those towns or on the roads between them where there were frequent parades of troops on forced marches. Rodak knew the crucial element of surprise would be of much less value when the enemy was ten times your size.

At thirteen going on fourteen, Zalaman was not bothered by his lack of self-control when it came to dealing with his erections, and now, away from his mother, with dreams of Anna in his head, he began to consider himself a world-class masturbator. Sleeping in the same room as Stanko and Rodak (operating in shifts), he was drawing late night requests from both Rodak and Stanko to "keep it down." The marching powder probably didn't help the situation. Rodak provided some of this magic elixir to Zalaman when he went out on guard duty. "In case you get tired," he said. But Zalaman saved some for other judicious uses, because it not only gave him more energy, but it also made him happier and it aroused him. His experience with *krupnik*, which had taught him about 'not doing too much,' he applied to the marching powder. He wondered why he was unable to show the same kind of restraint regarding masturbation.

> <

He was a little less successful than he imagined, concerning the judicious use of marching powder. He took some, sniffed into the nostrils, before going mushroom hunting with Lena. She announced she was going to be going into the woods, up the hill, and Stanko said OK, Zalaman could help her, he would watch the rest.

Rodak was, as usual, off scouting.

Following her into the dark woods—the leaves, brilliant, still clinging on—to find the mushrooms, a musket strapped to his back, Zalaman, maybe inflamed by the marching powder, became transfixed by the body, the legs and ass he imagined under Lena's dress. She excited him even more than Anne, or so he thought at the time. Unless he was mistaken, he had sensed that despite the real gulf between them age-wise—not just a couple of years as in the case of Anna, but more like a couple of decades—Mrs. Gmerk might be interested in him *that way,* maybe even more than Anna was. She looked quite a lot like her daughter, was perhaps even prettier, although Anna was very attractive. Her mother was a bit heavier—voluptuous, in fact, whereas Anna was willowy. Their features were alike. Lena's face reflected decades of compromise and worry, yet despite the lines thus formed, Anna's had more character.

Lena glanced back. She caught him staring. He blushed and she grinned at the sight. Zalaman wondered if perhaps she thought of him as being no more dangerous than her ten-year-old son. Why else would she ask him to accompany her into the woods to look for mushrooms. Unless . . . unless she enjoys his presence. She had been quite insistent that he learn how to find mushrooms and that he must spend some time in the glory of the exploding fall colors. Zalaman hoped for even more.

They were in a thickly wooded area when, without warning, without hesitation and without a word, Pani Gmerk turned and embraced him. They kissed. They lay back on a colorful bed of leaves, none of which could compare to the flushed pink color of Lena's breasts when she showed them to Zalaman, who, despite being able to partially crush a Cossack with a rock, almost passed out from lust. This plus the marching powder was maybe too much. He gratefully fondled the proffered breasts. She seemed to want him to suck them or nibble them or something even stronger. She filled his mouth with one of them and moaned. There was a simultaneous removing of clothing, which became too frantic on Zalaman's part—he felt himself close too exploding—so she slowed him down and told him he shouldn't make so much noise, panting and grunting even if they were "likely" out of hearing range. She could tell he was a virgin, so he should follow her. "With patience," she said, "with restraint." He did his best with that request, but then, this was his first time, so she understood that he had satisfied himself, but not her. They'd been laying back, side-by-side, clothes askew, for maybe two minutes, when Zalaman admitted, it was true, this was his first time. Lena was happy he was secure enough to say so. She told him she wished she'd been able to teach him a little more about restraint and how such restraint can give him power over a woman. Zalaman began fondling and nibbling her and she realized she might have another teaching opportunity. She gently pulled away from his kiss and admired his erection. "Speedy recovery," she congratulated him. "In all my years . . . I had to wait for a boy so young I should be ashamed to be with him."

Zalaman was too embarrassed to say anything, so he filled his mouth with her instead. "I forgot how it can be with a young man," she laughed. "You are a man, Zalaman. You just proved that. As you've proved it against the Cossacks in much bloodier fashion. Now, let me show you how to prove it to a woman."

After the next bout, a much more satisfying one from Lena's perspective, having been under her direction the entire time, Zalaman was exhausted. He offered her some marching powder, but she refused it, saying he should be careful about putting things up his nose. He had forgotten all about the mushrooms and wondered if they had ever really been on the agenda.

Mrs. Gmerk did still intend to hunt for mushrooms, but before they saw to that she realized that she had a responsibility as Zalaman's mentor. She doubted he appreciated it as he should, having such an experienced first lover. "Do you know how girls get pregnant?" she asked him. "If I was a young girl and I didn't know what I was doing, you could have given me a baby. Did you know that?"

Zalaman had a rudimentary idea—as with horses and goats—so he knew that what they'd just done was a key element in the process. He thought of Anna when she said, "if she was a young girl" and thought that she was perhaps counseling him against trying anything with her daughter—although, later, he was able to convince himself that she had, in fact, been giving him permission, just making sure he would be careful with her. At the time, he lay back on the leaves and stretched and promised himself he would do his best to practice her advice regarding the act of sexual congress and avoid getting anyone pregnant and becoming a father.

Pane Gmerk had enough of sprawling on the leaves. She got up and pulled him up. "Spending any more time away would be too risky," she said as they dressed. She uncovered a field of fungi beneath the leaves right where they were just lying. She demonstrated the proper way of digging them. "My husband is no dummy. I know I don't have to tell you this, but, of course, we did nothing here. Nothing happened except for these mushrooms."

Zalaman agreed, but of course it had happened and he hoped it would happen again. In fact, the next opportunity for a tryst with Mrs. Gmerk presented itself just two days later. They both willingly took advantage of it.

The entire family and the three partisans were gathered around the big dining table. It was rare for them all to sit down together, but Pan and Pani Gmerk had made a special request, saying it was a kind of harvest festival.

"It's been a very good harvest, thanks to your help," she looked at the partisans, "but soon will come a second harvest." She paused for effect and the other Gmerks smiled and watched the three look both bewildered by the comment and dismayed at the thought of more farm labor. "You have begun to treat us as if you trust us, as if you believe our sympathy with your cause. We have come to believe that you are men who do as they say and we need to treat you accordingly. We've grown rather fond of you," she said, willing herself to not look at Zalaman.

Mrs. Gmerk thought she was issuing them a warning when she told them about the Cossacks—how they would be coming to take what they claimed of the harvest—which was usually more than what they left for the Gmerks—taking an unconscionable share of their labor. There would be a dozen or so Cossacks, so it would be best for the partisans to leave while they had the chance. Rodak and Stanko were stunned. They did not take Lena's announcement as a warning, but an invitation.

"They tell us it's payment for protecting us," Mr. Gmerk said. Then he started shouting, "Protecting us from what? That's all I want to know."

"When will they come?" Stanko asked.

"Soon. But there's still time for you to disappear."

"Why would we do that?"

"They come after the harvest. They always seem to know when that is. There's never any advance warning. So, you can come back when they are gone and continue your scouting."

"Ridiculous. This is the opportunity we've been looking for." Rodak was angry they'd waited to tell him about this and yet grateful now to know.

"For the last two years, they've come on my name day," Anna said, and everyone turned to her. "The first of October, don't you remember? Well, not more than a week before or after." The rest of the family thought she might be right. They hadn't thought about it in relationship to Anna's name day. It was simply an inevitable and horrible annual event. The first of October was only two weeks away.

"Seven or eight of them come on horses and in uniform," Mr. Gmerk said, "armed with their rifles and sabers, looking for anyone who might threaten their rights. It's extortion."

"We had to be sure of your intentions," Lena told Rodak. "You would have done the same. The important thing is you still have time to avoid their notice and you'll be welcome to come back after they leave."

"Glory to God," Grannie added. Was she cheering the idea of the trio leaving or the promise of them coming back? Zalaman guessed it was the former.

"Impossible," Rodak said. "We're here to fight the Cossacks, not run away from them." He asked Lena for details. She was an impressive woman, he thought. Competent and good-looking.

He liked to imagine being with her, but she was married to Karl and Rodak respected, if not the institution, at least Lena. At his age, he figured he should probably be resolved to content himself with prostitutes (as he had for the past two decades), but when he listened to Lena, he couldn't help but feel lust along with admiration.

"You'd fight them here? Please, no," Mr. Gmerk said. "Don't bring that on us. You're badly outnumbered in this case. There could be a dozen of them. You'd only be helping the Tsar."

"Three to twelve—that's about normal for us," Stanko said. "You have to be kidding," Anna said.

"9 to 12 would be better odds still," Rodak said.

His statement was met with silence until what he might mean sunk in and Anna, who deciphered it first, asked, "You want us to fight with you?" She was shocked. But she was intrigued.

"The element of surprise is worth a dozen Cossacks."

"You said 9 to 12," Anna spoke with her hands propping up her face, elbows on the table, eyes riveted on Rodak and then taking in the other two.

Zalaman read her stare. He did not want to see any harm come to her or Lena. "They're not passing though. They live here." He turned to face the family and Bern. "What do you . . ." he started, but gave up in the face of the Gmerks' disputation.

The murmuring and exclaiming, with little shouting, came from everyone but little Karl: Rodak and Lena, and Zalaman and Anna, as well as Flora, Stanko. Karl, Granny and Bern. The most common noun was "revenge," the most common verb was "flee."

Anna used her crutch to stand and grab their attention. "The truth is, and we know this, these three crazy people are not going to flee. Neither are we," she said, "never have." She leaned toward Rodak on her crutch, "I will join. I'll fight with you—If I like your plan."

"Me, too," little Karl piped up. Lena slapped him on the head. They waited, everyone wanting to hear more. The partisans learned that the Cossacks would come armed with rifles and sabers, trailing a big wagon to fill up with our harvest and the harvests of others. Rodak took this as good news, that the Gmerks corroborated: "fill it with the fruits of our harvest—and our neighbors' harvest—the Cossacks are primarily looking out for not being cheated, not for armed partisans. They are used to 'enthusiastic' cooperation. They no longer search the house as they once did—but they always *might*."

"I think you should leave," Lena said. "Cover your tracks. And, by all means, come back when they've gone."

"A wise man knows when to retreat—so he can advance further when it's time to do so," Flora spoke up for the first time, looking at Stanko.

Mrs. Gmerk wasn't only afraid of the violence that was being suggested, she had been thinking it might be good to try and rid themselves of these partisans sooner rather than later. She was feeling very little guilt about Zalaman, but she didn't want to hurt her husband. And she was not happy about the way her eldest daughter stared at Stanko, which was even more upsetting to Bern. Stanko was attracted to Flora, but he didn't want to make an enemy of Bern, so he avoided her advances. Lena was even more concerned about the looks she found Zalaman exchanging with Anna. She wondered if she should warn her younger daughter, but, decided it was just envy and a shameless desire to keep the boy for herself. The whole situation was ridiculous.

"Time to eat," she announced.

"And have another drink," Stanko added.

Over the next few days, it became clear that they were not taking Flora or Lena's advice. They were preparing to greet the Cossacks. Everyone got a role to play, a position to take when they arrived. The success of their ambush would be dependent on rigorous sentry duties—the responsibility of Zalaman and/or Bern, Flora or Karl alternating at different vantage points—high ground where anyone coming from the east or west could be spotted early. Their arsenal now included the Gmerks' two muskets. After Rodak, Bern and Pan Gmerk were the best shots, while Stanko and Zalaman showed some improvement. The Gmerk women also knew how to pull a trigger.

Stanko concentrated on preparations, doing his best to ignore the looks of longing from Flora. Zalaman was less prudent.

He was in a field doing target practice with Anna and Little Karl. A pretend target practice without bullets to avoid attracting a neighbors' attention and so a target practice of limited value, aside from demonstrating techniques he'd learned from Rodak.

Little Karl, a perceptive kid, sensed his sister wanted to be alone with Zalaman, so he left early to relieve Bern from his sentry duty.

Anna had remained a mystery to Zalaman. He thought he might be in love with her. Not only was she beautiful, and maybe untouchable because their two- or three-year age difference somehow seemed larger than the twenty years separating him and her mother, but also, even with her mild infirmity, she did twice the work of Flora—and moved with more grace. He liked following her as she tended to the farm animals—collected eggs, churned butter, cleaned, made preserves, sewed, baked breads, did laundry. It didn't matter, she made them all interesting, her slight limp never an impediment. She moved so sensually that to Zalaman's eye it had become a dance, fluid and purposeful.

After Little Karl left, he followed her when she said she had to milk Mitti. In the barn, he first watched her comb through the long, white coat of a goat, calming the animal's normal belligerence to make the milking process easier.

"I once asked what you would do if you found your parents threatened at gunpoint, like I found mine when I knocked you on the head," she talked while she milked the goat. "'Knocked,' You make it sound so harmless," he said.

She laughed, then apologized and asked if it still hurt, when she already knew it didn't. He had told her so. "You never answered me, and I think it's because we both know you would do the same thing—'knock' me over the head."

Zalaman was lost in the wonders of her flesh. It wasn't just the squeezing and squirting, it was the exposed nape of her neck, and, below, the calf she exposed when she'd hoisted up her skirts to sit on the milking stool. She hoisted them again as she nudged the stool over so she could sit down beside the Baltic sheep with its crown of spiral horns. Assuming the best posture for success with the weapon-bearing sheep, her elbows splayed out to achieve the freest movement while protecting against any quick jerk should the sheep start acting less sheep-like. She sensed Zalaman's interest, not for the first time, but after years of longing for someone at least close to Zalaman's age and good looks, she now felt a warmth and dampness below as she spread her knees to cradle the wooden milking pail and revealed a bit more leg in the process. She didn't mind his staring. No, it was more than that. She invited it. For his part, Zalaman was not embarrassed to stand closer than usual, desire was assuming control without having said a word, without a touch. Neither Zalaman nor Anna was opposed to the idea of letting desire take over silently.

"Yes," he agreed with her assessment of his acting like a man. "I would. Or I 'hope' I would, because how can you ever tell how you would act in such a situation until you are in it. That's what I think. I never thought I could kill someone."

She looked up at him and smiled. "Do you think I'd be fearless enough to do what you did?" Zalaman thought it should be self-evident, so he didn't want to say a thing.

"So, you forgive me?" she asked. He looked at her, with what he hoped was a loving look, without answering. He tried to picture himself coming upon Papa and Mama and Keila and Davin all tied up and held at gunpoint by Anna and Lena. He wondered if his family had received his message. He knows he would risk his life to save them, if it ever, hopefully never, came to that.

"What do you think of my legs?" she asked, Zalaman leering with his mouth half open and embarrassed by her question. "I was born with legs of unequal lengths," she said, exposing the other leg while hiking the whole, long skirt even a bit higher.

"You can't tell," he assured her and he meant it. "They're beautiful," he said, a bit breathless. In fact, stare as he might, he could detect no defect in them. He ached to touch them. She could tell and it brought another smile to her face. She finished with the last goat and said she was excited to be fighting alongside him. "We would all like to see the Russians sent back to the other side of the Bierbza."

They moved on to the milk cow, Mitti, and sat side by side on two stools, alternating pulling on the teats, squirting Mitti-milk into the pail. They were sitting so close that when the milking was done, they kissed and kept kissing, and before you knew it they were rolling in the hay, clawing unabashedly at one another. "Mooo!" Mitti complained, but the lovers were deaf to anything other than their own animal sounds. Zalaman incorporated everything he'd learned from Anna's mother, including, successfully but with great difficulty and regret, Lena's advice about withdrawing just when it seems most unnatural, requiring a tremendous act of will.

Later, spent and lying side by side, Anna and Zalaman were naked under all the clothes they'd slid under. Anna was trying to divert her attention from what she'd just done with this 'child,' but she was less successful at this than her mother had been. Anna was, of course, unaware of Zalaman's activities with her mother. She hadn't thought much about the way her mother sometimes ogled Zalaman because it seemed harmless.

"As a Jew," she said, "you are probably not aware that I'm named after St. Anna. My name day is her feast day and that's the day after tomorrow." The name day that portended Cossacks. "Ever since I can remember, my family has feared the Russians. And why not? The Russians have given my family nothing and have taken plenty. It's not fair. But . . . they're stupid. They believe the Gmerks are loyal to the Tsar. Worst of all, they smell like their horses."

Zalaman was nervous about the Cossacks—and now here they came, just when he found himself in such a wonderful situation. Almost fourteen years old, and he'd just gone from no sex and total ignorance—to this! Anna and Lena. Well, the Lena part would have to stop no matter what happened in the battle. Anna put her fingers to her lips as he started to say something and heard the voices of Anna's father, Karl, and Stanko, approaching the barn, talking about hunting, yelling at the whining dogs to quiet down. Anna and Zalaman grabbed their clothes and, as best they could, they hid in the newly mown hay, holding one another, hearts throbbing, holding their breaths. Anna didn't want to imagine what her father would do if he found them. The difficulty of holding their breaths was intensified by their proximity, wrapped in one another's arms in the fragrant hay. But not for long, for the dogs started making a ruckus outside the barn. The naked couple was sure the dogs could smell their presence. How could they not? But Stanko quieted the dogs, still excited by the hunt, the strong odor of the newly mown hay hid all other fragrances, or so they imagined.

Stanko said they should go check on the sentries and the two walked on by the barn. Zalaman and Anna felt a great fondness for Stanko when he told her father they should go check on the sentries.

"That's the second time Stanko saved my life," Zalaman whispered. Anna wanted to hear that story, but for the moment, both could breathe easier. They lay there, not really wanting to move and soon their breathing grew heavy and uneven again.

> <

Surprise, as usual, would be the key. Rodak emphasized this to Stanko and Zalaman—and the Gmerks, who all agreed. Surprise the Cossacks before they have a chance to dismount.

That's why Stanko and Karl were checking on the sentries, making sure they were where they were supposed to be and staying alert. Rodak, Stanko, Mr. Gmerk, and Bern were the best shooters and were exempt from sentry duty. They had to stay closer to the farmhouse now that the day was upon them. Lena, Anna, and Flora had their own dangerous roles to play. Rodak even had a role for Granny.

Anna's name day came and went. There was no opportunity for Zalaman to be alone with either Anna or Mrs. Gmerk. Rodak, worried that Zalaman was secretly having his way with one of the women (and he suspected it might be so), made sure everyone was too busy for any business beyond watching lookout and joining in their assignments whenever possible—cleaning rifles, muskets, and revolvers, sharpening sabers, putting the family and his comrades through practice drills.

Zalaman and Karl, having the best eyesight, were often on sentry duty, to be regularly spelled by Bern and Flora. The dogs should be a reliable alarm, but they couldn't be counted on. Rodak placed the sentries at the two most elevated spots on either side of the farm, and although the Cossacks were likely to come from the east, they had the west covered as well. An alert sentry might provide a considerably earlier warning than the dogs. Especially, the eastern post, where they kept Zalaman's spyglass.

There was very little traffic on the road either way, generally limited to carts hauling just-harvested produce to market. It was boring duty, but Zalaman tried to make the most of it. The view to the east was magnificent. Through the magic of his spyglass, he could watch hunters tramping through the broad, post-harvest valley of vine-littered fields and into the multi-colored autumn hills that framed the whole landscape. Still, sentry duty seemed even longer than it was. There was only so long you could enjoy just sitting around and staring at the world, even with the added pleasure of bringing far things close with the spyglass, or the consolations of marching powder. He slowly pivoted his glass, scanning up and down the road, trying to imagine Cossacks trotting up, stopping in front of the Gmerk's farmhouse where they would be riddled by bullets to lie bleeding. Dying. Perhaps Rodak did, but he, Zalaman, did *not* look forward to that.

He did not want to see any blood outside of the Benowitz' butcher shop in Lahkvna, but he knew that's what was coming. During the Battle of the Seven Cossacks, he'd had no time to think about what he was doing, dropping that big stone was simply his natural reaction in the moment. That battle had resulted only in the loss of Russian blood, the pain was the pain of others. This time it could be his friends, Anna or Lena—or him.

Turning his glass in the other direction, he could look down on the farmhouse, or at least its front entrance, where he could see up so close that he could pick out the two new chinks in the low stone walls that flanked the path from the road to the Gmerks' front door. The walls were the crumbling artifacts of an earlier age; the chinks had been fashioned to stabilize Rodak's and Stanko's rifles. He couldn't see the weapons that were already hidden there.

In the ideal scheme, Rodak and Stanko would fire from the same side of the path so they wouldn't have to be afraid of shooting one another. Pan Gmerk would be on the roof with his hunting rifle. Zalaman would hide in the barn with a breech-loader and revolver. When the Cossacks were close, the women would come to the front door in greeting. They'd always greeted them there but this year they would be holding weapons behind their backs.

CHAPTER SIX

Battle at the Gmerks

It was midday and Zalaman was at his sentry post, the day he noticed a large spiral of dust on the northern horizon. It was the dry season and these little dust devils churned up frequently. But this one kept growing. He focused his spyglass on the base and saw a wagon bringing up the rear of a column of eight men on horseback advancing at an alarmingly brisk trot.

As he ran to the farmhouse, he recalled his first battle, and it made him shudder as he ran. He spread the alarm and took his assigned spot in the barn. Mitti's moos were drowned out by the dogs, already barking, more likely from all the activity and rising tension, than a reaction to the approach of Cossacks. He concealed himself behind the partially open barn door and wished that everyone would perform their allotted function, because the barn was where the Cossacks might go first to gather their rewards if the partisans and their collaborators weren't perfect in their execution.

Rodak and Stanko were on the ground behind the ancient wall, well-hidden but for the tips of their rifles. Big Karl and Bern were on the roof's far side, where they could peek over and watch and wait for the partisans' first bullets. Little Karl was still away at the western lookout and would be unlikely to know what was going on until he heard gunfire.

Zalaman could hear the hoofbeats but couldn't see and wouldn't stick his neck out. To do so would be even more dangerous here than it had been when he was on high ground, hiding behind a boulder, peeking down at unsuspecting Cossacks. It seemed this kind of work always involved a blind. It was like hunting. And he shuddered to realize it *was* hunting. His job, once Rodak and Stanko had fired, was to shoot whichever Cossack was closest.

Flora, Anna and Lena were standing at the front door as the Cossacks reined in their horses to dismount. It was at that moment that the women scurried inside to avoid the fusillade. Their retreat caused the Cossacks to hesitate in their dismounting. Was something afoot? They had a heartbeat to check around themselves before Rodak's bullet blasted an older, wildly mustachioed officer out of his saddle and Stanko's lodged in a second Cossack. Big Karl and Bern fired simultaneously from the rooftop—one of them, successfully (both claimed that success)—and the Cossack force was already nearly halved.

Zalaman partially emerged from behind the barn door and into a melee of blood and hooves to get his shot. He winged the Cossack closest to him, but it didn't drop him. Good thing that Rodak had already reloaded and was able to pick off the wounded man Zalaman had shot before the Cossack could return fire. The front door swung open and there was Anna, musket propped in the crook of her crutch. She fired and there was one less Cossack, then she went back inside to reload and join her mother and sister who were holding their own weapons close.

As the three remaining Cossacks dismounted, one of them shot up at Bern on the roof. Bern lost his grip and slid off the back of the house, landing on hard ground. The sound of his femur cracking could have been mistaken for another rifle shot.

The Cossack shooter stood close to the other two so they could form a triangle back-to-back-to-back. The six-legged creature edged toward the door, firing rifles. One of their rifles was a truly amazing weapon, a rifle that kept firing bullets each time the shooter pulled the trigger. Zalaman was back in the barn to reload but he had to get a look at the source of this rapid gunfire, thus exposing a bit too much of himself. A bolt of heat flung him onto the barn floor. He lay, stunned, sticky blood spreading down his back and as he looked down at his front, he saw that his vest was soaked. He was leaking blood, front and back. He passed out.

The wedge of three Cossacks was broken before it reached the front door: the one with the repeating rifle who shot Zalaman was taken down by Rodak's Lefacheux; another was stopped by a bullet from Stanko; and as the last remaining Cossack wheeled around to shoot at them, he was stopped by the saber Lena shoved through his chest.

They could only find eight—dead or in the process of dying—of the nine Cossacks Zalaman had seen through his spyglass when at his sentry post. What was missing was the supply cart Zalaman had described. No one could remember seeing it during the fray. Lena wanted to know where Little Karl was—and then, there he was, walking back unharmed to clear up the mystery. He told them how the missing Cossack, a supply sergeant, had escaped, but the wagon with his supplies had not.

When the shooting began, the sergeant had pulled so hard on the reins he was barely able to keep his cart upright and on the road. He headed his horse west at a gallop—away from the shooting to save their arms and booty. From his lookout post, Karl heard the shooting, grabbed his musket, and started scrambling down the hill. As soon as he got down to the road, he saw the sergeant, horse, and cart speeding toward him. He knew what he should do from Rodak's drills. He took a deep breath as Rodak had taught and told himself to be brave—and he was. He knelt in the road before the oncoming vehicle, balancing the big musket on his ten-year-old knee, positioning his arms as he'd seen Rodak do it, then fired, hitting the horse in a foreleg. It skidded on the wounded leg and dropped to the ground not more than twenty meters from Karl. The cart overturned, pitching out its cargo, including the sergeant. He was hobbled by the crash, but before Karl could reload, the Cossack used his functioning arm and leg to scramble off into the woods like some deformed creature. Karl noted where he disappeared, put the poor horse out of its misery, and rushed home.

><

Lena, Anna, and Flora tended to Zalaman and Bern. Stanko, Rodak and Pan Gmerk took the best hunting dog and left immediately with Little Karl, who showed them where the sergeant had disappeared. Mr. Gmerk and the dog gave chase through the woods. Rodak and Stanko paused for a moment by the overturned cart with its spilled load of arms and produce. They smiled and clapped one another's shoulders. They had come through the battle relatively unscathed—hoping the best for Zalaman and hopeful for his recovery under the care of Lena and Anna. They had not only killed eight Cossacks, but also had been rewarded with this trove of rifles, at least one of them a repeater like the one that had wounded Zalaman. They took off into the woods to catch up with Mr. Gmerk.

The dog seemed to keep having second thoughts about the right direction. The men trying to keep up suffered numerous cuts and scratches from the undergrowth. They had to admit it—the sergeant had escaped. Even if he was as badly wounded as Little Karl claimed, it was possible the man might make it back to his comrades and report what had happened.

"It's inspiring what a man is capable of when he's running for his life," Rodak said, walking back to the wagon with its spilt load still on the road.

"What he left us is a nice consolation, though," Stanko said. "We have to assume he will make it back to his headquarters."

That meant they would have to leave. Rodak turned to Karl, "He left without seeing what actually happened at the farmhouse, so you and your family may be able to talk your way out of this, but you should probably leave, too."

><

Pan Gmerk was not ready to give up his farm over this. But Rodak insisted, for the sake of his family. "Just until this blows over. The good thing is the only Cossacks who saw us shooting Cossacks are all dead."

"Except for the sergeant who saw Karl," Mr. Gmerk said.

Pane Gmerk had cleaned Zalaman's wound and bandaged him up. She announced that the boy would live. She hadn't had to remove any bullet because it had gone right through him, in the front and out the back, and had not hit any vital organs. He'd lost a lot of blood, but he was intact and had passed out from the pain, as had Bern from the agonies suffered at the hands of Flora and Anna when they straightened then set his leg using sticks and muslin.

When Zalaman woke his gut was on fire. "Don't worry too much about the hole in you," Stanko reassured him, "according to Mrs. Gmerk you are intact." But he didn't feel intact. Stanko stuck some marching powder under his nose and that helped clear his head. Anna smoothed his hair. At least he was among the living.

"You were hit with the repeater," Rodak said. "Now we have more than one apiece for ourselves." The thought of more shooting made Zalaman close his eyes.

Stanko was pleased with himself, watching Flora apply one of her herbal balms to Bern's leg. He hadn't let his instincts overcome his scruples. Still, he would like to have received at least some minor wound so he could be getting such tender treatment from her. He and Rodak had already been back at the overturned supply wagon, while the two Karls had started the considerable task of digging a big grave for eight. When Rodak and Stanko finally joined them, they were in a good mood, especially for gravediggers. They'd collected enough weaponry to arm an uprising of their own. The Cossacks had obviously been doing their tax collecting at several stops and now those collections belonged to the partisans. The wagon itself was still in working condition, so they could take it if they modified the exterior a bit so it wouldn't stick out as a Cossack wagon. But the biggest prize was the rifles: five Spencer repeating rifles.

A formidable arsenal and an incriminating one: "Made in the United States of America" embossed above the triggers. A close second prize was the Cossack strong box, which they had pried open to reveal a modest stash of silver and coins and a stack of banknotes bundled with twine. Before they buried the Cossacks, they stripped the least-bloodied uniforms from three of the bodies—one big and two medium-sized—to take with them.

Now, back in the large central room of the farmhouse, Lena was explaining where things stood. "Despite my sunny words, Zalaman is not yet out of the woods."

"It doesn't matter whether the supply sergeant makes it back to his fellows or doesn't," Rodak said. "The party of Cossacks we destroyed will be missed. And so Zalaman . . . he's going to have to be leaving with us and very soon."

On his cot, Zalaman tried to sit up, but was thrown back down by the deep, searing fire raging through his middle. Stanko gave him another dose of the marching powder. He wanted Zalaman to stay awake and understand what had to be done.

Rodak said that, excluding the weapons, they would divide this booty four ways—the three partisans getting a quarter each and the Gmerks the other quarter. He thought they also had a responsibility to bring something to HQ at Syp. "We'll give them one Spencer and some old muskets."

Zalaman was in no shape to participate in their planning, but the pain in his gut mellowed a bit from some combination of the marching powder and the salve Flora had applied to the wound. It was also gratifying to hear Rodak consider him an equal partner. He would have one of those deadly, marvelous Spencer machines.

"They can fire multiple bullets without reloading," Rodak told him. "But you must learn how to shoot them. They're not so easy to aim." Then he addressed the Gmerks, telling them that it might take the sergeant a day or two to get to the garrison at

Ostro. "But the Cossacks who were killed might be missed even earlier. Either way, we need to leave and, if you're smart, you will, too. Let's just hope Zalaman is in good enough health to travel."

A burning in his stomach all the way to his back traced the bullet's path. Zalaman's brain was starting to work again despite pain. He was thinking maybe he should stay with Anna and Lena and let Rodak and Stanko go on without him. No, he couldn't do that.

Besides, the Gmerks, too, might have to leave.

The older sister, Flora, the woman with the preordained skill with herbs, explained how the fever stemmed from corruption left in Zalaman's body by the bullet as it sped through. It would be dangerous for him to travel until his fever broke. And when might that be? Flora shrugged. "It's different with different people. But he's young and that's always an advantage."

"It doesn't matter," Rodak said, "we leave tomorrow morning."

"You'll have to wait and see how he is," Anna said.

First, Rodak and Stanko had to cover all evidence of their presence. They defaced the Cossack supply wagon beyond recognition and packed the rewards of their battle into both wagons, the new wagon and Georg's.

Zalaman's fever brought him dreams that night. They alternated between death and good fortune. One endlessly recurring motif featured Zalaman staying behind with the Gmerks. In another he was discovered by the Cossacks and tortured. One of the dreamscapes was decorated with ridiculously high piles of coins. Banknotes had the power of speech, warmly congratulating him on his new wealth.

Anna didn't think she and her family should run. She did not want to stay on the Bierbza with relatives as her parents were suggesting. She suggested the family stay put and feign ignorance when the Cossacks arrived. “We can say we were bound and gagged the whole time.”

Lena disagreed. The Russians were too unpredictable. “Even if they believed us, they might choose to slaughter us anyway, just to be safe.” Karl and Bern and the others sided with Lena.

Before dawn, Zalaman’s fever broke just a bit. Traveling with his injury, it was decided, would be less life-threatening than staying put and waiting for the Cossacks. He was still weak and delirious enough to agree to be carted off by Rodak and Stanko, after the Gmerks, Lena and Anna in particular, appealed to the cousins that he should stay with them. They could hide him. A part of Zalaman’s brain was still functioning and it was picturing a quiet time for healing. That’s what he was going to need, though he knew, in some other part of his brain, that this was not to be. Could things stay ‘quiet’ with Anna and Lena around? He wondered, with his injury, whether he would ever again be capable of physical love. He’d miss them. He was in love with Anna, but both had provided an exceptional initiation. Once healed, he believed, there would be more adventures, more women. And more silver. So, he told them, Anna and Lena, he’d stay with Rodak and Stanko. “The Uprising needs me,” he told them. They tried to keep a straight face but couldn’t. Lena shook her head and smiled, knowing he was less than enthusiastic about the Uprising but that his leaving was probably for the best. She was surprised when Anna found it impossible to stifle tears over his leaving.

There had been little opportunity for individual goodbyes, short of the intense hand-holding through the night with Anna and, after she went to bed, with her mother. Zalaman was so adamant about seeing her again and she laughed and said she believed he was on the road to recovery. She told him he was sure to have many successes with women and he could detect nothing in her voice that might suggest she knew about him and Anna. But then, he wasn't in the best condition for detecting anything. Best to ride off with his comrades. It would be getting colder soon, but their new wealth should make winter easier.

At first light, Rodak and Stanko settled Zalaman into the special seat Stanko had fashioned out of parts of an old gun crate, using some straw and adding a bit of old sacking to make it comfortable.

"Don't worry about us," Lena said. "We might get lucky and the Cossacks will just take our harvest and not burn down our house while we're gone." She gave Zalaman a very gentle (his wound would be painful enough when the wagon was bouncing along), but very loving hug. The Gmerks hugged Stanko and Rodak, while Anna hugged Zalaman, who was strapped down in his seat. He held on to her and practically had to be pried off. She'd whispered in his ear the name of the cousins—"Wiecki"—where they would stay and said she'd be waiting for him—either there or back here. He said he would do everything he could to see her again.

It was a crisp fall morning, chilled by breezes from the northeast pushing heavy, dark purple clouds. Zalaman was warm in his swollen vest, about as comfortable as his wound would permit. As they rode away from the Gmerk farm, he turned as best he could to watch the receding forms of Lena and Anna and the other Gmerks. He pulled out the spyglass Stanko had put in its scabbard by his side. When Zalaman found the Gmerks in his lens and brought them into focus, they were still together, watching their comrades-in-arms disappear. The image recalled the first time he'd first seen the family—spying on them from the woods with the same glass.

Stanko was driving the wagon, slowly for Zalaman's sake, but its movement wouldn't let him hold the glass steady enough to keep his eye on the Gmerks. He whispered a goodbye, then sheathed the spyglass and turned to the front. He should be facing the direction they were headed—the future.

It was so light, that neither Rodak nor Stanko, busy driving the vehicles, noticed the tiny snowflakes. Zalaman watched as they gathered like dust in the folds of his vest—the first flurry of winter. It didn't amount to much snow, but it was a reminder that winter lay ahead and might sometime bury them under a blanket of snow. But for the moment, he couldn't help but feel buoyed by the stuff. The first snow always put him in a good mood, one of joyful expectation. It did so now, such that he forgot his pain, but only for a few minutes and then Stanko hit a bump and the torture in his belly returned. Stanko apologized when he heard Zalaman cry out, promising to drive more carefully. Zalaman wondered if he could focus on the joy the snow gave him to forget the pain. He remembered other first snows—how they always changed the light. Whenever the first snow came at night, he could tell when he woke up, before even looking outside. He remembered playing in that white softness with Davin and Keila. He pictured them making paths so that he and his friend, Aron Benowitz, could chase one another through fields. He recalled snowball battles in the *kvadrat* with himself and Davin against Ev and Aron. He remembered target practice which meant throwing snowballs at Doozy Kurtsak, the big wooden chicken that was the Benowitz' butcher shop sign. He recalled that he and his friends threw snowballs at unsuspecting strangers and then ran away on their pre-established route. Then another jolt travelled right through him, interrupting his daydreams. But for the most part, the snow was having a positive effect; it was starting to pile up on the road and soften the bumps. He watched it settle on Stanko's shoulders, then fly off when he flicked the reins. As best he could from his strapped-in position, Zalaman scooped up enough of the stuff to fashion it into a ball, which he threw, hitting Stanko on the back of his head. Stanko flinched but was not going to give Zalaman the pleasure of thinking he even noticed. When a second snowball missed, Stanko told him he was a better shot with snowballs than bullets.

Maybe he shouldn't be allowed to use the new Spencer repeaters. Zalaman would have to wait until he recovered before he could fire those.

> <

When they were well away from the Gmerks' valley and the snow grew more intermittent, they stopped to look at maps and discuss where they were going. They used it as an excuse to try out the new Spencers. Zalaman could only watch as the cousins fired more bullets than they'd ever dare waste prior to this gift from the Cossack supply sergeant.

"Once you get the hang of it," Rodak said afterward, "the advantage of using the repeater is even greater than the advantage of a rifle over a musket. It's the North's great equalizer in the American War of the States. That's where these probably came from—Abraham Lincoln gave many to the Tsar as a thank you for his support, for the Russian warships he sent the North."

Stanko held one up one of the Spencers for Zalaman to inspect. "They will make us just like the American North," Stanko said.

"Tsar Alexander?" Rodak asked. "'The Tsar who freed the serfs'? He sees himself as the Abraham Lincoln of the East. Lincoln is The Great Emancipator and Alexander is The Great Liberator. I have known partisans of the Uprising who travelled all the way to America to join in their fight. Yes, they did it for the money, but also to tweak the English."

"Thing about the Spencers," said Stanko, "is that if you can't take a good shot, you can waste a lot of bullets really fast. With other rifles, you shoot, reload, and shoot again in the time this Spencer shoots twenty bullets—and that can get expensive."

After the first couple of days on the road, with no sign of any Cossack pursuit and well out of the Gmerks' valley, they slowed their pace. By dusk, the third day, they were in open country covered in a thin white sheet of snow. They had a good, sweeping view in every direction. They could sleep under blankets in their carts without fear of anyone sneaking up.

Zalaman's wound had started to heal and the pain was less, attributed in part to Flora's ointments and in part to the use of a little more marching powder. Stanko was treating the wound as Flora had instructed. That night, in the light of their campfire, he unwrapped the linen bandages, front to back, and applied the medicine Flora had given him. Stanko had a light touch for such a big guy. The salve itself consisted of wrinkled, old, withered, yellow flowers whose stems produced a kind of golden oil when he squeezed them. Gently dabbing this oil gently on Zalaman's wound, front and back, Stanko patted over the oil with seeds of some sort that Flora had crushed into a grainy powder. Then he re-tied the linen bandages.

They were still days away from the Syp HQ, when Zalaman discovered they were not planning on going directly there.

"Do you want to spend the winter in a tent drinking meatless soups?" Stanko asked. "Because that's what we'd get in HQ." Rodak said it was more about the roads being too dangerous at the moment. He was sure the Cossacks were looking for them.

"If I am going to suffer through the winter, I want to do it in a nice warm bed," Zalaman shouted—then winced with the pain brought on by his excitement.

"We have money now. We can afford 'creature comforts.'"

Creature comforts was a phrase Zalaman's mother used, but he thought Stanko's definition of a 'creature comfort' might differ from his mother's.

"Which creature's comfort did you like best?" Stanko asked him. "Lena's or Anna's?"

Zalaman was not going to admit it; he was not going to reveal that Stanko had guessed correctly. Did he know? Did everyone?

"Don't answer Stanko's question," Rodak warned him. Rodak, being a close observer of their young recruit, was the person who had first alerted Stanko to this possibility.

"Don't tell him a thing, unless Stanko's willing to talk about Flora."

"Oh, no," Stanko said. "As much as I wish it had been so. It wasn't. It never happened. Not because I wasn't interested, I was, but Bern was always in the way."

"I could see she was interested, too. It was noble of you to not act on your desire. Too bad we can't say the same of young Zalaman here."

"Alright, it's true," Zalaman admitted. "But it's not like I really had much control over the situation." He stopped short of saying "they were both after me," because it sounded like bragging. Plus, that wouldn't quite do justice to his role.

To Stanko, the important thing was commemorating this momentous, first-ever in the young man's life—"The loss of your virginity requires a celebration"—so he went for the *krupnick* they'd found in the Cossack's supply wagon. It had been quite a while since he'd had any of the liquor. It went right through Zalaman directly to his wound and then to his head and he thought he saw his father pouring *krupnik* for the customers in his shop. Stanko picked up the cup Zalaman dropped and prodded him back into awareness. The shock of seeing his father, or picturing him so vividly and so briefly, made him worry about delaying the trip to HQ where he hoped they might have received some response to his message home. The partisans made him feel a little better by assuring him that even if a response had not been received, they were sure that by now his parents had gotten Zalaman's letter.

After a week or so on the road, Zalaman's wound had healed enough that he could sometimes abandon his special seat and drive the supply wagon or Georg's cart. It was tricky going in the snow. He hoped they would soon concentrate on finding a winter refuge, a place to hibernate—although rather than hibernating, he knew they would try to be active partisans. Luckily, the options for such pursuits would be much more limited in the winter. They would lay low, out of the snow, and stay alert.

They wended their way through drifting snow, a task made more difficult by the load they carried, advancing now into a more populated region—populated with Russians and Poles, but mostly Prussians and 'former Prussians.' They chanced going into a village where the people spoke a low dialect that contained so many Baltic Prussian words, they found it easy to communicate with farmers and villagers. They kept their weapons under wrap and there were no unfortunate encounters with Russians, although this land was firmly in Cossack hands. It seemed to be so, except for those villages that consisted of little more than a dozen or even half-dozen houses and barns—inconspicuous dots on Rodak's map.

Late one particularly uncomfortable, bitter cold afternoon, Stanko and Zalaman were already struggling with the carts and horses when their breaths were taken away by an even icier blast. They stopped to catch their breath and let the horses catch theirs.

Zalaman missed the warm hearth of his crooked little house in Lahkvna. He loved sitting by the fireplace when it was cold outside, listening to the crackle of the flames and his mother reading to him.

He and Stanko huddled into themselves and waited for the return of Rodak who was supposedly off doing advance scouting in an upcoming village that he thought looked promising on the map. Despite the biting cold, Zalaman was content. He was living an unheard of adventure and he wasn't ready to go home. They would find warmth. They had money. It was so unlikely, what he was doing and, he told himself, maybe that's why he liked it. Mama would not approve, but she would appreciate the way he was handling himself. This adventure had not been of his choosing. It had been foisted on him—at least originally. Getting *chappered* was supposed to have been a death sentence—yet he'd escaped. Or at least the death sentence had been commuted. He might shiver in the cold and long for a warm bed, but now he was almost a seasoned partisan. When he got home in the spring—and he would go home then, even if he had to set out on his own—he would be bringing home silver.

He wondered how far away they were from Lahkvna because it felt like they were heading further and further away from home. He didn't really know if this was true, because the map showed only a small portion of the places they'd traversed since the death of Georg. He wanted a straight answer from Rodak and Stanko.

Rodak returned from scouting with nothing encouraging to report. Zalaman asked if they could look at the map. Rodak showed them where they were, but all the landmarks that showed up on the map had been swallowed up and smoothed over in the leveling whiteness. He, too, had struggled all day, breaking track through a half-meter of new snow. Now, with more of the stuff swirling around their heads, making it hard to see, they managed a get a fire going to warm up and to better read the map. Rodak pointing out where they'd been and where they might go. The provinces of Sandomierskie, Podlaskie, and Lubelskie.

"Can you show me Lahkvna," Zalaman asked. "It's not on the map," Rodak said. "Navharadak, then."

"No, not there either," Rodak said, exasperated. He asked Stanko to hold the map out flat, oriented as best he could east to west, then he trudged off into the darkness from which he shouted, asking Zalaman if he could see him. "No," Zalaman yelled back, "It's too dark and you're too far away."

"Well," he shouted, "the map would have to stretch all the way to me to include Navharadak."

Zalaman hoped he was exaggerating.

That night they kept from freezing by donning the Cossack uniforms collected after the battle. They put the uniforms on under their own clothes and slept in them through the night, waking in the morning to find it had stopped snowing but had buried them under a good six or seven centimeters overnight.

By midday, the sky had cleared, but it was even colder and they were plodding through deep snow. According to the map, up ahead was Punie, a small town, smaller than Navharadak, but for this region it was one of the larger communities. Rodak rode up ahead to look, and when he returned he told them, "There are about a thousand souls in Punie. The odd thing is, not one of them so much as looked at me."

"Well, you're not all that much to look at," Stanko said.

"No, this was very studied 'not looking.' They were intentionally not staring, not out of indifference, but fear." He told his partners, "Yes, there are Cossacks about, but not too many. The commandant warned me, the people around here are opposed to the Tsar, but they are also afraid of him. Rightly so. Talking to strangers—apparently even looking at them—is not in their interest."

"You want to stay?"

"There was something . . ." Rodak said. "An Inn. Nice and warm, with its own restaurant and saloon. They have rooms at a price we can afford. And there is an acceptable stable where we can keep our vehicles and animals and store the weapons. It's secure, not secure enough for our valuables, but for the rest."

They didn't want to attract attention when they arrived in Punie, yet they now almost qualified as a wagon train with armaments, so they took their time. It would be better not to appear in broad daylight. They would pose as Polish traders sorting out their business for the approaching winter, while as partisans they got the lay of the land, got to know the civilians, found out what's what and what kind of opportunities there might be.

"Punie is a small lemon," Rodak said. "It won't take long to squeeze."

CHAPTER SEVEN

Punie

At a leisurely pace, they passed a small church, a few stores, townsfolk who, as predicted, paid them no notice. They slowed more as they approached the extensive inn near the center of town. As they passed the inn, its doors swung open and a small group of men emerged and, like the others, they paid no heed to the three partisans. Of course, the three partisans were not upset by this lack of recognition. On the contrary, they felt more than sufficiently welcomed by the warm, smoky air and the delicious smells of cooking it carried, wafting by them as the doors swung back shut.

They drove on past the inn, to the public stables where they roused the young stable boy. The winter season was upon them and there were few travelers, so he was happy to have their business, the stable well-stocked with hay and oats. They found room to park the wagons as well and promised the stable boy something extra if he would keep his eyes on them. The weapons were well hidden, wrapped in two padlocked crates that took up most of the space in the wagon. They did not leave the two hessian bags, nor the satchel stuffed with banknotes, silver, and jewelry. They took those with them to the inn.

The temperature was dropping, a freezing day becoming an even colder night, making the cosy glow from the saloon's gas lamps look even more inviting. They entered, so grateful for the warmth it brought tears to their eyes. The gaslight revealed worn and withered beams inside that propped up the facade outside. It felt familiar to Zalaman, a lot like the off-kilter architecture of Lahkvna, where the ramshackle style predominated. In Punie, it was referred to simply as The Inn, but it was more restaurant-saloon than hotel. It had only three guest rooms, but the newly arrived 'Polish traders' could have their pick—there were no other guests.

The innkeeper's name was Januariusz Gerszewski, and Jan was delighted to have paying guests, especially those who offered to pay up front. His Frau, Gierta, always complained about how hard it was to justify keeping the Inn's guest rooms when they could make more money by getting rid of them and using the space to enlarge the saloon.

"The younger generation," Jan explained, "they have grown up with all the conveniences of modern civilization and they are now so spoiled they don't dare venture out in winter. In my day, winter was the best time to travel. There was little farm work to do and, certainly we had our challenges, yet we would head south. That was, of course, before we purchased this inn . . ."

Jan could have and would have continued if his new guests hadn't started making it obvious they were tired and hungry and wished to get along with it. They assured him they appreciated his attention, but it was true—they *were* tired and hungry. Jan said they should take care of their hunger first. Gierta was a renowned cook. "A real *szef*! The best chops in Punie and people come from all around for them," he claimed. As an astute innkeeper, Jan knew when to tell tales and when to leave his guests alone, especially paying-in-advance guests such as these. Stanko and Rodak could stay together in the largest room and Zalaman would have a small one, a quarter the size of the cousins,' but he didn't care—it was his own room! The first time in his life he would be able to enjoy such private extravagance.

"I apologize for asking," Jan said before handing over the heavy keys, "but I have no choice. The Tsar's officers will ask who my guests are, where they're coming from—and where they are going to."

"We are a family of Polish merchants from Navharadak on our way to our southern markets. We have been successful enough this summer that we can afford to wait out a month or two of the winter. Thaw out."

"That's good. It's true there are some suspicious characters who come through here—at least the Russians find them suspicious. If any of my guests are hiding something, the Russians inevitably find out and then of course I get the blame. A lot of trouble. But, never mind all that, I've been in this business a while and I can tell you are good, honest citizens." He showed them to their rooms and waited while they splashed water on their faces from a basin and brushed off their outfits as best they could, then escorted them into the restaurant.

The restaurant was the largest and most conspicuous part of the inn, with many nooks and crannies creating anterooms of differing character, but the saloon downstairs provided the life blood of the inn. It was well-lit, brighter than the restaurant, and it was cavernous—lively but usually not overly raucous, though mostly male. Cossacks and Poles (and others more exotic), sharing the same space, if not the same conversations. The restaurant upstairs served men, women, and families, but at this late hour there were many more drinkers in the saloon than there were diners in the upstairs restaurant. To the Bartos cousins, the lodging-saloon-restaurant was altogether more than they expected to find in such a small town. The less worldly Zalaman took it all in stride.

Having no standard by which he might judge the inn, he assumed it must be the norm.

Jan showed them to a table, repeating himself about how customers came to eat from towns and farms all over the region. "The best inn south of the Dzeszow," he proclaimed again before he excused himself—a claim that was buttressed by the fact that it was also the *only* inn. Drinks were served until the barkeepers could no longer stand.

Upstairs in the restaurant, the gas lamps were turned down to discourage late arriving customers like Rodak, Stanko and Zalaman. Gierta and her assistants were done cooking for the evening, but she would find them something. The restaurant was comfortably warm and that was the greatest pleasure after all the cold-weather riding; the warmth here from the residual heat off the kitchen's now-silent ovens and a roaring fireplace. The few people still there, when the three were seated by Jan, included a local tradesman and a table of three artisans, textile workers with blue-dyed hands lifting their knives and spoons. None of the famous chops were left, but the hot meat soup and fresh baked bread were, all three swore, the best they'd ever tasted. Rodak said the *zurek*, compared favorably with Pane Bartos' own soup, even the sourest version. They soaked the bread in the soup and when they were full, they found they still had a thirst, so they ambled down the candle- and gas-lit stairs to the saloon and ordered a round of *krupnik*.

Zalaman knew his limits and tonight he would pay attention to them. Or so he told himself. But after the first *krupnik*, he must have lost a little of his resolve. Stanko complained that by limiting himself to one *krupnik* he, Zalaman, was disrespecting their accomplishments, not appreciating the opportunity ahead, and just when he and Rodak had started thinking he could be an equal partner. Rodak shook his head at his cousin's nonsense, but Zalaman's first *krupnik* had given him just enough leeway to justify one more. "For just this one night," Stanko said and Zalaman agreed, "Just one night," when he acquiesced to the third and fourth.

There were quite a few Cossack officers in the saloon, along with the Polish administrative types, but the more they drank, the less the partisans felt restricted by the Russian presence. To Zalaman, everyone of the officers looked haughty and overbearing. Their uniforms were clean if not resplendent (Punie was hardly a major outpost) and they were obviously living well off the taxes extracted from the citizens.

Zalaman was reminded of Linards, the DPPO officer back home, the peacock who he'd dreamed of when he was tied up in Georg's wagon and who had taunted Minya Benowitz in the butcher shop. He was surprised to discover that Stanko and Rodak knew of Linards. He had a reputation. Zalaman was not surprised to learn that Linards was no better liked in Navharadak than he was in Lahkvna. It was enough to encourage another drink.

The saloon looked to be as popular with Cossack officers—the keepers of order and collectors of taxes—as it was to the local gentry, the people who were being kept in order and from whom those taxes were collected. But it wasn't a one-way, parasitic relationship; there was a symbiosis, a partnership between the subjugated and the gentry. The exploiters took their cut, but, at least for one 'Antek,' that burden was lightened by Russian rubles. The Poles and Russians didn't mix, but for the gregarious, boisterous character everyone called Antek. To Zalaman, he seemed to be the rule-proving exception to the segregation, a friend to Pole and Russian alike it would appear.

"A whoremonger," Stanko said.

"A person who sells women to men for sex favors," Rodak explained, though Zalaman scoffed unconvincingly that, of course, he knew what a whoremonger was. "He's everyone's friend."

"Might have to introduce myself," Stanko said, "Just watch, he'll introduce himself before I have a chance." But it was not to be that night.

In addition to the officers, there was a less well-dressed contingent of Cossacks comprised of rough and tumble veterans fresh from the war in the Caucasus. It was a war that seemed to be slowly petering out—just like the Polish Uprising. The veterans extolled their military exploits and the local officers bragged about their own, nostalgic for the years before they were stuck in

Punie. Then there were the local civilians, gentry, tradespeople, and artisans—all of them trying, and largely successful, to ignore the Russians. Other than Antek, they stuck to their own side of the room.

But a dark mood came over Zalaman. Too much *krupnik* and the warmth of the room transported him back to Lahkvna and Papa scolding him for breaking the one-sip rule. Zalaman grew dizzy. He fell off his chair and the crash went right through his wound. He cried out, waking Stanko and Rodak who had themselves dozed off at the table.

It had been a long, cold day, so the cousins pulled Zalaman up from the floor and dragged themselves to their rooms and slept long into the next day.

><

When Zalaman finally did wake up, it took a while for him to remember where he was and when he did, he was pleasantly surprised to find himself 'in his own room.' The bed was narrow but still took up most of the room. What he relished was that it provided far superior sleep to the branches and leaves of the last weeks, so, despite the overindulgence of last night, he felt well-rested. There was a small fur rug on the strip of floor not covered by the bed. It felt good on his bare feet. A room all his own. He would have liked to bring Anna here, but she was far away—hopefully, safe.

Last night, he'd begun to feel this dark melancholy. He realized he was missing home, maybe regretting things he'd done—like killing people who hadn't harmed him, loving women and then abandoning them, although to a lesser degree than the killing. But he would no longer regret not going home. He would go.

He was sure he would, eventually, get back to Lahkvna, but for now he was on his way to making something of himself. It was too bad this might require more violence and danger, but he was sure his father would agree that he was fighting for the right side.

And it would give him independence. He wouldn't necessarily have to grow up to be a peddler in the *shtetl*. The light streaming in from the tiny window gave him hope. He hadn't slept this late since the Gmerks.

Later, in the cousins' much larger room, ignoring the smell of their clothes and bodies, they inspected their loot. They were uncertain of the value of the various coins and banknotes and had no idea at all regarding several brooches, necklaces, and rings they found in the Cossacks' strong box.

"Stolen or extorted from their Polish subjects," Rodak said, exonerating themselves from any taint of unethical behavior.

"There is enough here that we can afford to stay all winter," Stanko said, hopefully.

Rodak smiled, denying it. They didn't really know what they had—and "We need to find a way to augment our purses."

They divided a portion of the coins into three equal stacks. Each stack should easily be enough to keep them in beef stew and krupnik for weeks. In exchange for a note of assurance from Jan, they stored the remainder in his safe box. No individual one of them could touch the box without the knowledge of the other two.

While Zalaman was in Jan's back office with Rodak and Stanko, he noticed several shelves of books the innkeeper offered as a library for guests. He let Zalaman borrow the two copies of *The Sorrows of Young Werther*—one in Polish and one in the original German. Zalaman thought he might improve his German but would only be able to do so if he also had the Polish version for reference. His mother had declined to read him this book he'd heard so much about. "You'll have to wait till you're a little older," she would say. Jan said he thought Zalaman should be old enough to read it now.

"But," he cautioned Zalaman, "*Vorsicht.* In the wrong hands, this can be a dangerous book. You mustn't take it seriously. In my grandparents' generation, some did. They killed themselves in imitation of their hero, Werther. I can't explain it because I can't understand it myself. They did it, I suppose, to show how emotionally deep they were, how strongly they felt about some imaginary love."

"Don't worry. I've always wanted to read it once my mother told me it was the book Napoleon carried with him on his Egyptian campaign. And our best horse was called Marengo. Mama had no qualms about my reading *The Count of Monte Cristo.*" And maybe that helped him regard this life of adventure, of weapons and treasure, as something nearly familiar. He had the urge to tell Jan that he was more musketeer of Dumas stories than a Werther of Goethe's. But he, Zalaman, was masquerading as the junior member of a Polish trading family and wasn't supposed to say anything that could lead to exposing his real life as a partisan of the Uprising.

The first time he met Lechsi, he was sunk in the wonderful goatskin armchair at the far end of the inn's restaurant but near the kitchen, reading *Junge Werthers*: *How happy I am that I am gone. I will enjoy the present and the past shall be the past.* He let the words sink in. It was like Goethe was speaking directly to him. Maybe that was why Mama had told him to wait. Reading a book like this made your own problems seem less foreboding by making them part of a grander picture. What he was doing wasn't insignificant. The Uprising was part of a much bigger story. Now he would be a part of that story. It could be a scary story; it could be a deadly one. But it could also be a good one.

He noticed a girl watching him. She was eating Gierta's chops with an older couple he took to be her parents. The poor light concealed as much as it revealed, but there was a dark eye shining on either him or his book. Strands of black hair fell over her other eye but over this one, there was an arched eyebrow, so he was distracted and kept forgetting what he'd just read.

On her way out of the restaurant with her parents, Lechsi stopped to tell him "I hope you like the book. I loved it." She was gone without waiting for a reply.

He kept reading after she left, but the book changed. This beautiful girl was now Charlotte.

Chapter Eight

Lechsi

And one afternoon just a few days later, as Rodak and Stanko were out exercising the horses, Zalaman saw her a second time, again in the restaurant with her family. This time she seemed not to notice him at all, except that it was a studied not-noticing, like the people of Punie intentionally not noticing strangers.

So, when they left this time, Zalaman followed them. It was a very cold afternoon and emerging from the poor light of the inn, the wind whipping the snow into white whirlwinds, he couldn't tell whether the snow was rising from the drifts or falling from the grey sky that intermittently opened with streaks of sunshine. The cold was as shocking as the beauty. He could barely make out his prey and counted himself lucky when they reappeared. The plank sidewalk was iced up and dangerous, so he had to pay attention to walking. He felt ridiculous. Spying on her? He should be back in the nice warm inn . . . And then Lechsi and her parents turned off the road and traversed a narrow path that went right up to a substantial house.

He kept on walking straight ahead, like an innocent newcomer, just exploring. As he passed her house, he imagined a rustle of curtain in one of their front windows and after a few minutes he turned to look back and there she was, walking toward him. She had been looking out of her window as he passed by. He'd been caught.

When she got within a meter, she stopped and regarded Zalaman, her arms crossed in front of her, mittened hands tucked under armpits. The light was fading with the winds, but it was still brighter than the restaurant. The light exposed smooth cheeks and shining dark eyes, her hair as dark as it had appeared under gaslight, and there was still a looping strand trailing from under her fur hat. She smiled.

"So, I want to know how you like the book or if you were just pretending to read it in order to impress me . . . make me think of you as a romantic hero?"

"I thought I was already reading the book when you came over and said you hoped I liked it, but maybe I'm mistaken. I might have done much worse things to get your attention. So, thanks for at least not accusing me of spying on you."

"Which you were just doing," she reminded him. Then, standing there in the snow, she changed the subject and warned him of the dangers of the book—that young people had killed themselves emulating Werther. He told her he had heard those stories. She told him they had banned the book in Leipzig. He hadn't known the government could ban a book.

"I'm Leschi," she said curtsying and he bowed slightly from the waist as he'd seen in Mama's illustrateds and said "Zalaman." They talked and walked up and down the path a few minutes, though never beyond the vision of her father, checking on their movements. But he wasn't her father, at all, it turned out, but an uncle, who, with her aunt, had raised her after both her parents perished of consumption. Zalaman felt the kinship of orphans and told her about his '*chappering.*'

"I'm not comparing," he assured her. "That's awful about your parents, I can return to mine whenever I want. Well, not quite whenever I want."

"If you are not being held against your will, you should return home to let them know you are OK." Zalaman told her he would. But not in the winter. The look on her uncle's face in the front window, told her she should return home. He walked to the front door with her, but before she opened it and disappeared in the house, she turned and said, "The first time I saw you reading *Werthers,* I not only wondered if you were showing off, I also wondered if it meant there was to be a romantic relationship between us."

Hanging out in the saloon at night, the three were getting to know some of the local gentry while keeping an eye on the Cossacks. One night they were closely watching a small, boisterous group. Maybe, too closely. One of them, a handsome Cossack officer, separated from the group and swaggered over to their table, introducing himself as Colonel Aleksey Domnantovitch. He asked them what they found so fascinating about his group, intimating that there was something annoying, if not suspicious, about it. Rodak explained so convincingly that they were merchants and were hoping to make a sale and to spot wealthy Cossacks . . . that the Colonel said, exasperated, that he was not interested, but that the traders should be more discreet . . . if someone was to get the wrong idea, well, spies were dealt with harshly.

The three became more circumspect in their spying. They maintained a lower profile in front of the Cossacks. When they were not out scouting, they were fraternizing with the locals, playing the tradesmen, looking for buyers of their goods as they would be expected to—not that they had any goods, but they used it to identify patriotic Polish citizens who might be of use and help ferret out the Russian sympathizers among them. Zalaman tried to convince them that he should spend time with Lechsi as a means of infiltrating Punie society. They were suspect of his reasons, but when an opportunity arose for him to see her, they didn't discourage him from taking it.

It was their first scheduled rendezvous. They went for a drive in her uncle's *droshky*. Wearing long coats, flying through the freezing, grey-white world, they were forced to snuggle close. At one point, Zalaman had to pull over onto a branching path to let a faster vehicle pass by and it provided the opportunity they had both been looking for and without a word, without asking for permission or even acknowledging what was about to happen, they simultaneously pressed their lips to one another's and held that kiss. Even after the *droshky* plodded slowly on, their lips stayed together and Zalaman knew this was like no kiss he'd even had before. Not chaste, but not too deep either, soft but not too soft. He pulled her to him and she didn't resist—until he put his hand on her thigh and she removed the hand and straightened up.

She told him they had to turn back to Punie before her uncle came looking for them.

Zalaman thought she was mad at him for being too forward, but when he asked if that was the case, she denied it. "Remember what I told you about me wondering if you and I were to have a romance. Well, I don't know about that, Zalaman. But rest assured there is no one else for me in Punie. The only interesting young men—yes, there were two," she laughed, "they both left long ago for Minsk. Young people leave Punie for Minsk because there is good work to be found there. Freeing the serfs created a lot of new business."

"Minsk is still in the Russian Empire," Zalaman said.

"I know that," she said. She told him about the poor treatment her uncle had more than once received at the hands of the Cossacks. Zalaman said he was in sympathy with her feelings in that regard. He could not tell her about his life with Rodak and Stanko, but it was evident to her it had something to do with Cossacks.

><

He was daydreaming of her in the saloon, all by himself, holding *Young Werthers* but not reading, when Pan Antek, a stein in one hand, materialized beside him like an evil spirit.

"Excuse me, sir, but is this seat taken?" he asked in Polish.

Zalaman and his partners had been observing Antek since that first night, they had had a few laughs over his ability to change smoothly from one face to another as he switched from one group to another. So Zalaman was prejudiced against him, but he was interesting.

He introduced himself, and said, "I thought you might be waiting for your friends."

"Cousins," Zalaman corrected him, introducing himself.

Antek proceeded to ask Zalaman about them—what they were doing in these parts and how long would they be staying, and if it was true about their being traders as Jan said. Zalaman said it was true and asked Antek what he 'was doing in these parts.'

"I have lived in Punie all my life. I know everyone here. And I do business with all of them."

"You are Polish, but you do business with Cossacks."

"Of course, I do," he said. "I do a lot of business with them. They have the rubles. And, for the most part, they are honest men. You are a Jew, despite your story about your Polish cousins. I would say the Russians are as honorable as the Hebrews." Zalaman didn't deny his religion but didn't answer. Antek laughed. "Look at you, a handsome example of the Hebrew race. I have nothing against Hebrews. I have partnered with them in business and have always found them not only honorable, sometimes even profitable partners."

Zalaman was about to question this but held back. Antek read his feelings anyway. He lowered his voice. "You should watch yourself, Zalaman. Take Aleksey Domnantovitch seriously. He gave you some good advice the other day. You must watch yourself, young man. Watch your tongue when it comes to our

Russian friends. Colonel Domnantovitch has been known to do much worse than offer advice. How old are you, anyway? You can't be a day over fifteen."

"I'm sixteen," he lied.

"Well, I hope we haven't gotten off on the wrong foot, Zalaman. I am impressed with you—even if you are really sixteen."

"You're probably right about being cautious," Zalaman said. "Thanks for the advice." All Antek was trying to do was offer friendly advice.

"We see remnants of the Uprising around here from time to time and they usually look like your cousins, especially the one who calls himself Rodak. Have you heard about Timas and Erkme?" Zalaman shook his head. "They were a couple of partisans." Zalaman was feeling uncomfortable and didn't want some squeak in his voice to reveal this, so he smiled and shrugged.

"I try to help Polish-Russian relationships," Antek said with a grin. "Business relationships. I do a good trade in tobacco and opium products with the Poles. With the Russians, well, I bring a little love into violent, but drab lives."

"Love?"

"A kind of love," Antek said, resigned to the foibles of his fellow man. He was certainly not shy about describing to Zalaman how he procured whores for Cossack officers and, occasionally, for bored Polish husbands, but Antek did not use the word whores.

They were "his ladies—respectable young women . . . well, relatively young, who don't mind making money selling pleasure. None of my ladies take pleasure in their work, or won't admit to it, but they do 'love' the extra income." Antek sold that love to lonely Cossack officers right in the saloon. His ladies never had to appear there, although they did sometimes wait in the inn's restaurant. "I trade in tobacco, spirits and a variety of opium tinctures and pastilles, but the ladies are by far the most lucrative business. You're too young to appreciate why that would be."

But Zalaman said he'd had some experience with women, which made Antek laugh—a laugh of approval rather than derision—when he doubted it could be bought.

Zalaman described his family trading business—cloth and spices, mainly, he said as he and the cousins had agreed—then changed the subject, asking Antek if he really felt he could trust the Cossacks when they were here stealing the fruits of his countrymen's labor.

"Cossacks are like American Indians," he said. "Noble Savages. Magnificent. But they can be wantonly brutal."

"That's not true," Zalaman said. "The Cossacks are not fighting to protect their piece of earth, like the American Indians. They are fighting to take what belongs to others."

"Yes, but if not the Russians, then the Prussians, or maybe the Germans. What can you do? They're here."

You couldn't deny it. But to the question, 'What can you do?' Zalaman thought he could offer several answers.

Zalaman was invited to Lechsi's house where he listened to her aunt attempt some Chopin. Then Lechsi, with her uncle's blessing, accompanied him to the inn to have a drink in the restaurant. Stanko and Rodak were conveniently away. When they arrived, he offered to show her his room and she made him promise not to take any liberties.

He did, but was doubtful of his resolve and noticed a little tremor from Lechsi which made him wonder about the strength of her willpower.

He lit his small oil lamp just inside the room, the afternoon sunlight having little effect from the nearly opaque little window. She was amazed at the smallness of the room—little more than a bed, which both realized was both the problem—where to sit—and the opportunity—where else?

Zalaman apologized, sat on the bed and with forced nonchalance patted the spot next to him in invitation. She froze in place. Not thinking it contradicted the terms of his promise of rectitude, he decided they at least deserved a little privacy and he leaned across the bed to partially shut the door but in doing so brushed up against her arm with his. She grabbed his arm and she held on to it and he couldn't tell if she was trying to stop him from going further or encouraging him, responding to his touch. He tried to lower her down onto the bed and sensed her tense again, but only for an instant and then there they were, face to face on the bed, their mouths finding one another and kissing and the kiss deepening, mouths slowly opening. This time he would show some restraint, like Lena had taught him. Lechsi seemed to be of another mind entirely. She undid laces and clasps and showed him her breasts and then let him touch them. He kissed them and knew he had never been so excited and that he couldn't stop—which wasn't going to be necessary, it seemed, as she tried to undo his trousers. She had difficulty with the buttons, so Zalaman gave her an assist, stood up and let his pants drop to the floor. Lechsi gasped—whether from his bullet wound or swollen prick, he didn't know. He was hog-tied, pants around his ankles. He dropped to his knees and was confronted with her open legs. Tossing aside her heavy skirts, there was a flash of flesh and underthings.

And then she jumped up, almost knocking Zalaman over, and scooted out the door, saying she had to find a toilet. Zalaman waited, debating whether or not he should put his trousers back on, imagining some female ritual Lechsi might be performing preparatory to sex. Maybe she just had to go to the bathroom. She'd be back as soon as she finished whatever she needed to do and he was still excited, amazed, and delighted by her show of lust.

She was taking a long time. She was going to come back. Wasn't she? It seemed like she'd been gone long enough. He hated putting his trousers back on; it was like admitting defeat. But he did them up and looked down the hallway, checked the toilet and then the rest of the inn. Nothing. She wasn't coming back.

Zalaman was confused and heartbroken. And there was the embarrassment of having been abandoned with his pants around his ankles. His partners were not much help.

> <

He got little sympathy from them, but they did supply a distraction in the form of their two whores—in fairness, they referred to them as ladies, in the spirit of Antek—Daiya and Ewa.

He'd knocked on the cousins' door to tell them what had happened between him and Lechsi, thinking that they might have some kind of explanation, though he would be skeptical, keep an open mind. He heard some muffled voices and scurrying about before he was invited in and introduced to the two women—Daiya, draped over Stanko in his bed and Ewa similarly sprawled against Rodak in his.

The faces of the two women were so hidden beneath layers of powder and paint, Zalaman thought it might prove difficult to recognize them cleaned up. The bodies of the two women, from the neck down, were more exposed. Everyone seemed to be quite drunk. There were large, empty ale flagons at the base of the beds, and they were all in jovial spirits, even Rodak. When Daiya offered Zalaman two opiate confections, he popped them in his mouth much to the cousins' amusement and before he knew it, he was sprawled on the floor between the cousins' beds, expounding on the fine qualities of the girl, Lechsi. But he did not talk about their recent misadventure.

The cousins did not want to talk about their Cossack-scouting progress, but made it clear they had some good news to share with him in that regard—"with respect to our work." Zalaman told them about his run-in with Antek.

The ladies, of course, knew all about Pan Antek. In slurred speech, they professed to hold him in high regard—but when they said it they could keep straight faces for only a moment before they broke down and laughed.

"He's an asshole who would shell anything to anybody, or *anybody* to anybody," Daiya claimed. She meant "sell." "Including his own children," said Daiya. Zalaman couldn't be sure if her speech was slurred or it was an effect of the opium on his brain. Ewa extolled the generosity of Rodak and Stanko, but Zalaman was beyond worrying about their finances.

"Not many out-of-town guests in the winter," Ewa explained. "Not mush local business for us."

"But then here *you* are," Ewa said, "jush traders taking some time off." The two whores had already expressed their regrets for having to submit to the debased urges of the Russians. The cousins assured the ladies they would not be in Punie any longer than the snow kept them there. Their money was short, they insisted, and trading demanded they get back to business.

"In Punie," Daiya laughed, "anybody's bizhness is everybody's bizhness." They made Punie sound just like Lahkvna. They had even had semi-official gossip mongers, Timas and Erkme, who, Zalaman said, sounded a lot like Osher and Henzel back home.

Hadn't Antek said something about Timas and Erkme? "Except our Timash and Erkme weren't really gosships, they were gosship inventors, and, as it turned out, getting information on the Cossacks."

"They made a lot of it up, too," Ewa said. "Timash and Erkme showed up in Punie a few years ago. Their act wash maybe like your Osher and Henzel. They'd make up shtories about people—they weren't meant to hurt anyone."

"But they did," Daiya said. "They'd shay shomething like Antek wash feeding the Cossacks false information. Or he wash overcharging for certain black market items."

"Or the shtory about Dr. Bebchuk working secretly for the Tsar."

Zalaman was thinking the gossip of Osher and Henzel was pretty innocent, but then he wondered: What about the disappearance of Heri Benowitz? He tried to remember their position on the Tailors' Revolt.

"Timash and Erkme were partizans of the Uprising." There was not a flinch or glance from the three tradesmen, drunk or drugged as they were. "What they were trying to determine all along wash who were friends of the Russians and who were not." The three partisans were not too drunk to be startled at hearing something so like their own story but tried not to show it. And Daiya and Ewa were not so stupid or drunk not to note the interest on the 'tradesmen's' faces.

"They were trying to ferret out citizens who would shupport them in their fight againsht the Russians."

"So, what happened to them?" Rodak asked nonchalantly.

"Who knowsh?" Daiya answered. "They were successful, I would say, because they got out of Punie with their lives."

"Just don't get us pegged as Timas' and Erkmes," Rodak said, suddenly serious. "We are traders—and please make sure your boss is aware to that."

"Sure," Daiya agreed, whatever Rodak wanted.

"Fuck, Antek, anyway," Ewa fumed. "Who caresh what that asshole thinks!"

Zalaman had never heard a woman talk like this before.

"Doesn't he get you this work?"

The cousins made it clear that whatever used to be the case, from now on, for the duration of their stay in Punie, however long that was, the two ladies were exclusively theirs. They would need no other customers. Forget Antek.

"That would cosht you a pretty penny," Daiya said.

"He'll want his cut," Ewa said. "You can't just say 'forget Antek' and pretend that's that."

Rodak and Stanko agreed. They would pay and the ladies could share with Antek as they saw fit. "But if he asks—" Rodak said.

"—We'll confirm that you are definitely traders," Ewa finishing his sentence. "Wealthy traders he should treat with reshpect."

After the ladies left, Zalaman expressed concerns about their admission that they 'cosht a pretty penny."

"We can't touch the safe box without everyone's approval, Zalaman," Stanko said. "And remember, anyone can do whatever he wants with his share."

"And, better news," Rodak said, "we will soon add to our purse. We saw several patrols today, well-armed, so of course we stayed out of the way. So, what have you been doing? We haven't seen much of you lately."

Zalaman had mentioned Lechsi to them before, but never told them much more than that she liked the same books he did. He gave them a detailed description of 'the deception of Lechsi.' Stanko said she might not have been deceiving him at all, just frightened after seeing his monstrous cock. Rodak said she was likely a virgin and had second thoughts.

"Second thoughts?"

"—about losing her virginity," Stanko said.

"—to a Jew," Rodak said, but Stanko kicked him and apologized—"to a young boy."

"I think she got cold feet," Stanko explained. "Old story. It doesn't matter who the other party is, once it's lost, it's gone forever."

"More important," Rodak said, "what have you learned about the Poles of Punie while we've been out scouting?"

"I've learned that the people of Punie blame the soldiers," Zalaman said. "They blame the Cossacks, not the Tsar, for all the injuries they suffer, all the insults they endure, and the heavy taxes they pay for the privilege. They don't think the man who freed the serfs would order Cossacks to do these things.

"If Timas and Erkme did have local support, wouldn't they have been more successful?" No one had an answer. For all they knew maybe they *had* scored some successes.

> <

After dismissing Ewa and Daiya—having provided them with dinner in the inn's restaurant—Zalaman joined the cousins. They ordered more drinks and Zalaman ordered Gierta's goat stew, a spicy concoction of vegetables with only a hint of goat.

Stanko raised a glass to Daiya and Ewa. "If a whore likes you she can be an excellent resource for information. Their customers are careless and so a prostitute often knows more than most about what's going on in town."

"Whores are often drunk or drugged," Rodak disagreed, "like their customers. I'm not saying whores are intentionally treacherous—it's the effect of their profession, to sell their loyalties, like their bodies, for a few rubles. But you may be right when it comes to Ewa and Daiya. They are not like the others. We owe them for much of what we know."

They all drank to that. Then they explained to Zalaman why they would be riding out of Punie the next day to scout along the Nurzec River. On their forays out of town, Rodak and Stanko, with the aid of Zalaman's spyglass, had looked for patterns of activity among the Cossack regimental patrols and couriers from large training maneuvers involving dozens of Cossacks, often armed to the teeth, to smaller, more manageable groups. They'd come upon a group of three who rode in from Dziedzow every month.

Three was a very manageable size, but two of the three were reported to be special sharpshooters. They appeared in Punie around the first of each month, collecting taxes like a landlord his rent, riding from their headquarters, one long day's ride away. They collected in other towns as well, before and after Punie.

"Two of them are young sharpshooters and they are accompanied by a heavy, old officer I call 'The Quartermaster,'" Stanko said.

"The fact that it takes only three to collect the tribute is testament to how entrenched the Cossack are," Rodak said, "and how complacent they are. They ride about with their earnings with no fear that any town council or trade group or farmers will interfere."

"We couldn't ambush them here in Punie," Zalaman said. "It's crawling with Cossacks."

Rodak smiled at Stanko. The young Jew, the young *man* was learning.

"The road they travel to get to Punie is long and lonely," Stanko said, helping himself to a mouthful of Zalaman's stew. "When they come to Punie, they arrive around midday, unless weather has delayed them, and they leave Punie the same day, even if it's late, to ride on to the next town and make more collections."

"Unfortunately, that lonely road is also wide out in the open," Rodak said. "There are no woods close enough to the road for a blind."

When they set out for the Nurzec, they were deeper into winter and its snow. Travel was hazardous, but the weather had been calm for a while, cold but dry, and if they postponed their scouting trip the snow was only going to get deeper. They left just before daybreak, doubly wrapped—Cossack uniforms underneath for the added warmth—breath steaming from human and horse. Zalaman was happy that they were not on their way to battle.

This was a reconnaissance mission, perhaps a prelude to violence later. Their greatcoats covered the Cossack uniforms as they did the weapons they carried just in case.

Otherwise, they travelled light, no wagon or carriage, just the three on horseback, following the road north in the direction from which the Cossacks would be riding. Everything was snow-covered, but because it had been dry lately and the road was well-travelled, the riding was easy. By the time the sun had risen over the hills to the east, they came to a fork in the road. The Russian tax collectors would take the less-used fork on their way to the last stop on their monthly collection route. An ambush on the side-road—not too far from Punie, not too close to Bibin and away from the busier roadway—would be wisest, but they would have to figure out a way to entice the three Cossacks off the main road to accomplish this.

The sun was shining fully in their faces, blinding in both its direct and reflected brilliance. But it was bitterly cold. The only warmth Zalaman felt when riding was when he could bend over, as far as wound and saddle would permit, and get close to his horse. He recalled winter rides on Marengo, holding tight to Davin's back. The memory made him feel further from home. The only familiar thing here was snow.

They stopped at a bend in the road. There was the sound of rushing water. A stream was hiding under the snow. Shading their eyes against the glare of sun and snow, they followed a line of trees that bordered the banks of the meandering, hidden stream that flowed out of the hills. Rodak found a declivity in the powder—seldom used in the winter by the look of it—that followed along the trees. The horses broke through the snow with each step. It wasn't deep, but it was tricky. Stanko's horse followed Rodak's with Zalaman last. They slowly ascended until they came upon a small, thick wood where they dismounted, left the horses, and walked over to the stream, the wood stopping right at the edge of its bank, about a meter-high, straight down to the water. The water was not covered in snow; it rushed, clear under thin, sometimes broken ice, and then in a sharp rumble over a low falls.

Zalaman thought he heard Stanko say something about this being the Nurzec. It was hard to hear over the whooshing of the falls.

"This is a branch of the Nurzec," Rodak said. "And it might be our answer. We have two kinds of camouflage here. The woods, and the noise."

"We're far from the road," Stanko said "We'd have to lure them someway . . ."

"They're going to be wary; they're carrying a lot of money," Zalaman said.

"The woods are close enough to the path," Stanko said. "All we have to do is find a place where each of us can pick off one Cossack. But how do we lure them here?"

"What if we wore our Cossack uniforms on top instead of underneath?" Zalaman asked. Rodak nodded, encouraging him to go on. Zalaman hadn't really thought it through. "So . . . let's use those costumes like we wanted to. They'll think we're Cossacks—and that gives us the upper hand, somehow. . . . Anyway, the uniforms allow us to get close."

"Until we get within talking range," Stanko said, "That's how long we can keep them thinking we're Cossacks. If we're lucky."

"Close enough to shoot maybe," Rodak said, "but I don't like our chances—especially with you two. The men on either side of the quartermaster are their best sharpshooters." Zalaman and Stanko objected so Rodak had to admit that at least in target practice they had shown some improvement.

The rushing falls was too loud for them to talk easily, so, after finding the most advantageous spots to position themselves if they could lure the Cossacks off the Punie-Bibin road, they moved away from the water and got back on their horses to discuss strategies for luring Cossacks while taking sips from Stanko's flask. They came up with quite a few plans, fanciful and otherwise, but decided they should go back to the warmth of the inn and sleep on it. They turned their horses and walked them slowly so they could continue to pass the flask back and forth, back down the icy road to Punie, joining the traffic, such as it was—just the odd horseman and carriages coming and going, every hour.

They must come up with a plan, Rodak said and Zalaman agreed.

"*My* plan is to let the Spencers do the talking," Stanko said.

"We'll have two wear our *papahkas*," Rodak said to Zalaman, referring to the cylindrical sheepskin hats that were a common feature of the Cossacks' informal uniforms. They had only been able to scavenge two of them when they took the Cossack uniforms and neither was big enough for Stanko. Instead, Stanko had a knitted version, featuring ear flaps. He thought the ear flaps made him look funny, so he would wear it only in the bitterest cold.

The plan otherwise remained vague. They did pledge to stay away from excessive *krupnik* and poppyhead tea and the like.

And midday, on the first day of the Christian New Year, 1867, just like any other first day of any other month, the three Cossack tax collectors rode into town to fulfill their duty to the Tsar. Rodak, Stanko and Zalaman watched, happy to see the Cossacks were sticking to their schedule.

Rodak and Stanko took off on their own for a couple of days—walking their horses through deep snow—to see if they could get close enough to the Cossack HQ to observe unobserved, and, if they were lucky, spy on the three Cossacks after they left Punie. Stanko was feeling very positive about their prospects, having managed to cajole Rodak into allowing him to take along his flask of *krupnik*. They'd been sober when it was required, he argued, but this reconnaissance trip would be too cold without it.

Under the eaves of the huts in Punie, snow had been shoveled into impressive piles to make the streets and sidewalks navigable. Everywhere else the snow was deep. The town's sharp edges were hidden under snow, everything rounded, softer, small buildings blending into a white landscape. Zalaman stayed in Punie to keep an eye on things—Antek, the Cossack officers, Punie, in general. There had been no sightings of Lechsi or her aunt and uncle.

Rodak and Stanko returned excited about their success in spying on the Cossack headquarters, watching a troop of several hundred Russian soldiers on the road, "parading around in uniforms much nicer than the ones we have." On the way to the Russians' HQ, they'd been spying on the three tax-collecting Cossacks that were their eventual target. The cousins followed those three as they travelled to Dziedski after Punie, collecting tribute, stuffing their bags with banknotes, coins, rubles and *zlotys*. The overweight tax collector, who often rode in the middle between the two sharpshooters, was a colonel, according to the insignia on his uniform. Stanko described the corpulent colonel's jowls, comparing his cheeks to his expanding saddlebag of banknotes. Rodak mimicked the vain bodyguards, twirling their mustaches, but he also pointed out their excellent marksmanship, he and Stanko having watched one of them bring down an elusive game bird with one bullet.

February was a short month, but there was plenty of time before the three Cossacks returned. They went back to drinking—moderately, as far as Rodak and Zalaman were concerned—and taking opium doled out by Daiya. When they were alone, the three talked about a plan, but never got beyond the idea that they were going to surprise the Cossacks, somehow using their

Cossack uniforms to get close to them, and then—it got a little hazy here—get them to give chase up that little side path and waylay them from the edge of the forest close to the noisy little tributary of the Nurzec.

During that month, the three partisans went far outside Punie, away from Cossack ears, to practice with their Spencers. Zalaman found these sessions a welcome distraction.

He'd become so frustrated with Lechsi, who'd led him on, or so he felt, and then run off before he had a chance to consummate their relationship. He decided, it must have been embarrassment as Stanko said. He vowed to act but was too afraid of failure. He couldn't bring himself to go to her house, uninvited, and confront her. When he went shooting with the cousins, he found he couldn't fire a Spencer accurately because he had to hold it against his shoulder and each shot hurt his old wound.

Rodak showed him how to make some changes in shooting style, alleviating the problem, but the changes made Zalaman a poorer shot. So, when the cousins were not just sitting around and waiting for the first of the month, but preoccupied with Daiya and Ewa, Zalaman started going out on his own to sharpen his skills.

Near the end of the month, Zalaman rode Beth a good distance outside Punie. He was still brooding over Lechsi, but the humiliation was fading. He took easy-to-retrace paths until well away from town, eventually finding himself in a field of dazzling, white, unbroken snow. There was a stand of young beech trees to serve as targets. He shaded his eyes from the glare and when they grew accustomed to it, he was able to focus. He practiced a bit with his revolver and the difficult Spencer, shooting from horseback, because even though they hoped to aim the Spencers at the Cossacks from solid ground—propped up on tree limbs, say, for added stability—shooting rifles from horseback was both more demanding and could be needed if the plan went awry.

Shooting a revolver while on horseback was challenging but that was the point. Plus, the snow was so deep he didn't really want to dismount. Beth was used to gunfire, knowing what to expect when she heard the click of the hammer. He fired off six rounds in succession, flushing a grey hare in the process.

When the echoes from the shots died, he sat, quietly in the saddle, feeling only the gentle expansion and contraction of Beth's chest. He inhaled the quiet. He was surrounded by nothing but snow and the soft susurrus rattling the mostly leafless beeches. He broke the silence, firing and missing a branch then firing again and again until he hit it, and fired and hit it once again. He stopped, the bullets' echoes died, and the smell of gunpowder persisted. It struck him that it was just last winter that he was playing snow games in the *kvadrat* with Davin, Ev and Aron. Would they recognize him now? He hardly recognized himself.

His bullets were hitting branches with greater accuracy. In the process, he flushed that gray hare or another one just like it from the trees. The hare twisted its nose a few times and sprang, sinking only slightly in the snow, adept at running as if it were weightless. Zalaman raised his right arm and straightened it, leading the hare. Hares are not known for running in straight lines and this one was no different, jagging to the left at the sound of the bullet, or perhaps, with those impressive ears, hearing some click that occurs just before the report. The first shot missed and Zalaman shot again and perhaps the target practice was paying off, but this time the hare jigged when it should have jogged and ran right into his bullet. The animal flipped into the air, then lay twitching, the snow around it reddening.

He was uncertain he would be able to do it again, but he'd shot a running rabbit—with a revolver from horseback! That was no small feat for anyone, but for Zalaman it was extraordinary. He rode over to the still carcass. It was a big rabbit, though not especially plump as this deep in the winter its forage was limited to the dry branches of beech trees. Still, it would make a welcome addition to one of Gierta's stews—creations in which meat was often more implied than actual.

With some trepidation, he dismounted to retrieve the hare and sank up to his chest. He had incorrectly gauged the softness and depth of the snow and was shocked breathless. He tried to extricate myself, but he was stuck, bound like he'd been tied up in Georg's rug. He had to laugh at his predicament. It was frightening, but it was mostly exhilarating—all alone and stuck like that.

Thankfully, he wasn't quite all alone. Good old Beth hadn't strayed. And then there was the steaming hare, right in front of him, almost at eye level, staring at the immobilized Zalaman, the furry lump much larger than he had imagined. And he remembered something he'd nearly forgotten—how, when he was much younger—he'd have these strange experiences, lasting less than a minute, but seeming longer; seconds in which small things would grow larger. A twig would be as thick as a branch, a branch like a tree trunk. The feeling was rapturous. Almost sexual, though these experiences happened to him long before adolescence. When it happened, he suspended disbelief—let it play out. It didn't make sense; it wasn't the real state of things and yet he wasn't afraid. He never wanted to break the spell. This rapture came over him dozens of times when he was little, but now, as he squirmed in the snow, he could no longer say for certain how many times. It had been so long ago. Once he'd been riding in the back of the cart pulled by Schwartzele, Papa driving with little Zalaman in back, jostled by the potatoes and cabbages as they hit ruts and gullies. As he sat among them, the vegetables grew many times their normal size. He could feel their great weight in his hands. The fragrance of the vegetables grew stronger, too. It was ecstasy—he didn't have a word for it—like a spell. Afterwards, he'd think maybe these events were just a normal part of growing up, but he never heard anyone else mention anything like it. He'd asked his brother, Davin, who seemed to think his brother was a little strange or was perhaps making up a story to make himself seem more interesting. Encased in the snow, Zalaman wanted to talk to Lechsi about it. Yes, Lechsi. He resolved he would do so. The thought of her brought him back to the present. The dead hare was still staring him right in the face. It no longer seemed quite so monstrously large.

Zalaman's body heat had warmed enough of the snow around him that, although he was thoroughly soaked, it no longer tightly encased him. It was still difficult to move, but he kept turning and twisting, creating wiggle room. He was glad there was no one other than Beth to witness his gyrations. He called her. She'd been the most docile horse after Georg had been killed. She came when he called. He grabbed the riding straps and gripped them, repeating her name to calm her and keep her steady, as he dragged himself up, drenched, the weight of his soggy clothes adding to the struggle. But he eventually got up in the saddle, brushed off the snow and nudged Beth closer to the kill. He leaned over to easily hook the hare from underneath with his rifle barrel and plop it into his saddlebag. He shook his head, laughing at himself for having been so awkward and dismounting. He could have stayed dry, but now he was so wet he feared freezing. He turned Beth around and headed back to Punie, carrying stew meat for dinner and a new confidence in his shooting ability. On his way back, shivering in his wet clothes as the outer layers iced up, he promised himself he would keep his resolution and no longer brood over Lechsi, but would confront her and find out what he had done wrong, though he didn't think he had done anything wrong at all.

When he got back to the inn, his teeth chattered as he handed the hare to Gierta. He splurged on a hot bath. Never had hot water felt so wonderful. It was melting things inside him that had frozen solid. After bath and the rabbit stew—it was delicious, with more than a hint of meat in it—Rodak and Stanko let Zalaman regale them with stories of his adventure. The cousins enjoyed and encouraged his enthusiasm, but Rodak reprimanded him for his stupidity. He should know better than get soaked like that. He could get frostbite. What good would he be to the Uprising with no fingers?

The weather was mild on February 27. It was just two days before their opportunity to waylay the tax collectors, but instead of putting his head together with Rodak and Stanko to refine the plan, Zalaman was hiding around the corner from Lechsi's house. Not hiding so much as spying. He was carrying through on his resolution. There was little activity on her street, just a few people on their way to market. While he watched and waited, he replayed the scene of her flight: the way she looked that day, her desire, grabbing his arm, her deep kisses—undoing his pants! Her thighs. And then—gone without even saying goodbye. He avoided picturing the way she left him standing there alone, trousers around his ankles.

Around midday, he saw Lechsi's aunt and uncle come out of the house and ride away in the little *droshky*. Zalaman turned away as they passed right by him. There was now an excellent chance that Lechsi was alone. Couldn't he go up and knock politely on the door? What if she ignored his knocking? That would be consistent with his current assessment of her feelings.

But his dilemma was short-lived. Not long after her guardians had driven away, Lechsi came out her front door carrying a shopping basket. Zalaman was uncertain what he needed to do next, so he hid, letting her pass. He weighed his options, afraid of making the wrong decision. He'd been less fearful when he was being shot at by Cossacks. Yet here, too, like trying to figure out the plan for the Cossacks, there were unknowns, unforeseeable reactions that made him anxious. Any decision would be dangerous, but wouldn't it be best to just go ahead?

He was still debating when he saw Lechsi returning from the market, a loaf of bread sticking out from a basket weighed down with other items. There was simply no avoiding it any longer. He scooted over to the sidewalk, positioning himself directly in her path. The snow was piled on both sides of the walkway, which was barely wide enough for two, so she couldn't pass without confronting him. She hesitated for only an instant when she saw him, then kept coming.

"Hello," she said, curtly. "Please step aside so I can get by."

"Let me help you with the basket. It looks heavy, let me carry it for you," Zalaman begged. She kept going and he was forced to step back into the deep snow to let her pass. He was nearly stuck in snow again, but this time the snow only came up to his knees. Lechsi kept going. "I want to apologize for whatever I did wrong. Could you at least explain to me what that was," he pleaded.

She turned to look at him. She stared at him. He seemed sincere. She couldn't stop the grin on her face when he tried clumsily to extricate himself from the snow pile. It recalled the scene in his room where he'd been hog-tied by his own trousers. She blushed to remember. She was ashamed of her behavior in his room. She'd led him on and never explained. She wasn't sure why herself, except that it had something to do with fear and the loss of her virginity to anyone other than Young Werther—or Chopin. Neither was she sure why she should feel tears welling up in her eyes.

She nodded and held out her basket.

Zalaman took it and followed her home, to her front door, carrying her basket, trying and failing not to look overjoyed. She opened the front door and entered, then turned to Zalaman, standing on her doorstep with her provisions.

"It's not for *you* to apologize to me," she said, "it's for me to apologize to you." She asked him to put the basket in the kitchen and then led him back to the front room—a spacious, all-purpose space, surrounded with bookcases overflowing with books.

Lechsi had him sit. They regarded one another and he waited for her to expand on her apology. "It was a horrible thing I did to you," she said, "leading you on after all I'd said to you about never allowing that to happen—"

"—Yes, that's true. But also, I promised you I wouldn't try anything. I meant it when I said it, but then . . ."

"No." She couldn't seem to clarify her feelings, so she got up and poured them each a schnapps. And after a few sips, she let him know that she hadn't been avoiding him because he'd been so forward—she'd been just as bad—she'd been avoiding him, because she was embarrassed by her own actions. He wanted to know to which actions she was referring. Running? Fear?

He wanted her more than ever, but she was complicated. If she wanted him as much as he wanted her, they would be in one another's arms.

"What you did hurt," he admitted. "but I understand. People should be allowed second thoughts."

"Thirds, even." She blushed and got up to pour them another. "But just a second schnapps." They drank and she studied him. Rubbed her chin to stimulate insight. "You know, it's not like I *chose* to run away from you. It was more like I had to. Of course, society would say I showed great control by stopping us, what was going on, running away. But now I think it's just the opposite. Some other force was in control of me. If I'd truly had self-control, I would have stayed. What do you think of that?"

Zalaman thought he liked that, but before he had a chance to say so, she continued, "—and then we would have . . . well, who knows how far it might have gone? When I ran away, I think my parents were in control. Watching me. Not my aunt and uncle, who aren't impossibly strict, like my parents were. And, by the way, Aunt and Uncle, went to Bibin to see my great aunt." She smiled. “But don’t get any ideas—when they go to visit Auntie, they never stay long.”

“That’s a shame,” Zalaman said, getting up from his chair and coming over to her. He didn’t say anything else, but felt he’d been given permission to bend over and kiss her. She let him and their mouths stayed glued to one another’s for several breaths, before she broke away, gently, grasping his hand.

“Let’s go out,” she said, a bit breathless. He helped her up and got their coats and before she opened the door to let them out, she gave him a little kiss on the lips.

They took an invigorating walk, arm-in-arm once they were far enough away from the house and the walkway through the snow was wide enough to allow it. She asked about the wound she’d seen that night. He deflected the question after she got him to admit it was Cossack-administered.

She stopped and looked into his eyes. “Let’s go back to my house. It’s cold out here.”

When they got back, she stoked the fire. Zalaman took the liberty of pouring them another schnaps. “I lied to you,” she grinned. “They won’t be back before nightfall.”

They held each other for a long time, not talking much, until Lechsi mentioned it would be getting dark soon and her aunt and uncle could be back anytime. She went with him to the inn, back to his room, where she pulled him down on his bed and started undressing him. This time there was no attempt at flight. Every movement was dedicated to the opposite of leaving.

Afterwards, he walked her home and she told him he had to say goodbye before she got back. She said she was afraid she was going to look too happy. Her Aunt would see right through her.

He asked her what she knew about Timas and Erkme. She regarded him closely and the words she said made him wonder if he hadn’t divulged more than he’d intended.

"No one here likes the Cossacks," she said. "What my uncle told me about Timas and Erkme was that they meant well, but they asked the wrong people too many questions. Do you know what I think, Zalaman? I think that if the Tsar knew how his Cossacks acted here, he would have them shot."

She gave him a peck on the cheek, a squeeze on the arm and disappeared into her house.

CHAPTER NINE

Bebchuk's Cut

The next day was a day of preparation, but it was all for naught because that night Punie was struck by the blizzard of the winter. Ewa and Daiya told them they had such a storm at least once a year or it couldn't be considered winter; it was the storm they could talk about next summer. And it scuttled the partisans' plans, such as they were. The road was impassable. The Cossack contingent might show up next week or just wait till the first of the following month. They would collect their taxes. The snow was so heavy, neither Rodak nor Stanko had any interest in venturing outside at all. Zalaman was anxious to see Lechsi. He should have said something to her about his now-aborted plans, something that might have served as a decent goodbye without giving anything away or frightening her. Now he would have the chance. He was relieved that he wasn't going to have to put himself in danger, not this day, at least. He could wait, happy to put off the chaos. The evening of the 28th, the wind blew through every crevice in the inn; the snow so thick and heavy that when the partisans peered out the inn's front door, the nighttime sky was white instead of black.

Despite their disappointment, Zalaman and Stanko were having a good time in the saloon, absorbing the conviviality of a big crowd. Others who were not anxious to go out into the storm, were happy to dally with just one more drink. It seemed only Rodak was unhappy.

He regarded the Cossack officers enjoying themselves. He spat. "It puts everything off a month. I can't stand watching these wondrous Colonel Domnanovitches. Prancing around.

"Well," Stanko said, louder, always more insistent when drinking, "I always say if you have no choice, you might as well pretend it's all for the best. There will be a double reward next month."

"You are going to have to stop drinking so much. You'll end up screwing up the entire operation."

Stanko denied it and appealed to Zalaman for support, but it was true. "You're bigger, so, according to my father, that means you can handle more alcohol, but you drink more than me and Rodak, Ewa and Daiya put together."

Stanko looked innocent, wronged, and surprised by Zalaman's remarks. "You think so? You're exaggerating. I don't need to cut down on my drinking and I'll tell you why. I am always ready to work—fight, ride, anything—even when I'm drinking. So, you should mind your own business."

"We're all in business together, right?"

"All of this arguing gives me an even bigger thirst," Stanko said, and ordered another round for the three of them, but Rodak and Zalaman got up to say goodnight and left Stanko who stayed behind to finish the drinks himself.

When Rodak got to his room, he fell instantly asleep from the wine. He had a wonderful dream, waylaying the smarmy Colonel Domnanovitch on the road. Zalaman lay down in his room, but had trouble falling asleep, because Rodak was snoring on the other side of the thin wall that separated the rooms, and because the same wine that sent Rodak to dreamland, had given Zalaman a headache. But he finally fell into a fitful sleep and a troubled dream of being in the *kvadrat* of Lahkvna, out in public, where he tried to seduce a woman who was a mixture of Lechsi and Hadar, a red-haired Christian girl from Navharadak.

><

Daiya and Ewa and all the other inn's customers had finally gone out to brave the snow; the winds had thankfully died down.

Jan and Gierta were closing for the night, so they shooed out the only one remaining—a very drunk Stanko. He decided to go outside to take a piss and observe the results of the historic snowstorm. Snow was still falling, but soft and gentle now. Stanko trudged, struggling a bit here and there to breakthrough a drift, then almost falling over when he encountered an abrupt change in the snow level where the sidewalk ended. He caught himself in time but realized he might have had a little too much to drink. He would take his piss and then go back to his nice warm room, tiptoe in quietly so Rodak wouldn't have an opportunity to complain.

He plodded along. around the corner to the back of the inn where he undid the buttons of his trousers and relieved himself, marveling at the depth of the snow and the rounded, white landscape that featured mounds of snow, some still tumbling from the sky, like silver ghosts in the dark. White and black was all.

The first, faint light of a clear new day forced Rodak to open one eye and look over to Stanko's bed, which was empty and did not appear to have been slept in. He closed that eye, imagining Stanko still asleep in the saloon. He started to fall back to sleep, but now he couldn't. After a while, he got up and checked the WCs and the saloon.

The Inn hadn't yet come to life—but there was no Stanko. He knocked on Zalaman' s door and it took some real banging to wake him. They went outside. The plank sidewalk had not yet been shoveled. Breaking through the drifts, using their legs like plows as Stanko had hours earlier, they went to check the stables, but didn't have to go that far.

There had been so much snow that anything that was not white stood out stood out like a sore thumb. In this case, that was

Stanko, passed out in a huge snowbank and sticking out of it stiff as a board. He had passed out but was still breathing.

They dug Stanko out then carted him back to the cousins' room to thaw out. Undressing him, they couldn't help but notice his pants were unbuttoned and that his prick was red and badly frozen. It seemed he'd either fallen asleep in the act of peeing or doing something about which they didn't want to speculate. Stankos penis and a few frozen red fingers started turning white as his body warmed. Penis and fingers were not the main problem, it was his toes. For some reason, those on his left foot were frostbitten. They'd been lucky to find him before he froze to death.

Stanko was coming around, revived by the pain. "They're hot," he cried, pointing to his discolored toes. He looked at his fingers which were returning to a more normal color. "Feels like they're on fire." Stanko was not one to complain about pain.

Having heard about Stanko's plight from Jan, Daiya and Ewa brought opium. Stanko took some and passed out. The two ladies, Rodak and Zalaman shared the rest.

Ewa felt Stanko's gray-blue toes. "I've seen this before. When he wakes up his toes will be numb. They might be infected and if they are, it'll spread." And she left with Rodak to fetch Dr. Bebchuk. Bebchuk's was a name the partisans had heard mentioned in relationship to Timas and Erkme. Antek, too, had mentioned him. An apothecary-physician-veterinarian, he was known to Daiya and Ewa as a supporter of the partisans' cause. He was also Punie's most respected doctor. More veterinarian than physician perhaps, if you were to compare him to a real doctor, Daiya explained, like Dr. Karblakov of Bibin, who had been Bebchuk's mentor.

Stanko woke to find Daiya holding his toes. He could see she was holding them, but, ominously, he couldn't feel her holding them. "I am not going to lose those toes," he said. "I'm very attached to them." Zalaman gave him some more opium and told him Ewa and Rodak were fetching the doctor.

The amputation of toes and fingers, legs and arms, parts, or wholes, was common in these days with all the unregulated labor, resulting especially from farming accidents. There were also amputations performed on many of the defects of birth, although a malformed infant might be allowed to grow into adulthood before the amputation of the impediment took place. Such practices were only as successful as the sawbone's skills and tools, although even many of the best amputations ended in the patient's death. Veterinarians and most physicians blamed infections caused by mysterious and poisonous miasmas in the air. Dr. Karblakov of Bibin's student, Dr. Bebchuk of Punie, knew all the latest medical practices, including amputation, an art which required the use of the most sophisticated blades. The practitioners were called 'sawbones' for a reason.

Ewa and Rodak found Bebchuk in his clinic. Once they filled him in, he grabbed some quinine for the victim and trudged back through the snow to the inn. When they got there, Stanko was awake. His toes were now blue. Bebchuk introduced himself and gave the blue toes a tight squeeze, causing the others to wince, but producing no reaction at all from Stanko, other than "The whole foot's numb."

"Your toes are dead," a grim Dr. Bebchuk said matter-of-factly. "And now the foot is dying. Can you smell that?" he asked. There was a bad odor coming from Stanko's foot and it wasn't normal foot odor. "And see this blistering," Bebchuk pointed out. "The gangrene is infected." He looked at Rodak, then Zalaman, the ladies, and finally, Stanko. "It calls for emergency amputation."

Stanko wouldn't hear of it, but his complaints grew less resolute as Bebchuk described the consequences of inaction. To Zalaman it all seemed a severe judgment, arrived at too quickly.

But what did he know? The others agreed; he knew nothing. They were convinced Bebchuk knew what he was talking about.

"The longer we wait," Bebchuk told Stanko, "the more of you will start dying . . . the more of you will have to . . . go." His tone was meant to calm and it had that effect on everyone but Stanko—nor Zalaman, who was thinking of the biggest haunches he had carved with the butchers Heri and Adnon, none of the bones had been nearly as big as Stanko's leg. How was this doctor going to saw through that?

"You'll be surprised how fast you'll learn how to compensate," Bebchuk assured Stanko. He took Rodak and Zalaman out of the room so they could talk freely.

"How risky is it?" Rodak asked.

"And how much do you think you'd have to cut off?" Zalaman asked.

"We'll lose much of the leg—but only if we operate right away."

"The longer you wait—"

Rodak interrupted and said he agreed with the diagnosis but had to ask about Bebchuk's previous experience.

"I've done these before," the doctor said. "It should be alright. You are from far away, but even where you come from people must have heard of the famous Dr. Karblakov of Bibin. It would be better if he was here. He's the best there is. But we've no time to fetch him—even if he *were* in Bibin, but I know he isn't. He's wintering on the Black Sea. It's not like he's some miracle worker, it's just that he's always at the forefront, knows what's new in medicine. Fortunately for Stanko, I have studied with him and still do when he's in the area. I've learned things about infection from him, too. But most important, I have obtained, from him, the ideal cutting instrument. It's at my clinic, if I could get one of you to come with me."

Rodak wanted to stay with Stanko. "I promise to do my very best for him," Bebchuk said with conviction. They had no choice but to believe him. He and Zalaman left to bring the doctor's tools.

Daiya wept for Stanko, head on his chest. Rodak shuddered; he couldn't imagine a one-legged Stanko. Then the two of them, along with Ewa and help from the innkeepers, cleared out all the furniture and cleaned the room as Bebchuk had instructed, borrowed lamps from the restaurant and filled bowls with soapy water, then moved in a sturdy table that could support Stanko's considerable weight and cleaned that, too.

On their way to Bebchuk's clinic, he talked excitedly about the procedure he was about to perform. "I know I can take care of your cousin," he assured Zalaman. Bebchuk had no doubt about his ability to amputate and had no reason to doubt Zalaman and his cousins were not the traders they purported to be, though he was perplexed by Zalaman's looks. He did not look anything like the other two.

Zalaman was thinking about butchering—how much it might be like doctoring. He'd thought about being a butcher, never a doctor. He'd never known a real doctor.

Veterinarians, yes, but aside from the medic at the Syp HQ, he figured Flora, with her knowledge of herbs and tinctures, was the closest thing.

When they got to his clinic, Bebchuk sat Zalaman down. He had something to tell him and something to show him. "Since, as an apprentice butcher, you know about cutting through bone, I'll let you in on something—not that it's a secret, though I wouldn't want your cousins to hear it. Some years ago, I performed an amputation and the bone splintered! It was awful. It also splintered my confidence in the procedure. But last year I made an important purchase. The most advanced blade. Bought it from Karblakov."

Bebchuk showed Zalaman the shiniest, sharpest blade he'd ever seen. "The American Civil War has produced new tools and this medical saw is one of the best."

"Like the Spencer rifle," Zalaman said. Bebchuk nodded enthusiastically. "Karblakov charged me an arm and a leg for it, of course." Bebchuk grinned, but then apologized for the pun.

They took the doctor's carriage back to the inn, Bebchuk carefully cradling his tools, Zalaman weighed down with chemicals and sprays, explained to Bebchuk when he asked about the Spencers, that they, too, were a product of war, in this case the war America was having with itself. When Bebchuk asked, Zalaman wanted to tell him more about the Spencers—how Zalaman had come to this knowledge about rifles and the American War between the states—because he could tell the doctor was interested, but decided it was better to keep his mouth shut. He'd promised Rodak and Stanko as much. But Bebchuk knew a lot more about the subject than Zalaman.

"The American war also created new bullets. They have minié balls—and a propensity to shatter bone. They've created a whole new demand for amputations.

"Excellent," Bebchuk declared, when they arrived back at the inn to find the room clean, and all cleared out except for the good solid table in the middle. Bebchuk donned an apron and sent Ewa and Daiya to procure aprons for the rest of them, explaining it was "so you won't get your clothes all bloody."

As Bebchuk prepared the area, he never shut up, as if relishing an audience he could further enlighten about his work with the famous Dr. Karblakov. But what truly awed them were the instruments of Bebchuk's work. The expensive blade remained wrapped in linen. Stanko looked away while Bebchuk cleaned his other tools. "Pasteur's idea was that there exist little beings, animals so little they can't be seen without a microscope—and yet, they *do* exist—and they are guilty as charged of spreading disease. The medical profession holds that these little animals are a byproduct of a poisonous miasma. But I don't know about that. If you are wondering why you put all this hard work into cleaning, it's because cleanliness is all."

As he washed his hands in a bowl of soapy water, he demonstrated how Zalaman and the girls should do it, too. "After I've done my work, you will be responsible for keeping the wound clean. Always wash your hands, get rid of all the dead skin. Keep the wound clean and treat it with bromide solution or maggots. I don't have any maggots myself at present, but I do have bromide. You will have to change the dressing frequently. These new techniques have been proven again and again. Where? Why in that American War. The point, gentlemen, and gentlewomen, where you see this effect on the skin—here, you see what I'm talking about?" Bebchuk pointed to Stanko's foot.

"The blood has stopped flowing here. I can see it at work on the ankle and now it goes higher. It needs attention now. One could pray that the progress of the disease will stop, somehow . . . miraculously . . . or—we can amputate." He poked and prodded, measured Stanko's toes along with his foot and left leg.

If absolute cleanliness was not quite achieved, the room at least looked spotless.

Rodak and Zalaman were to hold Stanko down—completely immobilize his leg—when necessary. There was to be absolute stillness when Bebchuk used the saw. Stanko was feverish, writhing occasionally, aware enough to feel where Bebchuk applied the tourniquet. To minimize the loss of blood, he had to apply it high up on Stanko's thigh.

"I have to be sure to get all the dead parts," he said. "Above the knee is safest." Stanko could only moan in refusal. Bebchuk unfolded a linen package to reveal the gleaming saw. He sprayed the area with carbolic acid, soaked a sponge with chloroform and morphia and had Rodak hold it over Stanko's face till his writhing ceased. They wrapped what parts of him they could in blankets to keep him warm. Bebchuk and his saw began their work.

Zalaman had never watched any butcher so intently as he did Dr. Bebchuk. The doctor's hand moved back and forth with such precision! And Zalaman had never seen an intensity of focus like the doctor's as he sawed through bone. Zalaman had to look away and blood was flying. He wondered about his interest in bloody things like shooting and slicing. Butchering, shooting, or doctoring. He forced himself to attend to the procedure at hand, his eyes open and on the work. Despite the tourniquets, it was a process which proved to be bloodier than anything he'd seen in the butcher shop or on the battlefield. Bebchuk worked his wonders and avoided any splintering of bone.

Even with this fine saw, Stanko's thigh bone required considerable strength as well as precision. It was the biggest bone Bebchuk had had to cut and it tested him and the blade. The biggest and only animal he'd ever done an amputation on was a dog. He'd cut human thigh bones before, but on smaller men, women, and children.

Even with the chloroform, Stanko's body twitched, twisting though he was asleep.

Rodak, Zalaman and Ewa were sweating profusely but doing a good job of holding him relatively still. Zalaman noted Bebchuk's uncanny ability to anticipate Stanko's involuntary movements and stop sawing. Daiya wiped Bebchuk's brow, his steel blade moving slowly back and forth, back and forth, progressing millimeter by millimeter.

And then, suddenly, Bebchuk sawed through the bone. There was no snap, just a smooth, bloody, and final separation of Stanko from much of his left leg. The sawing seemed to have gone on forever, but it had only lasted seconds. A few surgical snips and Rodak was holding Stanko's lower leg. Bebchuk folded over the flap of skin he'd cut to cover the bone's end and started stitching. They'd used up all the inn's towels and everyone in the room was drenched in blood, but Bebchuk, Rodak and Zalaman had no time to clean up with the others—they were under Bebchuk's orders to apply tight bandages over the freshly sutured stump and then replace the operating table—wiped relatively free of blood—with the cousins' two beds, one of which would, for the time being, prescribe the dimensions of Stanko's world.

><

Daiya and Ewa stayed with Stanko—Daiya in charge of the chloroform should he wake up, and Ewa who volunteered to stay with her friend ("not too much chloroform," Bebchuk advised. "It could be dangerous. Don't overdo it.") while the others repaired to the saloon for a well-deserved drink where they celebrated Dr. Bebchuk and his saw. Rodak said if there was a bigger blade of that steel, he could surgically remove his enemies' limbs with one well-placed swipe. Bebchuk laughed and said he hoped never to become an enemy of Rodak. "Anyway," he said, "the price of producing such a weapon could pay for the arming of an entire regiment. Maybe we should put science to work finding new ways to heal people, rather than more efficient ways to kill them."

Zalaman thought this was true, but wasn't it funny how these advances seemed to all be tied to killing and war? For his part, he was happy they were not going to be dealing with any Cossacks this month. He'd seen more than enough blood.

Before Bebchuk left the drinkers, he got serious, cautioning Rodak and Zalaman about how they were going to be responsible for keeping Stanko's fever down. "Keep the wound clean. That's the secret. Also, once his fever is under control, he's going to want to move, and you won't be able to stop him for very long. And you need to find him a very strong crutch. You can fashion one yourselves or see what I've got in my shop. He'll be fine, but he's going to face quite a challenge . . . go through a big adjustment."

><

After three days of agony that included at least two bouts of madness once he had absorbed the truth that he had lost much more than his foot, Stanko began to worry about how having one leg might limit his activities. Everyone was there—even Lechsi who Zalaman had introduced around—when Bebchuk brought the crutch. First, he looked under Stanko's bandages and proclaimed that Stanko was going to be OK. Next, he demonstrated how Stanko could best use the crutch without hurting himself and let him take a few steps. Stanko quickly got dizzy and lay back in the bed.

"Take it slowly but—practice and use it. Stay indoors at first—it's too icy outside. Treacherous. If you can save up a few *zlotys*, you will one day be able to buy one of the wonderful new artificial limbs . . . very strong . . . once again, thanks to the industry created by the war between the Confederacy and the Union in America."

Stanko decided he was not going to let his new status limit his activities at all. But he swore off drinking and Zalaman and Rodak promised to hold him to it.

><

Clear weather returned to Punie, but it was still cold and it maintained its thick carpet of snow. Zalaman wasn't sorry to have to stay inside and help Stanko. He and Rodak encouraged his first wobbly steps. While serving as his bumpers, they speculated about their thwarted mission and what they would do on April 1 now that there were only two of them.

"I am going to be there," Stanko promised and no one wanted to deny the possibility in front of him, but it felt far-fetched. Rodak just said, "April 1st is going to be here before you know it." After that, Stanko's progress was rapid. But he went through periods of dejection. Zalaman did his best to cheer him up but didn't want to be annoying either. It seemed reasonable to him that Stanko would be dejected. He and Rodak tried to cheer him up by talking about how they would use the money from their coming assault on the Cossacks to buy Stanko the gold standard of artificial limbs—something on a technical par with Bebchuk's saw. They didn't want to entirely squelch Stanko's fantasy of fighting alongside them. Stanko even had a new plan wherein, instead of them being on horseback, they would use their Russian cart, wearing their Cossack uniforms and under a blanket, Stanko would be taking aim. Rodak appreciated Stance's ingenuity but said the big wagon would be too cumbersome; it would tie them down. They needed to be on horseback for mobility.

Two weeks after the amputation, Stanko insisted that he was ready to go outdoors and Bebchuk agreed—so long as someone accompanied him, because it was still treacherous in the snow. The fresh air would do him good. Stanko said he would be even more mobile on horseback, but Bebchuk insisted he needed to demonstrate greater stability on foot and crutch. "Eventually, once your stump heals enough for an artificial limb, you won't have to use that crutch, then you'll manage . . . Horseback riding requires a lot of knee strength."

The weather had warmed, there had been no new snow and the sidewalks had been shoveled wide, allowing Zalaman to walk side-by-side with Stanko, keeping him upright should his crutch fail him. Stanko had started affectionately calling him "Crutch." Every day, Stanko and Crutch had been making it a little further. Stanko told Zalaman he wished he could experience feeling his missing limb like he heard some amputees claim they could, but Zalaman told him it might interfere with the great progress he was making using the crutch. And Stanko got into the swing of it. Even on his two legs, Zalaman sometimes found it an effort to keep up with him.

><

Zalaman had just taken Lechsi home after taking her to lunch in the inn's restaurant, when he encountered Rodak and Stanko walking down the sidewalk. The three talked about home—Navharadak and Lahkvna. The two towers that distinguish the Navharadak skyline were mentioned.

"They're less than half the height they had been before the Council of Elders decided they were too old to maintain," Rodak explained to Zalaman, while Stanko was moving faster, edging ahead of them. "The Council of Elders decided they were useless for modern warfare." Rodak and Zalaman watched Stanko disappear around a corner. He looked quite steady, apparently no longer needing human assistance. "When Stanko was just a child," Rodak continued, "I used to play with him in that ruin of towers. They were our private towers—and there would always be invaders, other kids wielding bigger sticks, trying to take our towers from us. Back then, Stanko was bigger than most of the older children, so we always got by. Oh yes, what I was saying about the Elders who allowed them to fall into disrepair just to please certain ladies—maybe the ladies your mother visited in Navharadak for those book exchanges, or rather their grandmothers—can you believe it? They convinced their husbands that crumbling towers were more picturesque, painted a more romantic scene than they would if they were too well maintained."

When they arrived at the corner where they'd last seen Stanko, he was nowhere to be seen. Rodak scolded Zalaman for losing sight of him. Zalaman complained that he was 'The Crutch' not the watchdog. Hoping they'd find him safely at the inn, they walked back only to be treated to the sight of Stanko, riding up on horseback. He stopped Beth in front of them, showing off his skill, turning her with one knee and what was left of the left leg. He held the reins in one hand and his crutch in the other, pointing it like a rifle at his two friends. Rodak and Zalaman had to admit they were impressed by the display, but mostly they were angry about his disobeying the doctor's orders. Rodak said Stanko was irresponsible for such risk-taking—after all their efforts. Stanko laughed and rode off.

><

Later that same day, Stanko achieved another milestone: he managed to walk down the stairs to the saloon. His resolve about not drinking was not forgotten, but there must be a celebratory drink. Jan bought a round in honor of Stanko. Antek insisted on buying another. "I'll miss having the Bartos boys around," he said. The three Polish traders all gave him the same puzzled look. "I assumed, the weather having improved, that you would be going back to your trading business," he explained.

Rodak didn't think Antek believed their Polish traders story, but he certainly wasn't going to admit it. "I hope you won't miss us too much."

"Not so much as Daiya and Ewa," Antek said.

Rodak told Antek no one should worry. Stanko's recovery was not far enough along for them to contemplate leaving anytime soon.

But once they were alone, Rodak berated Stanko for endangering everything, behaving recklessly on the horse like he had and warned him that Bebchuk was not going to be happy about it either. Dr. Bebchuck was not but as he unwrapped the bandages and found what a good job Zalaman and Rodak had been doing to keep the wound clean and change the bandages, he told Stanko he was making excellent progress. "I guess you *can* handle a little horseback riding, just get off your horse frequently and walk around a bit with your crutch. And then get some rest." Stanko rubbed his stump and said that was alright, he needed some.

><

As April approached, the three rode out of town for some target practice with the Spencers and to test Stanko's abilities. It was a cold day but fine, a quiet Sunday afternoon, broken only by church bells in the afternoon. A few snowy wisps falling from some unseen place in a clear blue sky. And then they opened up the Spencers and Sunday's quiet exploded.

When the smoke cleared and the echoes faded, Rodak tried to impress upon them how important the first shot was. "To be able to shoot more rounds is good; it can come in handy, but we can't let it be a distraction. It's far more important to make sure about the first shot. Those sharpshooters surrounding Jowls only need the time it takes you to cock the next round." They fired more rounds, then discussed plans for disposing of the dead and how they would pack the night before and have everything ready in their wagons in the Punie stables.

"Don't worry," Stanko assured Zalaman, "you'll have your chance to say goodbye to Lechsi."

"If we're lucky," Rodak said. "We'll have an hour, two at the most, to say our goodbyes. We have to leave before morning light." The earliest the Russians could come looking for their victims would be the 2nd, but there was no way they could discover there had been any foul play before the 3rd, especially if the three of them quickly cleaned up the mess they hoped to make, and by then the partisans would be far away. Zalaman asked about April 1st. Lechsi had told him it was a day for pranks. Rodak and Stanko knew all about *prima aprilis* and had assumed Zalaman did as well.

"Anything you hear on that day is likely to be untrue," Stanko said. "It's a day when people are allowed to get away with things that would get them into trouble any other time. That can only be good for us."

"The Cossacks aren't sympathetic to these pagan traditions—to other people's traditions. They have their own traditions—and fairy tales—even more than Poles."

By the end of the practice session, Stanko's shooting was showing definite improvement. The stump, at least in practice, was not proving to be much of a problem.

CHAPTER TEN

Dziedski

April 4, 1867

DEAREST LECHSI

Here's what happened on April First.

It was the first sentence he'd written since his notes to his parents from Syp, but it was a start. He owed her an explanation for why he'd failed to say goodbye, though he realized she would already have figured out quite a lot. Now, four days later, he had some time and he wanted to paint her a picture.

I didn't show up as I'd promised and I am sorry about that. At the time, I was more than sorry, I was frantic. But by the time you read this, you will certainly have already figured out much of what I'm about to tell you—and why I couldn't come see you.

It's just four days ago that we left Punie, before dawn, but it seems like months. It was so dark. The gas lamps had been extinguished and the hearth fires were embers.

Pitch black was what we wanted. We were on our way to the stables, and we wanted to leave Punie unobserved. But, if we were observed, it would have been assumed we were either involved in some early morning prank (prima aprilis) or are in fact, really Cossacks.

If you had seen us, you would have had a good laugh. We'd dressed in comical and ill-fitting Cossack uniforms, not fitted for parading around. I'd grown quite a bit, at least four centimeters since we'd taken these uniforms from their dead owners when there hadn't really been time to try them on. You see Lechsi, I'm not going to hide the truth from you about what I have been doing. I looked like a serf in a private's uniform, no ornamentation on either mine or Stanko's. Cossack tunics should be loose, but it was so tight over my waistcoat, it pressed into my old wound. The baggy striped trousers completed the look. It would have to do and would—on horseback. We all three wore those round Cossack caps, only mine had to be pulled down to my ears to get it to stay on my head. Rodak looked the most Cossack, more like an officer with his cherkesska, *his long, open-fronted coat with its ornamental loops covering much of the rest of what he wore. These outfits, adjusted by Stanko, the tailor of our little group, are hand-me-downs, they are stories in themselves, clothing that's been handed down from one generation of Cossacks to the next. When Stanko would sew up a hole in one of our Cossack tunics or baggy trousers, say a hole from a bullet or a blade or just a spot that had worn-through, Stanko would show me where the garment had been previously let out, taken in, re-stitched and handed down through at least another generation, perhaps a son of the original soldier.*

But enough about the Cossack uniforms. I haven't written anything in a long time, aside from a note to my parents, and it takes some getting used to—not just my brain, but my wrist. In that early hour when we walked to the stables, Rodak and I stayed alongside Stanko in case he needed any assistance, but he strode with that crutch just as steady as a two-legged Cossack. He slowed down a bit and stopped momentarily to observe the spot where he'd fallen asleep in the snow resulting in his loss of a leg. He looked like a war-scarred Russian, his left pant leg so baggy it wobbled around him like a hobbled balloon, wide and blousy, and when he tried to hitch it up, it enfolded him in waves of green-striped fabric. He would have fallen right there hadn't Rodak and I been at his side. Stanko just laughed it off, but it was an expression of the nervous giddiness we were feeling—happy there was no one there to see us, no light to be seen by.

We didn't look so silly once we were on horseback. Rodak was in the lead, as he usually is, his long coat was flapping, revealing the Spencer underneath, forcing him to constantly readjust the scabbard to hide the rifle. He was followed by Stanko who rode very upright, his black Cossack cloak hid his stump and rifle. I was in the rear wearing the same black cloak as Stanko. It was cold that morning but the cloaks kept us surprisingly warm. The Cossacks know cold and their felt cloaks are warmer than you might imagine. I remember my wound was hurting and I tried rubbing it gently under my waistcoat, but that only made it worse.

Zalaman paused in his writing to look over at Rodak and Stanko. They were still asleep. He scratched his head with the dry end of his newly acquired stylus. He had to keep at it, write faster, or he would never finish at this pace. Maybe he was putting in too many details, but he enjoyed that, conjuring the things he'd noticed. He thought Lechsi would appreciate them. She held writers in high esteem. As far as his killing and robbing Cossacks, she might not like that. Or maybe she would since Cossacks had been her family's tormentors too. He tried not to think too much of how she would regard him when she knew. And by now, as he wrote, she certainly already knew, if she hadn't guessed earlier, that the real business of the Bartos Brothers Trading Company was a Timas and Erkme venture, if of another sort—the successful kind.

It was a white landscape. We rode at a canter all the way—to the bend in the road where there was a little side path we'd discovered on an earlier scouting trip. It forked to the right, flowing hidden under the snow following a tributary of the Nurzec. We had to re-break a trail we'd broken earlier in the winter, before Stanko's misfortune, to the woodland we sought for hiding—the key to our success. Beyond the woods, the stream rushed on, exposed where the ice melted back to its banks and then it went over a waterfall. The waterfall was a key, too, like the woods—a curtain of protective noise where we would wait, just a few hundred meters from the Punie-Dziedski road. It was close enough that we would be able to see the three Cossack riders who, after having collected their tribute from Punie, would appear at that bend in the road as they rode north toward Dziedksi.

We dismounted and let our horses rest and drink. They lapped up the water from the stream. I sat by the edge where, in the roar of the waters, it was restful. The sun was shining, each of us aware this was the calm before the storm. I stared at the reddish-brown mud bordering the stream and felt happy. When I was a child, I always felt reassured seeing the promise of new life, of spring under the snow and here there were pale green shoots emerging from the mud. The fact that everything seemed so bright and shiny might be attributed to the marching powder we'd sniffed but I think it was more a tingling inside in anticipation of what was to come.

There is some correspondence between the powder and battle, as if they affect the same part of the brain. The thrill of the wonderful and the horrible.

I watched Stanko balance on his crutch to dip his remaining foot in the stream, but he pulled it out at once, swearing at the cold. Rodak stared at the road through the spyglass. It could be minutes or hours before they arrived. We had already debated about how to lure the tax collector and his sharpshooters to this place, this perfect blind for shooting. We would be as likely to scare them away as to lure them anywhere.

Rodak and I exchanged our scarves for the papahka we'd scavenged, the sheepskin caps that are so common with the Cossacks. We pulled them down to our eyebrows. Stanko did the best he could with his knitted version, turning it so that an ear flap covered his nose, turning it into a mask. We judged that he looked too suspicious that way. We fixed our cartridge tubes on the Spencers, aware, as Rodak warned us, that in the few seconds between our first round and the next, there is enough time for the sharpshooters to return fire.

Stanko and Rodak woke to find Zalaman still at work on his 'diary.' Stanko told Rodak that Zalaman must lead an interesting life to have so much to write about himself, then went back to sleep. Rodak watched him. He came over and tried to read over Zalaman's shoulder. "What language is that? No, never mind it doesn't matter." Zalaman went back to writing. "I'm going need some lessons," Rodak said.

Zalaman agreed to do it. Another time.

We rode to a better vantage point, but the waiting seemed to go on forever. We watched an eagle soar over us and scream. Rodak passed out a bit more of the marching powder. Stanko and I were on our usual mounts, (I was on Beth, who you met), but Rodak had picked an old Cossack horse we'd acquired before we came to Punie. Always thinking ahead, he wanted a horse strong enough to pull any dead horse or other carcasses to the river. Though she was an old nag, Rodak said she was still strong and dependable. She had been through so many battles, engagements that involved the firing of canons and exploding bombs, that she had lost much of her hearing. She lived in a quiet world of her own that would make her a good, steady perch for him during a gun battle.

In the afternoon Stanko now held the spyglass, and said he spied a smudge on the horizon. He handed it to Rodak who then handed it to me, and I saw the smudge resolve itself into three distinct smudges: three riders, riding north, three abreast on the road from Punie.

As soon as the tax collector and his guards passed the bend in the road, we galloped after them, reaching the road, a slushy mess, in no time. We then followed behind them, north toward

Dziedski. Stanko and I were taking our cues from Rodak, praying he had something in mind. He slowed and so did we, cantering till we were a few hundred meters behind the Cossacks, but we were slowly closing in. At 200 meters, we drew our rifles from our scabbards, and rested them against our thighs, hiding them under our cloaks. Rodak was still having difficulties with his long coat. His rifle kept catching on it, but he got it under control when we were about a hundred meters from our quarry, nearly within hearing distance of them.

We hailed the Cossacks in Russian as "Friends and comrades." "Camarades!" Stanko hollered on the left. "Tovarishii!" Rodak yelled in the middle. "Druzya!" I shouted.

The Cossacks stopped and turned around in their saddles. The two marksmen on either side of Jowls, the overweight tax collector, seemed to relax just a little when they saw our uniforms. Jowls had his hands on an overstuffed saddle bag. They returned our greetings.

But, of course, this ruse would not last long. It was up to Rodak to decide when to give it up—what was too close for comfort and too far for accuracy. Our costumes would not pass too close an inspection. I didn't want Rodak to overestimate my shooting prowess, despite the new accuracy I'd demonstrated in target practice and in shooting a hare from horseback. There was no time for idle thoughts about marching powder and violence. Now there were no thoughts at all.

We advanced close enough to make out the faces of the three Cossacks, our three opponents. When I saw their faces, the three Cossacks became men. My heart stopped, yet it was pounding so loud I was sure everyone could hear. My finger was fixed on the trigger. I kept thinking we should have fired by now. Rodak was prolonging the approach to make sure Stanko and I were close enough that we couldn't miss.

When I was sure we were close enough, if not too close already, though I had to trust Rodak on this, Colonel Jowls, asked,

"Kakoy u tebya polk?" and the hands of the marksmen went to their holstered firearms. We needed to respond. I hoped we were finally going to let our rifles do the speaking, rather than our bad Russian.

We were—but Rodak's rifle caught in his coat and then got tangled in the reins. And then that most dependable, tried and true, battle-hardened Cossack nag of his stumbled. Not a shot had been fired, but you couldn't blame her given all the tumult with the rifle. Rodak tumbled onto the snow and the startled Cossacks took their eyes off Stanko and me for just a moment. We both fired. My first shot missed the Cossack right in front of me and hit his horse. The bullets from the Spencer hit the horse so hard it threw the Cossack to the ground, and he nearly landed right on top of Rodak.

Rodak scrambled to his feet and grappled with the Cossack, wrapping him in a bear hug. The Cossack was a head taller than Rodak, but Rodak was strong and he held the sharpshooter tight and low, pushing him toward me. I'd only fired one round to Stanko's rapid one-two-three shots he got off before the Russian in front of him had a chance to fire even once. His Cossack slumped in the saddle, dead, I think, before the third round hit him and knocked him off his horse.

On the ground, Rodak had pushed the tall Cossack backward right up against my horse. I had my saber ready and ran it cleanly through that place where the neck meets the shoulder. I know this spot well, Lechsi, from my days playing butcher—it's where you cut a lamb to get the best neck cutlets. I plunged it so deep I couldn't pull it back out. It required much twisting, but I'll spare you a description of the blood and bone.

Zalaman paused, his wrist was tired, but he couldn't stop in the middle of the battle. When Lechsi got this letter, he wanted her to read it with such rapt attention that when she saw he'd written "Lechsi" she would know he was trying to be thoughtful.

She would at least be grateful that he has spared her the worst, but she might also wonder "How much worse could there be?"

As soon as the first shots were fired, Colonel Jowls of the bulging cheeks and saddle bags, had bolted in the direction of Dziedski. Stanko wheeled his horse with the confidence of a two-legged rider and took off after him. If he stopped to shoot the money-carrier and missed, an important aspect of the mission would fail. Rodak yelled at me—I should go help Stanko. So, I left the dead man slumped, saber still in his back—I hadn't seen his face—and gave chase.

The Tax Collector, with his heavy saddle bags, was losing ground to Stanko and I was gaining on them only slightly when Stanko caught even with the man and, at full gallop—dangerous even with two legs, let alone one, on the treacherous ice and snow—pushed himself up on the saddle and using a stirrup and his good leg, swung over the saddle, and leaped on top of the fat quartermaster, taking them both to the ground. The snow provided a forgiving landing. But now, heavy as he was, Jowls had two-legs and the advantage. He tromped away through the snow. I was focused on him since Stanko was paying him no further attention; he was interested only in the saddlebags—our reward for all this bloody work—and the saddlebags were still on Jowl's horse which was galloping away. Stanko had pulled himself up onto his own horse and took off after the one with the saddlebags.

I dismounted and as patiently as possible took careful aim at the fat colonel. He was not doing well in the heavy snow, trying to get as far away as he could, away from the road and into the woods. I had two rounds available. I judged the distance to be about twenty to twenty-five meters. Jowl's size and slowness made him a much easier target than a zig-zagging rabbit. It looked like he was crying. From fear and from the frustration of trying to run in that snow. It must have been like trying to run when you dream. While he ran, he tried to extricate his revolver from its holster but was having a tough time of it, like Rodak wrestling with his Spencer under the cloak. I pitied Jowls but wasn't going to let the feeling get the better of me. Still, I thought this was a different kind of killing—perhaps unnecessary. Then I thought about those Cossacks who threatened to rape you and caused your uncle such pain. I shot before Jowls had the chance to draw. He had colored the snow red by the time I got to him and stopped his pain. I'm afraid of what you may be thinking of me now. Now you know. It was not even a year ago, Lechsi, that I first killed someone, and the act made me shudder. How fragile we are. How fleeting life is. But this time, I was less bothered. I did not shudder at all.

Later, Stanko and I told Rodak we were sorry that we couldn't compliment him on his riding. He blamed the long coat, then the rifle, then the horse. Looking through the saddlebags quickly assuaged his anger. We had to see to cleaning up the mess we'd made, which would include hauling five carcasses, three Cossacks and two horses (Rodak's had broken her leg in the melee and had to be put down, plus the one I'd shot), to the tributary of the Nurzec to hide the evidence of the ambush as much as possible. But first we would inspect the contents of four saddlebags, a double tax collection for March and April. Quite a haul, as you and the citizens of Punie have seen by now. We discovered additional valuables hidden in Jowl's clothing. It seems he'd been trying to take a cut for himself. I told them it served him right that the extra weight had slowed him down and allowed me time to take a good shot. The combined booty filled three Cossack saddlebags. And we'd found a special pouch with silver coins along with the valuables in the tax man's clothing. The pouch was a beautiful velvet, fit for a rebbe's yarmulke, and inside were coins, stashed apart from the rest, and probably not accounted for in the ledger. There were gold pieces—some old ones, slightly tarnished, but still glowing when rubbed, the double eagle on one side and on the other, a queen—minted to commemorate the coronation of Catherine the Great. There were others, also pure gold, but more newly minted in commemoration of the coronation of Alexander the Liberator. We'd earned much more than we'd hoped to.

In one of the saddlebags, I found the ledger upon whose unused pages I am writing to you. When we deciphered the meaning of the columns, we found the ledger's used pages revealed many things. The first thing we realized was how much of what we had was taken from the people of Punie and we agreed that we would return a portion of that, as you know by now, keeping a sum in payment for the gratitude Rodak thought the town reasonably owed for ridding you of the oppressors.

The tax man's ledger had attracted Zalaman's eye almost as much as gold. The cover was supple, well-stitched, red leather, embossed with the Tsar's eagle. Zalaman had removed it from the Cossack saddlebag with a stylus tied to it, opened it across his lap and found accounts with dates going back years, listing the assorted sources and specific amounts, including towns visited—all calculated in rubles. Zalaman's ability to read Jowl's cyrillic was limited, but it was easy to see the day's final entry was "Punie." He also noticed how, dating back several years, there were conspicuously large amounts collected from the town of Dziedski, much greater sums than in Punie.

Dziedski was the town that would have been the next on the Cossacks' route and was obviously a much more prosperous place than Punie. Much more was collected there, than in Punie.

Zalaman pointed this out to Rodak and Stanko.

"It seems we've saved the people of Dziedski a lot of money."

"Oh, don't worry," Rodak said. "The Cossacks will still collect you know, eventually. We haven't solved anything. We've only disrupted things."

"We killed three Cossacks and have been richly rewarded," Stanko said. "That's not so bad." Zalaman pointed out the latest "Accounts Receivable" figure from Punie and said he assumed that amount would be returned to the people of Punie. Stanko objected, but Rodak shut him up, telling Zalaman he should be careful what he assumes. "But you're right in this case. Minus a fee for our service. Next time, the Cossacks may extract even stiffer penalties than usual, you know, if they think the people of Punie were complicit in our crimes against the Tsar."

"Dr. Bebchuk told me that when his teacher, Dr. Karbalov visited Dziedski, he was able to extract bigger fees," Zalaman told the cousins, who didn't see the point, but suspected Zalaman was about to suggest something. "You once described Punie as a lemon, Rodak. Dziedski must be a juicy peach." The cousins regarded one another with raised eyebrows. Was their conniving little Jew about to make some audacious proposal?

"Our victims were on their way to Dziedski," Zalaman said. The other two waited. "And thanks to them we now have more convincing Cossack uniforms."

Stanko laughed. "What I think you're going to suggest is preposterous."

"Look at the official saddle bags. The Tsar's own ledger. We could easily be mistaken for the Cossacks the Dziedski town council is expecting right now this evening."

"We might be mistaken from a distance," Rodak said. "But we'd have to perform their roles in ways that are beyond us."

"And in Russian," Stanko added. Stanko was less surprised than Zalaman that Rodak seemed to take a preposterous idea seriously enough to bother with these objections. He knew it was sometimes the 'preposterous' that most attracted his cousin.

"They're waiting for us right now," Zalaman said, worried now that he might have gone too far after trying his best to ignore that side of him that couldn't believe he was even suggesting such a thing.

"Maybe it *would* be a shame to disappoint them," Rodak said with a grin, shrugging his shoulders as if he didn't really believe such a thing was possible."

"I can't believe we are talking about this," Stanko said. "Those were pretty big numbers from Dziedski," he said to Zalaman, "but they're big because Dziedski is big, bigger than Punie—and with more Cossacks. I don't understand what you're proposing."

"We first have some work to do. Bodies and carcasses to bury," Rodak said. They started the clean-up process and as they worked, they continued playing with the idea. It still seemed far-fetched. They wouldn't be able to get to Dziedski before dark. Night could create problems, but also opportunities. It could help them avoid detection, although they guessed any local Cossacks would have given up waiting for Jowls and they might only have to deal with the local authorities. There were too many variables to consider. They should either go for it—all out—or forget it.

"You could carry the official ledger and the official collection pouch," Zalaman suggested. "Stanko and I on either side, playing the sharpshooters, showing the Spencers."

"Yes," Rodak said, "intimidate the Dziedski authorities by *showing* our weapons—and hopefully not have to use them."

It was dark by the time they'd deposited the dead—men and beasts—in the Nurzec, their own horses dragging the carcasses on a canvas tarp they'd brought for the job. They watched the bodies float away, slowly sinking, one-by-one. They covered all evidence of bloodshed with snow as best they could. They hurried it a bit, conscious of the dying light. It wouldn't matter all that much how careful they were—the Cossack hounds would find the spot sooner or later.

After having tidied up and taken the spoils of their success, which included all documents and the ledger, they arrived at the fork in the Punie-Dziedski road where they would have to decide. They could take their new found wealth to the left, back to the Punie stables where everything was packed and ready for their departure, or they could take a right to Dziedski, two hours to the north, where they might multiply that loot many-fold.

"Whether it works or not," Rodak told Zalaman, "it's too good an idea not to give it a try. With that much money we would be able to do a lot of good for the Uprising."

"The money's the goal this time," Zalaman said, "not just a bonus."

"I hope I don't have to get off my horse in the course of this transaction," Stanko said as they rode on. "I can shoot better now from my horse, rather than standing and leaning on my crutch."

><

Poor light and the long Cossack cloaks helped obscure the fact that one of the armed guards arriving in Dziedski that night had only one leg. If the partisans had to dismount, Stanko's leg might draw unwanted attention. One reason the scheme might work is that in each town on the taxman's route these collections were public transactions, handled out in the open, usually before the city hall, if one existed, for all citizens to witness. The monthly process consisted of handing over of the money and getting a receipt, so it drew little public interest.

Torches were already lit when Rodak dismounted and announced himself to the Dziedski official. Zalaman and Stanko remained on horseback. Rodak, wearing Jowl's epaulets, with his official collection pouch thrown over one shoulder and the official ledger in hand, introduced himself. He spoke passable Russian, but the official looked suspicious. It was late and there was something highly unorthodox going on, right here on the sidewalk in front of the town hall. He glanced at his aides. He asked Rodak about the health of the Lt. Limonev, but Rodak, who sensed this was ploy but couldn't be sure, feared that putting more than three Russian words together would expose his real origins. He didn't respond, but kept to his brief, rehearsed introduction. The light was dim and flickering, but Zalaman and Stanko read the suspicion on the faces of the local authority and his aides. Perhaps they'd missed some facet of the formal 'handing-over money for receipt' transaction that had been so clear-cut in the smaller town of Punie.

Mounted on their horses, Zalaman and Stanko didn't point their weapons at anyone, they just moved aside the long Cossack coats and exposed the Spencers to everyone's eyes. Zalaman and Rodak had figured this tactic would be enough—no actual gunfire would be required. And through a combination of foresight, luck, and gloom of night, they proved to be right. They would never be certain whether the Dziedski official who handed over two months of tax collections after seeing the Spencers, did so out of fear for his life, or whether simply exposing the rifles convinced the Dziedskian officials that they were the Cossack officers they claimed to be. After all, in this part of the world, only Cossacks possessed Spencers.

The Dziedski episode, successful as it was, never made it into the pages of Zalaman's letter three days later. That part would be easier to explain in person—something he had no doubt would happen—eventually. There was no actual battle to recount, so it wouldn't make very exciting reading. He didn't want to admit in writing to Lechsi that Dziedski had been his idea. Yes, it was a blow against the Russians, but wasn't it also a blow against the citizens of Dziedski? It sounded too much like a robbery and he wasn't sure she would admire his ingenuity. So, the letter he'd written was never finished. There was no final "With Love, from Zalaman." There was not going to be time.

By the time they got back to Punie it was close to the first light of morning. No time for goodbyes. Once they got to the stables to collect their vehicles, into which they had previously packed all their possessions, there was no time for Zalaman to see Lechsi. But the inn was so close to the stables that Zalaman ran there anyway, despite Rodak's order not to. He wanted to leave something for Lechsi. He woke up Jan and left him the velvet pouch, stuffed with banknotes, and instructions on how to distribute the wealth to the citizens—especially to Lechsi herself. A small consolation, he hoped, for not saying goodbye. But a heroic gesture, nonetheless.

Three days later, his right arm was still sore from writing in the ledger. Zalaman realized he might never be able to send it. He hoped it wasn't just the story of a fight written for himself, tucked away, never to be read, in a ledger in which there were still many lined and unlined blank pages. How he would ever get the pages to her, he had no idea, unless at some later date he and his friends felt it was safe and found their way back to Punie. He'd made the cousins consent to his Dziedski plan. They listened to him now.

Maybe, someday, he would figure out a way to talk them into returning to Punie. Rodak and Stanko claimed they would like to see their girlfriends again, too. He knew he could post the letter, but his handwriting was large so there were many pages. It would be a package more than a letter. To post what he'd written would require ripping those pages out of the ledger, which might destroy it and they wanted to keep it intact with all its information of interest to the Uprising, the Commandant at Syp especially. Besides, ripping apart the beautiful ledger would be an act of desecration, despite the attraction of his transforming a logbook of evil into a message of love.

They were a third of the way to Syp. For two long days and nights following the bloodshed, they pushed the horses, shaking and rattling the carts as much as they dared, stopping only when necessary. They were trailing five horses in addition to the ones they were riding or those pulling their vehicles. It had been one year since the previous visit to HQ. The cousins thought better maps might be available for the coming summer's work. They needed a rest in a safe place, and they could get that at Syp where they would provide the commandant with some of the booty. Most of it they would bury. Zalaman hadn't announced his intention yet, but he planned on going home in the summer once the snow had melted and the roads were passable. He would return home a wealthy hero. He insisted to the cousins they would only give the commandant the pages from the ledger with the Russian accounts. He would keep the parts with his letter and its remaining pages, and they agreed.

Rodak and Stanko were all charged up by the success of the mission and had no intention of not continuing their lucrative and patriotic work in the summer once things calmed down. They wanted a bigger nest egg before returning to Navharadak. Zalaman thought maybe they were being too greedy.

"From an Israelite! Do you believe it?" Rodak laughed. Who knew what they would be able to receive for some of the banknotes in their possession. The double tax collection had included a lot of large notes that might prove difficult to exchange at face value rates—and they could attract suspicion.

Along the road there were green shoots emerging from the snowpack, indications of spring. Zalaman missed Lechsi and it was different from missing Anna or even home; it was sharper. Maybe it would pass.

They'd slowed their pace, wagon and cart rocking gently over the soft packed snow. They'd had two straight days of sunshine and the sun had melted snow from the large, flat rocks near their road. They stopped to stretch their legs and rest saddle sore backsides on those rocks. It was warm enough to take off their coats and, using them for pillows on the warming rocks, they rested. When they woke, it was nearly dusk and they were groggy. Using the glass, Rodak spied a stand of oaks down the hill where the ground was already mostly clear of snow. They would stop there for some real sleep and have a decent meal. On the way, Rodak brought down a grebe. "Much easier," he assured Zalaman, "than shooting a zig-zagging rabbit."

They camouflaged their wagons and eight horses in the thick stand of oak, one of several groves that outlined farms on the low rolling hills to the south and west, the fields still partially buried in snow except for muddy patches displaying the re-emergence of the vegetable world. Stanko thrust his pike into the ice-encrusted stream that fed the oaks. He and Zalaman scooped up its water for drinking and cooking, but it was so cold they had to let it warm a bit before they could drink.

Stanko complained about his stump, but he told Zalaman he didn't want to look at it. It was so snugly wrapped, he worried about his friend's ability to redo it nicely. He just wanted to have a good meal. "Now that we are well off, shouldn't we be sleeping on soft mattresses?" Rodak promised he would have one in Syp—and a real doctor, as well. They didn't pay too much attention to Stanko's objections and unwrapped his bandages to look. The stump looked bruised as would be natural from all the activity, but it was healing.

While Zalaman went to work on the grebe, Rodak fetched more water to wash the wound before he rewrapped it. Zalaman said the bird should have been soaking first, but he could show them the right way to pluck it. "The kosher way," he said, "though the bird cannot be kosher, given our . . . situation." The cousins watched as he plucked the feathers, then singed off the pinfeathers, cut off the head and snipped two little white veins from the bottom of the neck to let out all the blood. He sliced off the ends of the wings and toes and, after another rinsing, covered everything with salt, sliced the grebe in half with Rodak's hunting knife and removed the parts that had to be removed—stomach, intestines, kidneys, liver, and some blood clots. The cousins looked on approvingly.

The sun was setting as Rodak built up the fire with the dry kindling he'd found on the oaks' sunny sides. The branches and twigs were so dry they made little smoke. Even though it was getting dark, they didn't want to announce their presence to any farmers emerging from winter hibernation who might want to investigate. Stanko said they shouldn't have to fear the people here all that much. They were on the right side of the Uprising. "Still," Rodak said, feeding the fire slowly, "you never know." The bird sizzled, emitting an intoxicating smell, mingling with the fragrant wood smoke. The three were drooling.

"This poor grebe," Rodak said, "was migrating too early in the spring. Grebes are such slow flyers, they're easy targets in the air. Normally, she would have dived under the water to avoid my gunfire. But the water is under ice, which made it easy for me."

The grebe may not have been the juiciest—the bird had burned off a lot of fat during its migration. No matter, they agreed it was juicy enough and that in fact they'd never tasted better.

They didn't do much more talking until they were finished with the grebe. They figured that the Cossacks must have at least narrowed down their search to Punie. Punie would be crawling with Cossacks. The three of them might be getting a reputation.

They agreed they'd been very lucky. Rodak passed around some marching powder. They were feeling well-fed and positive about their success and they indulged in some self-congratulations.

"Summer is coming," Rodak said, "and summer is the best time to put more holes in the Tsar's army and his pocketbook. We won't have to worry about any damned snow. At Syp, we'll get new maps and information. Maybe there are larger operations underway, somewhere where we could have a big impact, make the Tsar sit up and take notice."

"I didn't think we wanted to draw the Tsar's attention," Zalaman said.

"Fuck the Tsar! Now I want his attention. He may have helped your father, Zalaman, but he's still harassing Jews, just like the Poles. Oh, and by the way everyone—Happy Easter." The cousins laughed, but only a little. They all knew Easter was a dangerous time for Jews—in Poland and elsewhere in the Christian world, thanks to their role in the killing of Christ story.

"You may have it in you to become a true partisan," Rodak told Zalaman.

Stanko agreed, saying "It has nothing to do with your being a Hebrew or Christian. The Jews may be guilty of killing Jesus, as they say, and if that's true, well, you will never be forgiven. But who knows what really happened? That was so long ago."

"My father suffered at the hand of the Jews," Rodak said, "and he instilled his hatred in me. I thought he taught me all I needed to know about the subject, but now, it's just not important to me." Zalaman wasn't sure what he felt about Rodak's enlightenment. "And I'm starting to realize not all Christians are as stupid as I'd always heard," he said.

><

For the remainder of the journey to Syp, the change of seasons consisted of snow flurries alternating with sunshine that melted the new snow and old. They took their time, loaded with arms and vehicles that created a strain on yokes and animals. It was never-ending work to keep control of the wagons, constantly grasping and pulling the reins to guide the horses over snow that was hard packed by many wheels, crunching it down for days of good weather, then the hardpack softening to mud that sucked at wheels and hooves. Each morning, before they broke camp, Rodak made Zalaman give him writing lessons.

They agreed they would turn over half of what they'd taken at Dziedski to the commandant at Syp. Otherwise, the Dziedski portion would feel tainted. Zalaman rationalized the largesse as being like Robin Hood. He asked the cousins if they knew the story and they said they did—at least the barest outline of stealing from the rich and wicked to give to the poor and honest. Stanko knew enough to ask Zalaman if he was equating the Tsar with the Sheriff of Nottingham and Zalaman said "No, the Tsar is King Richard. The Sheriff of Nottingham would be—"Linards!" They laughed together, each of them knowing Linards and hating him equally.

Later that day, before arriving in Syp, they buried their valuables.

Looking over the unburied remainder, the Syp Commandant was pleased. The exploits of these three partisans—the veteran Rodak, his giant, young cousin, Stanko, and even younger Jewish partner, Zalaman—while not yet in the category of legends, were celebrated and, at the same time, were causing reprisals, bringing new pressure against the Uprising. The commandant did not welcome the pressure, but if this was the reward—the treasure as well as the harm to the Russians—then he *would* welcome the three, for at least a while.

When they'd first arrived at Syp—entering with their laden carts and horses to a confusing and tumultuous reception—Zalaman thought HQ looked even sorrier than it had the previous year. Once he and the cousins had distributed their largesse, sorting out and delivering arms, ammunition, and horses, the commandant expressed considerable enthusiasm for what they had accomplished. But among the other partisans bivouacking at Syp, they sensed an undercurrent of resentment. The Cossacks were unusually restless, and the men held a theory that the accomplishments of Rodak and company had something to do with the new retaliatory Russian campaigns against them. The soldiers at Syp had heard the Cossacks were preparing an attack and they were not happy about it. Partisan spies confirmed this rumor, but the commandant said his scouts had not yet seen evidence that the Russians were preparing anything at all.

Then the commandant apologized to Zalaman—here had been no response from his parents. He assured Zalaman the message *had* arrived at Lahkvna, but the truth was the courier who'd carried his message had never returned. Meanwhile, the new telegraph lines were impossible across borders and no rail lines connected Syp to the rest of the world.

Zalaman and his partners at first doubted they were the main source of the Cossacks' ire, but as they came to accept that it was possible, they had mixed feelings about it. Pride, yes, but some responsibility for stirring up a hornets' nest. They wouldn't stay long at Syp and risk their location becoming known. Zalaman was upset, feeling he was traipsing around the world while his parents remained ignorant of his fate, and he was sure they were suffering as a result.

The medic cleaned Stanko's wound every day. He also seized an artificial leg for him, something they had an ample stock of at HQ. Zalaman would occasionally leave his wooden stool in front of their tent and get in the cart with his ledger and stylus, ready to continue his letter to Lechsi. But nothing came of it. He would read what he'd written and cross it out. He was glad he hadn't sent any pages.

It was a June day and they were lounging on the bank of a stream that carved the border between the town of Syp and the encampment. The spring snowmelt had swollen that borderline and it now offered convenient places to do the cleaning of Stanko's stump. Stanko sat half naked, soaking his stump in the cold waters. It was the warmest day of the year so far, but the water was still cold as ice. Stanko claimed not to feel it. Zalaman helped him out of the water and watched him strap on the new wooden leg the medic had made specially for him and to which

Stanko was just growing accustomed. It was a Russian-issue artificial leg, barrel staves and a steel kneecap, copied from the latest American version—another wartime innovation. Stanko still needed a crutch, but less so. "I'm ready to be on the road," he said. Summer was the best time to stage ambushes and summer was here. Rodak, too, was anxious to leave Syp. He wanted to go deeper into Cossack-controlled regions.

The commandant's spies had told him the Russians knew Syp was harboring certain enemies and the Cossacks were organizing an operation. Perhaps an attack could be avoided, they suggested, if the commandant would turn in all three. The commandant would not go that far, but he welcomed the three's decision to leave. The commandant had been putting his troops through exercises to prepare them for a battle, fortifying the lines along the road from Syp to HQ, but he would prefer to avoid a major confrontation. His troops were badly depleted. It would be best for everyone if the trio left soon. Once they had time to get far enough away, he would have his spies inform the Cossacks of their departure and thus, he hoped, avert disaster. He was both grateful and relieved when they left.

CHAPTER ELEVEN

Dzeszow

When Rodak, Stanko, and Zalaman left Syp they were no longer weighed down by excessive weaponry and ammunition and horses. There was a lightheartedness that came from escaping what had become a dreary place. Stanko, with his new limb, was feeling particularly fine. Rodak appeared to be looking forward to inflicting more damage on the Russians. Zalaman was no longer interested in fighting Cossacks, but he felt the new lightness, too, ready for new, open country, feeling invincible. They could do no wrong. One more—one last summer, he thought.

After they retrieved their valuables, fished with success in one of the unnamed watercourses that ran toward larger rivers and the Baltic, they found themselves in full-blown summer, the land was decorated in green, splashed here and there with violet-blue irises and sky-blue geraniums. It was a pleasure to ride over the gentle hills and along flourishing fields with the occasional woods that provided cover when they wanted it. They felt they were heading toward a region of opportunity.

It seemed to Zalaman and Stanko that they could do no wrong that summer. Rodak felt what they were doing—nothing—was wrong. If there were opportunities for strikes against Cossacks that summer, they missed them. In the towns where they rested and spent their money, they also spent more time enjoying themselves than studying the movements of Cossacks. Zalaman and Stanko agreed with Rodak that summer was their time to get to work for the Uprising, but Rodak was unconvincing in his complaint. He was as guilty as they were that the only killing they did was of edible prey.

Rodak, in fact, shot all manner of birds and rabbits, even a goat and a sheep that strayed from some farmyard enclosure. Zalaman cleaned and gutted them all and Stanko cooked. Stanko also did most of the eating. He taught Zalaman what he knew about cooking. Zalaman continued instructing Rodak in writing skills. They sporadically scouted for Cossacks, but the regiments they saw were too large, so they stayed well away, and the summer slipped away while they lived outdoors, away from towns, hunting and fishing and eating—and occasionally visiting a saloon in some town for drinks and companionship. Stanko was walking around like he had two real legs and the joy of his recovery affected even Rodak.

"What was it that made Robin Hood and his Merry Men so merry?" Rodak asked Zalaman. "Marching powder or *Krupnik*?"

"What's with Robin Hood again?" Stanko asked. "It doesn't feel like we're doing much to aid the oppressed."

"My mother said it was because they got along so well together," Zalaman said. "Getting along together held them together—not just hatred of the sheriff or their dedication to the Virgin Mary. I didn't know what she meant when she told me that at the time, but now I think I understand."

"What she didn't tell you," Rodak laughed, "was the meaning of 'merry.' Making merry meant they were very partial to the ladies."

Autumn crept down from the north and they stopped in the town of Dzeszow to discuss their options. Dzeszow was a prosperous place, larger than Punie, with stores of brick showing off their wares in glass windows. The town even had a circulating library and a stationery shop, as well as several hotels and saloons—one catering to gentry, one to the trades and working people. There were people of many political persuasions. And looking ahead to the winter, it looked awfully good indeed.

They took rooms in one of those hotels. Like the inn in Punie, it had an attached saloon and they ate well and washed it down with ale, discussing the predominance of Cossacks, the state of the Uprising in general and the future—whether or not they should extend their stay before it became winter and too late to do anything and before they knew it, it was too late. Zalaman put on weight. He relented in his previous opposition to prostitutes. When he was not engaged in eating with Stanko and Rodak or fucking Zika, he would visit the small library, where he found a translation of *The Delightful Historie of Don Quixote de la Mancha*, a big book he read by oil lamp throughout the entire winter. The days were short and nights long and it seemed to Zalaman that the whole white world and time had frozen solid. He read, ate, drank, and contributed to the Merry Men's making merry, but vowed this would be his last winter away from home.

><

In May, the weather warmed. The snowbanks receded. New life stretched and emerged. But when they left Dzeszow one early morning, resolved to see if they could scout out Punie to see if the Cossacks' interest in the town had waned, there was still a biting chill in the air. They were trailing a string of horses and carrying all their worldly goods in one remaining cart: clothing, provisions, and weapons. The banknotes and the multi-national collection of negotiable certificates and securities they now held were stuffed in their underclothes as extra protection against the cold morning and any unanticipated encounters with Russians. They had gold coins strapped securely around their thighs.

The greens were luminous after the long winter that had been devoid of any color other than the white of snow and the black of night; the snow now mostly retreated to only the highest elevations. There were carpets of the pink-purple blossoms Zalaman's mother had called 'heliotrope' and carpets of white flowers that you could confuse with remaining snow. "Crocuses,"

Rodak told him. The aroma of the land in spring, lindens and beech leafing out, little flowers shining, grasses and reeds flexing out of the runoff. But Zalaman was lost in thoughts of Lechsi and the possibility of seeing her in Punie.

They approached the turnoff to Punie with Zalaman riding in the wagon, Stanko driving, Rodak trailing their reduced string of horses—now a shorter string after having left some with the commandant. The road was in relatively good state, but their wagon was weighed down by the weapons and sliver hidden under rugs and hides.

Before committing to making the turn to Punie, they debated the idea of sending someone ahead to see whether the town was still congested with Cossacks before carting their wealth there. Zalaman was holding his ledger as they neared the turnoff, but he wasn't using it for writing to Lechsi; he'd used it that morning to test Rodak's writing.

They argued about who should go ahead to scout and the dispute, along with the squeaky wagon wheels, might account for their being unaware that a contingent of twelve Cossacks was riding up from the rear and was almost upon them. By the time they did realize what was happening, it was too late to run for it—not that they would have stood a chance with all they were still pulling. They held their breaths and pulled over to the side of the road to let the Cossacks pass, hoping they could avoid more than the cursory scrutiny they might receive in Punie. All three gripped their weapons under the blankets draped over their laps. They exhaled when the contingent rode right past without so much as a hello. The three exchanged grateful looks, having avoided the death they might easily have encountered, if, for example, they'd been wearing their Cossack uniforms as they'd earlier discussed and rejected.

When the Cossacks got fifty meters ahead, they wheeled—all twelve horses and riders as one. Twelve Cossacks faced them.

Rodak held up his hand and the partisans stopped. The Cossacks walked their horses slowly toward them as Zalaman put the ledger under the blanket and gripped the repeater.

There were ten regulars, a captain, and a lieutenant. The captain told them in Russian-accented Polish to identify themselves—"Polish traders"—and asked where they were headed.

"We are traveling on business." Rodak said, "after an unprofitable winter in Dzeszow."

The captain did not bat an eye or change expression. "I've seen you in the Dzeszow hotel," he said. "On your way to Bibin or Punie?"

"Bibin," Rodak said.

"So, why did you find Dzeszow so unprofitable, I wonder?" The captain asked stiffly, guiding his horse among the partisans and their carts, the lieutenant following.

"We were too busy having a good time," Stanko joked. The captain was happy to hear an honest response. He'd seen the group drinking in the hotel.

"We trade in potatoes and onions, cabbage, turnips," Rodak explained. "We had a good year last year so we took some time to rest and spend our money. We've spent it all and now we need to go back to work."

"'Spent it all?' What would I find in those saddlebags?"

"What's left," Rodak said as expressionless as the captain. "Not much for the Tsar, I'm sorry to say . . . barely enough for us to start out this spring."

"Start out small, but start, that's what we say," Stanko smiled.

The Lieutenant poked his saber into the saddlebag on Rodak's horse, prying it open so he could peer inside. They had, of course, hidden all the valuables, including the arms, the Cossack uniforms, anything incriminating, in the wagon under rugs and hides. This provided minimal comfort for the way the captain and his lieutenant poked around with their sabres.

"You should have been more circumspect in your spending last winter," the captain admonished and his lieutenant seconded that. They claimed they'd seen them with their whores in Dzeszow, too. The partisans denied it and relaxed their grips on their weapons, while still holding on to them. It didn't appear the Cossacks were going to ransack the wagon or look further in the saddlebags.

The captain wished the Polish people health and wealth—excepting, he mentioned, the remaining stray partisans of the pathetic Uprising. He lectured the traders that "after all these years," Poles, like the three of them, should feel honored to be welcomed as an extension of the Tsar's territory. Rodak said he couldn't speak for all Poles, some of them were certainly crazy, but he and his family certainly agreed with him about that.

Zalaman and Stanko pretended to be warming themselves under the blankets, hoping to get out of this alive. The captain motioned for his troop to turn their horses back in their intended direction and leave the Poles to their business.

But the lieutenant hesitated. He'd been staring at Zalaman. "You don't have much to say, youngster." He didn't look like the other two; he looked like a Jew to the lieutenant. "What are you, a Jew, doing with these Poles? Why aren't you home helping your parents instead of whoring all winter with these reprobates?"

"I'm as Polish as anyone else here, sir."

"He only looks Jewish," Stanko said. "We've kidded him about it since he was a baby."

"What's that?" the lieutenant asked, pointing to the ledger Zalaman had failed to completely hide.

"Oh, nothing," Zalaman said. "I've been writing." He opened the ledger to display a page of his letter to Lechsi, trying not to expose the embossing.

The captain told the lieutenant to move on. "Leave the Yid alone." The lieutenant recognized something about that ledger. He'd seen something similar before, flipped it over with his saber and saw the embossing and red leather and requested that the captain halt. He ordered a young Cossack to dismount and get him the ledger. The three partisans could not let the Cossacks see that ledger.

The young Cossack approached Zalaman in the wagon. He didn't look much older than Zalaman, who was wondering if this Cossack was a boy recently *chappered* into service. He had a nascent wisp of mustache, curled up with oil, while his fellow Cossacks sported extravagant beards or side whiskers. As he reached out to take the ledger as he'd been ordered, he noticed that Zalaman was gripping something under his coat. At that instant, Zalaman pulled the trigger, the bullet striking the young Cossack in the forehead at nearly point-blank range. The boy collapsed down one side of the wagon and the quiet spring day was shattered by dozens of rounds from the three Spencer's, reducing the Cossack troop by half in seconds. The high, thick sides of the wagon provided Zalaman substantial cover, though several bullets pierced the wood and rained splinters on him.

Rodak and Stanko took down four Cossacks before they fell themselves. Stanko fell with his horse and was pinned hopelessly under it. The horse was deadly still and Stanko bellowed in anger, unable to take another shot. Rodak had taken down both the captain and the lieutenant with his first two rounds, but he and his horse—he'd been riding Beth—had both been shot. Rodak lodged himself behind a bleeding Beth, using her as a shield. She absorbed more bullets and then stopped jerking. Six Cossacks were still on their horses, horses trained for warfare, yet rearing and kicking, surprised by the sudden attack, while Zalaman was protected behind the solid sideboard and Rodak at least partially covered behind Beth and Stanko struggled, his good leg pinned beneath his horse. Using Beth to prop his rifle, Rodak shot another Cossack in the act of dismounting. From behind the wagon, Zalaman picked off one on the ground, as well. Another Cossack managed to get off his horse and shoot Stanko who was lodged under his horse. The bullet hit Stanko's artificial limb, shattering it and then passed into the horse—but not through it. Zalaman winged that Cossack in the hip and Rodak shot out the man's other leg. He dropped to his knees. Rodak looked a bloody mess, but he got up from behind Beth and staggered over to put a bullet through the kneeling Cossack's head and out of his misery.

The three remaining Cossacks were galloping hard back toward Dzeszow. Rodak looked pale, sitting by Beth's carcass, attempting to staunch the flow of blood from his thigh and thankful for the coins strapped to his body that had impeded other bullets.

Pinned under his horse, Stanko was in agony, yelling about his "fucking leg"—his previously good one—not the now shattered artificial leg from the medic. Zalaman couldn't budge the dead horse to extricate Stanko, but somehow Rodak, limping in pain, using his pike as a crutch, a makeshift tourniquet above his wound, was able to join the other two and carefully, using the leverage of the pike, lower himself to the ground. He wedged himself, using the pike again, under the horse, lifting it just enough that Zalaman was finally able extract Stanko, who lay back holding his 'good' leg.

"We need Bebchuck," Zalaman said, grimacing. Speaking was somehow very painful. He felt his face and noticed there were jagged pieces of wood stuck in his skin like darts, shards from the wagon's sideboard that had pierced his jaws and cheeks and, at the same time, saved his life. Now that he was aware of them, they truly started to sting. He pulled out two of the larger splinters, one from his check and one from his jaw, and more blood flowed. Rodak pulled a splinter from his shoulder that Zalaman hadn't even noticed.

"We can be happy the three remaining Cossacks headed toward Dzeszow, not Punie," Rodak said. Dr. Bebchuk would be the best thing for Stanko's injuries—his good leg had been broken under the horse and his artificial limb had been destroyed by a bullet—if not Rodak's too. Punie was close—assuming the doctor was in Punie.

"But we don't know if it's safe for us to appear in Punie," Stanko said through gritted teeth. "I am not going to have my other leg amputated."

"You've broken your leg, not frozen it. Bebchuk can repair it," Zalaman said. "And we'll find you a new limb, too."

"Now you're the only one the with two good legs," Rodak said. "You are going to have to scout out Punie for us and find Bebchuk."

Before he left, Zalaman retrieved the large piece of canvas they used for hauling things over the snow—like dead Cossacks and horses—to the Nurzec, and there was still snow here, banked up by the converging roads over the course of the winter. It wasn't easy to wrestle with this canvas anytime, and now his hands were slippery with blood, so he washed them in the snow. With some assistance from Rodak, Zalaman got the tarp under Stanko and they dragged him toward the wagon, uncertain how, once they got him there, they'd get him up and inside. And then, unbeknownst to Rodak, one of the 'dead' Cossacks got up and came stumbling toward him, right arm straight out in front of him, pointing a revolver at the back of Rodak's head no more than three meters away.

None of the partisans were holding weapons. If the Cossack had fired then, Rodak would be no more, but, to ensure he wouldn't miss, the weakened Cossack took one more fatal step forward, allowing Stanko, on his back, to swoop up the business end of the pike, impaling the Cossack. It was a clean piking, as clean as Rodak's skewering of Georg, though in this case, technically, the Cossack had eviscerated himself, stumbled right onto the weapon, which opened his abdomen and midsection and released a rain of blood and organs, again, just like Georg.

What had looked so breathtakingly horrible then, barely fazed Zalaman now. He was more upset by the demise of Beth. Since Georg's death, she had seemed like their horse, not his.

Rodak hobbled around making sure all the dead Cossacks were truly dead. Getting Stanko in the wagon turned out to be easier than they'd thought, with help from the horses and thanks to the wagon's previously high sideboards having been reduced by the fusillade.

From the Cossacks, Zalaman took only bullets and rifles. They had to get away from the scene of this battle and to Punie now, before dark, before either Rodak or Stanko lost too much blood. They held a vigil for Beth before they left, marveling at how smoothly she made the transition from Georg to them. Zalaman thoughts strayed to Marengo and his brother, Davin; he remarked how horses become like a part of your family.

Zalaman never figured out how Rodak handled the wagon and horses with only one useful leg, for he, Zalaman, was riding up ahead of the wagon to be first to Punie, uncertain of what awaited them there. Rodak followed at a less jarring pace, alongside Stanko and their worldly goods.

Arriving at the outskirts of Punie, Zalaman tied up his horse at a familiar spot near their old target practice area. It was getting dark and he was nervous, although he figured the darkness was a blessing. But what if there were too many Cossacks? Would Dr. Bebchuk be in town and available? He might not even live here, might have taken off to study with his revered teacher, the famous Dr. Karblakov. And what to do about Lechsi if he saw her? What he would do he didn't know, but his heart was pounding for all these reasons and the urgency of his mission. He slithered by Lechsi's house. There was no light on inside, but it would be early for lamps to be lit. The Cossack presence appeared to be minimal at that hour, but he stuck to the long shadows, slinking through edges of Punie's *kvadrat*, skirting the inn, and, his luck holding, finding Bebchuk just as he was closing his clinic for the night. When Bebchuk saw Zalaman, he swiftly glanced up and down the street to check on witnesses, then reopened the lock, scuttled Zalaman inside and drew the curtains.

"The Tsar is looking for you," he said while he had Zalaman in a bear hug. He'd never expected to see the partisans again, after the wounds, physical and financial, they'd inflicted on the Cossacks. But when Zalaman did show up at his door, he was shocked by his appearance all the same, and got right to work, removing a splinter that had been missed and wiping the blood off Zalaman's face, explaining how worried he had been for over a year now with new rumors of their fugitive status.

Bebchuk knew the danger of following Zalaman to the prescribed spot outside town as he'd been asked to, but felt he had no choice. These men were fighting the Russians and he knew they should not risk being seen together in Punie. They would be recognized. So Bebchuk grabbed his medical supplies, including a primitive wooden leg, and threw a cover over Zalaman to hide him in the back of his carriage during the drive out of town. From his hiding place in back, Zalaman told Bebchuk how his amputation of Stanko's leg had been praised by the medic in Syp who had given Stanko an artificial limb like the ones the doctor had mentioned.

"But he's gone and ruined it and broken his other leg, as well," Zalaman said, explaining how the legs were broken and the blood spilled. He held nothing back because he hadn't the strength to try to make anything up. He didn't think the truth would be a problem for Bebchuk. Bebchuk was glad he'd hidden Zalaman under the blanket, otherwise he would have seen what Bebchuk saw: Lechsi walking arm-in-arm with an older man. As the man, someone he'd seen with her before, walked her home, she rested her head on his shoulder.

><

They arrived at the appointed meeting spot, but Rodak and Stanko were nowhere to be seen. "It's alright," Zalaman explained, "they had to take it slow." Zalaman told Bebchuck not to worry; he'd been peeking out from the cart when they passed near Lechsi's house and had seen her. "I'm OK. I'm glad you didn't stop. How could someone like Lechsi not have a man? It wouldn't be fair to think she'd wait for me. I'm glad she didn't." He didn't mention how his heart had stopped when he'd seen them and, despite what he said now, he'd felt bitter regret and jealousy. Lechsi had once told him there were no interesting men in Punie, except for him, so he'd held out some hope. Her boyfriend or husband or whatever he was looked quite sophisticated—and here he, Zalaman, was covered in blood and wanted by the authorities. He felt miserable, but she was not the cause. Maybe she thought of him sometimes. She did.

Rodak arrived hauling Stanko, all the goods and animals intact. They lit some oil lamps and Bebchuk got right to work on both men, starting with Rodak. He could take care of a bullet wound quickly—clean the wound, locate the bullet, as one had clearly not emerged from the other side, and get it out as carefully as possible. Stanko was another matter. His treatment required thought. He asked Stanko to explain exactly what had happened, while withdrawing Rodak's bullet, then tightly bandaging the thigh. "But not too tightly,' he said. "We don't want to stop the blood from flowing elsewhere." After as much consideration as there was time for—and there was not much time, they were sure, before the Cossacks arrived at Dzezsow and discovered they should head to Punie—he decided he should fix up Stanko's broken leg with a splint. Of even greater concern to Bebchuk was Stanko's ruined artificial leg. Bebchuk marveled at the sophistication, the precision of what was left of that barrel stave-leather-steel construction. It was completely wrecked. He shook his head in despair. "Much of the steel and leather is intact," he said, "but the wooden parts are shattered and some of the rubber bumpers are missing. It was an ingenious limb, wasn't it? I don't think you can wait around while I figure out some way to fix it. It's too bad you're in such a rush. I would like to try my skill at re-fabricating the limb . . . replace those rubber bumpers with leather."

But they *were* in a rush, so Bebchuk cleaned Stanko's stump, strapped on the new wooden leg, and handed them bandages for later. He cleaned and tied a splint on the broken leg.

"You're very lucky," he told Stanko. "Only someone as big as the horse itself could sustain such a minor fracture from an actual horse landing on top of him." Stanko said he didn't know why, but he wasn't feeling all that lucky.

"Our luck finally ran out," Zalaman said, as Bebchuk applied salve to his facial wounds.

"The fracture should heal in a month or two," Bebchuk said, "as long as you don't overdo it." Everyone, Stanko included, acknowledged that there was nothing for it; Stanko was certain to overdo it.

Bebchuk promised to pass on their regards to Ewa and Dayia—and Lechsi. Dr. Bebchuk had been very busy last winter and had hardly seen anyone other than patients. Men and beasts. Nor had he frequented the inn, but he would give Jan and Gierta their greetings. With great care, Zalaman tore the *To Lechsi* pages out of the ledger. He folded the sheets in a way that he thought would discourage Bebchuk from reading them and asked the doctor to give them to her. Bebchuk said he would and, before riding off, looked at him and the two crippled cousins and warned them there would be challenges ahead.

><

There were, but they were not insurmountable if they took their time, took it easy. They spent the summer recuperating, with Rodak and Stanko both hobbled and dependent on Zalaman for much. He felt he had no choice but to put off going home and help them.

By the end of the summer, Rodak's leg was almost as good as new. He was angry at the damage done to him and vowed revenge. Otherwise, he exercised his new writing ability, practicing on any velum he could get his hands on and handing the results to Zalaman. He didn't write about his experiences in the Uprising, but about the reasons for the Uprising, its justification. Stanko, having ridden in the wagon all summer, was still wagon-bound by fall when it grew too cold to sleep outdoors. The two invalids consoled themselves with opium and Zalaman joined them to be sociable. To avoid showing their faces in Cossack-controlled and patrolled towns, they took advantage of secluded farms as they had with the Gmerks, this time paying their supportive hosts well. If they were gouged by a farmer, it fell to Zalaman to intervene and negotiate. "You're still an Israelite after all," Rodak said. They still had plenty of resources. The gold coins themselves could have seen them through many winters.

One of their hosts, a newly-freed serf, now overseeing his own crew of farmhands, demonstrated insufficient hatred of the Tsar, angering Rodak. The ex-serf overreacted to Rodak's taunts and made the fatal mistake of going for his musket, but he never made it because Rodak drew his revolver faster. The dead man's wife said that now she herself felt emancipated. "You've done me a service," she said. It had taken full time effort to feed herself, let alone her worthless husband. Rodak enlisted Zalaman to help him bury the husband. When they'd finished and the widow bade him a polite, but not tearful or even solemn, farewell service. She told Rodak she hoped they didn't have to leave too soon. No, they agreed; they did not have to. Rodak liked her spirit, and he found some comfort in her arms for a good part of that winter. It was the kind of peaceful winter they needed, although Stanko worked hard all winter at his rehabilitation. His remaining leg, still supported by splints, was gaining strength and he hopped about the farmhouse with Zalaman who once again became 'Crutch.' Before spring arrived, after a few embarrassing and failed attempts, Stanko succeeded in mounting his horse. After that feat, it was difficult to persuade him not to overdo it. He felt a renewed desire to pursue Cossacks—once the weather allowed.

Zalaman was worn down from all the caregiving. He was missing home. He missed Lechsi. He wasn't feeling so merry. He turned sixteen that winter—the same age Stanko had been when he and Rodak first met Zalaman and dispatched Georg. Zalaman questioned why he was staying. Whatever had been exciting about what he was doing was less so. He thought he could probably find his way home on his own. He had enough money to be able to pay for transportation. But he didn't talk about this with the cousins, because just continuing, avoiding the issue, was easier. They no longer required much assistance. Rodak wondered why Zalaman wasn't talking about going home like he used to and it started to trouble him that the boy didn't.

"You've proven yourself," he told Zalaman. "It's your right to go home if you wish." Zalaman nodded, thoughtfully. He was not surprised that Rodak had been able to read his mind. Earlier, in Rodak's company, Zalaman had just been the unproven Hebrew partisan. No longer.

"You would be welcome back with us once you rediscover how boring life is back in Lahkvna," Stanko said, impressed with his cousin's mellowing.

"In fact, I think you *should* go home," Rodak said. It was not an order, but a friendly expression of concern, compassion even. He and his cousin were not ready to return to Navharadak. They'd squandered too much of their fortune and were intent on returning in a grand manner. Zalaman thought his share of the remaining gold coins and other loot was sufficient—at least enough to get him home and make him a hero when he did. Maybe he should go back. He'd think about it.

><

Rodak and the others said goodbye to the widow. It was the early summer of 1869. She had grown quite fond of Rodak and cried when they left. It was their fourth summer together, back once again on the path to new territory, but looking for places now where there might be fewer Cossacks, while Zalaman debated with himself. Would Lahkvna be boring? They camped out, hunted, and enjoyed the warm weather. At night the moon shadowed the hills, still showing snowy patches.

"You could both do something less dangerous," Zalaman suggested. "What about all the new rail lines being built? They need workers." Stanko and Rodak both hated that idea—too much work like that was harmful to the body and soul. Zalaman said "So, Stanko, you could be a tailor. Rodak, you . . . you could go into politics."

"You've never had much choice in the matter of going and coming until now," Rodak said. "I'm just saying you've earned that choice now."

Rodak altered their route and for a few days they didn't discuss Zalaman's leaving, though it was on everyone's mind when they were crossing a broad river on a wooden bridge near the town of Beltow. Rodak stopped his horse on the bridge and said the river rolling beneath them was the Ica. He got off his horse and the other two joined him. He pointed out a small barge in the distance. "That boat will be making a stop at the dock just beyond the bridge. Zalaman, if you can talk your way onto that barge, it can take you all the way to the Aiveikste. And the Aiveikste feeds into the The Daugava."

The Daugava emptied into the Baltic at Riga and Zalaman knew that once he made it to Riga, he could make it the rest of the way to Lahkvna, a few days more, a week at most, away.

Rodak's suggestion was sudden. Zalaman wanted to think. Maybe he should consider the opportunity of staying longer with the cousins in order to come home a richer man, someone with even more to offer.

The barge was much larger than it had appeared at a distance. It was getting closer and who knew how long it would stay at the dock? Beltow wasn't a major port by any stretch of the imagination. The barge might unload and load quickly. The situation demanded a decision.

"If I can't talk my way onboard, I can pay for it," he said. That was it. After all the indecision, just saying it was how he made up his mind. He had to see his family. It could be a long journey, but not as dangerous as staying with the Bartoses. Barge travel might even prove enjoyable.

"Come with me," he said, anticipating their answer.

They would see him back in Navharadak or Lahkvna one day. After all he'd been through, Stanko assured him, he had nothing to be afraid of. Rodak handed him a leather purse containing more than Zalaman's share of gold and silver coins, plus a little jewelry—none of the bank notes since he would have difficulty exchanging paper certificates. Paper was something with which Rodak had much more experience, so he and Stanko kept the certificates and gave their friend extra gold and silver. Zalaman hid as much as he could in the inner pockets Stanko had sewed into his trousers and jacket. The rest remained in the leather purse, strapped to his body.

"If you use your head and don't spend it," Rodak said, "when you get home, you will the richest man in Lahkvna. At sixteen! Watch out for ruffians on the way," he laughed, indicating Zalaman need no longer be apprehensive about such things.

From the wagon, Zalaman grabbed the hessian bag with his clothes, rifle, and spyglass. When he was putting the spyglass into his bag, he thought better of it and gave it instead to Stanko, telling him to keep it safe until they saw one another again.

There was no more time for talk. They all embraced. The barge, populated by pigs and chickens with only a small crew and little room for passengers, had passed under the bridge and was tying up to the dock. Zalaman told Rodak to watch Stanko's wound.

"Tell my mom, Pane Bartos—she lives on Czaki Road—that Rodak and I are fine . . ."

"Don't lie to her—but tell her we are safe and will be home soon," Rodak said.

"I hope that's true," Zalaman said. He mounted his horse. Rodak swatted it and the horse carried Zalaman away. He didn't want his young friend—a Jew! He couldn't believe it—to miss this opportunity. Zalaman slowed the horse and turned to yell at them: "If you don't come home, how will I ever find you?" But he was too far away and couldn't make out any response.

CHAPTER TWELVE

Return to Lahkvna

He tucked his purse inside his jacket and rode down to the dock where the barge was already unloading chickens and picking up more pigs. He dismounted, looked back, and waved at Rodak and Stanko standing on the bridge. He couldn't tell if they waved back, but he did see them turn away and disappear.

It was a bittersweet moment. He felt alone, but with it—liberation. It had been three years with the Bartos cousins, so he turned to face his future, which seemed to be the barge. Before looking for the captain, he took the cowboy vest, the thing Stanko had fashioned out of Georg's clothing, and put it on though it looked a bit battered. He stashed his wealth where he could keep it close, vowing to save as much of it as he could so he could distribute it to his family. His repurposed clothing would help make him appear to be poor, a good thing as it would discourage would-be robbers.

Whatever price they were going to ask for the ticket, he would pretend it was a difficult sum for him to pay. He no longer possessed a shred of clothing from his life in Lahkvna. Twice the size now, he'd outgrown everything from that era. But he hadn't purchased much in the way of clothing to replace them. It made for lighter travel. Stanko had altered some of his 'worn' things—'worn' meaning previously used by others, including Cossacks. So, it wasn't hard to look penniless, even if he had enough money to buy the barge, which he didn't. He stood on the quay, staring at the boat. Up close it seemed like nothing more than a huge, floating barnyard. He figured that would mean cheap passage, but he was wrong.

He argued the fee was excessive, but he had little basis for his argument, never having paid for travel, and that might have made his argument sound too tentative. The bargeman lowered his price slightly and told Zalaman he could otherwise look for another barge, although he would end up paying more. He didn't always take on passengers, most of the other barges would not be open to passengers at all. He'd been lucky to find this one, he said.

The fee would take a very small bite of Zalaman's purse. For payment upfront,the bargeman agreed to take him to the Aiviekste, where he could wait with pigs and sheep bound for the Daugava and, eventually, the market piers of Riga. There would be many stops along the way.

Aside from the bleating and oinking and shitting of his four-legged fellow travelers, and the noise and that dust that were stirred up whenever they tied up at a pier for loading and unloading, he remembered the journey as peaceful and less lonely than it might have been, thanks to the friendly bargemen and all those animals. It allowed him to miss Rodak and Stanko a little less. One cow reminded him of Mitti, the Gmerk's cow that had watched over him and Anna making love. His horse was right at home on the boat, part of the menagerie in the hold.

The bargemen introduced him to a new elixir they called *khat* that they added to their tea. After drinking some, he floated even more serenely down the Aiviekste, a tranquil river in any event. The bargemen were transporting the leaves of this plant from Ethiopia. *'Khat'* was the name of the plant, and they always kept a small portion of each shipment for themselves to make their tea. It helped them wile away the long hours between ports and they claimed it gave them more energy, comparing it favorably to marching powder, except that it was more laudanum-like. Zalaman thought they probably meant opium-like, finding it stimulated his brain and made him feel enthusiastic about things like cows and pigs. Marching powder had given him energy and helped with pain, but *khat* made him happy—in the daytime, happy just to be floating down the river with the friendly, smelly animals, recalling all the rivers he'd forded with Rodak and Stanko as he lay among bales of vegetables—including *khat* leaves—the tea worked quite differently, lulling him into a gentle sleep. He could imagine getting very attached to this plant he was now sleeping on, inside and out. He dreamed he was with Davin in ancient Jerusalem. And then Mama, waving a sheet of paper. Maybe it was his message from Syp. He woke before he could find out, but he woke happy. He would know the truth soon enough. Then he worried that if they hadn't received his message, his sudden appearance might scare them to death.

><

By the time the barge slipped past the Ogre and entered the Gulf of Riga, it was mid-summer. They reached the piers after passing by many beautiful buildings, a never-ending parade of wealth and engineering.

At the unloading pier, he thanked the bargemen. They gave him the address of a local *khat* dealer and helped him with his bags once he was back up on his horse. His friends from the livestock world were bawling and oinking as they were being rounded up to disembark. The bargemen suggested Zalaman pay for a carriage and be driven all the way to Navharadak. He could be there in less than a week's time. But though he longed to get home, he decided he would take a day to look around Riga and look up that *khat* seller.

Zalaman rode into the city, stunned by the size of it, remembering his father telling him about getting lost in these same streets when he was hiding from the threats he'd received during the Tailors' Revolt. Zalaman, too, looking for the *khat* dealer, got lost in the maze of streets and alleys. It was by far the biggest city he'd ever seen. Over a hundred thousand souls, according to the bargeman. The buildings were many times larger than grandest in Navharadak or any place he'd been with Rodak and Stanko.

The streets were wider than the length of two Lahkvna *kvadrats*, and they were busy with commerce and carriage traffic, with an endless green park along the Daugava.

Not all of Riga was beautiful. Many of the streets were ancient, dark, and narrow—just wide enough for horse traffic. Zalaman had his weapons, his rifle and revolver, but he hoped not to need them and told himself he would use them only if he was forced to defend his life—or purse.

In the ancient quarter, he noticed a few Jews and realized he had seen only one or two in all the rest of Riga. At the time, he wasn't aware of the Jewish quarter of Maskevas at the southern tip of the city. The Jews he did see looked prosperous enough. He found getting directions was most successful when he used the German language. It seemed by far the language of choice.

The *khat* dealer (he said "*kvaat*") opened the door to his shop, introduced himself and gave Zalaman a sample to try right there, not infused in a tea, but stuffed in a pipe, which he lit with an ingenious flint that looked like a pocket watch. He introduced Zalaman to others smoking at tables and chairs deep inside the shop. These smokers identified themselves as 'Latvian.'

Later that day, he repaired to a saloon with a few of these Latvians, and they introduced him to several who called themselves, specifically 'Young Latvians,' though they didn't look any younger than the plain Latvians. They were politically engaged students who told Zalaman about their hopes for a free Latvia. "Free Latvia" meant free from German oppression, rather than Russian. Despite that, Zalaman was sure Rodak would approve of them and their ideals. And, in fact, one of the Young Latvians, a beautiful and 'young' Latvian, said she did perceive a threat from Russia. The students were optimistic, nevertheless.

The beautiful woman who'd shown some interest in Zalaman, told him that for the time being, the German population in Riga was declining, while the Latvian population was surging.

The *khat* made Zalaman more talkative than normal. He sympathized with the Latvians and shared stories about his travels. He embellished these stories very little but omitted some of the more unsavory parts of his adventures, as he had with Lechsi.

Poppyhead tea was then served, and, when mixed with the *khat*, it produced a feeling of euphoria that made Zalaman fall fatally in love. He was a little too earnest in expressing this and she rebuffed him.

"I hoped you had a more serious purpose than sexual gratification," she scolded him. But even in his heightened state, he caught a hint of potential forgiveness in her tone.

"Political action and sexual satisfaction are both important," he said, recalling, likely conflating, things Rodak had written. "I believe, in fact, that truly effective political action and sexual satisfaction depend on one another . . . they are in many ways the same." He thought this idea might have come from the *khat*. She laughed at him, but he thought she was interested. "Just don't think I am going to bed with you," she said. He said he didn't have a place to stay in Riga, so how could he be trying to get her into a bed. Several cups of tea later, they were in her bed. It was the softest bed he'd slept in since Dzeszow and it was the best love making since Lechsi. He also learned a lot about the young Latvians and their dreams that night, proving his point about political action and sex.

><

In the morning, the *khat* fog cleared from his brain, Zalaman parted on the best terms with the Young Latvian. He was now anxious to get on the road to Lahkvna. Riga was tempting, but he didn't want to give in to its temptations, waste his money. He wanted to enjoy the ride home while it was still nice weather and the *khat* would make everything even better. Midsummer and fall already in the air, he rode much longer than he should have to get out of Riga, but its streets once again perplexed him—perhaps it was the *khat* he'd shared with the beautiful Young Latvian before saying goodbye. He was concerned. He enjoyed getting lost in Riga, its streets teeming with boasting tradesmen, whispering seminarians, swearing, laughing laborers. He watched the watcher: police watching young mothers with babies strapped to their breasts.

Zalaman saw other, slightly older mothers pushing bigger babies in wonderful little wheeled carriages of wicker or wood. Beautiful young women, although none matched his Latvian. And then he came to the river and the directions were clear. He crossed the Daugava and before nightfall was lucky to find a true country inn catering to travelers and their horses and carriages.

The inn took care of Beth. Zalaman had decided, for the sake of saving brain power, to just call this horse Beth as well—and in memory of. Beth was a stinking mess after spending so many days with mostly pigs and goats as companions, so he paid the stableboy to clean her up. Zalaman had an excellent meal and comfortable bed, but he couldn't fall asleep. He tried a bit of his new *khat*, but it didn't help. The life and beauty of Riga was still whirring in his head along with the *khat* and there was no Rodak or Stanko for distraction. There was only the image of the beautiful young Latvian and that finally did the trick. He overslept and almost missed the Inn's breakfast. He rode Beth refreshed and full of confidence. He should have come home sooner. But he justified the three years thinking 'what else could I have done? What choice did I have but to help my friends when they needed me?'

He leaned forward in his saddle as far as his old wound would allow, resting one arm on Beth's neck and promised her that someday they would come back and visit Riga. He was looking forward to seeing Mama and Papa and Davin and Keila and his friends. And he was bringing home money! He wondered if they would recognize him and he took his time. Ten days, riding through ever more familiar landscapes, into the Pale of Settlement at some point, unless it had moved again while he was gone.

He got closer to home and rode along the very road he'd often taken, riding in Papa's cart, in the back with the vegetables. And then he came to the very place where, when he was ten years old and his family was returning to Lahkvna after the nomadic years, the *Weg Heim* had gotten stuck in the snow. That was only six years ago . . .

Zalaman remembered it clearly. A day sometime in the winter of 1863. The *Weg Heim* was stuck in the snow, but it wasn't Shwartzele's fault. The mule would react attentively when Jossel pulled the reins, direct her to the side, and allow horsemen to pass. Shwartzele could also sense that if she got any further to the side, the wagon carrying Jossel, his wife, Lael, and youngest, Keila, would slide off the road and injure her passengers—and possibly herself. Marengo, the Aszer's horse, carried Zalaman and his older brother, Davin, behind the wagon, walking in the ruts made by the wagon. Zalaman had insisted on the name Marengo after learning that was the name of Napoleon's savior-steed. Marengo had little trouble negotiating the snow—the two boys were a light load compared to the heavy wagon and three people Shwartzele pulled. Davin was riding Marengo, but with Zalaman wedged in between the back of saddle and his big brother, hanging on to the smelly wool of Davin's coat to maintain warmth.

All that day it had been cold and snowing. Jossel, Zalaman's father, could take the cold —they all could. But the snow made the *Weg Heim even* more difficult to maneuver than it usually was. In spots, the drifts made the road nearly impassable, narrowing down into two tracks or less. Passing horsemen were forced to push their horses into deep snow to get around the *Weg Heim's* iron-rimmed wheels, a fact they were unhappy about and they weren't hesitant to express their dissatisfaction with, and contempt for, the filthy Jews.

They were so anxious to get to Lahkvna, prepared for an emotional homecoming, that Jossel was driving at night—Zalaman and Davin sharing a saddle on Marengo following in *Weg Heim's* tracks—what had he been thinking? That Shwartzele could see in the dark? The *Weg Heim* slid and got stuck in a drift. It was freezing. They saw no way of getting *Weg Heim* unstuck, short of breaking it into parts. The combined efforts of Marengo and Shwartzele weren't enough to dislodge the wagon and there were no other crazy people on the road that night, so they dug an ice cave in the drift and huddled there together under their blankets and furs. Zalaman thought it was nice and everyone eventually fell asleep.

The next thing he knew, the sun had come up and some passerbys were helping dislodge the wagon. The sun softened the new snow, leaving a paper-thin frozen crust that crinkled so much it muffled the normal creaks and squeaks of the wagon and the clomping of the animals. It was almost warm when Lael pointed out the twin spires of Navharadak's ancient cathedral in the distance.

And there they are. Zalaman smiled now, the towers still standing, of course, since it's been merely six years, but now, remembering Rodak's story about the willful neglect of the towers by the citizens of Navharadak, Zalaman thought perhaps he noticed new cracks. He thought how now, six years after his winter arrival here, maybe everything would look different. Everything *was* different. The family had been worried about losing Davin because he wanted to run off to the Holy Land. Not being very religious, Mama and Papa didn't want to lose their eldest son to biblical nonsense. Although most of those leaving the *shtetl* were emigrating to America, Papa was always declaiming that if Jews started leaving the *shtetl*—wherever they were going—it would be the end of the Jews. Zalaman's Mama didn't want Davin to go either, wouldn't let him, but she disagreed when it came to those departing for America like Heri Benowitz had.

She read to her children stories about foreign lands far outside The Pale—from Pip's London in *Grosser Erwartungen*, Zalaman's favorite, to the wild west of Randall the Trapper.

Mama read to him from her books and serials and journals, stitched and bound or single sheets unfolded from a box, made-up stories, and the histories that she consumed like Papa did hazelnuts and almonds. Battles of good and evil like the pretend fights Zalaman and his friends fought in the *kvadrat*. She translated Russian into Yiddish while she read. She said the Poles were the best writers—especially the Jewish ones.

Zalaman could still remember how, late that winter day in 1863, the day that had started off with their getting stuck in the snow, when they finally got to Lahkvna and home, Marengo and Schwartzele both picked up their pace, looking forward to the lean-to between the Aszer's house and the next-door neighbor, which was their favorite stable, where they would be fed and cared for in the space warmed by the two houses that formed the two sides of their shelter—two leaning, crooked, timbered and stone-and-mortar houses. The sway of the Aszer's place was the norm in Lahkvna where houses and shops had long settled into their own natural configurations.

There was a big celebration with the neighbors when they got home. Minya Benowitz said there was still no word from Heri. The only other thing Zalaman remembered from that celebration was his father's promise. He would no longer antagonize the authorities—like the DPPO. Zalaman remembered it clearly because Papa had qualified the declaration with "if I can help it." Mama said "of course, you can help it, now . . ." Everyone in Zalaman's family knew what Mama was referring to, or rather to whom she was referring. That same Heri Benowitz from whom there was no word—Papa's friend, who had also been his partner in complaints about those in power, had disappeared and was thus no longer around to encourage him.

Zalaman rode under the shadows cast by the towers and emerged into the sunlight of the Christian city: Navharadak, home of Rodak and Stanko—and Stanko's mother, Pane Bartos, who Zalaman had promised to visit at their house on Czaki. He wouldn't ride by there now because he would see her when he could see her. But he *would* pass by Hadar's house. Why not? It was on the way to Lahkvna.

He slowed Beth as Hadar's came into view. He didn't find it quite as impressive as he had five years earlier, when he met Hadar. He'd seen nicer houses in Riga. But, still, it was a grand house amid the few grand houses of which Navharadak could boast. He looked up at the uncurtained windows but saw no signs of life. One day in 1864, his mother had brought him to this house, the house of the Trade Commissioner. The same who would one day, in just a year's time, grant Zalaman's father a valuable license, allowing Papa to create his liquor dispensary—all thanks to the machinations of Zalaman's mother and thanks to Zalaman, as well. The commissioner's wife, Hadar's mother, befriended Lael as a result of their common interest—reading—that led to Lael being admitted to Aleska's Christian women's reading group. She was a non-practicing Jew, but a Jew, nonetheless, and thus an oddity in the group. Aside from Lael's friend, her one-and-only and the wife of the disappeared Heri Benowitz, the Jews of Lahkvna were insular, speaking Yiddish exclusively, and exhibiting a fear of the Christians of Navharadak that Lael simply didn't share.

The first time Zalaman accompanied Mama to that grand house, she'd gone in order to exchange reading material with Aleska. It was his earliest memory of venturing into the Christian city whose buildings were symmetrical and sturdy; the streets, not dirt, but nicely cobbled or planked. Zalaman had already seen marvels for someone his age.

Few eleven-year-olds had families that wandered like his. But wherever he'd been, whatever he'd seen, he'd never been in any house nearly as grand as the Trade Commissioner's. His mother was talking to Aleska about the reading material they were exchanging, when Hadar entered the room. Zalaman may have only been eleven, but love has no age limit. He laughed now to remember how he fell instantly in love with the tall girl with wild, dark, red hair cascading over a heart-shaped face with bright blue eyes like none he had ever gazed into. Somehow or other, he couldn't remember how it had happened that he and Hadar had started walking around Navharadak together. He remembered once planting a kiss on her lips and how she'd made a face and didn't kiss him back. But then she'd smiled and said she hoped she would see him again. But his foremost memory of that infatuation was of the time he had brought her home, causing great consternation when his parents found out her parents had not been informed. The reason he remembered this so well was the surprise he'd felt to learn he'd done a bad thing, surprised that Papa—who did not attend shul or temple—believed friendship should be limited by religion. That's how Zalaman remembered it, though it was not 'friendship,' it was love, and that was a different thing. Now Zalaman laughed to recall how he'd figured at the time that Papa would appreciate the potential benefits of his son's love for Hadar. "You should see their house," he'd bragged at the dinner table to Papa and Mama and his brother and sister. Papa nodded, he knew the house and Zalaman said,

"If Hadar and I got married, we could all move in." Zalaman got a big laugh from everyone, yet when Hadar's father awarded Papa with his alcohol license, everyone who'd been at the table later remembered Zalaman might have had some influence. Zalaman liked to think he did.

Now a full-blooded partisan, as he entered the *shtetl* on Beth, Lahkvna didn't appear to have changed much—except that everything seemed smaller, as had Hadar's house. Lahkvna wasn't what you would call an 'eternal *shtetl*,' but it was old. As he saw it, Lahkvna's crumbling architecture—after the shiny opulence of Riga—seemed to suggest a different kind of permanence, not decay, something ancient yet mutable.

Like his family in its nomadic years, Lahkvna, the *shtetl* was moveable. Sometimes, it would be in Galicia and then, the next thing you knew, it would be in the Duchy of Lithuania, or Poland, or in a disputed territory with no certain allegiance or permanent name. Talking, that is, arguing about disputed territory could turn discussants into combatants. People who had been united for years by their hatred of the Tsar (before a new Tsar started bestowing favors)—Poles, Galicians, Lithuanians, Jews, you name it—could, at the same time, hold conflicting opinions on the subject of dominion. At this time, the region, known as Courland or Kurland, was within the Pale of Settlement, an area Imperial Russia had decreed as "safe for Jews," who could, perhaps, not be legal landowners, but could at least be considered permanent residents. Around the time of Zalaman's birth, the Decree of The Kurland Dukedoms had been enacted which had the effect that many Jews were forcibly moved from place to place to enable the Governor in Jelgava to show his Russian overlords that there were more Jews or less Jews in a certain region, depending on the Tsar's wishes. In Lahkvna, at the time of Zalaman's return from the Uprising, the Jews of Lahkvna accounted for nearly a third of the 5,000 who made up 'greater' Christian Navharadak. The Jews were fully integrated into the economy and none more so than Papa. Not all was brotherhood and good-will, but for the most part, aside from the terrors of Easter, and the depredations of the DPPO, inter-communal relations between Christians and Jews were good. In Lahkvna, unfortunately, The Department for the Protection of the Public Order was the fiefdom of Officer Linnards.

Before he reached his house, he had to cross the kvadrat—the town square and center of the *shtetl's* principal commerce: news and other gossip. Some things hadn't changed: Osher and Henzel were still there, haranguing the crowd. And there at the far end of the *kvadrat* was Doozy Kurtsak, the crazy wooden chicken, still guarding the Benowitz' butcher shop. Next to home itself, the Benowitz' butcher shop was the closest thing Zalaman had to home, where his best friends, Ev and Aron, lived with their mother Minya Benowitz. After the father and Jossel's best friend, Heri, had disappeared, the new butcher and, later, stepfather to Ev and Aron, Adnon, appeared on the scene. It was Adnon who had taught Zalaman his butchering skills. But when Heri Benowitz was still living in Lahkvna, he and Jossel, the two least religious Jews in the *shtetl*, were the most active denouncers of Russians.

The Christian citizens of Navharadak thought of the Russians as oppressors, but it was the local Kurland authorities who carried out the orders of the Grand Duke and the Tsar, issuing edicts and warrants and other feared official papers along with permits and taxes and helping, by hook or by crook, to supply the Russians with their quota of soldiers. The same could be said of the *kahals* that made decisions regarding the *shtetl* society. Among the officers of the DPPO, Linards distinguished himself in his hatred of the Jews by priding himself in his tolerance. He would tolerate their repulsive eccentricities to have their support in maintaining public order. And he'd noted the change in Jossel who, since the disappearance of Heri Benowitz, had been heard praising the new proclamations by Alexander II, the giver of new rights, improving life in the Pale.

When they resettled in Lahkvna in 1863, Jossel promised Lael to mind his manners regarding politics, but since then he'd broken his promise many times over, complaining, loud enough for all to hear, usually with his friend and co-conspirator Heri, about the unfairness, the corruption of the Russians and their local arms.

The night before he disappeared, Heri had been extolling his vision of America—Chicago to be specific. He'd read all about Chicago in a novel Lael had given him—*Randall the Trapper*. It was a wonderland where Randall spent the considerable wealth he made trapping fur-bearing animals and avoiding the American Indians. That was the life Heri dreamed of—not a dreary *shtetl* under the Tsar's boot.

"What evil angel," he'd asked, shouting his frustration that night in the presence of 'sympathetic' listeners,' "had the sense of humor to give these DPPO criminals such a name? 'Protection?' 'Public Order?'"

"Perhaps that angel on the Navharadak coat of arms," Jossel answered.

"That's an evil angel. A sword in one hand. What's in the other?"

"The severed head of a Jew?"

Everyone one agreed that must be the case, although, in fact, the armored angel of Navharadak held a sword in one hand and in most renderings, such as those stitched onto the caps of the DPPO, there was nothing discernible in the other, just the angel's index finger pointing toward heaven.

The next morning Heri hustled Minya out of the house, sending her on a long errand to Navharadak, and everyone later agreed it was probably because he knew trouble was coming and wanted to spare her the sight of his being hauled away by Linards. But in Navharadak, the authorities, Linards included, swore they knew nothing of Heri's whereabouts, and in fact grew suspicious over his disappearance. Jossel was convinced his friend had finally made good on his threat to go to America—on his own—and why not, Jossel thought, since no one else, Minya included, had seemed interested in leaving.

Various theories, some involving the authorities, others not, evolved over the year and a half later when his letter from America arrived.

Zalaman remembered few details about the letter—how the Jews were treated better than the Germans or Irish in Chicago; how there were still wild Indians, and how he saw Black Africans, but what he saw mostly was factory workers; how he was in demand in a town where the railroads brought in hogs and cattle every day, so that he'd become a butcher of large beasts, where meat was a part of every meal. But he remembered listening, as his father read it out loud to Minya and thinking how odd it was that Heri had written to Jossel, rather than to Minya, though it had something to do with Heri's guilt and embarrassment.

What Zalaman mostly remembered though, as he stared at the second-floor window of the butcher shop from the *kvadrat,* was how, years ago, he was looking out of that same window, staring out at where he now stood. Zalaman had stared out the narrow front window of the Benowitz' apartment, listening to Heri's letter thinking how fine it was to have a view from the second floor, when two floors were the maximum height of structures in Lahkvna. The Benowitz' front, second floor window provided a good vantage point, overlooking the *kvadrat.* The window glass distorted the passersby below, who wavered as if they were underwater, maneuvered around one another on the plank sidewalk like fish in a stream. It was fascinating. Now, looking up from the *kvadrat,* he remembered how this distortion had added to the magic of Heri's adventures. They were like the stories he had heard from his mother. Grand adventures about leaving places like Lahkvna for faraway places. Today, on his return, he chuckled a bit and thought about how adventures really do happen—especially if you happen to have the misfortune of being snatched by a *chapper*.

Zalaman walked Beth to his house, but on the way, passed his father's liquor dispensary where he'd been snatched three years before. He was relieved that it was closed as he didn't want to be discovered just wandering around the streets, rather than coming straight home after a three-year absence, but he was reassured by the shiny, outward appearance of the place and a solid new sign: "Purveyors of Superior Krupnik."

When the commissioner had needed assistance with such things as carting produce on the Jewish sabbath when other God-fearing Jews refused to do any work, Jossel had no such compunctions. In the fall of 1865, in line with the deepening relationships between Lael and Aleska, Hadar and Zalaman, the commissioner called Jossel into his office. Jossel had been doing more and more work for the commissioner, mostly carting and other odd jobs and he was relieved when the commissioner smiled at him. "The Tsar," the commissioner said, "in his wisdom and compassion" (he grinned and raised his brow at the mention of 'compassion,' as if the compassionate nature of the Tsar might be called into question), 'in his wisdom' . . . has opened some concessions to the Jews of the Pale. And to you, Jossel Aszer, I am giving the license to be the exclusive purveyor of alcohol to the Jews of Lahkvna—*and* to the Christians on Sundays." Sundays Christians should be praying, certainly not selling alcohol. It was forbidden. Not for Jews.

And so Jossel got his exclusive license and the Aszers prospered, albeit modestly. Papa grew even less critical of the Tsar.

The 1863 Polish Uprising was declared over. "They should give up and make up," he'd said. "It's all just politics." When Zalaman and Davin had first started working for their father, Zalaman had not been fond of alcohol. In fact, he hated the tastes of all the forms it took. He'd cringe when, based on some dare, he would have to take a sip of *krupnik*, the honey-spiced vodka so beloved by all.

Jossel made the boys promise to never take more than a sip. To do so could be dangerous and detrimental to business. But Zalaman grew to hate the krupnik less and less. Once the burning liquid had moved down to warm his stomach, the potion left a sweetness in his mouth, like candy. He discovered his father had been right that he shouldn't take more than one sip when once, despite his promise to his father, he tried a second sip, and then a third. He didn't like the tipsy feeling which ensued and it threatened to put him to sleep. But he wasn't going to give up so easily. Just to be sure it was the *krupnik* (it was tasting better and better), he tried a bigger portion and, instead of falling asleep, he threw up till the *krupnik* and everything else in his stomach had been ejected. From then on, it was no more than a sip. Until Rodak and Stanko.

He led Beth on until they came to his house. He could tell his family was inside from the sounds, his father's voice, and the smells, Mama's cooking. If he'd been blind, he still would have known this was home. If anything appeared to have shrunk, it was his little house and the tilt seemed a bit more exaggerated. His heart was pounding. It was nearly unbearable to stand there. But he hesitated at the door. Should he knock? No, he simply opened the unlocked front door.

Papa in his favorite chair started to get up when the door opened. He was not standing quite so upright as Zalaman remembered—like the house, he was a little more bent.

They stared at one another, Papa looking right through him at first, not speaking, either not recognizing him or dumbstruck with recognition. But how could he recognize Zalaman dressed so unusually, his face covered in new facial hair—sparse but it was dark enough—and grown to twice the size he'd been three years ago?

Zalaman was met with disbelief, then joy, then anger, followed by more joy and more anger—emotional shifts occurring within the first minutes of his homecoming. Keila's mouth dropped and she blinked, then gasped, recognizing him right away but couldn't believe her eyes and blinked again. Mama stuck her head in the room to see why it had grown suddenly so quiet and instantly let out a shriek like nothing anyone had ever before heard from her. They fell into one another's arms and cried, stopping every now and then to look at Zalaman to make sure it was true. "It's really me," he assured Papa, looking at each one to make sure it was true. Everyone had aged, but no one had changed as much as Keila, who was now a young woman. Neither Mama nor Papa had aged appreciably in three years. Papa looked a little older, only because for the past few years Zalaman had been picturing him at a younger age when he carted Zalaman around with the vegetables. Mama had just a bit more grey in her hair.

Zalaman had never seen her cry like this.

"Could we all stop crying for a moment?" he asked. "I hoped this would be a thing of joy. Maybe I shouldn't have returned."

"Where in God's name have you been!?" Papa demanded. "That's a very long story."

We've got all day," Mama said. " "And night," Keila added.

"Did you get my note?" They had not. "Where's Davin?"

Zalaman couldn't believe Davin had been taken by a *chapper* when trying to rescue his little brother. But maybe it wasn't true. They knew only that Davin had gone after him and had been missing since then! Zalaman shuddered, imagining how he might have passed by his brother at some point and mistaken him for a Russian soldier. Papa assumed that the same the chapper who took Zalaman had taken Davin. Now Zalaman assured them it wasn't so. He'd never seen Davin.

"The two priests who came into the dispensary before you were taken?" Papa said, nodding his head, because he had thought about this so many times over the last few years, "I think they snatched Davin." Papa took responsibility for both *chapperings*, blaming his inattentiveness.

"Perhaps he escaped then," Zalaman said, though he very much doubted it could be true, "and he's in Jerusalem." Keila nodded with approval at her brother's attempt to invent something positive, but Mama and Papa looked doubtful, so Zalaman tried to comfort them. "You never know, it might be so. Look at me," he said. If he'd survived, Davin could too.

Zalaman couldn't imagine any reasons other than bad ones that would make Davin leave Lahkvna without saying goodbye. What Zalaman had done by returning home was unheard of outside the world of unsubstantiated gossip. No one survived the *chapper*. He gave his family an account of how he had survived the *chapper*, followed by an even more cursory account of the time since with Rodak, Stanko and the Uprising.

Neither courier nor telegram had ever arrived from Syp. Zalaman assured his parents he'd gone to a lot of trouble to send them a reassuring message. But they couldn't understand how, having been freed from the *chapper* after only a few days of captivity, it had taken three years to return home. Zalaman stretched the truth about certain aspects of those years to justify his long absence. He told them that if he'd tried to escape, it would have been a death sentence.

"It was always crawling with Cossacks. I didn't even know where I was. Plus," he said, looking at his father, "I had an obligation to these partisans for saving my life."

'Your higher duty is to your parents,' Jossel and Lael both wanted to say, but didn't, not wanting to spoil the moment. It could wait.

"The more I listen to you, the more I start to recognize you under all that hair," Mama said. "And so big! A mother never forgets her son so, unlike Papa, of course I recognized you immediately, it was just . . ." She stopped and hugged him again then she laughed. "All the time you were gone I believed you were alive and if you were, you wouldn't take the stories of derring-do I was always reading to you, too literally."

Zalaman—thinking Pip and Werther, and Robin Hood—assured her that the tales she told had served him well enough and might even be credited with his living through situations in which his life had been in jeopardy. Mama gasped and put her hand over her mouth. Zalaman, mourning Davin, started to cry for Davin and feelings of guilt over his disappearance. The others comforted him and he knew he'd done the right thing to come home.

Lael hugged him so hard it hurt his chest wound. She made him show her the scar. It was an ugly one, despite Flora Gmerk's best efforts.

"Your face, too," Mama said. "You've scars, cuts there, that's for sure."

"Just some splinters," he said. "I've brought back something for each of you."

He showed them the gold and silver coins, and the jewelry. Mama gasped again, Keila too. Papa looked suspicious. How had he come by such wealth? He said it was "legitimately" his. "Ours, I mean. And I worked very hard for it."

"Did you learn how to shoot?" Papa asked, eyeing his son's handgun and fancy new rifle.

"I learned how to shoot," Zalaman confirmed. Papa raised his eyebrows and nodded, putting two and two together. Shooting and the fortune.

That first night home, they talked and laughed and cried. Keila did much of the talking and Zalaman marveled at her transformation. What a difference between eleven and fourteen when perceived in an instant. She joked about Papa's cushy job as alcohol purveyor to the Christian community and Papa mentioned his concern about the Trade Commissioner's health (not good). They talked about Davin, focusing on the possibility, signaled by the return of Zalaman, of his return, too. Zalaman finally acquiesced to their questions and told them of his adventures with Rodak and Stanko, albeit without details regarding battles, blood, women. Papa couldn't understand how a Jew, *why* a Jew would get involved in fighting and killing with Polish Christian partisans, even if they had rescued him from the *chapper*, but Zalaman just said he had no choice in the matter, and they accepted that answer—for this evening—though Jossel was skeptical.

Mama told Zalaman how she'd dropped out of her reading circles—along with life in general—out of her grief over her boys but had recently gotten back to reading. It was a good way to hold the sorrow at bay. "I was sure neither you nor Davin were ever coming back," she said. "I knew life wasn't like a book of fiction. Life wasn't joyful conclusions. Stories of 'return' were just stories—stories of redemption, like wishes. I resigned myself to that attitude, feeling that if I kept hoping for something else, for you and your brother to come back—I would go crazy."

Papa admitted to having become very agitated, early on, wondering how Heri and then Adnon had been able to keep Ev and Aron safe from the *chappers*, while he, Jossel, had lost both of his sons. There was an inequity here—and with him being the Tsar's official liquor dealer. He had complained to the *kahal*, but the *kahal* claimed innocence in the matter, insisting, in defense, that they had no control over such things.

Zalaman asked him about Heri, but there was nothing new to tell. "He still sends letters to your father," Lael explained, "but not to Minya. Minya is no longer interested. Minya has Adnon now." The story made Zalaman think of the woman he and the cousins had stayed with after Rodak had killed her husband and how she'd fallen in love with Rodak precisely for that act.

They drank a fair amount of alcohol that night. Jossel had his own theory of why Ev and Aron might have had a kind of protected status vis-a-vis *chappers*: Linards' lust for Minya, despite her unashamed hatred of the man. "She despises Linards as always," Papa said and sighed. "Heri was my friend, but he abandoned me too, not just Minya, Ev and Aron. It's been eight years now since he left. I still miss him . . . but I think of him less and less."

It made Zalaman think about Rodak and Stanko. He didn't miss them constantly—but he was more than aware they were missing. He was surprised he felt that way having just been reunited with his real family.

Zalaman brought out his *khat*, telling them that if they wanted to stay up any later, they should try some, but they were not interested. Jossel was horrified. He had heard of this 'elixir's' affect and considered its use an affliction. Mama agreed, but Keila was curious. Zalaman apologized and hid the *khat* away. He hoped his father was sufficiently under the influence of the alcohol that he would forget all about it.

He asked about Hadar, the daughter of the commissioner—"The one you kicked out of the house"—and Keila said that Hadar was now practically betrothed to a distant relative. This bit of information was from the infallible lips of Osher and Henzel.

Zalaman smiled—some things never changed—when Mama said, "Don't worry about her. You can find a Jewish girl in the *shtetl*. Look at you—big, smart, handsome—even wealthy you say. You will find a respectable Jewish girl to marry."

An hour or so before sunlight, when he lay down on his old bed, it felt too small. He was a little drunk, but it wasn't the alcohol that kept him awake and made everything look so small. The night with the lovely Latvian woman in Riga was the last time he'd slept indoors and in a bed. He'd come to love sleeping outdoors, especially on the nights when the air was warm and full of flowers like this one. He would have gone outside to sleep, but on the Aszers' street there was nowhere to go that wasn't hard and rocky or you wouldn't put yourself in danger of being run over by a carriage or trampled by a horse.

The next day, he distributed the contents of his purse. He kept half of the gold coins for himself, just like he and the Bartos boys had before distributing their goods to the Uprising and the Commandant at Syp. They were grateful but weren't sure what to do with their new wealth. Jossel and Lael hid the coins and jewelry. There would be a time they might need them. Papa would love a carriage, but Mama thought it would not be a good idea to put on a display. Especially now, when Zalaman had just just returned—from the dead. Too much good fortune—his resurrection and the Aszers' sudden wealth—would be suspect.

Once they were alone, Papa told Zalaman he was concerned about how he had achieved such wealth. It didn't seem to Jossel that the Uprising, failure that it had been, should prove so lucrative. But he was 'a practical man' and accepted his share. Mama did not appear to be troubled by any misgivings—she and Keila were simply grateful.

Then Zalaman went to see Ev and Aron. He was less circumspect in telling them his adventures and they were awestruck. "We wondered where you might be fighting—if you were still alive," Ev squealed, giddy with joy and laughter over Zalaman's resurrection, "but you were fighting *against* the Russians, not for them." Zalaman didn't quiz them about Heri, but noticed his return gave them a glimmer of hope for their father, just as it had given his own family some hope for Davin. Someday, they said, we'll go to America and look for Heri.

When he left the Benowitz brothers, he took a quick ride on Beth, but soon dismounted to better inhale *shtetl's* familiar sounds and smells. It would be best not to advertise his return, so he avoided the *kvadrat*. But he wasn't going to slink around, either. If there had been any stories about the death of a *chapper* named Georg, they would have been long forgotten. However, it would be best not to have any dealings with the DPPO. He didn't really know if he was guilty of a crime. At least in the eyes of the *shtetl*. Everywhere he looked he saw Davin's shadow.

><

He went to Navharadak and introduced himself to Pane Bartos. She welcomed him in and insisted he call her Elizavetta.

He told her Stanko and her nephew Rodak were safe and sound, though "sound" might have been stretching the truth, glossing over the true story, but then they probably weren't playing it 'safe' either. Elisavetta was more than grateful for his assurances; she said she couldn't thank him enough and brewed them what she called English tea. As they sat in her small, tidy kitchen and drank the tea, she said that she appreciated his consideration of her age but said she wanted to hear everything. Zalaman didn't want to do that, but he did tell her how her son and nephew had saved his life, omitting the more unattractive details of the rescue. He told her about his life with Stanko and Rodak in farmhouses and inns and on the road—and some of the fun they'd had there. He didn't talk about the Uprising until she lost patience with harmless anecdotes and said she liked it all, of course, but didn't want to hear "any prettied-up version."

So Zalaman told her about the amputation of Stanko's leg. She sobbed, "I was worried about bullets and sabers, not snow" and chastised herself for not having foreseen this possibility.

Perhaps if she had, she could have prayed for his limbs, too. She laughed at herself, but before long she was crying again. She wiped her eyes and asked about him, Zalaman, "Why would a Jewish man, a handsome one at that, be inclined to support the Uprising with those two? Rodak has never hidden his contempt for your race. He's been fighting in this never-ending Uprising forever. Decades now."

He reminded her about Rodak and Stanko saving his life and said Rodak had changed with respect to his attitudes about Jews. "That would speak well of you," she said, just a bit skeptical.

After saying she didn't want to talk about Rodak, she started talking about Rodak—"there's no avoiding it." She poured more tea and told Zalaman she thought the Uprising was doomed from the start. She blamed Rodak for encouraging his 'not-so-innocent'—I know, 'little'—not so little—cousin to join him in this crusade. "Stanko, my boy, he should have known better, but I don't blame Rodak for Stanko's choice. Stanko has his own mind. And Rodak, well, he's only following his dream. He warned Stanko it would be dangerous, although I suspect he knew that would only attract Stanko more. When they came back on their furlough a few years ago—must have been when you were taken—Stanko sounded as committed a partisan as Rodak. They made a profit and that helped.

"You showed good sense to leave. You stay here now and be with your family. I've never had anything but admiration for your people, no matter what some priests say. I have always been treated fairly by the Hebrew race. There is a lot of anti-Jewish sentiment here in Navharadak—but of course you know that—how could you have missed it!"

"I'm sure some Jews, stuck away in their *shtetls,* only hear bad things about Poles, but there is good and bad in all people. Rodak's hatred for the Jews? It's a thing—the only thing—he inherited from his father." Zalaman assured her that Rodak had reformed, but she continued with her story. "It was a farm accident," she said. "There was a fire when Rodak was only seven. He lost his mother and family. Only Rodak and his dad, Etz, my brother, survived. Etz was not the best father, but he raised and fed the boy. Fed him a lot of hate, too. Rodak was the only one there when Etz took his last breath—and his last breath was a curse. It's hard to fathom, but he told Rodak that Jews had started the fire that took his wife and other children. And now, he told Rodak, convinced he'd been poisoned, 'they're killing me, too.' Etz blamed the Jews for everything, any bad luck he had over the years, Jews were responsible. It wasn't his fault if the crops failed. Naturally they were going to be responsible for his death as well. So, he uttered one final curse on the Jews—that was his legacy to Rodak. Of course, the church didn't help. His aunt, my sister, used to drag him there every Sunday and I'm sure they only confirmed what Etz had told him."

"I don't think the church part stuck," Zalaman said, and told her he would come to see her again, before the cousins returned wealthy men, as they'd promised to do. She found the wealthy part doubtful, but said she appreciated hearing it.

Zalaman quickly reintegrated into *shtetl* life, aided by the *khat*. Mama and Papa were intent on finding a suitable betrothal for him, something that would keep him in Lahkvna in case he ever got the itch to travel, something suggested by his frequent dreams of Riga. He vowed he would stay put and help through the winter. And after? Mama would ask. Zalaman was noncommittal. He knew he wouldn't be able to spend his life in Lahkvna. He'd seen too much. He would only promise that he wouldn't go anywhere before the spring.

And in the winter, he applied himself to learning more about butchering, having Adnon show him all he knew. Aside from time with Adnon and visiting Ev and Aron, there were visits with Pane Bartos, Elizavetta. He spent the rest of the time that entire winter enjoying the company of his parents and sister. Early in the winter, before the heavy snow, Elizavetta visited Zalaman and his family in Lahkvna and they got along well.

He did meet some girls his own age through Lael but he never took up the challenge of seeing any of them more than once. He thought doing so would commit him to life as a butcher in Lahkvna.

Memories of that winter would always be colored by what was to come with the melting of the snow, echoes frozen in time as a snow-white idyll. He was alert for *chappers*, wondering if anyone had ever been snatched twice. He thought about this especially when he went back to help Jossel at the alcohol dispensary.

And when he wasn't working, carrying jugs and casks for Papa, helping Mama and Keila cook, he experienced a new feeling of joy. Freedom. A burden was gradually being lifted. He had to be on the alert for *chappers*, perhaps the DPPO and Russians, but all-day-and-night-caution was unnecessary. He enjoyed the simple pleasure of walking in the snow when he didn't have any place he had to go to. Sometimes, he carried a firearm, thinking he might see a winter hare and pick it off like he had on horseback outside Punie. He'd take it to Adnon's to show him what he'd learned about skinning rabbits and then cook it for his family.

As he walked, he sipped *khat* tea from a small, blue stoneware flask he'd picked up from a merchant in Dziedzow. He picked his way through the slippery streets and icy pathways of Lahkvna to open country where he would find himself in fields of snow blanketed in places by higher drifts of even more snow. When the sun broke through the clouds and sparkled on jewels woven into dazzling sheets, he was happiest. The heavenly tea helping him avoid seeing everything as tainted by the absence of Davin. He walked on, the melting snow soaking his trousers from the knees down. Having drunk an excessive amount of the tea one day, he was wet and exhausted when he spied Stanko's missing leg sticking out of a nearby snowdrift. He plodded laboriously towards it, through deep snow, until it became clear it was only a birch branch half buried in the snow.

He didn't mind the cold when there when was a nice, warm home with Mama's cooking waiting. Lael would draw him a hot bath, a luxury they normally reserved for Fridays, but she couldn't deny him the pleasure she knew it gave him. He felt so at peace in that bath, he allowed himself to think he was someone who had actually returned from the dead, and then remembered something the cousins had said after one bloody battle. "Death," Stanko had said, "must be so wonderful, no one ever wants to come back."

"You think there's a choice? You can come back if you want to?" Rodak laughed. "It's eternal." Zalaman laughed at the memory, laying back in the warm water. He had only just turned seventeen, but he'd seen enough death to feel there was quite possibly nothing at all in the end. If you believed that, killing another man was a very heavy responsibility. So Zalaman felt good about having resolved to never kill another human being—unless someone was trying to kill him. He only had to stay away from situations that might require violence. Should Rodak and Stanko return, they would not be happy with his resolve. Despite that, he hoped they would return.

Working with Papa in the liquor store gave Zalaman plenty of time to explain his life with the Bartos cousins without Mama hearing anything. He revealed a number of less-than-lovely memories. Jossel decided Rodak and Stanko were nothing but a couple of bumblers who achieved nothing. Common criminals. Zalaman decided he had botched the job of making his father see. He'd made up his mind and that was that. But one day when spring had definitely arrived and Zalaman had had at least two sips of *krupnik,* he told his father that despite what he felt about Rodak, Stanko and the Uprising, when he was with them, he'd seen real bravery. Something in the way he said it made Jossel stop and regard his son. He nodded that he understood, albeit with a grim expression. “I will never again kill anyone,” he promised his father.

Chapter Thirteen

Childhood's End

Full-blown spring and melting snow made walking easier in some places, sloppier in others. On Easter morning, Zalaman had taken a longer than normal excursion, starting early to avoid the infernal bells of the new Navharadak church. It was a holiday that never meant good things for the Jews. Osher and Henzel had been warning the people of Lahkvna all week that they should stay indoors. But such warnings were as normal for Easter in the *shtetl* as messages of Jesus' resurrection in Navharadak.

The fields were still too frozen to start planting, but the sun was starting to thaw things as Zalaman traipsed through the mud, trying to be careful of his clothes, determined to restrict the unavoidable muck to the soles of his new boots—purchased from the best cobbler in Lahkvna using his own earnings. The shoemaker gave him a special price, or so the man claimed, telling Zalaman it was in recognition of the support his Papa had shown the tailors during that yarmulke war against the Jewish elites.

It was such nice spring day, so promising with its green shoots, that Zalaman felt like bathing in golden sun after a long winter, before he realized it was already afternoon. He picked up his pace, just in case there was any trouble—it was Easter, after all—and he might be needed at home. Papa and Mama and Keila would be staying inside to avoid any of the taunting they might encounter from the Christians of Navharadak—Christians looking for trouble. Rodak had warned Zalaman that Easter violence was on the rise and Zalaman himself had witnessed it in Dzeszow. A good day for Jews to stay safe inside while the Christians prayed in their church. The problem was that after church, some liked to come outdoors and drink and mourn the loss of their Savior. That was usually as far as it ever went. Papa had mentioned that the taunts on Easter had in recent years become more aggressive. So, that morning, Jossel had bolted the door and, just as a precaution, had hung the window with black crepe.

><

The church bell in Navharadak pealed in Easter celebration. Not long after, he heard the chant: "*Kristos prisikele . . .*"—"Christ is Risen." The church bells pealed again, and the chanting grew louder. Zalaman began to feel nervous. Not that there was anything threatening. He'd had a nice walk, fortified by the special tea from his blue flask, and now he was pleasantly exhausted—and full of ideas about the possibilities of life in Riga. If he was apprehensive at all, it wasn't about Christians, but worries about Mama's and Papa's reaction when he announced his intentions to them. He figured he could concoct some story that would placate Papa. He had a brainstorm! He would go to Riga to study! He could afford it. He didn't really need his Papa's approval. "It would be better. But he can't stop me," he said to himself.

Zalaman was formulating this story—how best to delude his parents—as he ascended a short hill where he could see the *shtetl* below. His daydream of Riga evaporated, interrupted by the chanting, "*Kristos prisikele!*" growing louder—not coming from the church in Navharadak, but edging closer to Lahkvna and sounding less and less like a joyous announcement, more and more like an angry menace.

From his perch, it didn't take him long to locate the source of the chant: a drunken mob of twenty or so armed men who were now entering Lahkvna. Fortunately, there were very few other people on the streets of Lahkvna. The few Jews who happened to be outside, including Osher and Henzel, who had been in the *kvadrat* all week telling people to stay home on Easter—were grabbed by the rabble and forced to lead their parade. Osher and Henzel had been trying to get an elderly couple off the street to safety, when the rag-tag army grabbed all four of them, tethered them to ropes and prodded and herded them toward the *kvadrat*. He felt for his rifle, securely in it's sheath for rabbit-hunting.

His immediate impulse was to run down the hill, confront this mob and demand they stop before they went beyond humiliation. If he'd learned one thing from Stanko and Rodak though, it was to size up the enemy before acting. They were still singing *Christ Is Risen.* They carried weapons—mostly clubs and long knives, but there were also pistols and a couple of old muskets—and it looked like they were ready to use them. Zalaman recognized some familiar faces—Navharadak authorities, Linards with them. Their presence made this appear to be a sanctioned event.

A few meters below him was an old stone wall. It reminded him of the ones in front of the Gmerk's farmhouse that Stanko and Rodak had used for a blind when the Cossacks came to collect their due. But he still hoped the mob's weapons were for show only, a threat to scare people, rather than to commit actual violence.

There were only three other people outside, as far as he could tell. The rest of the citizens of Lahkvna, like his family, were safe inside their homes, listening to the chanting grow louder and more menacing, the less timid observing it all from behind their closed curtains and locked doors. The three other Jews on the street were a young woman with two young men. They appeared to be laughing or arguing about something, enjoying the spring air and themselves so intensely they were oblivious to the chant—until the parade rounded the corner and it was too late to run. The club-wielding leader of the pack ordered the three to join their motley parade.

Behind the leader with the club and Linards, Zalaman recognized a plainclothes policeman from Navharadak who, like Linards, always threatened the Jews. The Christians were certainly not overly concerned about concealing their weapons, but Linards kept exhorting them to straighten up and not act as if they were drunk. The request was generally ignored. The mob had a mind of its own. They'd been drinking for quite a while, but alcohol was not the real fuel of this rabble—hate was. One of the young men—and, except for Linards and a few others, they were not much older than Zalaman—stumbled drunkenly and fell in the mud. He quickly picked himself up and looked around just to make sure he hadn't given anyone the impression he was under the influence of anything other than his love of Jesus and hatred of his enemies. Two of the men from the DPPO were not hiding their official positions but were actually wearing their caps with the Navharadak coat of arms—the angel in armor, brandishing sword and scale—adding to the sense of this being almost an official proceeding.

Zalaman walked down to the stone wall.

The mob had seven Jews in tow by the time they were approaching the *kvadrat*. They had been expecting to round up a great number of Jews and seemed dismayed to find the *kvadrat* empty. It felt to Zalaman like the horde hadn't yet considered what they might do with the Jews.

The afternoon had warmed the *kvadrat* into a muddy quagmire. Linards invited the seven Jews to relax. "Take a seat in the mud," he told them. When the Jews respectfully declined his offer, he taunted them—"Don't be so fastidious." And then, finally, "That was not a request. It was an order!"

The Jewish men protested. The two young men who been waylaid when they'd been having such a good time with their woman friend, warned their tormentors that they had friends in high places in Navharadak, eliciting laughter from some of the gang and anger from others. Their young woman tried to defuse the situation, asking if someone wouldn't give her and the older woman a hand so they could obey Officer Linards order and sit. Osher and Henzel helped them down and then sat themselves.

The rest grudgingly followed their example, each one gasping as they sank several inches into the slush, eliciting new rounds of laughter from the mob.

"We need more Jews," said one of the leaders.

"No, we need less Jews," laughed another who carried a lethal-looking club.

One of the mob stayed behind to guard the seven Jews in the mud while the others spread out into Lahkvna and started going house to house, demanding people open their doors unless they wanted them broken down. Those who foolishly opened their doors were dragged to the *kvadrat* which was now filling with people—young and old, men, women, and children. Many of them were people Zalaman knew.

He knelt behind the wall and drew his rifle from its sheath as the Jews stuck in the mud were told to strip. None of the people in the *kvadrat* moved. So, the man with the big club, who'd seen his request for "more Jews" richly fulfilled, selected one of the young Jewish men to demonstrate how he could use his weapon. He clubbed the man, again and again. It had started. Zalaman took aim at the man. He was big and offered a good target. But Zalaman noticed others getting up and disrobing, as the gang made hilarious and demeaning jokes concerning naked bodies. There was a pale, slender girl, a friend and contemporary of Keila's, trying to cover herself with her arms. One of the Christian mob grabbed her and started carrying her off—much to the delight of the gang—but he fell face down in the mud, releasing the girl who ran from the *kvadrat*. The big man didn't get up. They'd barely heard the report from Zalaman's rifle, they'd been making so much noise, but when they saw the blood, Zalaman watched them, pointing in fear toward the wall as he reloaded. That's when he saw Mama, Papa, and Keila, frantic, being dragged into the kvadrat, herded toward the naked group in the mud. Mama had a crazed look on her face that he would never forget. She was pulling fiercely on the hair of her tormentor until Zalaman's bullet pierced the man's midsection. He saw his mother glance toward the wall and he showed himself, waving his rifle, running toward her, Papa and Keila and the gruesome mayhem that now engulfed the kvadrat. He hadn't quite reached them when something crunched onto his head and the stars flashed, only to be swallowed up in a black void where he was oblivious to the crunching, slashing, and shooting that ensued.

When he eventually opened his eyes he saw only more darkness. The sun had gone down. He was alive, mired in the rapidly refreezing kvadrat mud. Quivers of light flared, exposing a nightmare scene of contorted limbs, an arm gyrating in an arc in the flickering torchlight. He was lying in a slaughterhouse, but when he tried to raise himself up to locate his family, he was unable, falling back from the pain in his arm which collapsed under him. Helpless as a turtle on its back, in addition to the arm problem, his head felt like it had been split in two. Then there was only blackness.

He woke in a panic, with the terrible pain in his arm whenever he tried, unsuccessfully, to raise himself. But he managed to stay awake and listen to the moaning and wailing. He joined that chorus, before passing out again.

When he woke the next time, there was Elizavetta Bartos. His brain was so cloudy from the blow to his head, it took him a while to recognize her. She held a torch in one hand, and was trying, as gently as possible, to lift Zalaman with the other. It didn't work because he could offer so little help. She stuck the torch in the mud so she could use both arms. The torch illuminated a deep slice in his right arm and it was still bleeding. She bathed it in cold water, then wrapped it to staunch the bleeding. Zalaman thanked her and she told him that once news of what had taken place reached Navharadak, a few horrified Christians, such as herself, had dared venture out to help. Horrified but brave, he said.

She helped pry him loose from the muck, a feat he couldn't accomplish with one functioning arm. He stood, shaky, in the middle of the carnage. The mob was long gone. The few torches supplied by good citizens of Navharadak didn't illuminate the entire square and that was a blessing. With Pane Bartos' assistance, he searched the monstrous graveyard, clenching his left fist. Moving was tricky in the poor light and with his injuries, but aside from his arm and splitting headache, he believed he was otherwise in one piece. He'd suffered that bang on the head from Georg, and the one from Anna, but this one felt worse. Elizavetta assured him that his head was not in two pieces but that one side was swollen larger than the other. He told her he'd been clubbed just as he saw Mama's frozen look, a look like she was searching for him and then saw him, turned, and attacked her tormentor.

When she found them, Pane Bartos tried to steer him away, in the other direction, but she knew he had to see. At first, he didn't recognize them, they were in such a twisted tangle: Papa, bent protectively, prayer-like, over Keila; Mama face down, one arm stretched out to the other two. Zalaman's knees buckled and Pane Bartos helped lower him gently to the ground. He felt the world had stopped and he couldn't breathe. He wished to go back in time before this. Pane Bartos covered the bodies with her cloak, rearranging them slightly so they looked more comfortable alongside one another.

Zalaman, shivering, got up but fell back to his knees before he finally got up to embrace each one. Mama, Papa, Keila. It had to be a dream, but he was too aware to even think it was not. Everything had changed. Happiness would be gone forever. He sat back on heels only to be treated to the inappropriate, blasphemous beauty of the coming sunrise. He stared as clouds of magenta feathers cleared a space for the sun still hiding under the horizon and dark storm clouds, afraid to face the horror in the scarlet-black muck.

Zalaman told Elizavetta he was alright and thanked her again but told her she should go home. He couldn't leave them, and she said she'd be nearby if he needed her.

She left to help other families. Zalaman didn't know how long he stayed there, shedding more tears, shocked, and immobile.

Later, when the burials took place, the rebbe said the *kvadrat* had been sanctified by the blood. It would no longer be a suitable place for commercial practice. For the Jews that were still planning to stay in Lahkvna—and no one knew how many that would be—the *kvadrat* would be a sacred burial ground. The *shtetl's* ancient Jewish graveyard didn't have room for the large number of the slaughtered, though it was easily over one hundred, and the kvadrat would now be Graveyard Square. Entire families had died, so with no direct family member to say the prayers for them, the mourning became communal—the burying as well. It spread to parts of the Christian community as well once the magnitude of the slaughter became known. Some people from Navharadak, like Elizavetta, came to offer comfort and medical care for the wounded. More Christians came to help than had rampaged on Easter. Zalaman's old girlfriend, Hadar, came with her mother, Aleska, and her father, the commissioner, to pay their respects to Lael and Jossel. They saw Zalaman, and at first didn't approach him. What could you possibly say, that would sound sufficient? But knew they must. The commissioner praised Jossel as Aleska did Lael and Zalaman hugged each other. When he embraced Hadar his emotions exploded, and he was still sniffling when she said goodbye.

He was joined in prayers by Elizavetta and by Minya Benowitz and Adnon. Minya's sons, Ev and Aron somehow escaped from the butcher shop where Adnon had bolted them indoors and went out to fight the Christian mob. They had not escaped the massacre. Zalaman helped Minya and Adnon bury them, although digging with only one arm made him less helpful than he wanted to be. And they helped him with his family, and others as well. Among the survivors, burying and praying, were Osher and Henzel, the two sages of the *kvadrat,* digging where their arena had been. Zalaman and Minya agreed the two old men must be eternals, having escaped with their lives and all their limbs despite being among the first who'd been rounded up.

Digging with his one good arm, he used a shovel he'd retrieved from his house. It was one of the few items he'd been able to salvage, the mob having ransacked his house and many others. He dug like a one-armed automaton, a *golem* with splitting head.

Even with the help of others, it was slow work. It took several days to bury the dead.

Chapter Fourteen

Leaving Lahkvna

A week after the massacre, Zalaman was once again in the mud, shivering, this time in a potato field. He wasn't precisely sure where this potato field was, but he remembered he'd been walking northeast along the Tervete all day yesterday after leaving Lahkvna.

After the burials, although his house had been desecrated and nearly emptied of contents, including the valuables he and his family had stashed but obviously had not hidden well enough, he'd still wanted to stay home. Elizavetta would hear none of it. He would come and stay with her in Navharadak at least until the state of shock subsided. She would feed him and take him to a doctor in Navharadak to see to his head and arm, which would be very lucky for Zalaman, since the two best doctors in Lahkvna were unavailable. One had been killed and the other had fled, leaving one animal doctor who Zalaman considered inferior to Bebchuk and would have been too busy to see him right away anyway. Zalaman's outrage against the people of Navharadak would make staying there difficult, yet he felt he had no choice but to accept her generosity. He would go home soon enough, he thought. He was so exhausted and semi-delirious he had no room in his heart for any feeling other than grief. And so, he allowed her to guide him to her home on Czacki Street.

There were days of nothing much more than doctoring, eating, and trying to sleep. The injuries to his head—his brain intact, it seemed—and arm had started to heal. But as his physical pain diminished, Zalaman's despair increased. He found it impossible to accept what had happened. It couldn't have happened. It was too monstrous. A fury would overcome him.

Pane Bartos pointed out that very few of the citizens of Navharadak had been involved and he knew that was true. He said if Rodak and Stanko had been there, they might have prevented it from happening. But he and Elizavetta had to agree that Stanko and Rodak would have tried to intervene and probably would have ended up dead.

"The men who did it are inhuman," Elizavetta said. "It's like Etz—angry with the Jews about everything. They're stupid! You know they blamed the Jews for the cholera outbreak in West Kurland."

Zalaman wanted to go to his family house, so he told Elizavetta he was going and that he would be back after he spent some time there. "Some time there" sounded unacceptably vague to Elizavetta, but she decided not to push him.

There was no one on the streets of Lahkvna. Maybe everyone had left. It was hard to imagine living Jews wanting to stay in Lahkvna, but he'd heard that most would. What would he do? He still felt like he was one of the dead. The emptiness of the *shtetl* made everything strange, because other than the quiet—the lack of people on the street—everything looked perfectly normal. He skirted the *kvadrat*, because he'd decided to visit the house, then come visit the graves.

It didn't make much sense, but every major piece of furniture—there had been a few—had been destroyed. As he'd noticed days earlier when he'd gone to the house and found the shovel, almost everything else, anything that could be carried away, had been carried away. Papa's rifle was missing from its perch on the wall, while Lael's books were untouched. The secret caches in the walls and floor, where they'd hidden their valuables, Zalaman's included, were empty. He did find his emptied purse.

He imagined what they must have said to Mama and Papa, what threats they might have made, before being herded to the *kvadrat*, to make them reveal their hiding places.

Revenge. It was demanded, but not yet. Not now. When he had the means to do it right. Later, perhaps, he would figure out what that meant—to 'do it right.'

He had nothing. No gold or silver, some items of clothing like his father's greatcoat and old hessian bag and what he'd been wearing that day—everyday clothing and hunting gear. He found two scarves in the house—one of Mama's and one of Keila's. A bar of soap. A small flint that had always been dependable for a spark. The hunting knife he'd held in his hand that day and the rifle. He put them in the hessian bag and carried it all to the stable where he'd kept his horse. But there were no horses and no people there.

He grabbed the hessian bag and headed to cemetery square. He stood at his family's grave and told them what he intended to do. He must have been spared for a reason and the only reason he could come up with, aside from some undefined form of revenge, was to keep their memory alive. He felt it was his duty to achieve something grand, something he could give them. They would say: 'Do not think about revenge now and end up getting in trouble. That wouldn't do anyone any good.' Above all, they would say 'Be careful. Pay attention.'

It took him a long time, thanks in part to the not-yet-healed arm and head, for him to find three reasonably imposing stones, each one nearly as heavy as the one he'd launched over the cliff onto the Cossack. He placed the three stones on the ground where he'd buried his mother, father, and sister. Between each act—selecting the stone, carrying it, positioning it—he would need to sit and catch his breath and steady himself. He thought it was probably a mixture of hard work, the bitterness and sorrow. Others had been doing the same as Zalaman—there were already commemorative stones at irregular intervals around the old *kvadrat*. He faced each stone and scratched in a name with his knife: J O S S E L, L A E L, K E I L A. It was hard work with his injuries, but he kept at it, not stopping until the names were etched deep enough to last.

He got up and dusted off his pants and stood in front of the three stones. He talked out loud to them, promising things he thought they would want to hear and which he could try to deliver. When he'd been etching their names in the stones, he'd promised them he would not give in to despair. Standing in front of them, he said he would try to do something that would make them proud. He said he loved them—and he said a "goodbye for now." In all his life, thus far, he'd never felt so alone.

He carried his bag as he walked away. The *shtetl* was so quiet, though he knew there were still plenty of people here.

He knew from Elizavetta that Minya and Adnon were not leaving. He wanted to just keep walking. He didn't care where. He couldn't leave without saying goodbye to Elizavetta, and to Minya and Adnon. But after saying goodbye to his family, he couldn't bear any more goodbyes. He would just stop and say goodbye to Elizavetta. In Navharadak, people were going about their business as if nothing had happened in Lahkvna.

Elizavetta was not at home, but he could not wait.

He had to leave here where everywhere felt like a graveyard or a mockery of one. He left her a note, thanking her for all she had done and promising he would return.

He walked. Walking was like medicine. Well into the evening, barely aware of what direction he was going, just up the Tervete, away from the source of pain. He kept going until he lay down late that night in a muddy potato field. He was still gripping the knife he'd used to cut potato vines for a mattress, the same he'd used to scratch in the names.

That was the field where he'd awakened this morning, shivering in the mud frozen onto his greatcoat after a night of nightmares involving the mutilations of Cossacks and Jews. It was a large field. The dry vines left there from the previous year's harvest hadn't provided much relief from the cold. He shook off the clingy ones and rose, shaky, stiff, aching, and hungry. He found one small, elderly potato with a wrinkled little face, hanging on to a dried vine he pulled away from his coat. He sniffed. Last year's produce, soft but not rotten. He took a bite. It didn't even taste like a potato. More like dirt. But he put the remainder in his pocket just in case.

There was a line of beeches running along the Tervete, the little river that divided Navharadak and Lahkvna, so Zalaman followed it upstream after turning back first to confirm he was already far enough away that the ruined stone towers of Navharadak were no longer visible. There was no smoke rising from any direction, no sign of a town, just the occasional farmhouse. Walking by the Tervete, he knelt and took a long drink, then rinsed his face and hair of remaining bits of potato and earth. He knew the Tervete flowed east toward the Tset and he got up and followed it in that direction, through woods and farmland, avoiding signs of people.

Long before midday, he gave into his hunger, sat and slowly chewed the rest of the poor little potato. It was so quickly gone, it left him hungrier than he'd been before. The clouds remained dark, but no rain or sleet fell that day.

Night found him in another potato field, looking for a place to throw his coat over the collected vines when he spied movement at his feet. Or perhaps he was delirious and unsteady. Then the field mouse skittered out of a pile of withered vines and hopped away down a lumpy row. Zalaman gripped his knife, but the mouse was long gone. He guessed maybe that was best for both. He had a flint, but he wondered if he could eat a mouse even if it was well-cooked. He was hungry enough to try, so he kicked at the pile of vines in frustration, but no creatures emerged. He stretched out, covering himself with vines as best he could with his barely functional wounded arm.

He cried himself to sleep, crying not from the physical pain, but from trying, unsuccessfully, to picture happier times, a world that no longer existed.

He woke wet, the sky still black as his mood. He'd just been having a dream of Mama—at first, not at all a nightmare—in which she'd been reading to him about Robin Hood from her Yiddish Popular Library series. Rodak and Stanko played Robin and Little John. But when he tried to look at his mother, he couldn't see her face. Was she crying? He woke to rainfall pelting his face, pooling in the folds of his coat. He got up, shivering—cold, wet, sore, and still hungry. *Khat* or marching powder would have helped, he thought, helped alleviate all these plagues—except maybe the hunger.

The streams were rapid with spring runoff, so it wasn't hard to get drinking water, but food was another story. The third day out from Lahkvna, the landscape stayed the same, but it wasn't possible to find even an old potato to eat. He was oddly aware of being semi-delirious. He tried to concentrate: Orphaned now. Like Pip. What would he do? Water alone is not enough.

All day he fought the desire to throw away the heavy bag and greatcoat. They would be needed. Just keep going. Get away from the terror. Talking to himself transformed into a dialogue with Mama and Papa advising him to "keep the coat" and keep going, Keila offering her own advice: "Find food, steal it. If you must." He thought she made sense, so when he spied the spire of a church, he turned toward it—a village where he would try to put her advice into practice.

He grew nervous as he approached the town. Punishment for stealing could be severe. He put on his greatcoat with its many long pockets, two of them in the inner lining, and one which would be big enough to hide . . . what? The carrots piled in display at an outdoor market. Not being in his right mind, he'd forgotten to put his best scouting techniques into practice beforehand. The moment of lucidity hit him just as he was about to snatch—he hadn't scouted an escape route—so he didn't grab anything and kept walking right past the carrots. When he came to the larger, busier central market, he told Keila he wouldn't make the same mistake. He scouted this time, determining the best escape route, but wondering more and more about the soundness of Keila's advice and then denying his fear. He was Zalaman, the Cossack Killer. He saw a table of produce that was attracting very little attention, due perhaps to its pile of sad looking vegetables. To Zalaman they looked delicious. There was a potential escape route. As he approached the table, it seemed that everyone was staring at him. Then someone bumped into his injured arm and he yelped in pain, attracting more attention. He kept going right through the village, out onto the road that led away in what would have to be the correct direction. It hadn't been pain that made him scrap his plan, it had been the fear of reprisal.

> <

More farmland. Most of the fields still held pockets of snow, not yet ready for tilling and planting. There were no edible vegetables for him to dig out of thawed places. He berated himself for screwing up the chance to snatch some vegetables. 'You can shoot Cossacks, but afraid to steal a carrot?' Keila asked.

Before he had a chance to explain, he heard scurrying, saw movement at his feet. A field mouse. It paused as he gripped his knife, careful to move slowly and smoothly, so as not to scare it off. The mouse twitched its nose and whiskers, sniffing for its own meal. But it stayed put until it became aware of Zalaman's knife and leaped—toward the blade. Then the mouse ran, essentially headless, the body dragging the nearly severed head, until it completed a rough circle and collapsed.

With the strength he had left, Zalaman was able to gather some dry vines and strike a spark with the flint and fan a fire to life. He cut a stick for a spit and skinned and cooked the little creature. It would be a few mouthfuls at most, but as the mouse started to brown nicely and the smell of cooking meat overcame him, he paused. Was it OK to eat a mouse? He sniffed at it—a smell of smoke and earth—closed his eyes and bit into it. He chewed deliberately, carefully. The taste was not pleasant, the meat stringy but juicy. Or so he thought, until he noticed it was not fat—the 'juice' was blood. He'd undercooked it. Still, he swallowed, and it went down. He held his nose and took a second bite, immediately spewing up both bites. Now his stomach felt sore and even emptier. He was going to die—he was convinced of this—unless he could find something to eat in the next village.

Around midday, the sun disappeared behind thick purple clouds, the temperature dropping in response. The winter was perhaps not quite over, and so he was grateful for the coat. The cold spurred him on. He'd rejoined a main road—a broad path connecting villages and farmers—where he encountered, without conversing, an increasing number of travelers, presaging civilization somewhere up ahead. The melting snow and mud had refrozen to form jagged, difficult-to-see hazards for the unwary or the famished. Being both, Zalaman stumbled, then looked up to see if anyone else had seen him. No one seemed to have noticed him.

Ahead, a town rising in the distance, a town of some size judging by the look of its church spire, not to mention the growing number of travelers. Some were on foot like him, others on horseback or driving carriages. Zalaman asked a couple of walkers the name of the town.

"Aknieste," one said.

"Zilupe," said the other and they walked off arguing and laughing about it.

Zalaman supposed it depended on your language. Whatever it was called, Zilupe or Aknieste, it was going to provide him with something to eat. It would be a cold night, so a greatcoat with ample pockets for stashing things quickly would not look out of place. Others on the road had wrapped themselves up as well.

He entered the town with his stomach and nerves in knots. He picked his way through residential backstreets, sticking to the shadows as much as possible, though the more he walked, the more convinced he was that he could pass for a normal citizen. This time he would do his scouting.

He made a few rounds of Zilupe's central trading square, ambling over to "Markovics Produce," an impressive and popular wagon, piled with quality produce. He walked with unnatural nonchalance, admiring the brightly painted sign and the produce.

Marcovics looked to be a prosperous merchant. At the moment, there were a few customers at the man's wagon. His brain being undernourished, he couldn't decide if it was a good thing that there were customers who might be distractions for Markovics, who was keeping an eagle eye on his wares. They might block Markovics view of Zalaman at the right moment, but the same customers could be a problem if they were to witness his theft.

Markovics looked to be on the short side, about Rodak's height, but without his muscle.

He took notice of Zalaman's scouting, and asked if he could assist the young man—who didn't look as though he'd be able to afford the quality of Markovics' produce—in any way. Zalaman simply praised his produce and Markovics thanked him but said the produce was there for purchasing, not just admiring. He asked only for a fair price.

Zalaman nodded and saw Markovics get distracted by a woman walking her horse up to the wagon. Mrs. Markovics? She handed the reins of the horse to Mr. Markovics and as she did so, Zalaman slipped a few turnips into his pockets, all in one movement, flawlessly smooth, especially considering his depleted condition.

Markovics missed it. Before Zalaman had a chance to run, the wealthy peddler turned and asked, "Perhaps you'd like to buy something?"

"Yes," Zalaman said, hesitating, suddenly unsure what to do, certainly not run. "Yes, I would. . . . Definitely. Like to . . ."

Markovics smiled and turned to secure his horse. Zalaman grabbed two apples and stuffed them in another pocket, just as Markovics turned back. Caught in the act, Zalaman took off running as fast as he could.

Mr. Markovics threw the reins back to his wife, jumped off the produce wagon and chased Zalaman down a road leading out of the market, yelling "Thief! Police! Help!" Zalaman realized he was running down a sidewalk that was taking him further into the center of town instead of away from it. He crossed the street and doubled back on the other side in the opposite direction. The maneuver allowed Markovics, in unflagging pursuit but on short legs, to make up some ground on the object of his pursuit. He had the advantage of having had a good night's sleep and not carrying a heavy bag.

Zalaman had to drop the bag to gain speed. He needed to put more distance between himself and the peddler. The few people they passed on the street would either turn away, cower, or enjoy watching the chase. But no one intervened.

Zalaman ran too close to a tree and a branch slapped him hard across the face, slowing him enough for Marcovics to pounce on his back and the next thing he knew he was on the ground, flat on his stomach, Markovics straddling his back, screaming "Police! Thief!" Zalaman managed to flip over. But Markovics stayed astride his chest. "Get up!" Papa yelled. The sky and Markovics spinning above him. The hunger and exhaustion and misery had caught up with him—along with Markovics. He didn't know if he was capable of more, when Papa yelled again, "Get up!" and Zalaman summoned all he had and pushed Markovics off so forcefully that the peddler went crashing through the leaded glass window fronting the sidewalk. Markovics stopped screaming. All Zalaman could hear was the breaking of glass. He hadn't meant to hurt the man or do so much damage.

Freed of Markovics, Zalaman took off running to the edge of Zilupe. He noticed how badly his coat had been shredded during his tangle with Marcovics. He could see no one pursuing him, so he slowed briefly to examine the damage to his coat. With the meagerness of his wardrobe and the coat's usefulness in his new line of work, he wished Stanko were around to mend it. At least he still had the turnips and apples. Hungry as he was, he started running again so he would be completely clear of the town and be able to enjoy his food fully. Approaching the low wall that marked the end of Zilupe and the start of open country, he ran what should have been the short distance to salvation, but felt himself suddenly levitating, his feet running on air, as he was lifted by two constables who had come up from behind, one on either side, and hoisted him from under his armpits as if he were a child weighing nothing.

That evening, Zalaman found himself wedged between the two constables on a bench just outside the local Magistrate's office. He was so worried, he'd lost his hunger. He knew about the treatments thieves received.

Inside his office, the Magistrate was finishing his evening meal and talking with the prosperous peddler Markovics. Outside the office, the constables were sitting so close to Zalaman it hurt. One of them pushed painfully against something hard in Zalaman's coat pocket. He looked and leaned away from the man as he reached into the pocket, slowly, like he'd moved with his knife so as not to alert the mouse. An apple. The constables had somehow—thanks no doubt to the many pockets—missed one of the apples. Without thinking about anything other than the reawakened complainer that was his empty stomach while listening to the Magistrate's and Markovics' chewing, guzzling, and burping through the closed door, he pulled out the apple and, before anyone could restrain him, took a bite. Too late, the constable on his right grabbed his injured arm to stop him. Zalaman yelped, but kept on chewing, a trickle of apple juice escaping down his chin.

"Aww, leave him alone," said the other constable. "Let the kid have something to eat for Jesus' sake. Who knows when he'll see real food again." The constable on the right shrugged as if it was of no consequence to him and released Zalaman's aching arm. He thanked them between chews. It was the best apple he'd ever tasted. The friendlier constable on the left chuckled and handed him a rag. "I've never seen anyone enjoy an apple so much," he said, motioning to Zalaman how he should wipe his face, before seeing the Magistrate. "How long since you last ate?"

"I don't remember," he said, dabbing at his face with the rag. A new welt on his cheek was a reminder of his being felled by Markovics. He was surprised by the amount of blood the rag picked up along with the apple juice. It reminded him of the bloody face he'd scared Bebchuk with after that battle. "Many days," he answered, trying to be polite.

"You look awful," the constable said and helped Zalaman wipe off more blood.

The door opened and Zalaman quickly stashed what was left of the apple. Markovics was escorted out by the Magistrate. They were old acquaintances who'd just shared supper while discussing appropriate punishments for the young thief. Markovics frowned when he came out into the hallway and saw Zalaman. He shook his head in despair but said nothing to him. He turned and bade the Magistrate goodnight.

The Magistrate ushered in Zalaman and the two constables. They told the magistrate their brief part in the story and were dismissed. The magistrate observed Zalaman while he tried without success to light his long-stemmed pipe. He was old and hard of hearing and Zalaman couldn't tell how much he understood about his justification for taking the apple, but when he mentioned "Lahkvna," the Magistrate stopped the lighting ceremony and nodded. He held up his hand, telling Zalaman to stop.

Zalaman got up, alarming the Magistrate, but he just wanted to help the Magistrate light his long pipe. The magistrate relaxed and let him. He had heard the story of the massacre in Lahkvna. Everyone had.

"You shouldn't have had to steal," the Magistrate said. "Surely, merchants would take pity on you and give you something to eat?"

Zalaman felt the remains of the apple in his pocket. His Mama told him to keep quiet in case he might say something he would later regret, like his current view of the Christian charity. He didn't talk, but his lips quivered.

The Magistrate released a long trail of tobacco smoke and told Zalaman how very sorry he felt for him and his *shtetl*. "I'm not sorry for your being saddled with your religion.

"Whether one is a Jew or Christian or Chinaman, it makes no difference to me. Those things were determined by God Almighty for reasons we cannot comprehend. I am of course very sorry for what happened in your *shtetl*, but even sorrier for what is bound to happen to you now because you stole, and we must follow the law."

He took another long pull on his pipe, then exhaled slowly. "And set an example." Another puff, then, "I wish I could say that what you are going to suffer is for your own good, but that would be a cruel joke." He was going to make a general amputation joke he'd made before under similar circumstances but stopped himself. "I imagine one-armed thieves are even clumsier than you."

Zalaman did not cry out or even weep, but exhaled and lifted his injured arm and assured the magistrate he was already used to life with one arm. He'd hoped the worst punishment would be the amputation of a finger, nothing so drastic as an arm. He pictured his shoulder looking like Stanko's stump. Maybe the Magistrate was just trying to scare him.

"If you'd taken two apples, it would be both arms."

Zalaman was sure that was a jest. The Magistrate was trying to scare him. Did he know about the other apple?

The Magistrate's smile was brief and grim. He called the two constables back into his office and ordered them to escort Zalaman to his cell. To Zalaman's disbelief, they'd somehow managed to bring back the hessian bag he'd abandoned during the chase.

They left him in a cell so dark, he only realized he was in a cell when he heard the rasp of iron against iron, like the turning of a bolt. He bumped his shins on a low bench. He sat there rubbing his various sore parts and eating the rest of the apple. Amid all his woes, he was surprised he'd been allowed to keep the piece of apple. Had they forgotten or did they do him a small kindness out of pity for him or for Lahkvna? It could be pity for the severity of his coming punishment. He stretched out on the wooden plank bench, filling its length from end to end. Unsurprisingly, he couldn't sleep. But he must have fallen asleep eventually because he was awakened by another rasping sound. He was cold, groggy, his mouth dry and his stomach still hollowed out. He had dreamed the sound. No. He'd heard something and now he heard footsteps disappearing down the corridor. Then silence again. He got up and stumbled against the cell door, almost falling out of the cell. The bolt has been pulled and the door left ajar.

He groped in the dark for his bag. He found it and snuck down the corridor and out the front door and then out of Zilupe, all the while in near total darkness. He disappeared into the landscape, without being able to see more than a meter ahead.

Who'd freed him? He'd first assumed it was the friendlier of the two constables, but it might just as easily have been the magistrate or the two of them, the constable releasing him with the magistrate's blessing, the magistrate unable to live with himself if he became another tormentor of the Jews of Lahkvna. "Christian or Jew or Chinaman, it makes no difference to me," he'd said.

CHAPTER FIFTEEN

Markus and Odessa

He walked through the night and into the next day, staying away from any towns, wanting to put more distance between himself and Zilupe in case he was being tracked as an escaped felon. He was still starving, one apple went only so far, trudging through fields with retreating snow still in the crevasses and north facing inclines. His bag kept getting heavier, but he'd resolved to keep it with him. He knew which direction he was going but he had no idea where he was headed. He only knew that he wanted it to be far away. He felt that despite the loss of the world as he knew it and the fact that he'd been hit, once again, on the skull, he was at least thinking clearly enough—although still hearing the voices in his head—to question whether he was thinking clearly. Mama said a damaged brain was no excuse for failure, only a reason for greater vigilance.

Zalaman realized he would never hear that voice again—outside his head—so he treasured his brain's tricks. He cried, missing her as he walked.

He didn't have to wait long for Papa to speak up. "I agree with Mama, and I think it's OK steal if necessary—but only if you follow Mama's advice and stay on your toes."

"There are no authorities looking for you," Keila informed him. He didn't question her as to how she could know that, because he wanted to believe it. "They took pity on you, because of what was done to us. You must be willing to accept this pity from now on, if you want to succeed like you promised us you would."

><

The next day, feeling safer by being far enough away from Zilupe—not to mention Navharadak—that he returned to the main road where he encountered people heading to or coming from Aknieste, the town that had been mistaken for Zilupe when he'd arrived there. Aknieste was a bigger town than Zilupe, practically a city and not too far by the look of the three odd-looking spires that now came into view.

It was not the Riga he was hoping for, not even a Navharadak, but it was a place of some importance in this part of Kurland, complete with modern industry boasting three belching smokestacks that he'd mistaken for church steeples. A riverside town, and the river, a traveller informed him, was the Dunupe.

He wanted to stash his bag someplace outside the town, so he could move more freely, should the need arise to do so. He left the road and followed a path, little more than two ancient ruts, still partly under snow and obviously little used over the winter. Then he walked away from the ruts, plodding through knee-deep snow to get to a solitary set of evergreens where he stashed his hessian bag near the roots that were tucked hidden under the branches where the ground was free of snow, but not too muddy. Aside from his many-pocketed greatcoat, with its occupational benefits, he needed to be unencumbered when pursuing this work. If he had to steal to get food—and he had no illusions about avoiding it—he was determined to do it right this time. He followed his footprints back to the path and took the main road into Aknieste, following the traffic until he came upon a large commercial area bustling with citizens doing their early evening shopping, many choosing fresh produce from the carts and shops.

He entered one merchant's shop that looked more prosperous than most. It was lit by flickering lamps and Zalaman thought the flicker might work to his advantage, Maybe it would impair the merchant's vision. Zalaman was determined to take a different approach this time. Inside the shop, the light from the lamps was brighter than it had appeared outside. There was movement everywhere. He would take his time. Pay attention," Mama said—to get used to the flow of shoppers and the trembling light, but not too much time which might arouse suspicion, like it had with Markovics.

He inspected the produce just like a normal shopper. Because of Aknieste's position on the Dunupe, river traffic brought a more exotic inventory than anything he'd seen outside Riga. There was a variety of fruits and vegetables that had been floated upstream from warmer climes to be distributed in Odessa and then up the Dniester to the Dunupe. The potatoes were like nothing he'd ever seen—reddish orange in color and, he was told by a fellow customer, they had to be cooked before eaten. With his hidden camp in the pines, he could see himself cooking these dense potatoes. It would take some time. When he thought the merchant wasn't watching, he snatched two of them, one with each hand simultaneously and then, in less than a heartbeat, thrust them into two inner coat pockets. He should leave and not tempt fate, but he knew he would—both for the challenge and because he was very, very hungry. He snatched a juicy-looking cucumber on the way out. And then he was out! He'd done it! He was better at this than he'd been able to give himself credit for. It was so much quicker than working. He took his treasure back to his camp in the pines.

His stomach had long ago stopped grumbling, but now there it was again. He started a small fire to cook the potatoes. He touched the smooth, red skin to see if they had softened, but it took a long time for them to do so. They turned out to be orange inside and had a completely different taste from other potatoes. At first, he wasn't sure he liked them, but his hunger kept him at it and by the time he finished both, he wished he had taken more. They were the sweetest potatoes he'd ever eaten. If they really were potatoes. Or was it his hunger that made it taste so sweet, like that apple in Zilupe. He was happy he'd escaped that one, but it was a fleeting feeling—it only served to sharpen his awareness of how unreachable true happiness now seemed. He would try to find another red potato tomorrow. He felt better than he had in many days, but he was still hungry, so he ate the big cucumber. He whittled some pine boughs to make a mattress, then wrapped himself in the greatcoat. He cried and slept without hearing any voices in his head.

><

For two more days he kept this up, practiced his art, visiting two different peddlers each day, improving his skills without getting caught. He snatched modest amounts, but once stole a loaf of bread. He began to regain his strength. His head and arm ached less.

He slept well on a fragrant bed in the evergreens. It was spring. He was getting less advice from the family in his head and his tears over their loss were frequent but briefer. He welcomed the warming spring but couldn't abandon the heavy greatcoat his work required.

On the third day at Aknieste, his health had improved enough that he became a little restless and wanted some new distraction. He walked to the Aknieste *kvadrat*, where he spotted a new peddler with a large, well-provisioned cart, doing a bustling trade. The more hectic the business, the more distractions to take advantage of. This new peddler's big cart was filled with a diversity of healthy-looking vegetables and had a crowd around it. There was a boy lurking about in a long apron. He was young, thirteen at most, and probably even younger, who was dressed like a shop's assistant with a long apron. But Zalaman somehow knew it was a costume. Like his own greatcoat. This boy was up to the same thing Zalaman was. He was sure of it once he saw him whisk a sizable bundle of carrots off the cart and into his roomy apron. Most astonishing—the boy was staring right at Zalaman when he snatched the carrots, not watching the peddler. He nodded, then placed himself right in front of the peddler, blocking his view of Zalaman. Zalaman moved quickly and snatched some carrots for himself, then melted into the crowd losing sight of his enabler until he came up right behind Zalaman demanding in Zalaman's ear that he return the stolen goods. He laughed, grabbing Zalaman before he could escape, introducing himself as Markus. Zalaman thanked him for his assistance and let Markus follow him to his camp in the evergreens, both chewing on their carrots, each expressing admiration for the other in terms of speed and daring.

"Although those are less important than other skills—things like knowing who and when to strike and avoid getting caught," Markus said. Zalaman agreed and told Markus he'd learned that lesson the hard way.

"Yet, you still have all your arms and legs."

"Well, I've only been at it a week or so."

"OK," Markus laughed. "Give it time. Most thieves are young, you know" Markus said, looking too young to be a veteran. "We get limbs amputated and die of infections or die of old age in prison. But not me. I like your little camp. The way you have it set up and all shows me something. Like what? Like you've been around. Sixteen? You are? Well, I'm not certain, but I think I'm fourteen."

"I don't think so," Zalaman shook his head. "It doesn't matter."

"I am going to go back to Aknieste now," Markus said, "We need meat to eat with those vegetables."

><

Zalaman couldn't help but be impressed when Markus returned in less than an hour carrying a chicken to accompany the vegetables. He no longer wore his shop's assistant costume and was carrying a small pack. They had a feast. Zalaman was glad they had no alcohol because he didn't think he'd be able to drink it without becoming a sobbing mess. He asked Markus about himself, but Markus was reluctant to talk about his past.He was not so reticent about his future. He was going to be leaving soon, he said, leaving the country.

Zalaman managed to talk a bit about Lahvkvna. Markus said he was sorry, he couldn't imagine . . . He grew quiet and then said, "Nothing I can say will help, Zal. People are mostly awful."

They were both silent, watching their little fire crackle. Zalaman said, "Not all of them." He told Markus about Rodak and Stanko.

"I've made a living from Russians, too," Markus said. "But I worked with them. Never had to kill any." He didn't want to talk about it, so he just said he'd gotten involved in some bad business in Russia recently. He was more interested in the future. He wanted to get ahead in the world. And that's why he was leaving Aknieste.

"I've had enough of this little outpost. It's too small. It doesn't have the kind of opportunities you can find in the city. You need a place with wealthy families."

"Aknieste looks like a city to me," Zalaman said. "I have been to Riga, if that's what you're thinking."

"No," Markus shook his head. "Odessa." Odessa—it sounded very far away to Zalaman. "You've just arrived a few days ago," Markus went on, "but I've been here too long. I'm taking off in the morning. That's why I brought my stuff," he said, patting his pack. He explained to Zalaman how the Dunupe flowed into the Dniester, which would take him to Odessa. He had located a barge and he would board early in the morning while it was still dark.

Zalaman reminisced about his barge trip to Riga, a voyage he remembered fondly. Of course, he did, it was before the slaughter.

"Come with me."

"No. Like you said, I just got here."

"But you did say something about getting far away from Navharadak . . ." When Markus spoke about Odessa it reminded Zalaman of Davin's enthusing about Jerusalem. The difference being that Markus knew Odessa, or so he claimed. It was attainable. Zalaman had seen it depicted on the commandant's maps in Syp. It would be considerably further from home than he'd ever been. Isn't that what he wanted? Rodak had told stories about Odessa. They always involved mystery and a sense of something very foreign.

"It's a long way," Zalaman said. "Here, I could maybe get a job."

Markus laughed. "A job? Why haven't you done so already? What's keeping you?" He shrugged. Odessa wasn't so far. He'd been all the way to Russia. He had the barge all figured out. "It's easy to sneak on board. Come with me, Zal. It isn't everyday, you are going to get this kind of an opportunity."

"Opportunity?" Zalaman had to laugh. Markus' swagger and self-assurance were attractive qualities. Zalaman thought he, himself, could use some of that. It struck him this was the first time he'd laughed since Lahkvna. It felt wrong to do so and he stopped, but he felt grateful toward Markus for making him see that laughing was a possibility.

"Odessa is all the things your friend Rodak told you it was," Markus said with a grin. "They call it Eldorado." He felt like a fisherman reeling in his catch. He grew serious. "Here . . . well, everyone you loved has been killed. What could be keeping you here?"

"The dead," Zalaman said. He heard them, the three dead people he'd loved so and had buried in Lahkvna, telling him maybe he should go. "Why not?" Keila asked. A cold shiver went down Zalaman's spine. He knew it wasn't his family saying this—it was him. He told his new friend about the voices he'd been hearing in his head since he'd left the *shtetl*. He let Markus regale him with stories of Odessa until they both fell asleep.

><

Markus woke Zalaman long before dawn. They gathered up their possessions, such as they were. Zalaman had very few and noticed Markus had even less. His new friend carried a formidable knife hanging from a scabbard on his trouser belt.

Other than that, he only carried a small bag on a strap over his shoulder. "To leave my hands free," he said, "when I need them." There was only dim moonlight. Walking back to the road and then into Aknietse. Markus led them cautiously. Zalaman never came out and said, "Yes, I'm with you to Odessa," but he followed Markus that morning as if he had. He lagged behind Markus, preoccupied with the idea of traveling so far away from Lahkvna, although, as his mother reminded him, it was what he'd wanted.

She assured him it would be OK.

Up ahead, Zalaman saw Markus stop alongside a coach and horse. He turned and made a little bow toward Zalaman, flourishing an arm as if he was offering Zalaman a ride. When he caught up, Zalaman could see the diligence was parked with a horse already in harness and a coachman who had fallen asleep on his perch, awaiting some early morning customer. Markus jumped up onto the seat behind the coachmen's bench and held a knife to the man's throat. It seemed to Zalaman that the coachman could easily overpower Markus but for his fear. Zalaman jumped up and helped Markus hold the coachman. "Drive on and make no other sound," Markus told the man, directing him to drive out of town rather than toward the docks as Zalaman expected.

They were not heading to Dunupe where the barge would be. Instead, they drove out of town and into the woods where Markus kicked the coachman out, and, leaving behind the outraged cries, turned the carriage back around and headed toward the Dunupe. Zalaman was reconsidering his decision to go to Odessa with this person. He asked Markus what was going on, but Markus just shrugged his shoulders and said, “Trust me.”

There were few Aknietse harbor officials about at that hour. Markus pulled the carriage over to an embankment overlooking the Dunupe. He took his bag and told Zalaman to grab his. As soon as they were free of the carriage, Markus slapped the horse to send it on its way. And then they slid down the icy embankment to the pier jutting out into the Dunupe. There were few Aknietse harbor officials about at that hour, but Markus put his finger to his lips when Zalaman had another question. He led Zalaman to an enormous barge. It was twice the size of the one Zalaman had taken to Riga.

The sky was allowing color back into the world when the loading began. Horse and oxen-drawn wagons piled with crates and sacks of dry goods appeared, only to disappear into the waiting barge. The crates and sacks joined bales of ‘who-knew-what’ (perhaps *kvaat*). The wagons rolled right up to the barge, then up a wide gangplank.

There was much dust and creaking loads, animals bawling and neighing. The scene had a grandeur of commotion that put to shame Zalaman’s earlier, more peaceful experience with livestock on the barge.

Markus, anxious to get on board before the daylight got any brighter, tapped Zalaman’s shoulder. Without a sound, he hopped up on the bed of a passing wagon. Zalaman took a deep breath—this was the moment to commit—and did the same, envying Markus’ limberness, his smaller size, when they wedged themselves between stacked crates of onions. The wagon rumbled up the gangplank onto the barge and then continued all the way to the prow for unloading. While the bargemen unloaded the onions from one side of the wagon, the two stowaways squeezed out the other side and hid behind a pile of steel two meters high, wedged now between steel and onions. It was an uncomfortable position to have to maintain over the course of a long voyage.

Zalaman complained.

"We couldn't ask for a better barrier than a wall of iron," Markus said, assuring Zalaman they would be able to move about once the vessel got underway.

"Not iron. Steel," Zalaman corrected him. "A commodity that's very important to the new industrial revolution. Do you know what I'm talking about?" Zalaman wanted to impress Markus with his knowledge, gained from his years with the Uprising, not the shul back home. But he got no satisfaction from Markus. The kid wasn't open to enlightenment.

He asked how long it would take to get to Odessa.

Markus shrugged his shoulders. "Not long, I hope." He shrugged a lot, Zalaman noticed, dismissing things he didn't want to talk about. It could get aggravating, Zalaman thought.

The cramped quarters were harder on the longer, larger Zalaman, so it was worse for him when he felt a shudder of movement and the barge cast off from the pier and started moving slowly downstream and Markus announced that since they were in the prow of the ship it was too light for them to move about without being discovered and thrown overboard.

They didn't emerge from their cramped confinement until dark. Zalaman's legs were so stiff he had to lie low and stretch until he could move less painfully. When asked, Markus admitted he knew nothing about this barge except the direction it was going. It would take them to the Black Sea and Odessa. When he asked Markus for details about Odessa, Markus laughed and said he'd never been there before, but wasn't Zalaman happy that Markus had talked him into coming along? Zalaman didn't look happy.

"OK, so, I've never been there. I never said I was, you just figured I had because of my stories about the place. Well, don't tie yourself in knots. Those stories are all true. I heard them from my Russian business associates, and they wouldn't lie about such things."

"Sometimes you sound so well-travelled and experienced, but now you sound so innocent. I haven't met a man yet who wouldn't lie about such things." Zalaman remembered how Davin used to tell him stories about the Holy Land. His stories often sounded real—even though Davin had never been there. They were so important to Davin they became real to him. "What about all of the amazing people and their riches you told me about?" he asked Markus

"Don't worry. It's all true. We just have to find the friends of the Russians I know from back in Russia. They may be willing to help you, too—like they will me."

"I don't know about working with Russians. They've mostly been on the receiving end of some weapon I was firing or throwing at them."

"Zal, that's *your* problem. I hope it won't be our problem. And you know, being a Jew in Odessa might not be so bad. I've heard Jews run the city."

"Well, things in Odessa can't be worse for Jews than what I've seen back home. Based on what I saw in Riga, I'm thinking maybe bigger cities, because they have more people, a bigger variety of people, are more tolerant of others—of people not like themselves."

"I agree. So long as you stay in your own enclave."

"We call it a *shtetl*."

The trip took longer than they had hoped. They broke up the long summer days pretending. To the bargemen, they were tradesmen or merchants accompanying a shipment of some

commodity or other. To the tradesmen on board, they pretended to be bargemen. They stole as a team when stealing was required, using distraction and deception. Markus was very quick with his hands as well as his feet.

Fortunately, papers were never demanded of them, but they didn't push their luck—if their stomachs or other organs demanded they move about, they did so, but they stayed by themselves. Twice they were able to beg for some tea—*khat* tea, no less!—from a friendly bargeman who likely knew they were stowaways but didn't care.

They traded stories to wile away the time. Markus spoke about shady exploits in Russia and Austria. His stories lacked detail, so Zalaman figured they were Markus' romantic fantasies.

Zalaman told Markus stories of his childhood, of Rodak and Stanko, but especially those of his nomadic childhood and his life in Lahkvna before last Easter. To Markus, who claimed to have been orphaned at an early age, it was a childhood that sounded too good to be true and he decided it was just Zalaman's wishful thinking.

Meanwhile, they had plenty to eat if you liked onions and other raw vegetables. They used the most distant corner they could find for a toilet. Despite misgivings about the other one's commitment to truth, they decided they made a good team and should stick together once they got to Odessa.

It took longer than they'd guessed it would, but then there it was, spreading before them—the sparkling Black Sea. It appeared to be open endlessly to the south, afloat with bigger ships than they'd ever seen, ships from everywhere—Russian, Ottoman, the Mediterranean, the Holy Land—the world.

At the port of Odessa, they disembarked just as they'd embarked only in reverse order, unnoticed. Dropping their two bags on the beach, they ran plunging into the cooling waters of the Black Sea, waters heated by the sun, wonderfully warm on the surface and cooler below. They were equally poor swimmers and didn't go in over their heads, but stood in it up to their waists, soaked up its warmth and the heat of a sun stronger than any Zalaman had ever felt. He hadn't experienced the sensation of feeling clean for since . . . when? He guessed it was when he got caught in a downpour after leaving Lahkvna. That drenching had only washed off the outer layers of dirt. The little creeks where he'd camped had been very cold and only big enough to stick his face in to take a sip. He felt like he was now in another world—one of huge ships, endless sea, the southern sun. And he had not yet even been to Odessa proper.

Zalaman was anxious to explore Odessa and Markus wanted to find his Russian contacts, one of them named Vojin, so they let the sun dry them while they watched ships from unknown parts of the earth unload their goods. Many of the big ships had Russian names on their prows; they rocked gently as they were unloaded, tons of grain from across the Sea of Azov, from Armenia, from the Bosporus and the Ottoman Empire. It had been the Russians who turned what used to be an Ottoman lake into an international seaway thanks to the protections offered by Peter the Great's navy. But it was Catherine who annexed Khadzhibei and renamed it Odessa.

Once their clothes were dry, they walked from the harbor up into the city via a maze of ancient sycamores which shaded marvelous stone buildings that looked more like those in the lithographs of Paris and Rome in his mother's books than anything he'd seen in Riga. When they emerged from the alley of sycamores, they wandered into a wide promenade, crowded with people, many of them immigrants like them: Greeks, Italians, Bulgars, French, Russians, Jews. You could tell who was who by their national dress, even if sometimes they only showed pieces of their old clothes with new. The promenade provided a breathtaking view of the harbor below with its two long curving piers and the sea beyond. Zalaman and his friend turned away from the sea view and entered a quiet zone of even more sycamores with wonderfully broad leaves, that were part of a park offering a green gateway into the city proper. After the sun and shimmering sea, the park was dark with shade trees, but when they left the park, the city's multi-storied buildings were once again bathed in bright sunlight, shaped by curves Zalaman never knew were possible.

They stopped at a broad intersection bustling with vehicles and people of every description. They managed to cross the street and avoid death by carriage, then wandered through both prosperous-looking commercial and beautifully groomed residential areas and those that were rundown, dirty and dark. Zalaman was entranced and feeling like he was high on *khat* without having taken a drink or smoked a thing. The odors of Odessa made a strong impression. Mouth-watering spices and pungent perfumes mixed with the smell of excrement from the various beasts of burden.

Markus, though he purported to be the world traveller, was transfixed by the moving carpet of costumes. He commented on the mix of opulence alongside poverty—wealthy merchants and beggars holding sacks, many of them Jews from Persia and the Ottoman Empire who were asking for some pennies because they were on their "way to the Holy Land to die."

Zalaman, on the other hand, was fascinated by all the clean-shaven Jews. Clean shaven Jews were a rarity in his experience. They wore silk yarmulkes but no beards!

The more orthodox of Lahkvna's *kahal* would be outraged—if any had been left alive.

These French 'Cabbalists,' as Zalaman would come to know them, loitered about, smoking cigarettes with other Jews, bearded and not. But for their yarmulkes, Zalaman would have found the French Jews indistinguishable from the Christian Frenchmen.

Just like the Frenchmen, these Jews wore high leather boots and flared waistcoats. Zalaman liked these outfits but was glad he didn't have to wear one in the heat. The sweat soaked through the Cabbalists' white linen neck wear.

Markus pointed out a group of prosperous-looking Greek merchants. "Maybe Bulgars. I can't tell them apart," he said. They wore long, collarless, richly embroidered, belted shirts over wide trousers that were tight at the ankles. Zalaman tried not to gawk at the women. Greek or Bulgar, whoever they were, there were girls his own age with dark hair, some crowned with wreaths, and there were more mature young women wearing aprons, hiding their hair under headdresses. Many of the headdresses were adorned with gold coins, as was the lace fringe of their aprons. Zalaman wanted to know if it was real gold. Markus insisted it was. Zalaman was skeptical. He guessed that Markus' assertion was based exclusively on hope.

Intermingled with all the fragrances and diverse clothing was an equally diverse chorus of voices. Dozens of different tongues speaking at once. They were in the commercial zone known as "Greek Street." They paused there and let the voices clarify a bit—mostly dialects of Yiddish and Polish; it was the domain of Jewish merchants and peddlers. No Greeks in sight. But their Jewish counterparts—inheritors?—were busy hustling flour, salt, feathers, raisins, jute, herring, melons, apples, pumpkin, plums, pears, among the onions, dried beans, carrots, and potatoes, on and on—you name it.

There was an obviously popular peddler who sold his produce from a smart-looking cart with "Edil" painted on both sides. Zalaman remembered how he'd been attracted—to great detriment—by Markovics' sign in Zilupe. Edil was not Greek, but an old Jew who feigned indifference at the interest Zalaman and Markus expressed in his wares. He squinted his aging eyes to make it clear he saw them. Saw *through* them, and they'd better not try anything funny. Zalaman and Markus smiled their most innocent smiles and walked away.

Edil reminded Zalaman of Papa and he wondered if the old man had recognized Zalaman for what he was, what he'd become. A thief. Markus, on the other hand, was incensed by the dismissive look Edil had given them. Not just dismissive—threatening. And Markus had done nothing at all! He should have.

"No," Zalaman said. "No. Leave that old man alone." Markus scoffed. He couldn't afford a partner who was soft.

They walked on and gazed in the windows of the shops displaying perfumes and oils, coffee, spices, soaps, Turkish tobacco, Bulgar roses, again, on and on, like the crowds. The shopkeepers generally barred the entrance of the two vagabonds, so they walked up the hill to a different part of the city, into terraces of a residential neighborhood. It was beautiful, but they turned around, overcome by the cooking smells wafting out family kitchens and Zalaman's nose led them to a large Jewish sector of Odessa where vendors and cafes were serving familiar, tasty-looking dishes like *tzimes* and herring on rye bread. They had stumbled on a prosperous ghetto, the Bazama, not suffering from government-imposed restrictions. But they had no money to purchase anything. They would have to rely on their own proven methods. This would require being quick on their feet. Just like Zalaman in the evergreen grove outside Aknieste, they had to find a safe place to stash their worldly possessions. Markus knew just the place. They'd passed it, an abandoned shop, on their way to the Bazama.

><

Not much light penetrated the shop's one window. It did appear to be empty. It was locked, but there was no one nearby, so Markus forced the lock with his blade, and they entered. "Our

Odessa den," he dubbed it. "Until I find my friends and they arrange something better."

"Our sanctuary," Zalaman said. "How can they be friends if you've never met them?" He asked. Markus did his characteristic shrug, "Friends of friends, then." He found a weak spot in a wall near the wooden floorboards, a place where they could hide their belongings.

The closest commercial area was the Bazama and there they put into practice the team methods they'd developed on their long barge ride. First, they picked a likely target with a crowd of customers. Next Zalaman distracted the peddler, employing several languages to make an inquiry as to the price of a melon and holding the peddler's attention long enough for Markus to make his move. But Markus *didn't* move. So Zalaman re-engaged the peddler. Nothing. Markus just walked away, angering Zalaman who had put a lot of effort into distracting the peddler. He gave Markus a dirty look and left, puzzled and disgusted. Markus was nowhere to be seen. So Zalaman returned to their den and there was Markus, sitting on the floor with a tidy little pile of fruits and vegetables spread out in front of him.

As they gorged on Markus' successful theft, he bragged about how much practice it took, to be that deceptive that Zalaman didn't even notice him act. "It's simple but it takes a while to master it," he said, the pear's juices running down his chin.

Zalaman chewed, grateful for Markus' skill, but decided it was alright if he never achieved mastery. It would require devoting too much time to perfect the art, and like Markus had said himself, thieves don't live all that long.

Before Markus left to meet his Russians, he explained to Zalaman why he could not come with him, how Zalaman might screw everything up. "It might not be easy to find these guys but when I *do* meet them, it would be better if I didn't introduce you right away—because they're only expecting me, you see? I'm just going to be 'the new guy.' I'll let them know all about you once they trust me." Zalaman's skeptical look was getting as familiar to Markus as his own shrug was to Zalaman. "Don't worry, I'm not going to say a thing about this attitude of yours toward the Russians. When the time is right, I'll paint a pretty picture, so they'll *want* to let you in, get you some work. Let's just hope they're in Odessa like they're supposed to be."

Once he left, Zalaman wondered what kind of work it was that Markus was talking about and decided Markus himself probably didn't know, although it would likely be something outside the law. He leaned back against the den's stone wall. It was not someplace you wanted to stay unless you were there to sleep. He thought longingly about his cozy little room at the Punie inn, picturing Lecshi in it with him. He had to find a woman.

There were many attractive creatures in Odessa. And here in the den, it was lonely and claustrophobic. He should be out enjoying the sights.

Outside, the street teemed with beautiful women. Or so it seemed to Zalaman. Of course, if he wanted to get anywhere with any of them, he'd have to have money so he could buy nicer clothes and then buy someone a drink. The eyes of some women suggested they might be for sale, but he didn't want that. And he did not want to do any more stealing. Good as he and Markus were, it was too dangerous. It was no way to improve his life—just to shorten it. It wasn't what he'd promised Mama and Papa, though he was grateful that they, along with Keila, seemed to have cleared out. They were silent, which he hoped meant his brain was recovering.

Feeling as well-fed as he had in recent days, he walked aimlessly through a perfumed night. The incense of night-blooming flowers infused the air over the cobbled, winding streets, helping mitigate the smell of kerosene from the lamps that lit the way. In Riga, as in Navharadak, gas lights illuminated the streets, but here gas-oil lamps shed a different kind of light. The shades and fragrances inspired a sense of emotional warmth and longing in Zalaman as it had on other newcomers from other lands. As he walked, he felt tears welling up, suppressing them by concentrating on where he was, not where he'd been.

Everything and everyone looked softer and more attractive than normal. It was quiet for such a busy scene. Peacefully active. As he walked on, one woman caught him staring and he averted his eyes. He'd been gawking. The local police eyed him suspiciously—or so he imagined. He walked back to the Jewish quarter, and in the dim light, he thought he recognized someone. But, no, that person had died in Lahkvna. Right there on the sidewalk, Zalaman almost started crying. He let out one sob and stopped himself, but that one sob attracted the attention of a man wearing a sash. A policeman? He was heading toward Zalaman, so Zalaman slipped down a dark street where there were none of those gas-oil lamps. If someone was going to rob you, this would be the ideal place. He heard a door suddenly swing shut and he decided it was time to go back to the den and see if Markus had returned.

He hadn't, but when he did appear later that night, he found Zalaman already asleep, so he woke him to announce he hadn't found his friends–just some *khat*.

"We can't start a fire without attracting attention to our lodgings," Markus said, and he made a spark from Zalaman's flint, which he used to light a pipe stuffed with *khat*, blowing the smoke in Zalaman's face. "I know how much you prefer this to that tea on the barge," Markus grinned. "I didn't steal it," he said when Zalaman asked. "I got this from friends. "New friends. The ones I'm supposed to meet—Vojin, Timor and Bogdan—weren't there."

He handed Zalaman the pipe and they handed it back and forth as long as there was *khat* to burn. "What we are smoking is a gift from people who gave me the benefit of the doubt. I told them I was looking for Vojin and his colleagues, and as soon as I mentioned their names and told them I was doing business with Vojin and his mates, these men took me under wing and insisted on buying my drinks. I'm telling you, those names mean something. At least in the Gnazdo, they do. People fear them. I know that's the only reason they befriended me."

"Well, then, let's hope they don't find out you are lying about doing business with this Vojin . . . that you've never even met him—because then these new friends would likely kill you."

"That may be true—*if* I was lying, but I'm not. I will be in business with them. And now I can see it must be major business that they do . . . So, we have nothing to fear."

Zalaman was now more convinced than ever that he did not want to get mixed up in Markus' 'work.' He didn't want that kind of life here if he could avoid it. Better the peace and quiet that comes with lower paid work. Whatever that might be.

"This *khat*," Markus puffed, "these people don't smoke it. They chew it. It's supposed to be much better that way—once you get used to the taste." Markus puffed. "By the way, Zal, you can't get what *you* want through honest labor."

"And what is it *I* want?"

"You want some new clothes. A nicer place to stay. The ability to make those bastards from Navharadak pay for what they did. You'll never be able to avenge your family and those of Lahkvna by yourself. You need resources, powerful allies. It's not something you can achieve through honest labor."

"That's ridiculous. When have I ever even mentioned revenge? What I want is a woman."

”Anyone would have to be thinking about revenge. You don’t want to talk about it now, that’s fine. Forget I said it. Let me tell you about the Gnazdo, where I ended up tonight. It’s not like any saloon you’ve ever seen. So full of bad behavior even I was shocked.” Zalaman grinned at Markus being ‘shocked.’ He preferred this enthusiastic Markus to the one who just shrugged with feigned indifference. “All I had to do was mention that I was supposed to meet Vojin and his friends, and someone gave me this *khat* as a gesture of goodwill and welcome to Odessa. Vojin and his men are away but are returning from Moscow soon.”

Zalaman lay back, trying to chew the stuff. It was not pleasant. He told Markus he’d stopped hearing those voices in his head.

“Good. Otherwise, you could be mistaken for a crazy person.”

“How could I not be crazy?”

Markus shrugged. Zalaman did have a point. He tried to imagine what Zalaman must feel toward the men who slaughtered his family and friends. He couldn’t blame Zalaman for not feeling ready to face his enemies. Even old Russian enemies.

“I’ll stay in the Bazama,” Zalaman said. “There’s a lot going on right here in the Jewish quarter.”

The next morning, Markus said he was going back to the Gnazdo, or the Gambrinus, or elsewhere to wait for his Russians, but before he left, would Zal like to steal a little breakfast with him?

They’d been in Odessa one week, when Markus disappeared.

They’d been successful, just barely, in avoiding serious trouble and yet still managed to have enough to eat. They’d been caught out during the attempted theft of a loaf of bread. During the chase that ensued, Zalaman, remembering the horrible (if exhilarating) details of his failed attempt to outrun Markovics in Zilupe, again promised himself this would be the last time he would do anything so stupid. Luckily, this time the chase was abandoned when they split up and disappeared and later reconvened in the den. They enjoyed the bread with a nervous energy from the close escape. Nothing serious had happened but it would have been dangerous to show their faces in Bazama too soon after.

Vojin and his friends were still missing, so one night Markus and Zalaman walked all the way back to Greek Street where they again encountered Edil, the merchant who had growled at them their first day in Odessa and who reminded Zalaman of his father. It was the eyes. Obviously, a successful peddler. His large, colorful horse-drawn cart with his name on the side carried a greater variety of fruits and vegetables than many of the permanent merchants whose shops lined that street. He peddled premium produce that included a variety of exotic species from the Levant and Africa. He sold the local Black Sea cod from a pail on his cart. Zalaman noticed how every morning Edil parked his wagon in its privileged position on the street. How he attracted a good number of customers and spectators—he wasn't a peddler at all—he was like Markovics, a merchant who happened to be on wheels.

Zalaman steered Markus clear of Edil's wagon. He wanted to avoid his disapproving-father eyes. Markus, on the other hand, was incensed all over again about the old man's attitude. Edil would be a problem, he said, yes, but stealing from him was a challenge they had to accept. Zalaman disagreed, but Markus wouldn't be denied.

"Then you'll have to do it yourself." Stealing from Edil would be like stealing from his father. It would also be impossible, because Edil seemed to already be on to them. That was the argument that won over Markus, not Zalaman's insistence that there had to be a safer way to live.

When they got home, Markus went off to the Gnazdo or some other Russian-frequented restaurant or cafe to look for his Russians.

He didn't return the next morning, nor the next few mornings. Zalaman started wondering if he would ever see Markus again. He thought about going to look for him but didn't relish the thought of nosing around by himself in the Russian quarter. He hoped Markus had found his Russians and would return when he was ready.

CHAPTER SIXTEEN

Edil

Zalaman decided he'd visit Greek Street. He hadn't been there since that last day with Markus more than a week before. Maybe he'd been unfair to Markus, never agreeing to his plans for Edil. If he ever was going to steal again, why not this old man? He wasn't Papa after all. And Zalaman was hungry.

He walked up to the back of Edil's wagon while Edil waited on a customer and gazed at a temptation that was too large to act on—yellow melons, bigger and brighter than any he had ever seen. He prodded the rough skin with a finger.

"*Tsi nit*," cautioned Edil, a man who, after years of dealing with young, irresponsible, sometimes starving, kids, had developed eyes in the back of his head. His Yiddish was calm, but unequivocal. "*Mach nichts.*" He repeated it in several other languages in case the ragamuffin wasn't as Jewish as he looked. You couldn't tell these days with all the races on Greek Street—in fact, all over Odessa. But that rich mix of so many races and nationalities was also one of the things Edil was going to miss about Odessa. He would *not* miss having to deal with things like the young man poking the melons.

Probably such people were everywhere. It will be the same in the Holy Land. But he contented himself that once he was there, he wouldn't care about ragamuffins like this.

Zalaman returned Edil's glare but apologized for poking the fruit. They stared at one another for a moment, until Edil spoke up. "Do you know what you are poking to death there?"

Zalaman hemmed and hawed, not wanting to admit he didn't know what this sweet-smelling thing was, so Edil introduced him to the grapefruit.

"It's also called The Forbidden Fruit. The Fruit of Paradise."

"Really? I'd been misled into thinking that was an apple."

Edil begged to differ. "It has a bitterness that is sweet. And it is much more expensive than an apple, so don't play with it."

He didn't want to dismiss the young man unfairly, so he introduced himself and Zalaman did the same, then leaned over for a closer look. Surely the old man couldn't object to his sniffing. Something of the lemon, something of the orange, yet different from both.

"So, what happened to that disreputable, angry, and very skinny partner of yours, the one you were slinking around with before?" Zalaman wasn't surprised Edil had noticed and wasn't going to give him the satisfaction of looking surprised. He just told him Markus had disappeared. Edil nodded his approval of this fact. "I had to turn over a couple of young crooks to the authorities recently," Edil continued. "They tried to stage a scuffle, something I'd already seen thieves do to distract me and seen it performed more convincingly."

Edil was settling into this, holding Zalaman's interest while keeping tabs on other customers. "The best of all the thieves was this old woman selling violets. Her scheme didn't last for long, but only because her husband would no longer play her accomplice. Then there's the thief who comes at you with a story-that-never-ends while his partner makes the snatch."

When Edil described the Zalaman-Markus routine, Zalaman, despite himself, couldn't suppress a smile that the old man correctly understood as an admission of 'That's me.'

"Watch out. *Tsi nit,*" Edil warned, wagging a finger. "I haven't heard what happened to the would-be scufflers I caught. I had to turn them in and I fear the worst." Zalaman didn't ask what the worst might be because he didn't want to hear it and he didn't want to appear as if this could be of any interest to him.

Edil had to turn away to answer an inquiry from a customer concerning the freshness of the cod. He was a master of easy banter. He not only looked, but he also sounded like Papa. It wasn't just the eyes and the age. He listened to Edil compliment "Mrs. Kolodi." Edil sympathized with her when she complained about her miserable husband. Then he made some not-quite-indecent comment which made Mrs. Kolodi laugh. Edil waved over at Zalaman to join them.

"Mrs Kolodi is such a beautiful creature, Zalaman. Don't you think? Of course, you noticed. Could you guess this woman's age?"

Zalaman nodded his agreement that Mrs. Kolodi was a beautiful creature, though Mrs. Kolodi was anything but. He knew what he should do because this was an exercise in flattery straight from Papa's alcohol dispensary. He knew he should say a number less than he figured she was without being too outrageous and be taken as a joke and fail as flattery. He'd never been good at guessing older people's ages. They were either in the category 'old' or they were 'very old.'

"Thirty-five," Zalaman said. This was greeted with great frivolity by Mrs. Kolodi. Edil nodded in agreement. He secretly guessed she was in her fifties.

Mrs. Kolodi loaded up with three cod with Zalaman's and Edil's encouragement—"It's just caught and serving it to that husband of yours might be just the trick to get him off your back," Edil said—along with numerous vegetables Edil suggested would go so well with the fish. Zalaman ran around retrieving her purchases and wiping them clean.

Once Mrs. Kolodi was gone, Edil said, "Zalaman, you could earn some money doing things for me. Couldn't hurt, could it? Might make you an honest man. Help me clean up the mess all around the wagon here and feed Goliath and then I'll give you a bite to eat. Not the forbidden fruit, but something good," he promised.

The assistant to the peddler sounded just fine. Apprentice to a butcher. None of it appealed all that much, so one thing or another. Anything other than work that leads inevitably to amputation or worse. It was not what he'd had in mind when he'd stood at their graves, and promised he would make them proud. He would work hard and be successful and, doing so, he would honor their lives. It was honest and safe, and it would keep him fed.

Edil's produce felt like home right away when Edil introduced his straw broom and his horse, Goliath. Zalaman stared into the horse's truly large eye, telling Edil how he'd been on and around horses his whole life, about two of his own, as well as the two Beths and Krysa, grooming and feeding them, appreciating them. Goliath was a Stanko of his species, big and powerful looking. Zalaman loved the feel of him, his soft hide, and the muscles that shiver rippled underneath his hand on Goliath's neck. He observed the worn teeth. Goliath was not young. Edil said that was true—he and Goliath had been together many years and he would be sorry to leave him. Zalaman marked that but didn't have time to ask Edil what he meant about 'leaving.' Edil directed him to sweep up and then feed Goliath.

When he was done, they took a break and Edil provided a welcome meal. He claimed that business was not good, but this was contrary to Zalaman's impression. "You just arrived, so you don't know Greek Street," Edil explained. "You should have seen it just a few years ago. Haven't you seen the empty shops?" Zalaman nodded without mentioning the den.

"Maybe it's for the good," Edil sighed. "And yes, as you can see, I've got plenty of business myself. That's in part thanks to those who left and who left me with new customers. And it's certainly easier to cross the street these days without getting held up by the crowds or run over by carriages."

"That sounds like Odessa today."

"It's an echo of what it was. The Jews are emigrating, leaving for Palestine. That's why so many shops and stalls are empty."

"My brother Davin always wanted to go to the Holy Land. I hope he made it—but I doubt it."

"I'm going, too. So, I'll look for him. One of these days. Sooner rather than later." Zalaman wondered if Edil wasn't a little old for such a journey and such a major change. He didn't say this, but Edil saw the look of concern. "It's not so far as it used to be. Now there are dependable boats." He tried to size up the young man. "Do you even know where you are?" He pointed in the direction of the Black Sea. "The other side is Istanbul, then, Greece—and Jerusalem! It's not such a long journey considering how far you've come—and I know from your speech that you are from the northern Pale."

He told Edil how Davin had run off to save him when he, Zalaman, had been snatched by a *chapper* and how no one ever found out what had happened to him.

"He's probably in Jerusalem," Edil said. "You and I were destined to meet. My brother is also in the Holy Land. I am going there, in part, to see him again—before I get too old for the journey. It shouldn't have surprised me when my previous assistant ran off to the Holy Land, as well."

Zalaman could work for him every day, if he wanted, like the previous assistant, but he should take a bath and get some new clothes or at least clean and sew what he was wearing. Edil gave him a few coins, trusting him to return, smelling better, in the morning. Zalaman realized his dip in the Black Sea had been quite a while back.

Maybe that was why the women of Odessa had been less than friendly.

When he got back to the den, he noticed Markus' shoulder bag was missing from their hiding place. He must have been there that day and taken it. No one else would know how to get in or could have found the hiding place, and who wouldn't have also taken Zalaman's hessian bag and the *khat*? He was angry at Markus for not contacting him, not even leaving a note. But at least Markus was still alive. Maybe Markus didn't know how to write. Maybe he didn't know how to read. Zalaman sat and chewed some *khat*, thankful Markus had left it. He'd now come to associate the taste with pleasant times, and that somehow mitigated the bitterness.

The next morning, he was already on Greek Street waiting for Edil when the peddler appeared, carting a fresh supply of goods. He sat upright for his age, Zalaman thought, comparing him to Papa, on his bench in the wagon pulled along by Goliath. He looked the prosperous peddler. When he saw Zalaman there so early, he gave an approving nod. Zalaman patted Goliath and helped Edil down from his perch, although Edil hadn't indicated he wanted any assistance. He thanked Zalaman and said he was happy to see him so bright and early. Even earlier, he wanted Zalaman to know—when Zalaman had no doubt still been asleep—he and Goliath had already been at the central market, filling the wagon.

It was high summer. The first full day of Zalaman's employment. He helped Edil stack and clean carrots, beans, peas, turnips, celery, a variety of cabbages, onions, and potatoes. Before they parted ways at the end of that day, Zalaman had added leeks, brussels sprouts, and cauliflower to his vocabulary. Goliath didn't require much in the way of caring. Along with his great size, the horse was calm and intelligent and he would nod his big head in appreciation of Zalaman's attention. Zalaman's interaction with customers was limited to fetching this or that—he was not involved in the selling or accepting of payment. But that very first day, he caught a lad, even younger than Markus, trying to steal an apple. Edil was busy with a customer, but he was watching out of the corner of his eye as Zalaman wrested the apple from the boy's grasp.

Zalaman let him break free and run off and Edil approved. *It takes a thief . . .* , he recalled the old proverb.

It was hot by high noon and the customers were home taking a midday nap, so they sat and drank tea, Edil leaning against the wagon, Zalaman, standing, leaning on his broom. "This Markus of yours," Edil asked. "Your would-be accomplice—what ever happened to him?"

"Markus is OK. But he's disappeared. He's had it pretty hard in his life—if you can believe him. Yes, I do. He's tough for someone so young. Maybe he's found his Russians and is away doing whatever it is they do. He doesn't really want me involved, at least yet—which is a good thing."

"I agree," Edil said, "but have you looked for him?" Zalaman said he was planning on doing so that night after work—in the Russian Quarter. "There is no Russian Quarter in Odessa," Edil explained. "The whole city has become a Russian enclave."

"Markus mentioned a saloon—the Gnazdo."

"Good. Yes, there is no Russian quarter, but if there *was* one, it would be the Gnazdo or the Gambrinus. Those taverns would be the Russian-quarter cathedrals. But be careful." He gave Zalaman two coins so he could get inside and buy a drink, assuming he first got cleaned up.

><

In the Gnazdo that evening, a reputable-looking and better smelling Zalaman was looking closely for evidence of the depravity extolled by Markus. It was a cavernous tavern. A lot of alcohol was being consumed by Russian gentlemen, tradespeople, and merchants. He noted a Russian couple sniffing marching powder or something that looked like it. He asked at the bar about Markus, but got nowhere, so he sat and drank and watched the ladies.

Were they prostitutes? They clung to the men, but were they clients or pimps or lovers? The Russians in the Gnazdo didn't look menacing like Cossacks, but that didn't mean they weren't dangerous. Maybe more so. It might be wiser for him not to mention Vojin and the others. He didn't want to draw attention. He was already getting more of it than he knew.

There was still no Markus later when he got to the den. He ate and chewed some *khat*. It was late, but after the hubbub of the saloon, he was restless in the dark, stuffy den, so he walked all the way down to the sea. It felt good to be out in the cool air above the beach. At intervals, there was a waist-high cement embankment lit by electric torches. Zalaman leaned against it, turning his face to the breeze that blew across the sands from the sea and he was washed with salty dew that mixed with tears. There was something about all that water, water that he knew was full of life, that made him think of its opposite. He wiped the salty dew from his face and stared out over the dark sea. There were illuminated ships bobbing on its waters. Life on them this late.

He was profoundly alone. Why had his family had to leave? Did he owe them some kind of revenge? What could revenge possibly look like? Repaying violence with more violence would surely not be the way to pay homage.

The Russian ships were slowly dancing at anchor, their onboard lanterns cast stripes across the bowing hulls and lapping water. As his eyes adjusted to the dark, he saw that there were people, dozens of them, sleeping on the beach. The air was so temperate and he was suddenly so tired—the labors with Edil, the effects of the *khat*, the alcohol at the Gnazdo—it would be comfortable to lie down for a while on that soft sand still warm from the sun.

He walked down to the beach and lowered himself down onto the sand. The fresh air made sleep, which had eluded him in the den, come easily, as he wondered if perhaps Edil would agree to watch his bag so he could use this beach as his residence as others were obviously doing. So he should leave Markus a note where to find him. If necessary, Markus would find someone to read it to him. Content with these plans, he fell asleep.

But before long, a watchman was slapping him on the legs with a cudgel. "No sleeping on the beach overnight," he ordered. Zalaman picked himself up and headed back toward the embankment, crossing the sand where the dozens of people he had seen before had now disappeared, evidently aware of the night watchman's schedule. They had retreated to the embankment to avoid the watchman. As the watchman moved on, they were already reemerging to return to their comfortable sandy beds.

"Don't let the watchman catch you a second time," the man next to him said. "He can arrest you." He also told Zalaman that the watchman wouldn't come again until the crack of dawn. The man said he'd grown so used to the watchman's routine that he automatically woke up before his second round. He offered to wake Zalaman. Zalaman said that was very generous. "Everyone knows," the man said, "and no one makes a stink."

In the morning, Zalaman had been awakened so early that he didn't have to run in order to be ready and waiting for Edil and Goliath when they arrived at the central market to get enough produce for the coming day on Greek Street. The watchman's interruptions were a small price to pay for the accommodations. Edil agreed to keep Zalaman's bag in the wagon, so Zalaman could abandon the den. He paid a last visit that night, taking the remaining *khat* and leaving Markus a note saying he could be found at Edil's on Greek Street. And so, the Odessa beach became Zalaman's permanent bed. Once, in advance of the watchman's first visit, he went to look for Markus, this time in the Gambrinus, but to no avail.

Working for Edil was not taxing. He learned about herbs and new vegetables—that there were three different varieties of cabbage alone: white, red and savoy. *Khat* seemed to be the only herb Edil didn't sell. He felt about *khat* a lot like Papa did.

As the weeks passed, Zalaman began to participate in some of the commerce—the selling itself. Edil had to reassure himself that Zalaman was becoming an honest man. He saw he was scrupulously fair to the customers.

Zalaman befriended a cute flower-lady on the far end of the *Bazama* where the flower ladies congregated. He convinced Edil, against the peddler's better judgment, to add flowers to his list of goods. Zalaman had forged an alliance with his flower lady in which she provided him with blooms to give away free to each of Edil's customers as a way to make them fall in love with the exotic and fragrant flowers. And they were beautiful, Edil had to admit. Cut flowers were not a necessity, but they turned out to be a moderate success anyway—the free flower trick had worked to a degree. The flower lady got her piece and no one lost money over it. And the flowers made the wagon more attractive.

But Zalaman had hoped to make some money, so he was feeling frustrated. He told Edil he should branch out. His nights on the beach made him think about seafood. Edil said there was no more room in the wagon.

"You should get a bigger wagon."

"There is no bigger wagon. Nothing bigger is allowed on Greek Street."

"Then get a real shop."

Edil laughed. He was going to be leaving for the Holy Land so what did he want with a shop? Besides, what Zalaman didn't know was that a Jewish clan controlled all the properties on Greek

Street, including wagon spaces. They decided who was permitted. They were just like the Port Jews who controlled half of the docks and all the fishing out of Odessa. The Port Jews were the reason Edil would never sell more fish than the occasional bass—or cod like they sold Mrs. Kolodi—from a fisherman friend. He said he had no choice but to work with the Odessa clan of Jews—they just referred to themselves, domineeringly, as The Odessa Jews—but he refused to work with the Port Jews. He didn't explain why, but when Zalaman badgered him about it, he said they were corrupt and unreasonable. So were the members of the Odessa Jewish gang, only a little less so.

The Odessa Jews were not the only clan running the city. There were other, more secular clans, all of them little more than extended gangs in league with the Odessa authorities like the *kahal* with the DPPO. As one of the beach-dwellers had explained to Zalaman one night: the Port Jews had a Russian counterpart on the docks who controlled grain shipments. The Port Jews controlled everything else: fishing, manufactured goods, even human sea passengers.

Zalaman visited both the Gnazdo and Gambrinus, but after looking almost weekly, he was now too busy with Edil, and would visit each only one more time. The work with Edil that had started out so easy and simple, had changed since Zalaman got it in his head to get ahead. He had little time to look for Markus. But he looked. This time he had a few coins in his pocket and the pockets were not those in his greatcoat but in a new pair of pants and jacket, more Odessa-style than the old outfit, the pants raggedy and too small. He hoped he'd stopped growing so he wouldn't have to spend so much on clothing. He felt he was tall enough already, usually among the tallest in the room. But the costume made it easier to gain entrance to other cafes and saloons, some nearer Greek Street, as well as the Gnazdo and the Gambrinus.

No matter what part of Odessa one spoke of, The Gnazdo and the Gambrinus vied with one another for the honor of being most licentious of the Russian drinking establishments and, thus, the most popular among all the saloons. Zalaman didn't find Markus in either place, but he didn't ask like he had originally, because the asking had gained him nothing but wary looks. Women were finally taking notice of him. He took them to be whores with their provocative smiles. One of them always lavished him with a special look no matter which Russian businessman she happened to be on the arm of that evening. Once she had approached him and he had to explain he couldn't afford her. She lost interest in him after that. He wondered if maybe he'd been unfair and shouldn't have assumed she'd been about to proposition him. He'd been so frugal at the time. Had to be. But he should at least have found out how much. He nursed his drink, looking at her studiously avoiding his look. But not completely. He believed she approved of his new costume. He thought about drinking in the Punie inn's saloon and how Rodak had questioned Antek's right to use Daiya and Ewa and make such a profit from their own hard work. He hoped Rodak and Stanko were alive and healthy.

"The watchman does not dare roust *us* out of our beds—and beds they are even if they are beds of sand." This was the way Bar, one of the Port Jews, introduced himself to Zalaman, the young man who had been asking so many questions. "I may not look like it, but I am one of the Port Jews no one wants to trouble." He said it with a sigh, matter-of-factly, not like he was bragging. Bar had been watching Zalaman on the beach from his privileged spot—higher ground, reserved for the Port Jews.

Bar explained he was not simply a member of the clan but was also an "over-the-sea" shipper, owner of an iron steamship and two barges who simply didn't like to sleep on rocking boats at night, even if they were his. "I like to sleep on solid ground whenever I can, when I'm staying over in Odessa—in the summer," he explained to Zalaman as he showed him the Port Jews' semi-private beach. "I get tired of rocking boats, especially on summer nights like this" he said, deeply inhaling the mixture of sea air and the fragrances of Odessa.

Bar told Zalaman he'd seen him on Greek Street with Edil and before Zalaman could say anything to defend his boss, Bar said it wasn't necessary. He respected the old man. He told Zalaman he should sleep here, with the Port Jews. As he said, the watchman does not bother anyone here. Zalaman thanked him and was grateful to be able to sleep through the night unmolested.

The next week, when Bar sailed away, Zalaman kept his spot on the beach. And when Bar returned, Zalaman thanked Bar for the privilege he'd shown him and asked if he'd had a good voyage and would like to chew some *khat*. Bar laughed, then thanked him and said Jews shouldn't need these things.

Bar explained the relationships between the Port Jews and the Odessa Jews—they had to maintain positive connections—and said that the bad relationship with Edil was Edil's fault, not the clan's. He painted a picture of Edil as unrealistic and idealistic.

"The docks belong to the city of Odessa, but the piers belong to us. It's always been this way, even before we—the Port Jews—built the two major piers. The Russians control the grain because they grow most of it. It's easier this way."

The talk of clans and rights reminded Zalaman how his father had supported the tailors of Lahkvna in their revolt against the *shtetl's* elite over the right to wear velvet *yarmulkes*. Bar knew about The Tailors' Revolt and grew quiet.

"You're from Lahkvna," he said. Bar travelled quite a bit. He'd heard about the massacre of the Jews but could see Zalaman did not want to talk about it. He sympathized with the boy's agony and wanted to do something for him. Bar told him he too was idealistic. He wanted a world where there were laws—religious, secular, it made no difference—rather than lawless gangs. Yes, he referred to them as gangs. And yes, he had to do business with them, at least with the Odessa Jews, although the gang didn't control itinerant peddlers.

He hadn't then told Edil anything about Lahkvna. At first, he had consciously avoided the massacre. But once the kvaat loosened Zalaman's tongue, he repeated some of the conversations he had with Bar. Edil said yes, there was a clan of Jews that controlled—claimed to 'own'—the commercial part of Odessa that included Greek Street. They controlled the shop owners, but they didn't control itinerant peddlers like him. Zalaman wondered if the valuable spot Edil's wagon regularly occupied made him less 'itinerant.'

Edil compared the Odessa Jews under their headman, Royt, to the Cossacks under the Tsar. Zalaman laughed, but not because he found the comparison absurd. On the contrary, he'd been thinking the same thing.

"The Odessa Jews may not be as bad as their Russian counterparts, but they can be violent," Edil said. "Why do I do business with such people? Because there is no other way to do business here safely. I don't have to do business at the port."

To Zalaman this meant Edil *could* do business with them if he would do it on their terms. He told Edil of the atrocity at Lahkvna. The slaughter of his family. He and Edil cried together. Edil said he couldn't fathom the depth of Zalaman's pain, but he claimed to have felt something amiss all along, a haunted look in Zalaman's eyes. "Odessa has had its share of these massacres of Jews," he warned—"another reason I'm happy to be leaving."

"You think in the Holy Land there won't be clans and gangs?"

"No, I suppose men are the same everywhere. Maybe it will just be the Jews doing the massacring."

Edil owed the boy nothing, but, like Bar, he wanted to do right by him. He thought about giving Zalaman the wagon and throwing Goliath in with the deal. Deal? What would he get out of it? That was easy—thinking about it made him feel good. He was leaving anyway, wasn't he? He had no relatives left in Odessa to leave his business to.

He'd saved enough money for the voyage to Jerusalem—across the Black Sea to the Sea of Marmara, the Aegean, and Mediterranean all the way to Palestine or at least to a port not too far away. He couldn't subject Goliath to such a voyage. If Zalaman took over his cart, his customers would still be served.

Zalaman was touched when Edil explained all this to him and cried tears of joy—it seemed tears came easily to Zalaman these days—though he was not surprised.

"You hadn't said anything about Goliath and your wagon—your business, so I figured you were taking the vehicle and the horse with you. Seems like they might be of some help to you during a long voyage." He didn't add "your being such an old man." Edil said they'd just get in the way.

Zalaman's time was all taken up practicing his role as "New Edil." That's how Edil introduced him to the men in charge of the wholesale markets. Zalaman didn't want to be "New Edil." Patting the wagon bench, he said he was Zalaman Aszer, Pretender to the Throne.

Edil took him to the outskirts of Odessa, to a village called Bogdanovka, where he stabled Goliath in a barn. Near the barn was a cottage where Edil stayed, but he could not offer it to Zalaman because, though it would soon be getting too cold for him to sleep on the beach, the cottage was not Edil's property. The owners could return at any time to reclaim it and he had no way of contacting them about Zalaman.

Meanwhile, he suggested Zalaman sleep in the barn with Goliath until he saved enough money that he could afford other arrangements "when the barn gets too cold."

His date of departure nearing, Edil started informing his customers that he was soon off for the Holy Land. Some applauded, some censured him, all regretted losing him—which is when he would introduce or reintroduce Zalaman, "The New Edil." Later, when Zalaman reprimanded him for this, Edil, did a Markus-like shrug and said, "You know all you need to know. The only secret is hard work. It's just damn vegetables after all."

There would be winter snow in Odessa, but not in the amounts Zalaman was used to. Working hours would be even longer once Edil left, leaving him with all the work.

Before that happened, he decided he would pay one more visit to the Gnazdo. It had been many weeks. Months, perhaps.

He took a Turkish bath so he could feel confident with women and when asking after Markus.

The saloon was buzzing when he got there and so was he, having added a tincture of opium to his drink. He nursed it, trying to imagine what the most beautiful, but respectable women might look like under all those clothes. Undressing them in his head, he found the well-dressed excited him more than the whores whose costumes left little to the imagination—although they excited him, too. Among the better-dressed young women he disrobed was a dark-eyed beauty he'd spied more than once before. She was always alone and she never smiled when their eyes met. Whenever they did, hers were quickly diverted, which may be one reason he never approached her—nor did any of the other men in the Gnazdo. When Zalaman asked his waiter about Markus and Vojin, he got no response from the waiter, but when he asked about the solitary beauty, he got a 'no-no' shake of the head that reminded of him of Edil's "*Tsi nit*" when he and Markus had been eyeing Edil's produce.

Despite his misgivings about Markus, it would be good to have him back in Odessa. He'd grown to love Edil, but he wanted a friend closer to his age. His only friend in the *shtetl* had been killed. A hero. He hoped Stanko was OK and had a new leg. He sipped, and wondered if Rodak and Stanko had heard about Lahkvna. If they were still fighting in the north, would they have heard anything? It seemed everyone else in the world had. When he next saw Rodak, he would ask Zalaman how he was going to avenge his people. It made Zalaman sick to his stomach to think about that, even the thought of being confronted by Rodak with this. Whenever these thoughts entered his brain, he pushed them away, but the opium let them seep back in. What if he could kill all the perpetrators, how would that make him feel? Relieved? Proud? Disgusted?

What, short violence of, could be revenge?

Bar had pointed out to Zalaman that the Jews still alive in Lahkvna had some rights as Jews of the Pale. They had some legal course open to them, did they not? Yes, Zalaman said he was probably right. But he couldn't imagine it getting them anywhere. "Navharadak's Council of Elders will never do anything for the Jews. The presence of the DPPO at the slaughter practically made it a sanctioned event. I certainly have no power or influence." "'*Sanctioned event,*' Bar said. "But that's good. The case is against Navharadak, not just the rabble."

Zalaman finished his drink. The best thing he could do now was to put all his efforts into this opportunity Edil was handing him. He would make something of himself. He would have no power until he did so.

> <

Before he moved into the barn, he spent one last night at the beach talking with Bar, making sure it would be possible, once Edil was gone, to add fish to his wares, and asking about Bar's idea of Lahkvna's legal recourse against the city of Navharadak.

"The Council of Elders, or whatever they call themselves," Bar said, and in fact that was what they called themselves, "you're probably right about them. They're not going to do anything about the slaughter because their own people are implicated, their DPPO was for all intents a party to the thing." Zalaman nodded, hopeless. "So," Bar continued, "we have to appeal to a higher power."

Zalaman smiled at the "we," and asked, "You mean ask the Holy of Holies to intervene."

"Oh, we must go higher than that. We need the Tsar."

As the day of Edil's departure loomed, he and Zalaman also spent more time talking. He told Zalaman he thought the grief he was experiencing over Lahkvna would slowly fade. Zalaman had heard this theory before and wanted to believe it, but he didn't.

"Each day," Edil promised, "just a little bit more. It's still early for you to feel this relief, the blood of Lahkvna is not yet dry. There's something else you should know. Acts of violence against Jews are becoming more common everywhere every year. Not on the scale of what happened in Lahkvna, but attacks are becoming regular events right here in Odessa. Since 1821, every ten years or so. Jews in Odessa—we all think about leaving, but we reassure ourselves that since the last violence was, say, just last year, we ought to be OK for a while, maybe another ten years, a few more years of peace before it bubbles up again. Wishful thinking. It's like the plague. You don't get advance notice. The Christians of Odessa, like those in Navharadak, blame the Jews for crucifying Jesus Christ, for the plague, for the failure of the previous harvest, for just being Jews. A few years ago, there was a new twist here. Some of the Jews right here on Greek Street, were deemed to be too successful. Especially one of our merchants. The Christians, which is to say the Russians, argued that the Jew had made his success at the expense of poor Christians. And so, he was murdered—a symbolic act. Kill one Jew to resolve the problem of Jewish prosperity."

"But what about the Odessa Jews, the clan. They did nothing?"

"No. And I respect Royt for deciding against total war."

"I appreciate your warning me against becoming too successful. Thank you for the vote of confidence in my abilities." Edil laughed. It was true.

><

Edil drove Goliath one last time on the evening he was set to sail. In the wagon, in addition to the remnants of the day's sales, were Edil's leather traveling bag and Zalaman's hessian bag. Edil was leaving for Palestine and Zalaman was moving into a straw bed in the loft above Goliath. Edil apologized to Goliath for leaving him but assured him he would be in good hands. He told Zalaman there were many kinds of horses, just like there are many kinds of people, good and bad. Goliath was the best horse he'd ever known and Zalaman the best horseperson. They would make a good pair.

"We've had a talk, Goliath and me," Zalaman said, stroking Goliath's massive neck as they approached the dock. "He understands that you have family waiting for you. A new life. He told me he's happy for you."

Bar was watching his dockworkers assisting embarking passengers when he recognized Zalaman with Edil. He observed them as they said goodbye, saw Edil hug his nag, then Zalaman. It was a long hug, yet when they broke, neither looked all that sad about parting. It was not a tragic event. Edil was fulfilling his lifelong cherished dream, family and a new life waiting for him at his destination. And Zalaman was starting a new life as a business owner.

Edil said he would write to 'Zalaman of Edil's on Greek Street Market' and let Zalaman hear all about his life in the Promised Land and he made Zalaman promise he would write back and report on how he and Goliath were doing.

Zalaman wished him a safe voyage and hoped that he would find his brother in good health. Maybe find Zalaman's brother, too.

Chapter Seventeen

Odessa and Katya

But for the companionship of Goliath, Zalaman would have been lonely after Edil left. He threw himself into work, adding more seafood to his wares with Bar's and the Port Jews' assistance. Bar suggested Zalaman talk to Royt, the head of the Jewish gang that 'administrated' the Jews of Odessa—those who were not engaged in shipping, the business of the Port Jews. If Zalaman really wanted to expand his business, perhaps find a permanent shop, Royt's support would be essential.

The weather cooled and Zalaman found himself spending more time in the Gnazdo where he got to know Kogan, an Antek-like, Jewish-Russian pimp. Kogan introduced him to Mehtap, and once Zalaman thought he'd had enough of the incomprehensible poetry she wrote and insisted on reading to him after sex, Kogan introduced Rosabella, a whore with uninhibited and unending political opinions. He settled into an alternating pattern with the two.

His favorite item in the Gnazdo was not the whores or the drink, but the *kolbasa*. That and the dark-eyed beauty who drank alone but whose attention he could never attract, at least not until one evening when he was too enthusiastically tucking into a stew featuring his beloved sausage and choked, spewing the spicy, juicy *traif* over pants and vest and earning a generously exaggerated laugh from Dark Eyes.

One day in the cold of late fall, he broke into the deserted cabin near Goliath's barn and moved in, warmed by the wood stove where he cooked his morning and evening meals, luxuriating at night with a book and an oil lamp, dreaming of Dark Eyes or Lechsi or Hadar, a girl from his childhood.

At work that winter he was accosted by a heavyset man who introduced himself as "Izzy." It seemed Bar had spoken to Royt who was Izzy's boss. Royt was arguably the most powerful Jew in Odessa, so it was an honor that Royt wanted to meet him. That meeting took place in Royt's opulent apartment in the hills above the city, where Zalaman listened as Royt encouraged him to reach beyond his mentor, "Old Edil," who Royt dismissed as "just another fanatic running off to the Holy Land." He knew Zalaman's story from Bar, and he commiserated with the tragedies of Zalaman's life. He said Zalaman deserved better and Zalaman was quick to agree. A shop on Greek Street? Yes, Royt could facilitate such a thing. He liked Zalaman's spirit. But what he wanted would require Zalaman to do something for him. Something big enough that might qualify Zalaman to be an honorary clan member. "Anything," promised a grateful Zalaman, acknowledging that nothing was free and he was determined to improve his circumstances.

Celebrating his good fortune in the Gnazdo, he grew emboldened to approach Dark Eyes. When he did, she laughed at him, but quickly complimented him on getting the *kolbasa* stains off his vest. He told her he couldn't understand why such a beautiful woman was always sitting alone but supposed it must be because others considered her dangerous She looked like someone who was guaranteed to break hearts. "Not so much hearts as heads," she claimed. She asked him why he'd been inquiring about Vojin, her absent boyfriend, the breaker of heads and the reason others were afraid to approach her. Zalaman said he was glad he didn't know any better. Having been bored and lonely all winter, she was attracted to Zalaman's audacity, just like Royt had been. She also liked his looks and suggested they meet somewhere far from the eyes of nosey Odessans.

A few days later, Zalaman was summoned back to meet Royt at another fashionable apartment he kept in the middle of the city. He could tell how impressed Zalaman was by wealth and laughed when asked how many places a person needed in one city. Royt explained how his family's wealth went all the way back to their roots in Russia where they'd once enjoyed a near monopoly on the domestic tea trade. Zalaman wanted to be a part of this world. Royt, sympathizing with Zalman's desires, offered him an opportunity to participate in it. All he had to do was kill one Major Tushayev, someone responsible for many crimes against Jews, the death of more Jews than were slaughtered in Lahkvna. It was an opportunity to extract a measure of revenge and better his situation in life. Something that should be easy for a man who had killed so many Cossacks. Zalaman told Royt he appreciated the offer but didn't want to make his mark that way. It would be more than dangerous to kill a Russian officer in a town half-controlled by Russians. He'd promised his parents he would no longer kill. Royt said he believed Uritsky's shop on Greek Street would be vacant soon, Uritsky decamping to the Holy Land like Edil and so many foolish others. Zalaman hesitated. Perhaps permanently disabling the man would be good enough? Royt said Zalaman was fooling himself if he thought he could pull off such a feat without it becoming fatal. "But OK," Royt said, "I can find someone else to do it. A shame, though. I would have liked to have you in the clan."

Hidden in the shadows that flickered beyond the oil lamps, Zalaman followed Tushayev in the night. He followed him all the way from the saloon to his home where the Major shared a meal with his wife and children who acted as if they loved this Jew-hater. The scene at dinner made him sad, thinking of meals with his own family. Later, following the Major down an alley after leaving his loving family on some errand, Zalaman, rounded the corner and was confronted by the Major pointing a cocked pistol directly in his face. Zalaman had not been the quietly alert scout he thought he was. The Major wanted to know why he was being followed. Was he working for Royt or the clan? Tushayev was asking angily and that was probably why he didn't hear Izzy as he emerged from the alley and shoved the blade into Tushayev's neck. The Major collapsed, still gurgling about Royt. Izzy said he was happy he'd decided to follow Zalaman and see how he would fulfill Royt's request. Zalaman assured him he was happier. Izzy didn't want Royt to know he'd done the killing. He wanted Zalaman to take credit for it. Izzy had too much business to do with the Russians to even be a suspect. That, and the fact that Izzy was impressed with the courage Zalaman had shown when he refused to divulge Royt's name to the Major—even with a gun in his face.

> <

For a long time after he moved into Uritsky's store and opened his very own produce shop, Zalaman wondered how it was that Uritsky had decided to depart for the Holy Land so soon after the demise of Major Tushayev—a murder about which neither the Russians nor the Odessa Police seemed to have a clue. Perhaps the Major had not been the revered figure Izzy had thought he was and hadn't been the number one case for the police nor a great concern to the Russians. Perhaps Royt had pulled some strings or called in some favors.

Throughout that harsh winter, Zalaman was able to keep the shop open, even profitable, thanks in part to the now full-time employment of Sandr, his previously part-time assistant, and his nights were warmed by the cook stove in his little cabin. How quickly the cabin went from seeming like someone else's, to feeling that it belonged to him by possession.

Occasionally, his nights were warmed by Katya. It hadn't taken long from Katya's "see you soon" to Zalaman's meeting her in the Bazama and bringing her to the cabin. He couldn't believe his new position in life. But on those nights with her he felt it strongly. He was serving wine to the most beautiful woman in Odessa—even if she did belong to someone else—in his own cabin! He served more wine and they talked and drank more wine and then they made love and felt happy—as happy as Zalaman had allowed himself to be since Lahkvna. He still was surprised he had the capacity for it.

And it never lasted long because Katya could never stay long. She had to take pains to avoid detection.

For Katya, Zalaman provided a release that had been a long time coming. She came to the cabin only when she felt it was safe to sneak away from her home, from her neighborhood, without being seen by Vojin's friends or relatives. Those rare evenings when she did come to his cabin, they both found remarkable. After long, difficult winter days, when he and Goliath returned home exhausted, and Katya was there, he found he still had plenty of life left in him. Those were truly warm winter nights, but they were few and far between. When Katya was not there, which is to say by far the greater number of nights, after saying goodnight to Goliath, he would cook something and then read into the night. He was training himself to be able to concentrate on whole pages at a time, which meant avoiding feelings of dread or despair which would interrupt a story. Reading once again became part of his life. He couldn't get enough.

The work of running a shop was harder in the winter due to the increased travel times between cabin-stable-markets-Greek Street. But, what a pleasure to have a shop relatively free from the tyranny of the weather. That was a bonus, but the most exciting part is that he was already, even in winter, making a small profit.

Katya did not want to run into Zalaman at the Gnazdo. She said it wasn't safe, so they both more or less stopped going. He preferred having a drink in his own place, now that he had his own place. He preferred having that drink with one woman and now he had one, even if she didn't come but once every few weeks. He was so busy making a success of his new shop, he needed all the sleep he could get.

On Easter Sunday 1871, he rode Goliath into the hills above Odessa where he spent the entire day remembering Papa and Mama and Keila and Davin and his life before. He relived it; it was all still fresh, almost too raw. It struck him that he would need to do more to honor their lives than just make a success of himself. There would have to be revenge.

It turned out to have been a good day to be out of town. The Odessa Jews who had been in the wrong place suffered that Easter. There were no deaths, but there were plenty of injuries inflicted by the unruly Greek Christians on the bodies of those few who had forgotten what day it was. The Jews suffered property losses whether they'd stayed home or not. Some Russians joined the Greeks in their crimes, a bad sign for the future of Jewish-Russian relationships. But Royt's clan managed to protect most of Greek Street, including Uritsky's, Zalaman and Royt agreeing they should wait awhile before they changed the name to Aszer.

But the Easter terror brought back the agony of Lahkvna and Zalaman suffered. Both Bar and Izzy noticed his black periods and tried to talk to him about them. Perhaps talk him out of them. They thought they already knew what was bothering him before they even asked: the massacre of the Jews at Lahkvna. What they uncovered was something else: *revenge* for the massacre of the Jews of Lahkvna. He admitted to sometimes feeling the weight of it even more as time went on. Izzy advised him to consider 'their' killing Major Tushayev as a measure of revenge. That at least got a laugh from Zalaman, who questioned Izzy's 'their' killing and the entire idea, reminding him again, "It was the Poles not the Russians."

"Christians, all the same."

"No," Zalaman insisted. "You know that's not true."

"No, you're right, it's not true. The Russians are in a class by themselves."

"Besides, it's not really *The Poles*, either is it? It's *those* men . . . those specific twenty men."

Katya couldn't excuse her fellow Russians for having joined the Greeks in the Easter mayhem. And she was fed up with waiting for Vojin, although, to be fair, since she'd gotten to know Zalaman, she might not be seen as 'waiting.' She did her best to make sure her neighbors knew nothing beyond the fact that she had a sick relative she had to visit occasionally. She went to the Gnazdo rarely, just to keep up appearances. When she told Zalaman she was truly fed up with Vojin, Zalaman wanted to believe her, but next thing she'd get some report that Vojin was on the way back to Odessa, was even nearby. She was once told he was imprisoned in Russia.

"Yes," said someone else, "but he's soon to be released."

"Hah," laughed someone else, "I've heard he's living it up in decadent fashion in Tbilisi."

The imagined sightings of Vojin reached Katya whenever she went to the Gnazdo, providing both a reason to go—she wanted to be prepared—and a reason to stay away—the sightings always turned out to be false. She was feeling very attached to Zalaman, despite the rarity of her visits. She had to keep her attachment secret. If anyone asked where she'd been on such-and-such a night, she would say she was caring for a sick aunt. She still feared Vojin.

Life went on for the two of them, throughout that winter and the following summer and another following that. Zalaman's business prospered—grew like his love of Katya and the length of her stays with him at his cabin. She would explain to anyone who cared that her aunt was getting sicker.

Before long, Zalaman had enough work to hire an assistant for Sandr—Moishe, recommended by Izzy. His produce and seafood sales made it possible to pay an additional hand. He let them run the business for one summer week so he and Katya could get away to spend that time together. It was a surreptitious escape, a day's ride away to the Black Sea beach at Zatoka. Katya hadn't heard a thing from Vojin, not even any sightings from people in the Gnazdo. She told Zalaman she no longer felt she owed any allegiance to Vojin.

But when they returned from Zatoka, Katya found a letter and a package waiting. In the letter, Vojin apologized for his lengthy absence. Writing earlier had been impossible, he wrote, without saying *why* it had been impossible. He would be back soon and hoped she liked the necklace. The news was a sobering reminder of things as they were after the Black Sea romp—sobering because, given the fine jade necklace, this time she believed he meant it.

Zalaman was both deflated and strangely energized by this prospect. It was about time to get rid of this impediment to his happiness. He would fight for Katya. Meanwhile, she lay low and he buried himself in work. Katya had a feeling Vojin would show up in the summer—this summer—when the weather was favorable for travel. On one of her rare appearances at the cabin, Zalaman scolded her for coming so seldom and for her fear of Vojin. She told him it was a very rational fear. Vojin had the reputation of being a violent character. "Never toward me" she said. "I've never really seen that side of him. But I hear about it and I can tell when he's boiling under the surface." She claimed she didn't know what his business was and didn't want to know. Knowing too much could only get her in trouble.

It was midsummer, 1874, when Vojin and company floated into the Gulf of Odessa on a large Russian trawler on which two decks had been re-fitted for passenger travel. The lower deck was cramped and unhealthy, but if you could afford it, there was an upper deck, comfortably free of smoke from the smokestacks, though not from the smoke of a dozen burning cigars. The upper deck smokers were well-tailored in typical Black Sea fashion, which is to say international motley. Their wives and children were at the railing watching Odessa grow larger as the men smoked and discussed Bismarck and how the Egypt-Ethiopia war was affecting commerce. The war was interfering with that commerce, they mostly agreed . . . yet, perhaps something good could still come from it.

One of those puffing away on his cigar was Markus. He'd accompanied Vojin and Bogdan for three years of profitable, if illegal, 'trading' in Mother Russia. He'd aged at least ten years, looking quite the world-weary fifteen-year-old—a few pounds heavier, nicely filling out his clean Russian tunic and trousers. Zalaman would not have recognized him except for that familiar shrug and sneering grin as he blew smoke rings to intertwine with those of his two Russian partners and business associates, Vojin and Bogdan.

In the minds of Vojin and Bogdan, Markus was not quite a full-fledged partner. He was too young, too green, too young and at times, too much of a show-off. After all, chronologically he wasn't much more than a child. But there were qualities in Markus that were a real benefit to their work. Both men respected his original way of looking at things and taking action and his bravery in executing them. Being so nimble was a big benefit when circumstances called for physical activity—doing things the aging Timor would have found impossible, transforming his sometimes-obnoxious braggadocio into an unexpected act of bravery. Since Timor's untimely death—his old body had slowed him up during one caper—Markus had been a valuable replacement, though it had taken Bogdan a long time to reach such a favorable assessment. At first, Bogdan had been opposed to Markus, considering him too young and innocent for their kind of work, but he was quickly disabused of that opinion. Anyway, it was Vojin's decision. He had the final say in this and every matter and he insisted on giving Markus a chance.

Even before the problems with the aging Timor, Vojin had known they needed younger blood. And you couldn't get much younger than Markus. Vojin had been right about Markus, and Bogdan told him so. After a couple of successful years, ruthless in stealing or smuggling anything that was worth stealing or smuggling, big jobs, and little ones, they had been creative and lucky, sailing back to Odessa rich men.

When they were about to dock. Vojin pulled the cigar out of his mouth and sat up, waving the smoke from his eyes. As he surveyed the Odessa skyline, the familiar landmarks of Baroque towers and monuments, he was not thinking about Markus or Bogdan. Vojin had missed his adopted city, never imagining he would be gone for so long. What he was thinking about now as he got closer, was what he'd missed most: his beautiful Katya. The one common trait of the women he had been with in Russia was that each one made him miss her. They were all inferior—especially, sexually. It had been a long time since he'd left Odessa, but he believed she would remain faithful.

He'd made it clear, three years ago, that that was what he expected. If she had been faithful, he would marry her. He was a wealthier man, and he would share with her and their children. And he wanted children now that he could afford their healthy upbringing—an upbringing befitting an important father and a beautiful mother. If, on the other hand, Katya had not been unfaithful, he would kill the bastard or bastards and find someone else to marry.

><

Once they arrived, Vojin left directly to see her after sending Markus and Bogdan on their way. Vojin could have announced his coming by messenger, which would have given her a chance to freshen up as women like to do, but that wouldn't have been his style. He'd wanted to surprise her. He wanted to see the expression on her face when she saw him before she had a chance to 'compose' a face. And if she *had* broken her promise and taken a lover while he was gone, surprising her might be surprising *them*.

She was home in her apartment when Vojin arrived, but it hadn't been many days since her last visit to Zalaman's cabin. Despite herself, when she saw him, she found it easy to look overjoyed at his return, though a cold shiver ran through her body as he hugged her and held on tight. It felt strange after the years with Zalaman. She'd sometimes felt she'd been overly careful, but now she could tell that was wrong. You couldn't be too careful when it came to Vojin. She had to admit, Vojin did look good. He was as handsome and almost as tall as Zalaman. And yet they were so different. Vojin had blond hair and blue eyes and a light complexion. She decided that she found Vojin even more handsome than Zalaman. Vojin was more impeccably dressed than he had been years ago when he'd left. His current costume was very Russo-centric, not what the grander, more cosmopolitan Odessans were wearing these days. Even Zalaman, poor as he was, when he wasn't in his apron selling fruits and vegetables, looked more modern than Vojin.

They made love. It lasted all of three minutes, but Katya knew, lying next to him, close, staring, that this was just the first in a series—unless Vojin had changed more than he appeared to have.

Katya didn't like to discuss their sex practices. "We don't have to talk about it," he said and hesitated, wanting to say it right. She was a very demanding, precise, and aggravating woman when it came to speech. "I just want you to know that *you* are the best. The. Very. Best."

"And how do you know that my friend? To whom are you comparing me?"

"I've been in Russia, working hard. That's all. And you?" She raised her eyebrows in sincere innocence when he asked her, "Have you been faithful?"

She glowered back at him. "Have you?"

He stared back. They were both guilty of infidelity, but fidelity was, after all, only expected to apply to her. He was a man. Katya looked like she was disgusted with him for asking. But, at the same time, she was supposed to be pleased that he cared. Vojin, found the anger in her disgust reassuring. It seemed genuine. It would be belittling to her to demand a yes or a no. He found the look on her face more convincing than a verbal denial. She was clever, he knew, but not a good enough actor to fool him.

Vojin visited the Gnazdo with Markus and Bogdan. Everyone reassured him that yes, Katya came to the Gnazdo when he was gone, just like she had done years past when the two of them were a couple, but no, no one was with her, in fact, they didn't see her in the Gnazdo much at all lately. If the people he asked said no, they hadn't seen her with anyone, this meant only that they would rather avoid the issue entirely. Offending Vojin was a reckless thing to do. The wall of isolation formed around Katya by her sensible fear of Vojin, had, until the advent of Zalaman, made her a lonely woman, sitting by herself, but this was of no concern to Vojin. He was quite happy to find that Katya had been loyal, and his happiness encouraged him and his buddies to drink to excess, celebrating their return and their success in Russia. They bought rounds for everyone in the crowded saloon.

Everyone was soon feeling very good, radiating newfound bursts of camaraderie.

Just before closing time, one of the celebrants, a soused old man everyone called Bovo, one of Katya's many jealous admirers, whispered something so interesting in Vojin's ear that Vojin dragged the man outside so he could hear more clearly, so he could be sure he understood correctly what Bovo was trying to tell him in the boisterous saloon. Once outside, accompanied by Bogdan and Markus, he asked Bovo to please repeat what he was trying to say.

"There was this . . . Israelite," he said. "Someone who came up to Katya not long after you left the country. I noticed . . . it seemed to me—because I always wanted to keep an eye on her for you—it seemed to me that she let this Hebrew sit with her for quite a while. I know, sounds like it looked quite innocent. But I'd never seen her allow this before. Soon after, she pretty much stopped coming to the Gnazdo. I thought it was suspicious and wondered why she stopped coming—like she'd found something better to do."

Vojin thought about Bovo's story, but only briefly. "Well, I hope she found something better than this dump," he laughed at Bovo. "She likely stayed away because she got bored seeing the same old faces every night—like yours—with no one to even talk to her, because, like you say no one wanted to offend Vojin. How stupid."

"Yes, that surely must have been the case," said Bovo. He'd had enough of being dragged about—a humiliating and painful experience that had put a rip in his trousers. But before Vojin turned away, Bovo remembered that he hadn't finished what he had to say on the matter. He was still sitting on the ground when he grabbed the tail of Vojin's cloak, making Vojin bend closer to hear, "although . . . this same Jew?" Bovo said. "I used to see him in the Gnazdo before the time he sat down with Katya. Then he, too, stopped coming." Vojin had heard enough about this Jew. He just wasn't interested.

But Bovo held fast. "But when he used to come, he was always asking for you and your friends—and some fellow named Markus."

As soon as he heard Bovo say 'Markus,' Markus knew *he* was that Markus. Even before, when Bovo said, "Israelite" he thought *Zalaman*. He almost whispered the name out loud. Bogdan and Vojin looked at Markus. Markus avoided the temptation to say, "What a coincidence," but that would be stupid because there were probably many Markuses there that night and countless other Markuses in Odessa . . . but he did not say it, there was only one Markus associated with Vojin and Bogdan.

"Zalaman," he said to Vojin. He'd told them both stories about Zalaman. But he lied and said he doubted Zalaman would have a ruble for Gnazdo. Markus had been away for years, so, Vojin asked, how could he know this man's current finances? Markus added that he didn't think Zalaman even liked girls. "If they did meet," he said, "you can be sure it was innocent." He offered to find out from Zalaman himself the next day.

Vojin asked if Markus couldn't please see his way clear to take care of it now—that night.

Markus didn't want to give up Zalaman, but, knowing which side his bread was buttered on, as he left Vojin at the Gnazdo, he knew he might not have a choice. If Zalaman had been with Vojin's girl, and, despite what he'd told Vojin about Zalaman's not liking girls—Markus knew differently, according to Zalaman's account—he wouldn't put it past his old friend, but . . . he didn't want to hurt Zalaman. Zalaman had been hurt enough. Markus liked Zalaman. Zalaman was a survivor and wise beyond his years, just like Markus himself was, at least in Markus' own estimation. Years ago, when he and Zalaman had been together, Zalaman had told Markus about some experiences he'd had with women. In fact, to Markus, who was only fourteen at the time, Zalaman seemed quite experienced for someone his age. Markus had never witnessed anything that would make these stories seem more than bragging, but now they made him uneasy.

It was late when he got to their old hideaway, but the den had become an occupied shop with a different lock on the front door. He was relieved, thinking he would avoid the discomfort of a necessarily uncomfortable situation, when he realized he was not going to be able to locate Zalaman that night. The city was asleep. Who knew if Zalaman was even in Odessa? It was a warm night, so Markus found a comfortable spot on the promenade where he would be able to sleep undisturbed. He tossed and turned, assailed by worries about Zalaman. Who knew if he was even in Odessa? When he eventually fell asleep, he dreamt about great financial rewards heaped on him by daring to be the truth-bearer to Vojin.

Next morning, it turned out to be very easy to find Zalaman. Markus had hoped he might at least see the peddler, Edil, on Greek Street and ask the old man after his friend. Zalaman was now a successful merchant on Greek Street, if not the owner, although he acted like one, ordering about two assistants, at least the man running Uritsky's.

Zalaman didn't appear to have changed much. He'd shaved his beard since, so more of him was visible than three years ago. His wardrobe was what you'd expect of a successful merchant with shop assistants. Markus sat and squirmed, uncomfortable about what he was about to do, watching his friend sell his potatoes and onions, even Black Sea cod and a long stem of irises.

Zalaman must have worked hard. Being a successful merchant made it easier to believe Vojin's girlfriend might have been attracted. Markus didn't know Katya—though, after years of listening to Vojin's stories which mainly consisted of overly detailed accounts of their bouts of lovemaking, he felt he did—but he supposed some women might consider Zal handsome.

Vojin had been gone a long time. Markus hoped there was nothing to Bovo's tale. But even if what Bovo said was true, he was talking about one night years ago. A drink in the Gnazdo, that's all. Everything else would be speculation.

Zalaman recognized something about the man when he came into the shop, something about his walk. When Markus said "Zal" that was all it took and they were hugging one another, Zalaman asking his friend where he'd been all this time—and wondering if Vojin had returned as well.

Zalaman left Sandr in charge and he and Markus repaired to the nearest dining establishment and after having had a laugh about saving money and stealing vegetables, they put in a brief attempt to catch up on the past three years. Zalaman told Markus about Edil and Bar and Royt and his business. Markus said he'd just returned from Russia and apologized that he couldn't discuss a lot of what he'd done there, but he'd been in Russia almost the whole time and had done very well. Zalaman asked him where else he'd been and Markus just said their work involved many border crossings, but he couldn't give Zalaman details, wasn't even sure most of the time what borders they were crossing. Zalaman told Markus how he'd looked and looked for him in the Gnazdo, in the Gambrinus, everywhere, for days and months after he disappeared, asking after him and Vojin, the Russian friend he'd been looking for. "Did you ever find him, Vojin and the others?"

"I did. Made my fortune with him."

Zalaman asked if they'd become friends and Markus hesitated, thinking about the word, but then nodded, "Yes. He's a hard one, though. Not someone you want to upset." He gave Zalaman a nervous little smile. Zalaman gestured with open arms—"What?"—but all Markus gave him was his characteristic shrug. "Hearing about Edil and your business success is boring, Zal. Who have you been drinking with all this time? Who were you smoking *khat* with? Who were you fucking?"

Zalaman was grateful Markus put the question so directly rather than try to catch him out regarding Katya if that's what he was doing. "I can't say that I've been so busy that I've denied myself such pleasure," he said, noting revived interest on Markus' part and, for just a moment, the look of dread on his face. Markus clearly didn't want to be the messenger of bad news. Being the friend of someone who'd been fucking Katya, would, in Vojin's mind, practically make him an accomplice.

"Yes, of course I've been with women as I'm sure you have. Money helps, doesn't it. I used to shy away from whores—but not any longer. No time for romance, so I spent most of my time with two—Mehtap and Rosabella. They've kept me very busy. I'll introduce you."

Markus relaxed a little. "Vojin left a girl behind. Katya. Seems she was friendly with some Jewish man in the Gnazdo."

"I know a Katya or two. Not well."

"A Jew who'd also been asking after Vojin . . . and me . . ."

"Of course. I asked about you and Vojin in the Gnazdo. I've already told you that. You left without even saying goodbye. Those are the names you left me with Vojin and Bogdan . . . and Timor."

"I'm only concerned with Katya."

"As a matter of fact, I stopped going to the Gnazdo because people there became unfriendly. I figured I was being too inquisitive. Katya? Maybe? Masha, I remember. Women before I no longer had time for anything but a short evening with Mehtap or Rosabella."

Zalaman was either really good at this or he was telling the truth. Markus couldn't decide which. It was entirely possible that he spoke to some Russian woman years ago. Why shouldn't he?

After another drink, Markus could not contain himself; he was moved to speak about his adventures in Russia. He told Zalaman how proud of him he was. He, Markus, had not managed to detour onto a straight and narrow—legal—path. In

Russia he had done well, it was true, but he wasn't easy about it. He didn't think he'd ever go back. He hoped no one from the "private markets" they had traded in was going to come looking for them. Markus' thoughts ricocheted back to Vojin and Katya. He should have gotten back to Vojin before now, but relieved, he decided he could honestly say there didn't seem to have been any funny business between Zalaman and Katya. He excused himself and they agreed to get together again soon.

After Markus left and left him with the bill, Zalaman congratulated himself on a convincing performance. It had been wise of Katya to insist on jumping through all those hoops to keep their love hidden. He'd been sure for years that she was overdoing the need for secrecy and he'd been wrong. But not wrong it seemed, in his understanding that Vojin was dangerous.

The barrier of distrust between Vojin and Katya had been partially dissolved by Markus' reassuring report. Katya could feel the positive shift in Vojin's attitude during their next, longer lasting sex. "Are you satisfied?" she asked him post-coitally. He thought she didn't like to talk about sex after having sex and especially not request an evaluation.

She laughed. And said that was not what she meant. "I'm sure you've asked everyone in Odessa about my fidelity."

"According to Bovo, you were seen drinking with a young Jew."

"Bovo? Well, if you are going to believe drunks and crazy people, what am I supposed to do?"

"Just be honest with me."

"It's preposterous."

"What's so preposterous? That a beautiful young woman would get lonely? This Jew was a friend of a new associate of mine who replaced Timor—Markus. You'll meet him.

"Anyway, Markus talked to this Hebrew—Zalaman—and he says it's all rubbish. So, I want to believe you." He smiled and pulled her close. "No, I *do* believe you."

Katya hid her smile inside. But all was not perfect. How and when was she going to see Zalaman? She quickly rejected the idea of using the sick aunt ruse with Vojin, too many things could go wrong, assuming he didn't see through it immediately. Seeing Zalaman while Vojin was in Odessa was a hopeless fantasy—and a dangerous one, too, for her and for Zalaman.

Markus and Zalaman were back together sooner than expected, this time in Zalaman's cabin, drinking wine and smoking *khat* and telling stories. Markus was markedly more relaxed and not just because of the *khat*, but also because he was no longer playing Vojin's spy. He was trying to distance himself a bit from his boss. He wasn't sure in what sense he was still working for Vojin anyway. He wasn't on any payroll and there were no jobs on tap in Odessa as far as he'd heard. Distancing himself from Vojin and Bogdan was easy, because Vojin had already suggested that the three of them not spend so much time together—at least for a while. Vojin had heard from a very credible source that someone they'd done business within Russia, someone from one of those private markets, was unhappy with Vojin. Were they unhappy with Markus and Bogdan, too? Most likely. Temporarily laying low was a healthy idea. The source of this rumor, this warning, was Andrei Shavradsky, the Number One of the number one Russian clan in Odessa. He was Royt's Russian equivalent. Owner of the Gnazdo and profit-participant in much Odessan commerce. His clan was everywhere Royt's wasn't. Shavradsky was a decent sort from a Russian family as illustrious and monied as Royt's. The two were respected clan leaders and they maintained a good relationship with one another—for the sake of the family businesses.

Markus told Zalaman he'd given up *khat* at Vojin's insistence and was only doing this for old times' sake. He said he didn't think it was so good for Zalaman's brain. Also, if Zalaman didn't spend so much of his earnings on *khat* he might be able to move into a nicer place. Zalaman insisted it *was* a nice place—especially when you compared it to their den, or the beach or a hay loft. Markus described the opulence of the St. Petersburg apartment he'd shared for a while with Vojin. Zalaman listened to Markus holding forth in good old Markus fashion on his many exploits in St Petersburg, adventures up and down the Neva with Vojin and Bogdan. The women. The money. Zalaman, hungry for details, encouraged him to continue. They'd known hardship together. What was real money like? Where Markus had previously remained silent, now, thanks in part to the *khat* and wine, he elaborated. He first told Zalaman he couldn't say anything specific and then proceeded to reveal how he and Vojin and Bogdan had smuggled tea and opium in a Russian grain ship and made a killing, evading not only any payment to the Port Jews for shipping, but also the Russian tariffs. They'd already delivered the opium to their customer, while the tea was safely warehoused and awaiting its distributor. Zalaman was to say nothing about this to anyone, of course.

Zalaman swore he wouldn't. He said he didn't like to brag, but he'd been making a profit every month and he was quite happy with his cabin despite Markus' feelings about it. It was rent free. "I'm saving my money. Obviously, I have not been spending it on furniture. Not whores, either, if that's what you're thinking. At least not lately."

><

But the mention of whores brought up the idea of visiting some and resulted in an impromptu rendezvous with Mehtap and Rosabella. The two ladies complained that Zalaman had been ignoring them. Where had he been for so long? Then they paired off and went to their individual apartment-boudoirs—Zalaman with Mehtap and Markus with Rosabella.

Relaxing after sex, Rosabella started complaining to Markus about Zalaman. She hoped Markus wasn't going to be like his friend, who, until tonight, had disappeared for such a long time, she'd worried he'd fallen for that "dark-eyed beauty" he talked about. "His 'dark-eyed beauty' of the Gnazdo. She was unapproachable for some reason, and I think it was the 'mystery' of her that attracted him, the fact that the other men in the Gnazdo seemed to be afraid of her, made her irresistible to Zalaman . . ."

"That doesn't seem like Zalaman to me. Being a dark-eyed beauty would be enough."

"—and because he is a passionate young man, and I knew he wasn't having sex with Mehtap or any of Kagan's other ladies, I thought well, you know."

"No."

Well, anyway—here he is back with the living—and he brought you!"

There was no way Markus could reveal what he now knew for certain: Zalaman and Katya had been lovers. Zalaman had lied about it, which was only natural as he knew the consequences if Vojin found out. Now Markus felt it wasn't *if* Vojin found it, it was when. If Zalaman's love affair with Katya had been revealed so easily to him, without his even trying, it wouldn't be long. It would be better if Vojin found out about it from him.

He would then be considered Vojin's most trusted, if not to say 'most intelligent' partner. He could never be as intimidating as Bogdan, given the latter's size, but he could be Vojin's right hand man. What was his obligation to Zalaman? Nothing. And Vojin deserved to know what the supposedly loyal Katya had been up to. The dilemma was that he wanted to take credit for the information, but he did not want to be present when Vojin found out. He'd be furious. Anyway, Zalaman owed him, rather than the other way around.

Markus was having this conversation with himself as walked from the Gnazdo to Vojin's place. But the real dilemma came down to a choice between fear and friendship.

Markus feared Vojin, but he didn't like him. Vojin could turn on him, any minute. Zalaman would not. He feared Vojin, but he liked Zalaman. Markus shrugged. He wondered which path he would take. Could he take both?

><

Zalaman was not prepared for Markus' news.

He'd been having a very good day before Markus came to tell him that Vojin knew or was about to find out—Markus wasn't immediately clear about this distinction—about him and Katya. He had not been as clever as he thought he'd been that morning, congratulating himself on having won back his friend, who seemed to have had a satisfying tumble with Rosabella, and having not been caught out regarding Katya. She was all that was lacking on this brilliant late summer day. Red sycamores lined the thoroughfares that funneled Goliath pulling and Zalaman driving the *Weg Heim II* toward Greek Street and *Uritsky's-soon-to-be-Aszer's.* The trees rustled over the creaking carts on the street and Zalaman reveled in it and in the clip-clop of animals, and in the human voices, sounds carried on the salt breeze off the Black Sea and right into his face and Goliath's muzzle, refreshing to man and beast.

They'd been running a little late. Zalaman had spent a little extra time tidying up the cabin in case Katya found a way to get away from Vojin and needed someplace to hide. He knew the chance of her managing to come was slim, but knowing Katya, it was possible. Goliath had been feeling fine too, having had an extra hour of rest as Zalaman tidied up, and enjoyed shaking the salty mist from his mane. Zalaman was, however, both missing and worried about Katya, but he believed all their efforts at concealment—the subterfuges she'd so wisely insisted on—had paid off. Life would be less interesting in Odessa if Vojin remained and Zalaman was unable to see Katya. But the day was beautiful and he was happy to be on the way to his own shop—he was still unused to the idea of having his own shop. "And you," he said as he patted Goliath's sensitive neck. He said a quiet thank you to Edil.

Now Markus was at the shop, revealing that he should be less concerned about losing Katya and more about losing his life. Vojin knew or would soon know and would no doubt try to kill him.

"What do you mean? Does he know or doesn't he?"

"So, it's true." Markus crossed his arms and let out a big sigh and was met by Zalaman's stony-faced silence. "How?" He finally asked Markus.

"Rosabella," he said. "But don't blame her. She didn't know what she was doing. She was lamenting you not being around. It doesn't matter. Rosabella. Bovo. Who's next? He's going to find out."

"How? You? I understand you think you must. In fact, I think it's OK. But—not yet. I need to secure my shop. the key. So . . . thank you for coming and telling me. But can you wait two days before you tell him?"

Markus shook his head. Every hour of delay increased the risk to him. And he could lose his advantage to some other informant. He agreed to one day. He wouldn't say anything until then. "One day. What'll you do? I hope you're going to spend the next day closing your shop, until things are resolved—however that happens—and jump on Goliath and leave Odessa."

"It might come to that. But I don't have to close the shop. I have assistants who know what to do." Zalaman didn't want to run, he wanted to fight. But fighting Vojin and his gang was more than he could handle. If he had Rodak and Stanko with him, they would make a preventive attack. He didn't, but that didn't mean he didn't have other resources.

"When you come back, I'll be gone. Or, if not, well . . . we'll see you then."

Markus grabbed Zalaman by the shoulders as if to shake some sense into him, repeated unequivocally, "When I come back in twenty-four hours, I hope you are gone, and that Vojin hasn't been here first with a small army." Zalaman told Markus he wished them both success, however it might be constituted.

When Markus had left, Zalaman told Sandr and Moishe to keep things going at the shop—he needed to take a walk. He walked as long as he felt he could, trying to think, berating himself about how he should have known that even with all their careful planning—Katya even staying away for long periods to avoid detection—it would come to this. He was grateful for Markus' warning—he'd risked his life to do so. His fear of Vojin had been palpable, like Katya's. Zalaman had observed their fears and had let himself be infected by them. It was probably a healthy fear. Vojin was not someone to take lightly. He walked back to Greek Street to find Izzy, who took him to Royt's current address.

Royt thought what Zalaman told him about the smuggling of opium on the Russian ship would be of high value to someone like Shavradsky. The part about the teas enraged Royt. Tea was the source of his strength. "Not medicinal, commercial." Zalaman told him he knew that from Izzy and that's why he had come to him.

"This Vojin," Royt said, "I wouldn't be surprised if Shavradsky and his clan aren't already looking for him. There's been talk about a ring, a new syndicate of smugglers who are supposedly encroaching on Shavradsky's businesses and there's a rumor, not much more than gossip at this point, about people and goods being sought. That's why your friend told you his gang was lying low and staying separate."

Izzy wondered why Markus had told him all this. "It would seem to be against his interests to turn on Vojin."

"He didn't turn against Vojin. He might not even remember what he said to me about the smuggling. He wanted to impress me about how far he'd come since his days—our days as common thieves. He came to me because he thought it was in my interest." And Zalaman told them about Katya. In the telling, brief as he kept it, he grew anxious, worrying about her.

Royt smiled as he listened to Zalaman, recalling his own youthful indiscretions. He suggested it might be best, as his friend Markus had advised, to leave Odessa for a while "until things have sorted themselves out. Shavradsky will be very grateful for your information. I wouldn't be surprised if Shavradsky protects you from Vojin by eliminating him as a threat. But maybe not today. This won't happen overnight. Don't try to see Katya. Too dangerous. Vojin has the prior claim."

"Claim? She's a free woman. And I know she prefers me to Vojin."

"You leave now for someplace nice. Surely your friend Bar has a ship going up the Dniester. Be sure to write once you settle somewhere and let me know where to write to you so I can keep you informed about things here in Odessa."

He shook his head. Zalaman left. Izzy brought up horses for Royt and himself, thinking they would ride to the Gnazdo and talk to Shavradsky. But Royt stood there in contemplation.

"We should go," Iz said.

"You're quite enthusiastic about this aren't you. I'm surprised." "It's a matter of honor. It's the right thing to do.

"An affair of the heart. Zalaman should have known better. You know how he claims to have had a lot of experience—and, yes, he does for someone of so few years. But this Vojin is certainly the more wronged party as far as love is concerned. Don't you see that, Iz?"

"Yes, but still Vojin is the villain here. He's not only cheated the Russians, but he's also cheated us!"

"Which is why we're going to see Shavradsky." Maybe the kid had it coming. But not mortal, physical violence. Royt had said he would intercede and his word meant something. He'd go see Shavradsky. But he sniffed his wrist—he needed a bath first.

He wasn't going to go to see the faux-aristocrat Shavradsky without wearing his best. An hour wouldn't make a difference, so he sent Izzy ahead to the Gnazdo to hunt down Shavradsky for a meeting.

><

Zalaman went back to his shop. He invoked Katya's excuse, telling Sandr, "I'm leaving town to visit a sick aunt and hope to be back soon." He was leaving Sandr in charge but he, Zalaman, was taking Goliath and the wagon. He hitched Goliath to the *Weg Heim II* and drove to the cabin to collect a few things including his savings from its hiding place behind the kitchen wall.

He would come back to the cabin when the Vojin gang business was finished and he hoped that when he did so the owners of the cabin wouldn't have returned and taken possession. If the cabin wasn't available and Sandr ran the shop efficiently, Zalaman reasoned he would be able to buy something even nicer. Who knew how long it was going to take to clean up this mess or to simply dispatch Vojin and any other threats?

He started to organize what he would take with him in the *Weg Heim II*. Yes, he could leave Katya, hoping she'd be a truly free woman when he returned, but how was she going to survive Vojin? Would she try to escape?

><

Locating Vojin had not been easy for Markus, but he did finally find Bogdan and by the time they found Vojin it was close enough to twenty-four hours that he was sure it was safe—for Zalaman—to tell him about Katya and Zalaman, how he'd tricked a Gnazdo whore into revealing that everything Bovo said about Katya and the Jew was true. "I didn't want to believe a friend of mine would do this," he said, "although he was innocent of you and her at the time."

Zalaman's innocence at the time was beside the point. Zalaman was guilty. Vojin was angry at himself. He should have known. But he was even angrier at that whoring Katya, who would pay for this humiliation, but this Jew would pay with his life, as Vojin had promised himself when he had a premonition of this as the boat docked in Odessa.

Vojin didn't want to gather any more of their associates for this because he didn't want to do anything that would attract attention. It was something he and Markus and Bogdan could handle. He could take care of the Jew by himself. He envisioned a certain, very simple performance: Markus making sure Zalaman wasn't armed, then Bogdan holding him while Vojin worked him over then cut him. Maybe burn down his place. He'd take a torch, just in case.

It was already getting dark by the time Zalaman had everything stashed away in the *Weg Heim*: clothes, his bullets and gun, his spyglass. A few mementoes from the Cossacks, but even fewer from Lahkvna, all into the old hessian bag, itself the oldest memento. Goliath neighed and shook his mane, letting Zalaman know he'd forgotten something. Zalaman patted Goliath on the rump, then grabbed his one remaining empty saddlebag and went inside to retrieve his savings—three years of savings, hard earned banknotes, and coins he'd been hiding behind a loose board in the wall. He'd been doing so for three years and didn't realize until now, as he spread it out on the floor in front of him, what a considerable amount there was. Would he be able to stuff it all in one saddlebag?

"Good Lord! That is something!" Markus exclaimed, emerging from the shadows into the fading light. Zalaman jumped, frightened out of his wits. "Don't let me disturb you," Markus said. "Get it all in the bag." Markus had a pistol, but it was tucked away in his belt.

"I'm just about to leave," he said, slowly gathering up the remaining paper and silver coins. "You can go tell your story to Vojin."

"Too late for that now I'm afraid, Zal."

Goliath whinnied outside. Markus was looking about. He hadn't come alone. "Just take this," he told Markus, thrusting the bulging saddle bag at him, "and let me go."

"Too late," he repeated, but took the bag. "Sorry."

The sound of horses and men outside bothered Markus. Vojin and Bogdan? Zalaman jumped at Markus' loss of attention and grabbed for the saddlebag. But Markus, always the quicker of the two, remained so even in his stouter version. He shouldered his way out the front door, weapon in one hand and saddlebag in the other and stumbled immediately into an impressive group of men on horseback waiting for him—impressive in terms of arms, costumes and horses and the trappings on those horses. Markus dropped his weapon but not the saddlebag. A man holding a bruised and battered Bogdan introduced himself as Shavradsky. Markus hardly shook at all when Shavradsky unsheathed his saber and used it to pluck the saddlebag from his hand. Vojin was nowhere in sight, but Markus recognized several of the horsemen as regulars from the Gnazdo, heavyweight clan members. One of them tied Markus' hands, assuring him he had nothing to worry about. They would get along fine. He would help them find Vojin, who would help them find the masterminds behind their crimes. Before they left, Shavradsky gave the saddlebag to Zalaman. He stayed, looking down at Zalaman from his horse after the others rode off. He told Zalaman he owed him.

Zalaman said, yes, you've saved my life.

Shavradsky laughed. "If I were you," he said in muted Russian, like someone who was accustomed to having everyone's attention—and in this case, he certainly had Zalaman's, "I wouldn't consider your life saved until you are far away from Odessa.

"Vojin has friends here—and even once we've found Vojin you may not be safe, you won't be safe, because Vojin is just a small part of a rival who threatens the peace and stability of Odessa. Royt and I agree on this. He and Bar Zachar of the Port Jews are waiting for you on Bar's dock. He has a barge headed up the Dniester and it's waiting for you."

Zalaman tried to take all this in. Vojin, Markus, Royt, Bar, Markus, Vojin, Katya, and Shavradsky. He only had time to tell himself this was the best of all possible outcomes. Shvaradsky watched him struggle. "I do owe you something. I didn't bring any coins but take this—for now." He removed a glove, twisted off a ring, handed it to Zalaman and then rode off before Zalaman could thank him. He'd wanted to ask what would happen to Markus. The gold face of the ring depicted the same double-eagle insignia that had been embossed on the leather ledger he'd taken from that fat Cossack tax collector outside Punie.

Just as Shavradsky had said, Bar and Royt were waiting with a carriage alongside a loaded barge. The bargemen were watching. They'd been waiting for him, too.

"We hear Vojin got away?"

"They'll get him . . . or so they say. You've saved my life and—Bar! How did you get mixed up in this?"

"No time for that. We'll just say you had perfect timing."

"This vehicle seems too nice for your old nag." The voice was Izzy's as he descended from the carriage. Zalaman rubbed Goliath's muzzle and warned Izzy to be respectful. Royt said Zalaman was going to have to jettison the big wagon "Take only what you need, what will fit in the carriage. We'll store the rest for you."

Zalaman objected. The *Weg Heim II* had been had been a reminder of Lahkvna and family.

"Not enough room on the barge for the monstrosity," Bar said. "A lightweight, one-horse carriage is what you need."

"And it's a very nice carriage," Izzy said, as he finished harnessing Goliath. "It will attract women—wherever you end up." The barge would be heading north up the Dniester.

Zalaman understood he had no choice. As long as Goliath could accompany him, he was otherwise more or less indifferent. Everything had changed. He even felt a kind of euphoria with the prospect of a new adventure. He had to admit Goliath would probably appreciate the much lighter conveyance. "Oh, well," he said, "who's to say there won't be a *Weg Heim III?"*

The barge let out a blast. The impatient bargemen men were waiting at the gangplank. Bar waved in sympathy. He clasped Zalaman in a bear hug and so did Royt and Izzy. They asked to hear from him soon. He stepped up onto the carriage, recalling how Rodak and Stanko had hurried him to that first barge on the Daugava.

"What will happen to Markus? And Katya? I'll want to hear from you, too," he shouted. Royt, Izzy and Bar nodded in response and watched Goliath pull the carriage up to the loading plank and disappear into the barge.

><

A dozen or so years after Zalaman's escape from Odessa, Royt got a letter from him, written on the train from Vilna to Riga. In it, Zalaman asked Royt to share the letter with Izzy and Bar. He wrote that tossing around Bar's name had led to royal treatment from the bargemen all the way to Kiev, where the barge turned around and headed back to Odessa. He'd wanted to get further away from Odessa—to Vilna and eventually, Riga—but looking around Kiev, he was seduced by its beauty, including its attractive ladies. And so, despite the overbearing presence of Russian soldiers and the innumerable Russian Orthodox priests, he stayed for several years—until his money ran out. He and Goliath took odd jobs, but the Russian authorities denied him a permit to work as a butcher's assistant. He tried to economize, bartering with peddlers for his food and moving into a smaller, windowless apartment. He sold the carriage. He sold Shavradsky's ring. He spent what little he had left on alcohol and tinctures of opium and marching powder and didn't stint on the care and stabling of Goliath. Their rides through the countryside grew less frequent, but Goliath was his only remaining friend and the open spaces temporarily provided some light into the dark gloom that had descended over him. Generally, he bathed in self-pity, tortured by old wounds, scars on his body from Cossacks and scars and on his heart from the horrors of Lahkvna.

Broke and desperate, he rode Goliath out of Kiev. They were headed for Vilna and a new start, but halfway there, Goliath lay down and refused to get up. Zalaman sat with him, stroking his muzzle and bringing water and recounting stories of the good old days in Odessa with Edil. He fell asleep telling Goliath about other horses he'd known but were gone now—about Marengo and Krysa and the Beths—and he woke up to find Goliath had gone with them. He buried his old companion and walked the rest of the way to Vilna, entering the city with an even heavier heart and darker outlook than when he'd left Kiev, vowing, again, to give up his old bad habits. The more expensive ones were out of his reach anyway.

He confessed in his letter to Royt et al that he could not be sure how Vilna had become the home of the Uprising, but the Russians were even more firmly in control here than in Kiev. The Lithuanian and Polish languages were strictly forbidden, yet, to his surprise, on just the second day he was there, he came across a group of young people who spoke openly to him in supposedly proscribed tongues about their gang of thieves who practiced communal sharing and invited him to join. Hungry, lonely and, grateful for the company, Zalaman joined their ranks. He quickly developed even worse and more expensive habits than those he'd maintained in Kiev.

Many dissolute years he spent with the gang. They were not a clan like the Royt's—it was like in Oliver Twist without the Fagin. But eventually the euphoria, the nervous excitement of breaking the law, faded, almost disappearing after a visit in a dream (though he felt quite awake), from Mama and Papa, reminding him of his promise. He struggled against this but to his credit he could not. He told himself he could only find the strength to change his life by leaving Vilna. When two of his associates were arrested, he pilfered funds from their joint stash—but only what he figured was his share. He bought a ticket to Riga on the Daugavpils branch of the St. Petersburg-Warsaw railway. He loved the train like he'd always imagined he would. The movement was jerkier than a barge, but there was also a rolling motion in it that was relaxing and took his mind back to the barge trips, pleasant memories now, glossing over the anxieties. He asked the conductor for pen, ink and vellum.

After reading the letter, Royt folded the vellum to share it later with Izzy and Bar. At the end, Zalaman had asked after the health of all three—and about Katya and Markus. Royt would have to figure out how to get a response to Zalaman, how to tell him about Katya stabbing Vojin, who bled to death and whose killing led to her imprisonment, where—as Izzy had to remind

Royt when Royt couldn't remember—she, like so many prisoners, achieved an early death.

Chapter Eighteen

Riga and Maria

Zalaman had no idea how he would, once in Riga, get to the vexing problem of what to do regarding Lahkvna.

What could he do? He could at least go visit the town and his parents' graves. There was a new rail service to Kuldiga, just a couple of days of foot travel from Lahkvna. How much time had he spent—*with* a horse—traveling from Riga to Lahkvna seventeen years before? Ten days? Two weeks? Science and industry were changing the world so fast it made your head spin. He would deal with Riga first. He had to improve his financial situation before he could return to Lahkvna as a respectable person like he had seventeen years ago. Then, he'd especially wanted to impress his father and mother.

It was past midnight and raining hard when the train arrived at the newly constructed Riga junction. Zalaman did his best to stay dry, but it was impossible. He was quickly drenched, cold and miserably lost in the city's maze of streets and alleys. He was searching for the apartment of the *khat* dealer, the place where he'd met the Young Latvians. The one in particular, though, he couldn't remember her name, but he laughed when he remembered how she'd come to agree with him that "Political action and sexual satisfaction are equally important." This was before politics meant anything to him.

Perhaps young Latvians. One in particular could help him find work or at least a place to stay until he found work. He would avoid the *khat* this time.

Before Odessa, Riga had been by far the biggest city he had ever seen, with a population of over a hundred thousand souls. Odessa was beautiful and exciting with its great variety of nationalities and races, but Riga had even more imposing buildings, stylish and gleaming black in the rain. The streets were wide enough for commerce and carriage traffic, but there was little of that at this hour.

He was lost, but he was able to find his way to the river. He settled under a wide-trunked tree in one of the green parks along the Daugava that he recalled from his earlier trip. The tree had not yet grown its full summer foliage, but it provided some protection from the rain. He lay down, a blanket under and greatcoat over, and thought, *I made it. Now what*? He checked to reassure himself that his revolver was in his bag, then fell asleep for a few hours and woke to a brilliant, sparkling sunrise, the young summer sun quickly drying out the park and Zalaman.

He walked back into the part of the city he thought the remembered. Riga was not all shiny, imposing buildings. Many of the streets he walked down were just wide enough for single-file horse traffic—narrow and, dark even on a sunny day. The spoken language restrictions in Kiev were enforced here as well, so it was no wonder he heard only Russian from boasting tradesmen, gossiping women, whispering seminarians, swearing laborers, laughing children, and a policeman complimenting a young woman with a baby strapped to her breasts, and another mother singing a nursery rhyme to two children in a wonderful carriage of wicker and brass-jointed wood, bumping over the cobbles. There were very few yarmulkes in sight.

He stopped at a coffee house that seemed familiar. The coffee cost three times what he had ever paid for the drink, but worth the price, he convinced himself, because the coffee jolted his memory: he had been in this same cafe with the beautiful Latvian and she had mentioned that Riga had a big Jewish quarter, "Maskevas" on the southern end of the city.

So, he left the dark maze that was old Riga and walked south down the eastern bank of the Daugava, the grasses dazzling with dew on his right, crows and seagulls careening above, competing with fishermen on the banks and with one another over the flotsam bobbing along to the Baltic.

> <

Maskevas was bustling—a growing Jewish community, a newly prosperous ghetto made possible by the relaxing of rules that had previously restricted the movements of Jews and limited their commercial activities. When she'd first mentioned Maskevas in 1869, she said it consisted of only a few hundred people. Now there were thousands.

Zalaman's bag felt heavier and heavier, as he walked around—past all the shoemakers, tailors, furriers, cabinetmakers, financiers, doctors, lawyers—although he wasn't the only Jewish vagrant on the streets of Maskevas. He decided he should stay, use his few remaining coins to get a simple place to rest and try to find work immediately. After he ate.

He got a job carrying boards for a crew putting in a new sidewalk. A passing gravedigger, observing how many boards Zalaman could carry, offered him a job digging graves. He worked both jobs, though he preferred carrying the boards. The grave digging, no matter how routine it became, made him gloomy. The good part about the grave digging job was that, unlike the sidewalk work when the sidewalk was finished, the gravedigger never ran out of work. He went to work full-time with the gravedigger. As he dug, he thought about how he needed resources before he could go to Lahkvna, so he could have some small bit of power. He would need some in Lahkvna though he wasn't sure what he could do with it. Aside from hiring assassins.

He talked his way into a job caring for horses, exaggerating his experience with war horses. He was still able to do some grave digging on the side and now, after enjoying his work with the horses, he was able to dig graves without all the gloom.

When he had the time, he would visit the thriving produce market in the heart of Maskevas—the Maskevas *kvadrat*. Zalaman accepted a few jobs there, carting produce from Riga and the countryside. The Maskevas square itself was unexceptional when compared with the grand central market in Riga with its never-ending stalls and shops stretching from St. Peters to the Dom with all the delicious fruits, vegetables, and delicacies, including products from Scandinavia and Europe. The Riga central market was where he'd go if he was to go back into the produce business someday. That's where the money would be. He was never going to earn enough carting produce for others. But at least he had honest work. And he felt so much better exercising muscles that had never been used during his dissolute years in Vilna.

He'd been at this a month before he gave himself a day off and rode to Riga on one of the horses he cared for. His rehabilitated brain proved much better at remembering the right streets, and it got him to the *khat* seller's shop. The place was now occupied by an old man, not a *khat* dealer, who pointed Zalaman in the direction of the coffee house down the road—not the one where he'd had his expensive, thought-provoking cup on his first day in Riga, but a place with a younger, less affluent crowd where he did find some people who had been active Young Latvians back in that day and still were and who claimed to remember Zalaman. Unfortunately, the beautiful woman he'd slept with was not among them. The ones who remained were still the same—planning for a free Latvia, free of Russians—but they hadn't made much progress along those lines. Perhaps they smoked too much *khat*. Even so, Zalaman enjoyed their enthusiasm and high ideals and, finally, eventually, their *khat* too, once they convinced him—once he *let* them convince him—that too much clarity could be stultifying in its own way and become a burden. Before it got dark, he wished them well and rode off for Maskevas so he could keep his schedule the next morning.

Which he did, tending the horses, shoveling dirt for the dead, and saving as many coins as possible so he could buy a new outfit before he made his next trip to Riga. Which he did, just two weeks later.

He wanted better lodgings than the flophouse hammock he currently called home in Maskevas. He would need to make more money. He got up before dawn so he could get a good place in line at the Blackheads Guild in the ancient part of Riga. He'd heard on the street that the Blackheads, a brotherhood of successful merchants and ship-owners, might be willing to give him some assistance with lodging, maybe even employment. They were known for helping foreigners, including Jews, and would at least give him a hearing.

><

He left Maskevas early because he'd also heard that a line formed at the Guildhall later in the day. He walked north along the Daugava and though he got there before the Blackheads opened their doors, a line had already formed. The line was twice as long when he finally was permitted inside, after having listened to his line-mates talk about 'the first time' they came to the Guild—and the 'fifth time' they came. Inside it was chaos. Applying for help was a lengthy process and a humbling experience. He felt he didn't have the right answers to the Guild masters' questions about his history and his work experience. He left frustrated and disappointed, without a great deal of hope that the Blackheads would do anything to help.

As he walked down the impressive stairs of the hall, he was attracted to a wooden poster board displaying several lithographs.

One showed a striking image of a Viking ship and announced a museum exhibition of naval artifacts—"The Story of Riga and Navigation"—that had been supported by the Blackheads. The day wasn't half over. It would be too late to dig graves by the time he got back to Maskayas, so he decided that rather than visit the Young Latvians' coffee shop, he'd see if he could learn something. In Odessa, he'd visited the Archaeological Museum more than once, and felt he'd benefited from the experience, having learned things about his adopted city of which most Odessan's were unaware. In those days, he would report back to Katya what he'd learned. Did she know that way back in time, before the Tatars, thousands of years ago, Odessa was a Greek settlement? "Like in Greek Street?" she asked.

He arrived at the Museum of the History of Riga. He followed the hallways to the exhibition rooms where he read about the city and admired artifacts from sailing ships that had plied the Daugava and the Baltic Sea hundreds of years earlier and even earlier than that, before the city was "Riga." He was impressed by small dioramas that showed how the first known inhabitants, the Livs, an ancient Finnic tribe, operated a threshing barn near the harbor before there was a 'Riga,' a name derived from the Latvian word for threshing barn.

In the next room, one vast diorama took up the entire gallery. It showed Vikings in Riga and how they used its natural harbor as a trade route to Byzantium. He spent a long time reading about the Vikings and marveling at the artifacts they'd left behind—swords to weighing scales. But there was a distraction. One that was perhaps heightened by the daydreams Zalaman had enjoyed during his walk to the museum.

There was a woman with a young boy of about ten in tow. He assumed they were mother and son. Aside from two museum guards—one stationed by the door to keep an eye on the visitors and one who strolled up and down the corridors from time to time, Zalaman and the mother and son were the only people in the gallery. The room was darker than the others, allowing spotlights to highlight the details of the harbor's diorama. The effect of the lighting was quite dramatic, but he couldn't get a good look at the woman. Her form and her movement aroused more than his curiosity. Was it just an effect of the light? But no, there was a certain serenity about her movement, even though she was constantly being asked questions by her son about the exhibition. In German, he noted. She was quietly lost in the model of Old Riga, unfazed and unresponsive to the boy's questions until she finally declared in Polish "It's a shame."

It was more than a whisper and he was surprised to hear the forbidden Polish. She said it again in Russian. The boy said something and Zalaman edged a little closer to hear better. The woman wore a high collared black dress with a slash of red feather, the red flashing in the spotlight when she entered its orbit exposing beautifully high cheekbones, almost oriental, but not quite, a strong jaw, but not too, some freckles, a nothing of a nose. When the spotlight hit her in the face it revealed a pale complexion and green eyes and she smiled at him staring at her and then she looked away. She had a profusion of light brown hair, topped by a black hat with an upturned brim which was itself crowned with a burst of ribbons and bows. She was slender, but he'd learned you couldn't really know about women's bodies for certain, because these elaborate outfits exaggerated certain things and concealed others as dioramas did with whatever they were designed to emphasize.

He imagined she looked at him again, but this time didn't smile, and he felt embarrassed rather than encouraged. He'd been edging closer to her like she was some animal or Cossack he was hunting. He backed away.

"It's a shame," she grumbled one more time. She repeated it again in Latvian, a language that was also forbidden. He thought it must be dangerous for her to be using those languages, but the guards were Poles, not Russians, so maybe they didn't care and this was the way things operated. Maybe she was trying out languages to make sure he understood what she was saying.

"Excuse me," he said in Latvian, then, daringly switched to Polish, "but what is 'a shame?'"

"What isn't a shame these days?" she asked theatrically with a grin and introduced herself: "Maria Konopnicka and this is my young charge, Edward Abramowski."

Zalaman introduced himself to both and asked Edward "What's it like being a *charge*?"

The boy giggled but stepped back. She looked Zalaman up and down and explained that Edward was her student. She was his tutor and they were visiting from Warsaw. She looked him up and down again and asked him what kind of work he did, which was obvious, again he supposed, despite his attempt to improve his wardrobe. "Don't be embarrassed about working with your hands or your muscle," she said, speaking Latvian.

"As far as I am concerned, you couldn't have a better introduction. My life is dedicated to the working class and not just in an abstract sense." She could tell Zalaman wasn't sure what she meant by this—as had been her intent. "When I said 'What a shame,'" she continued, "I was referring to the fact that we are the only ones here. No one cares about history anymore."

He told her about the Archaeological Museum he had visited in Odessa and how, aside from his mother reading to him, "it was my introduction to history. My favorite wing was organized by time periods . . ." He hesitated, worried maybe he was going on too long, but she nodded, encouraging him to continue—though Edward tugged at her hand. "But the furthest I ever got was the 'Egypt, Ancient Greece and Rome' wing of the place. I could only absorb so much each visit and I never got past Rome. If I could go back, I would start all over again with Egypt and Greece and Rome before moving forward. There was so much more I wanted to know."

She stepped back. "And are you planning on going back to Odessa? Is that where you live?"

"No," he said, he lived here, in Riga. Another part of the city entirely. He bent down to talk to Edward. "Do you like ships?"

"Ship battles," Edward specified in a very formal Polish.

"I liked battles, too, when I was your age. My brother and I would pretend we were Cowboys and Indians. I didn't even know what a museum was back then, so you are a very lucky little boy to have a tutor who brings you to such a place."

"I like *real* battles," the boy explained. "I mean, to study them."

"So, neither Latvian nor Polish are forbidden if you're a teacher?" He asked Maria in Polish.

"It *is* forbidden. But we don't have to worry here. The staff is Polish. The Russians, at least the ones we see in Riga, like to take people's money, or shoot them. Protecting art is not a major preoccupation. They value their own skins—"

"—and vodka," he interrupted.

"—but don't give a damn about history," and then she lowered her voice just a little even though she'd maintained there was nothing to worry about, "and that's what makes them dangerous." She excused herself but said she and Edward had spent more time than they'd meant to and had to leave. They weren't here for the museum so much as the rally. "It's a political rally. Just across the roadway in Bastejkalns park. You should come if you plan to stay in Riga and find out what's what. It's a very impressive group of speakers."

He didn't think he wanted to waste his time listening to politicians, but Maria was another thing. He followed them to a large public park where a crowd was gathering around a raised platform supporting a dais with a half-dozen chairs arranged to face the audience. A crowd was gathering and two men were already on the platform, professorial types in deep discussion. Riga policemen lingered around the edges.

"A protege of Max Stirner will be speaking," Maria explained, graciously undismayed by his professed ignorance. "The topic is property. The ineffectiveness of the state." She couldn't tell if he understood her, but he told her to go on. As she'd done in the museum, she looked him up and down. Even though he'd worn his best clothes to visit Blackheads, the way she looked at him made him feel naked. He guessed he still had the look of the destitute.

"If you find yourself in difficult circumstances," she said, "you know you're not alone. Do you have a family?"

"I did," he said, but wasn't about to offer an explanation. "I'm in the city to talk to the Blackheads . . . about getting some employment help.

"And what experience do you offer?" But before he could even start to frame an answer, she continued, "You talk like an educated man—and in a variety of languages," she said. He denied he had much of an education but said he did read a lot.

"Then you are an educated man," she said.

The crowd around the stage and the hubbub were growing.

The speakers were stepping onto the stage to take their seats. "Depending on what it is you are reading of course," she said, though now completely distracted by the tumult.

She turned to face him. "You should certainly be interested in the rally. You can never tell; it may provide you with new hope. But now I must excuse Edward and myself. We don't want to miss Stirner's man. It's an important piece of Edward's education and we need to get closer. It's been nice meeting you! Perhaps we'll see you after the rally."

Maria and Edward melted into the crowd and left him all alone in a sea of laborers. People not unlike himself, not dressed all that much differently than him. There were plenty of the more affluent, however, Maria among them. Looking around to see where she might have gone, he couldn't spy any bobbing ribbons and bows. He was surrounded by professors and students, factory workers, dock workers, makers of sausage, paper, bricks, or soap—all identifiable by the details of their dress. No identifiable peasants, but a few men and women of various ages dressed as domestic servants. "Property," she'd said was the topic to be discussed, but the crowd was not made up of men of property.

He had no burning business back in Maskavas and, anyway, it was far too late to walk back and haul boards or gravel or groom a horse. He might learn something by staying, something valuable. But if this was a political rally, which he thought it probably was, given the waist size of the worthies on the platform, then he didn't want to get involved. He didn't want any trouble with the authorities. The authorities always meant trouble and the policemen of Riga bore all too close a resemblance to those of the Navharadak Department for Protecting the Public Order.

He was watching the police when someone thrust a broadsheet into his hand.

CALLING ALL WORKERS!
July 5 Bastejkalns, Rally for Workers Rights.

The noisy crowd was edging forward to hear, bunching up against the front of the platform on which four bearded men were listening and nodding to one another and to the speaker, who stood at the front of the stage within touching distance of the crowd. He was introducing the featured speaker, an adherent of Max Stirner, of whom Maria had spoken, one Dr. Reitzel, who had translated "the most important book of the decade:" Max Stirner's *The Ego and Its Own.*

Zalaman thought perhaps he should leave. It was a perplexing title and so was the speaker's description of Stirner's book. He used a lot of unfamiliar, mysterious words like 'nominalism' and 'abstract objects' and 'universals.' Zalaman's mind started to wander, his attention drawn to one of the bearded men seated behind the speaker.

There was something familiar about him—the way he jiggled his knee? He pulled at his beard as if he was surprised to discover its presence. He wore a long, black cloak just like the others on the stage and nodded his head in agreement with the speaker's points. The crowd was listening politely and intently. "Individualism" it seemed was all about independence, self-reliance. The crowd got behind that, Zalaman included. The speaker's final statement, the first to get a strong reaction from the crowd—applause and hurrahs—was the reminder that *Individualism* wasn't just an ethical concept, it was also a political movement. "It is the best, the most practical advocate for your interests, for our interests—for the interests of the individual. The individual takes precedence over the state." There was more applause, plus some curses and some laughs.

The man Zalaman had been watching got to his feet and walked to the front of the stage as he was being introduced by the current speaker. That walk was so familiar that the name came to Zalaman's brain at the same time the retiring speaker introduced him, promising the man would "have something to say about *the illusion* of property rights—our brother from The Latvian Individualist Movement, Roman Bartkowicz."

Chapter Nineteen

Old and New Uprisings

It didn't take long for Zalaman to see that under that beard and layer of fat, Roman Bartkowicz was none other than his old friend Rodak Bartos. It was true. He appeared to have aged a good deal more than thirteen years. But that change was understandable. What wasn't, was hearing him speak about The Latvian Individualist Movement. How was that possible for the old terror of the Cossacks, the dedicated soldier of the Uprising? Zalaman was spellbound, cemented in place, and listening to his words less than scrutinizing his face, constantly checking to reassure himself it was him, now having become a political rabble rouser for Individualism?

Rodak lowered his voice just a bit, having its intended dramatic effect—the crowd hushed. Zalaman decided he'd better listen and he noticed how Rodak's self-assured, calm manner held the crowd's attention. They strained to hear his words, words that were much more incendiary than his demeanor and referred repeatedly to "property," "theft," and "the ghost." The ghost meant the state. For Stirner, Rodak and Maria's mentor, property was theft. Rodak explained these ideas were based on Proudhon. Rodak would repeat a phrase like "The state is the Ghost," and the crowd would repeat it back. Rodak was very good at this. He had everyone's full attention as Zalaman muscled his way to nearly the front row of onlookers. Rodak seemed to notice the movement and his gaze settled on Zalaman without reaction—or was it simply hard to tell behind the beard. "Whoever knows how to *take*," Rodak continued, "to defend that thing, to him belongs property!"

There was cheering and Rodak did now smile at Zalaman, nodded his head as Zalaman did. He asked, staring directly at Zalaman, if anyone in the audience knew the legend of Robin Hood. The ones who did cheered, including Zalaman, who recalled how he and Rodak and Stanko had cast the Tsar as Prince John. But where was their Prince? If Stanko had been in the crowd, Zalaman would have spotted him towering over the others. Rodak was proposing something else. “The work of Robin Hood and his merry men is the least dangerous example I can give you of Max Stirner.” He lowered his voice theatrically and the crowd quieted. “Your self-interest is the legitimate reason for doing whatever it is you do—what you do to survive. We are from the many arts and crafts,” and here Rodak thrust out his arm in an inclusive gesture toward them, “and from many parts of the world. We are international! And we welcome all minorities!”

Zalaman wondered if Jews were a minority. Certainly not in Odessa, but here, yes, certainly. He’d seen Rodak change his attitude toward Jews as they spent time together. Now, he’d been transformed again. He was riling up the crowd, finally getting to his introduction of the main speaker, Professor Reitzel, a Stirner translator and expert. It seemed Reitzel was well-known and well-regarded, as he was wildly applauded—no doubt by Maria and Edward as well, though he still couldn’t see them.

><

“Roman Bartkowicz?” Załaman laughed at the man who rushed over to him after he’d excused himself to the others on the dais. They embraced as long-lost brothers would, then moved apart to study one another. “You’ve changed,” Zalaman said. “And I don’t mean your name.”

“Yes, well, hopefully we’ve both changed after all these years. Hopefully, it’s a progression. You’ve certainly changed. You look older and I understand why that would be.”

“You look older but bigger. My name is still Zalaman Aszer.”

"What's a name?" He moved into whisper in Zalaman's ear. "The Cossacks decided to put a name on some of their most embarrassing loses—and they chose mine. And then there was the business in Lahkvna. We'll save that for another time. Let's go somewhere where we can hear one another talk."

They moved away from the crowd, where they could hear one another speak without interference from Dr. Reitzel. Rodak said, "Before anything else, let me apologize to you, Zalaman, for my earlier self as Rodak."

"You want me to call you Roman now?"

"Yes, please, do that for me. As Rodak, I said awful things about Jews, and I can see how such ignorance leads to things like Lahkvna. In Lahkvna, for God's sake! I knew some of those killers from Navharadak. Christ, I might have been one of them."

Zalaman shook his head.

"Well, no, I don't think so either, although Pane Bartos wondered about the same thing. And, yes, she likes you too."

"She saved my life—at least as many times as you did. And Stanko. Who is . . . where?"

"He was fine for a while, after you left," Rodak said, shaking his head. "I tried to do what you'd done and be a good nurse, but by the time we got back to Navharadak infection set in. I nagged him about cleanliness. I kept reminding him about what you'd said and what Bebchuk said and the medic at Syp. I cleaned the stump when I could. Pane Bartos, too. But the infection just got too far along. Before he died, he predicted I would see you and he gave me instructions for when I did."

"I still wear the vest he made me," Zalaman said. "I finally grew into it."

"That's what he was doing the whole last year—making clothes—until the infection drove him mad and he shot himself."

"Instructions?"

"That I should tell you . . . he was sorry he hadn't been there, in Lahkvna, to help you. But we, he and I, did everything we could to help redeem the situation and hoped it would help bring you peace. 'Peace like I'm about to find,' he said, 'but by less lethal means.'"

Zalaman returned Rodak's dark grin. "I don't know that I'll ever find peace."

"You're young yet," Rodak said and Zalaman nodded that was true, though he didn't feel like it.

"How can you redeem such a situation?" he asked. "I'm working up the nerve to finally go back to Lahkvna and face them. I only know one way to get revenge—"

"Well, that way is closed to you now."

"—and one of their lives for ours—there's no vindication. . . . What do you mean 'closed?'"

"Don't think revenge, think justice. Justice has been served. The bastards are all dead and yours truly, Roman Bartkowicz, am responsible for the death of three of them—the first one with Stanko while he was still alive. I took Linards myself. He died a slow and very painful death, as you might appreciate."

"I'd like to hear that story someday," was all Zalaman, stunned, could say.

"You can return to Lahkvna and make it a peaceful return." Zalaman couldn't believe it.

"Maybe I'll go with you . . .

"You're full of surprises." He would very much like to have Rodak with him when he returned to Lahkvna. He also knew he wasn't ready to return in the style he wanted. Not to show off, but to show he'd made a success of himself. If the direct perpetrators were dead, he could wait.

Rodak excused himself to say goodbye to his co-speakers, saying he would meet Zalaman later at the Dzirnavu where they could eat and drink and tell their stories.

"Only if I get him first," Maria demanded, emerging from the crowd with Edward in tow.

Zalaman introduced her and Edward to Roman Bartkowicz, explaining to 'Roman' how he'd just that day met Maria at the museum. She bestowed a big smile on Zalaman—perhaps a show of greater esteem upon seeing him on such good terms with one of the rally's major attractions.

Rodak shook his head. Zalaman was still the ladies' man.

Maria looked like a well-groomed but less well-tamed animal. "So," she said to Zalaman, "you stayed for the rally after all!

I'm surprised. And you're a friend of one of the speakers. I'm doubly surprised—" She turned to Rodak/Roman, "—surprised that I didn't see your name on the poster."

"I'm just a regional functionary and new at this, not important enough to be mentioned on the poster."

"Hearing you speak," she said, "I don't think such modesty is merited."

"Your own name . . ." Rodak said, ". . . Maria Konopnicka . . . Where have I heard it?" Maria claimed she didn't have the slightest idea.

"She's a big admirer of Stirner," Zalaman said.

"From Warsaw," Rodak had heard her name in anarchist circles but wasn't sure she was a part of the movement.

"Yes," she confirmed her Polish identity. "I should apologize, Mr. Bartkowicz. If you've heard my name, it was probably in connection with workers' causes in Poland—and elsewhere. Or, although of less consequence, you might have heard of my latest book. It's title is *In the Mountains* and I'm afraid it's caused me some unwanted new celebrity—in some circles. In Warsaw, at least."

"'In the Mountains'? I'm sorry, it doesn't ring a bell. Travel memoir? No. History? No. Politics?"

"No. Poetry," she said. Zalaman and Rodak didn't know what to say about poetry, so she told them she would give them a copy. Zalaman told her what a surprise it was to have found Roman after many years. They owed her a debt of gratitude for getting

Zalaman to the rally. Rodak seconded that and again said he had to excuse himself. They decided Zalaman would walk Maria and Edward back to their hotel—she and Edward needed the rest after a busy day—and then meet his friend at the Dzirnavu.

"Before you go, Mr. Bartkowicz, let me say how greatly I wish that when you talk about the rights of the minorities—and such talk is of the utmost importance—how I wish you would include women's rights."

"I never considered women a minority."

"You should," Zalaman piped up. Searching the crowd for Maria during the rally, he'd seen very few members of the opposite sex. "Aside from Maria, did you notice any women in your audience? A few, perhaps, but it's a shame, isn't it—"

"Zalaman is always noticing women—even their absence."

"—that there weren't more. Every day, wherever I'm digging holes like a dog or carrying loads like a beast of burden, I see female workers who have it even worse."

"You should have been up there on the platform," Maria said to Zalaman.

Rodak apologized for having to leave that discussion for a later date and left reminding Zalaman about the Dzirnavu.

Zalaman agreed to walk with her and Edward to her hotel, but their hotel was on the left bank of the Daugava, too long a walk for her or Edward in their exhausted state, so she insisted on hiring a carriage and he reluctantly joined them, apologizing for not having the fare.

She told him to keep quiet about that. It was well within her means. Edward quickly fell asleep as the carriage rolled north along the Daugava. She pressed him about his financial situation, and he admitted to having an up and down relationship with money and to currently being a laborer but said he had had other experiences in other countries as a merchant—and Polish partisan.

"Never apologize for being a laborer," she told him.

She was not a political organizer, but she was committed to helping workers—and women and children—find better lives.

She did it mostly by writing. Her poetry-writing life had lately been overtaken by other duties. The essays and stories she wrote, along with her activities supporting the rights of women, organizing rallies, some not unlike the one they had attended earlier, kept her very busy. She was currently helping organize an international rally to protest Prussia's treatment of peasant children.

"In Poland," she said, "I am becoming recognized as a poet. As unlikely as it sounds, that's how I got this wonderful tutoring appointment." Edward had fallen asleep with his head in her lap and she patted it affectionately. "It seems a great many people have purchased *In the Mountains*. Your friend, Roman, doesn't read poetry anymore, I'm sure, than you do, so he probably heard my name here in the Duchy because I have been active in political circles—ones similar to his own perhaps, though I'm no anarchist."

"Rodak," he said, then quickly, "*Roman*, sorry, Roman says he's an anarchist, but I'm not sure I know what that means."

"To me it means simply 'no'—'No' to everything, to the state; all states should be demolished by any means at one's disposal."

Zalaman chuckled at that and explained, "My friend has changed a lot since I knew him. He used to be a violent man, not a public speaker."

"Well, of course, the man standing next to me at the rally said Pane Bartkowicz was involved with Johann Most, so perhaps he hasn't changed all that much. Most is a well-known figure. Notorious. Occasionally violent, though he seems to have disappeared to save his hide."

Zalaman didn't want to spend the rest of the ride talking about Rodak. He'd noticed Maria wore no rings, nor any jewelry at all as far as he could see."You're not married?"

"I am a *little* married," she admitted a bit mischievously. "I have six children—to them I am *very* married. As for a husband, I have moved on, away from him, and now have my own life in Warsaw. I left him back in Suwalki."

Maria Konopnicka was a good ten years older than Zalaman. She'd been raised a strict Catholic but had put that and her earlier life behind her when she abandoned Suwalki for Warsaw, bringing only her six children and enough of Jaroslaw Konopnicka's money to live modestly in Warsaw so long as she could earn money tutoring children of the city's elite. "Otherwise, it's not worth my time." *In the Mountains* had earned her such recognition that her pedagogy was now in demand.

"I would love to read your book," Zalaman said.

"I have a copy in my room. It's a pleasure to meet a man in Riga who reads and is interested in poetry. I feel that first I'm a poet. Only after that do I feel like I'm a reformer, or a tutor—or even a mother. I hope that doesn't sound awful. I love my children beyond anything."

"It must have taken courage—with six children in tow."

"Fortunately, I have relatives in Warsaw who are taking care of them while I am here with Edward, but, it was my duty to take them away from Jaroslaw. I couldn't leave them in that loveless household. If I had, Jaroslaw would not have hesitated to throw them out as soon as I was gone. It wasn't courageous what I did. I was afraid. It was necessary—for my happiness. Sometimes you must be selfish, and you find that in being selfish you are serving others despite yourself."

He believed he understood her and started to tell her something about his life in Odessa when the carriage pulled up in front of the hotel. But Maria wanted to hear more about Odessa, so with Zalaman in agreement, she ordered the carriage to take them to the Dzirnavu—and let Edward sleep.

He told her about Edil and Goliath, about his 'produce business' and Royt and Bar and Shavradsky, the clans that ran the city. And what did he love about it, she asked. He thought for a few seconds and said, "people I met there, from all over the world. Getting to know them through work—or pleasure. But also, the wonderful smells of flowers and cooking."

She smiled and he felt encouraged to go on.

"I'm sure the number of books I read in those years were far outnumbered by the intoxicants I absorbed."

"But you read."

"Whatever I could find in whatever language I could find it."

"Just so you understand, we are not going to be getting into bed together, even though I find you attractive. You have an attractive face, although you look older than your years and I'm not talking about your visible scars, and you have a literary imagination and speak several languages well and I am going to help you. Besides, Edward and I leave for Warsaw in the morning." He told her that her offer of help was very kind but unnecessary. They both knew that was a lie, so she found it easy to get him to admit it.

"You see me now a free woman, but it took me many years to liberate myself. Jaroslaw never approved of my writing, never approved of anything I did. It felt like I was locked in a cage. In fact, I was locked in a cage when I was with him. Do you know that feeling?"

Zalaman asked if it had to be a physical cage and she said, "it's almost always the spirit that's caged."

"It must feel wonderful to be free then," he said.

They had arrived at the Dzirnavu. She turned and held his hands. "Two words: 'Dr. Eriks Prokopovics. OK, three. I have been here in Riga for two days; yesterday, Edward and I spent with my friend, Dr. Eriks Prokopovics, to discuss translations. You will meet him. He'd like you and he could use your skills, your intelligence. I know you've had little schooling. Won't matter. You have languages. He likes handsome young men with a past—but don't worry, he's harmless. But he does have connections and he might be able to help you in a number of ways."

She got a card and stylus from the waiter and wrote "Dr. Eriks Prokopovics" along with his street addresses—home and office. She told Zalaman, "Eriks Prokopovics is my number one critic, confidant, supporter, and translator." She gave him the card. "He will at least listen to you, if you use my name. He could be a valuable key for you. So now that you have that, you have no further need for my help. But if you'd like to come later, after I've put Edward to bed—we'll have to be quiet, and you know the rules—I will give you a copy of *In the Mountains*. After your food and drink—don't drink too much with your old friend Roman—come to the hotel. If you'd like the book."

"I'll come, of course! But . . . do you come to Riga often?" She smiled. "We shall see."

Zalaman waited for Rodak at the Dzirnavu, his thoughts bouncing between Maria and Rodak. The saloon reminded him more of the Inn at Punie than the Gnazdo or any of the others. He would have to watch himself with Maria—not be too forward. But, like he'd learned from Lechsi in Punie, it wasn't easy telling when you were being too forward, until you were, because you didn't want to lose an opportunity for both of you to enjoy some good healthy sex that he found was usually desired even if that desire was denied. . . .

He was so absorbed in his thought, he didn't notice Rodak watching him until Rodak laughed, "Hello! You look so lost! Are you with me or is it Maria?"

"Both," Zalaman said, jumping up. They embraced, then stepped back to look one another over once again.

Rodak ordered two beers and two krupniks. “This is your lucky day, Zalaman—I should say ‘our’ lucky day, because one, we are reunited—and two, we both meet Maria Konopnicka. According to my colleagues, she’d raised funds and organized rallies in Poland like the one here in Riga today. And she is a known poet, can you beat that? *Meine Kollegen* are hardly what you might think of as literary people, even so, one or two had heard her name.”

“She gave me the name of someone she thinks can help me.” Zalaman handed Rodak the card.

“What? You need help? Let me help you,” he said reading the name she’d written. “I know of him. Dr. Eriks Prokopovics can help you more than I can. Maria’s quite a woman. The two of you were right to point out that there were very few women at the rally. It’s typical at these things. But, you know, sometimes things can get out of hand.”

“What about Lahkvna. And Linards. Please tell me about his ‘slow and very painful death’” The description involved an Orsini bomb ripping off Linard’s legs and his pathetic attempt to reattach one of them while bleeding to death—more than enough for Zalaman. He hadn’t foresworn violence completely, but he was trying to.

Maybe now, with the slayers slain or dead by other means, he could. They talked about that Easter Day in 1870. Zalaman was able to recount details of that day he’d never talked about before.

“We had a pogrom in Odessa, too.”

“Odessa?” Rodak raised his eyebrows and growled how he couldn’t wait to hear all about it. He heard a little about it, then told Zalaman how, after they’d returned to Navharadak and after the death of Stanko, he’d been disgusted with Navharadak, how he and a few others had had to take matters into their own hands to bring some semblance of justice back to its society, and then travelled to Germany where “they turned me into an anarchist.” He promised that discussion, too—how he’d fallen in with his mentor and hero, Johann Most—but for now, suggested they toast Stanko.

"But what about the Uprising?"

"I was hostage to that dream for too many years. I'd always been an anarchist, or 'individualist,' I just didn't know it. I was too busy being a Polish partizan to understand. But somehow, after all those years trying to kill Cossacks, and after being in Navharadak for a while and considering what happened in Lahkvna, well, I started reading. I read Proudhon in translation and then Stirner and finally Johann Most."

"I'd much rather hear about you—Roman—not political theories. Tell me if, despite your added girth, you've been lucky enough to have any special female friends."

Over Zalaman's protestations, Rodak professed not to be one to kiss and tell like Zalaman, but yes . . . in fact, he still did—back in Germany. "Auntie Elizavetta—" Zalaman clamped his hand over his mouth in shock. "—No, not that. Auntie Elizavetta, Pane Bartos, who professes to love you like a son, she is the one that had me read Stirner and others about the new anarchist movement in Germany. So that's where I went and where I met the woman, Rosa. OK, I will tell you. She isn't here with me because of Crazy Max Hodel. He ruined everything that had been looking so promising in Germany. Hodel was kicked out of the Leipzig Social-Democratic Association and aligned himself with the anarchists and then proceeded to ruin everything for us by shooting at the Kaiser. This was just two months ago. Hodel's death sentence will be carried out next week. Me and some of my friends in the Social Democratic Party, at least those of us who knew Hodel or Nobiling—you know, Karl Nobiling—we decided it would be wise to leave the German Empire for a while—until things calm down. So, I came back to Riga. You seriously haven't heard of Nobiling? Have you been living in a barrel?" Zalaman assured him that, yes, that was the case. "Dr. Karl Nobiling. He also tried to shoot Wilhelm just one month after Hodel's attempt.

But Nobiling was a better shot. It was only Wilhelm's spiked helmet that saved his life. Nobiling's genius was to shoot himself after the attempt on the Kaiser rather than face the embarrassing spectacle of the guillotine. After Max Hodel has his head cut off, sometime after that, things might calm down enough for me to go back to Germany—and Rosa. She's waiting for me there and I like it that she is. I hope you have a chance to meet her some day because you'd like her. She may not have the kind of physical beauty you seem to require, but she is funny and much less pig-headed than me. I miss her and want to go back, but it's simply too dangerous right now. I'll just wait and see. Bismarck is promoting a new law that would make it impossible to live in Germany if you are any kind of social democrat, let alone an anarchist. Do you follow? Good, but I don't think you do. You are trying. Anyway, Germany's too dangerous, so I will be here in Riga longer than I'd originally anticipated. This could be a good thing for you—for us. There is a great deal to do. You were always the best scout—and I need to find someone."

Zalaman apologized that he had to leave so he could keep a rendezvous with Maria, but assured Rodak it was only to pick up a copy of her book before she and Edward left for Warsaw in the morning. They made plans to meet the following day at Cafe Trenci. Rodak watched him scurry off to his rendezvous, considering how he might use Zalaman as an accomplice in his search for Johann Most. Most, his anarchist ideal, had been expelled from the Reichstag and was now in hiding, most likely in England, but maybe America. He could even use Worker's Brotherhood funds to pay Zalaman something, although considering what he'd learned of Maria Kronopnicka and her influence, if this Dr. Prokopovics wanted to take Zalaman on in some capacity, he, Rodak, would never be able to compete.

><

Maria's room was on the hotel's third floor, marking a new high for Zalaman in any man-made structure. There was a note stuck on the door of her room, advising Zalaman not to knock; she'd left the door open so as not to wake Edward. Upon entering, the first thing that struck him, after the warm look from the high-cheekboned, green-eyed poet, her profusion of light-brown hair now tumbling well down her back, was how his room in the inn at Punie would have fit in one of the closets. The third floor was high enough above the clatter of the street that he could hear Edward's regular breathing in an adjoining room.

She thought it best that they whisper. She held a copy of her book in one hand and with the other motioned him to sit. 'For just a minute,' she said, so she could sign her book. She asked about his dinner with Roman but listened for a few minutes and then said it was late. She handed him the book and gave him a goodbye kiss—a peck on the cheek. He reciprocated, giving her a goodbye hug. Meeting no resistance, he followed it up with a kiss on her cheek. It wasn't a peck, but more a caress, and once again, he encountered no resistance. Just pliant softness. He tightened the hug slightly, confirming she was as slender under all those clothes as he'd imagined. Her arms were around him as well. He kissed her on the neck, lingering there. She moaned slightly, or at least he thought so.

He had been so full and content after the food and drink at the Dzirnavu, he'd felt almost indifferent about having sex with Maria, especially after her previously stated opposition to any advances he might be considering. Now, he no longer felt so indifferent. Gently, a bit clumsily in the dark, he edged the two of them, like some four-legged creature, toward the bed. Was she resisting this? He didn't think so. They were both breathing heavier. He was pressing into her. To steady them, one of his hands grazed her breast and, like it had a mind all its own, stayed firmly there. She removed it and moved away, shaking her head. Shades of Lechsi. But no, despite moving away and shaking her head, she was smiling. Zalaman tried to apologize—he'd just forgotten himself. But she put a finger on her lips and shook her head and said he'd have to wait "—until I get to know you better."

"And what is the possibility of that since you're leaving tomorrow for Warsaw?"

"I'll be back. Soon. I must come back to work with Eriks, but before that I'll post a letter to him—for you." Maria did not sit down. She and Zalaman stood there, regarding one another. "You know, Warsaw is only a day and a night train ride away. Perhaps things will develop with my work, in fact, I will make sure they develop in a way that will require me to come and see you." She took his hand. "In the meantime, my friend, Dr. Pokopovics can help you."

"So, you keep saying. And I believe you, although I have no idea what I could do for him."

She smiled. "He may need your Yiddish."

Maria's card in his vest pocket, but Prokopovics' address already committed to memory, Zalaman stopped at the Trenci to see Rodak as they'd planned. The Trenci was a well-lit, cavernous place, immaculate, with highly polished marble and exotic woods that arched into the ceiling, the owners having cleverly recreated one of the great coffee houses that flourished in the Ottoman Empire a century earlier. The Trenci not only served coffee from its own deliciously roasted arabica and Turkish beans, but also chocolate and cooling sorbets flavored with lemons or roses. The Trenci's biggest sellers were beer, vodka and 'Riga balm,' a highly alcoholic herbal liquor that was delicious with or without coffee. According to the Latvians, who favored using it in their coffee (as well as to Jossel Aszer who had sold bottles of it in Lahkvna), the drink had proven medicinal qualities. Rodak drank Riga Balm Coffee, but Zalaman, after one mandatory drink to celebrate partisan-hood and one more to remember Stanko, not wanting to jeopardize his meeting with Dr. Prokopovics, stuck to non-alcoholic drinks.

Rodak wanted to enroll Zalaman in his efforts to spread the gospel of anarchism. He was in demand from workers' rights groups everywhere but Germany. And he had just discovered that in Germany, Bismark's Anti-Socialist law had been passed, meaning his exile would have to be extended.

Zalaman was so overcome with positive emotions over being with an old friend—the comrade-in-arms whose lead he'd felt compelled to follow when fighting Cossacks but whose current endeavors he could allow himself to follow freely—he would be able to free himself from the beast of burden work in the Maskevas. To that end, Rodak thought his friend's meeting with Prokopovics was propitious. Both Maria and Eriks were good social democrats and those types sometimes supported Individualist causes.

"This Dr. Prokopovics, if he likes you," Rodak said, "he could help your situation. I'd like to meet him myself, once you get things settled. He seems kind of a mysterious character."

"A 'philologist' she called him."

"Yes, a true wonder—an anarchist with a job."

"I don't think he's an anarchist. Philology is a trade?"

"Well, it's a discipline in the academy, in the universities. They study language, I think. Reading and writing. Don't ask me to explain! Ask Prokopovics. Maria Kronopnicka now, I find she's an organizer, a fundraiser, yes, a major contributor. A voice."

When asked about Navharadak and Lahkvna, Rodak said that when he and Stanko had returned to Navharadak, they found considerable remorse over Lahkkvna, but even more fear of reprisal for trying to take action to bring the perpetrators to justice. The *kahal* no longer existed and the Navharadak Council of Elders, who are still taking their marching orders from the Russians, condemned the guilty but didn't name them and didn't punish them, so to what they had been condemned was unclear.

Certainly, Linards and his fellows in the DPPO continued their lives and professions with impunity, except for the bomb-builder Ingatz Abramowics—"

"Not Ignatz Abramowics the shopkeeper!"

"One and the same. A story for another time. A couple of the cowards left town, a few died of mysterious causes. Stanko and I took care of the rest." Zalaman closed his eyes and thanked him. He was thanking him for all the dead of Lahkvna. Rodak apologized again for the Christians of Navharadak. Zalaman told him he was glad, with apologies to Rosa, that Rodak found himself stranded in Riga where he could see more of his old friend, and he would do whatever he could for the cause.

"I think you never know if a woman is really waiting for you. I hope she is."

"I hope she's no Katya. That's *my* story for another time."

Chapter Twenty

Dr. Prokopovics

He searched the streets of inner Riga for Dr. Prokopovics. The area was no longer the confusing maze it had been when he'd arrived. The professor's apartment wasn't far from the site of his original experience with the *khat* seller and the Young Latvians. But after repeatedly pulling the bell without getting a response, he decided to try the second address on Maria's card.

That address took him to the Riga Technical University where he entered the looming building that housed the University and proceeded down endless dark hallways, its doorways closed but for an open laboratory or theatre where students were engaged in their studies.

When he finally arrived at the right office number, his knock elicited no response, but an interior light leaked from under the door into the corridor and he heard a squeak from inside like you might hear if a chair was moved. He asked if Dr. Eriks Prokopovics was there and the answer was "No. Sorry, I just don't have time to meet with students today."

Zalaman said the magic words—"Maria Konopnicka." The chair squeaked again, and the door opened to reveal an exuberant professor who's welcome and demeanor contrasted vividly with the dismal building he inhabited. The man introduced himself as Dr. Eriks Prokopovics and shook Zalaman's hand. He was very well-dressed for a professor, Zalaman thought, although he truly had not had much experience with doctors outside of Bebchuk. Dr. Prokopovics was an older man of about fifty who would, nevertheless, have been considered the height of fashion in the Trenci, and he completed the image with emphatic, but not flamboyant gestures to emphasize a point, along with a monocle and a most original mustache, its well-waxed tips sticking slightly upward.

Eriks had somehow already received a post from Maria K. about Zalaman. A letter which included a second letter addressed to Zalaman himself. He immediately ushered Zalaman out of the dreary university building to a park that was the other end of the Bastejkalns, where the political rally had been held. Dr. Prokopovics said he was sorry he'd missed that rally, but at the time he'd been out of the country.

They sat down at a table in the park and were served coffee by a waiter in a long striped apron with a serviette neatly draped over his forearm. Any forebodings Zalaman felt in the university building, dissipated. He felt like he was on the right track toward a more bountiful and sophisticated life, one that might make him more respectable and stronger and thus able to return to Lahkvna. And yet, despite this positive feeling, despite the fresh Baltic air, he was just a bit uncomfortable when the professor handed him the envelope from Maria.

"She wanted you to read this before we talked."

Zalaman nodded his approval and started reading—some to himself, some out loud to Dr. Prokopovics. "She is well and hopes we, too are enjoying good health"—*and hopes that I think fondly of her as she does me*—"can't say when I'll be back in Riga as there is much work in Warsaw." *Doesn't specify what the work is. She advises I take whatever Dr. P has to offer as my improved financial situation will make it possible for me to buy a railroad ticket to Warsaw.* "OK, I will let you know why I'm busy.

"*In the Mountains* has put me in demand for speaking engagements and for writing essays and still, all the while, I must keep writing poetry and, thankfully, the poetry is what people seem to be most interested in. Oh, and how could I forget, there is the raising of six children, quite a task, but a job which I have somehow managed to relegate to a minor distraction, because my greater responsibility is to my public work, to the rights of children as well as those of women." *If it wasn't for all these things, she would be with me in Riga now.*

Zalaman didn't read these last lines out loud, but Dr. Prokopovics couldn't fail to notice the smile they provoked.

He looked up at Dr. Prokopovics who was smiling just like Zalaman. He thanked Dr. Prokopovics for the letter.

"You know very little about me, rebbe Aszer, I know. I would expect Maria to leave all the explaining to me—she'd know that's the way I want it. I teach philology to incompetent and undeserving but earnest students at Riga Technical. Riga Technical is nominally and theoretically a 'technical' university, so I am the only resident philologist on the faculty. *And* I am on the faculty of Columbia College in New York City in America." In fact, Dr. P. was uncertain whether he was still on the faculty of Columbia given the political turmoil in the United States that had recently forced him out of that country. It sounded unlikely to Zalaman—teaching in two different parts of the world at the same time, but the professor told Zalaman he was operating under an outdated assumption. Travel to America was no longer burdensome. "It takes me only ten days using two steamships, even with the transfer from England." Arrangements with both schools allowed him to take alternate semesters off, so he only had to make the trip twice a year, although he'd become very fond of those trips and "steamships like big beasts."

"When my father said someone was 'Going to America,' it mean"t he was crazy—like his best friend Heri Benowitz who left his wife and family for America after reading *Randall the Trapper.*"

"Haven't run into many trappers at Columbia. I am a native of Riga, and I find it enlightening to juxtapose visits to the old world and the new. That life has been postponed for a time being by the political climate in America, but with the new Arthur administration wanting to open things up, someday in the future I will no longer be *persona non grata*. I made the mistake of translating some anarchist tracts into English while at Columbia and the works were eventually determined to be subversive by the US government.

"As far as we, as far as you and I are concerned, Zalaman, I should explain that Maria knew I was looking for an assistant—life experience and flexibility are more important than academic experience and degrees. I know from Maria's letter to me only that you recently arrived from Odessa and Kiev and Vilna, but by your accent, and although I notice certain anomalies—language and pronunciation are a specialty of mine—you are Jewish and from the Kurland."

"Very good. It's a long story, I'm afraid. Some of those 'anomalies' might be the result of traveling from *shtetl* to *shtetl* when I was growing up, listening to many languages, learning to be adaptable. Surviving the challenges of being kidnapped, fighting Cossacks, getting arrested, starving, watching your entire family and friends murdered before your eyes. That's my education. I've learned to be flexible. If that can be helpful to you."

"Aside from the murders, you almost sound like you've enjoyed the rest."

"In Vilna, before coming to Riga, I came to realize that after you go through the darkest valley, the sunny peaks look even brighter." He told the professor about Lahkvna. Dr. Prokopovics listened, appalled, silent for a while after Zalaman finished. The professor expressed his sympathy and his understanding of how inadequate such expressions were.

He twisted his mustache's tips and pursed his lips, "Worse yet, these atrocities are proliferating. So, what can I do for you? Maria thinks you are a young man with a future, notwithstanding your past. I don't know how she can say such a thing with so much confidence, since the two of you spent such a short time together. From the look of you, perhaps she is smitten. Now, Maria is not a loose woman—though what do I know about that aspect of her actual life?—but she foments a lot of gossip. Her reformist political activities make her enemies, and her poetry is often . . . suggestive.

"She's very open-minded—certainly does not deny her sexuality, although some have suggested she prefers women. On top of that there's the unfortunate business with that husband of hers—Jaroslav. It's an impossible marriage. A male companion such as yourself might be just what she needs. She claims you are well read and that's a hard enough commodity to find, even among the students at the technical school. Would you like to walk?"

They walked through the park. At the professor's prompting, Zalaman told him what he'd thought of the rally. Dr. Prokopovics was a proponent of social democracy, and was interested, as a student and translator, in anarchism. He corrected Zalaman regarding his interpretation of certain issues but was generally impressed with the attempt to grapple with them. Should property be regarded as theft? Perhaps.

"I'm tempted to give it a try," the professor smiled cryptically. "Not really. Look, it's short notice, I know, but the truth is, I could use your help. As Maria knows, I recently lost my assistant, if you're interested, I'd be willing to give you a try at it for a week . . . see how we get along."

Zalaman accepted the offer, his heart racing. This wasn't like Edil, the peddler, offering to let him fill the position opened by his nephew's departure for the Holy Land. Dr. Prokopovics represented a new world for Zalaman, a world of which his mother would approve. Whether he should have been or not, he was not worried about his ability to get along with the professor. He was to have the previous assistant's room for at least the trial week, which meant he would be living in that same splendid house in his favorite part of the city where just earlier this morning he'd been knocking at the door. If he passed the trial-week, he'd get the room and board plus a "salary of some sort" for helping the professor do whatever the professor needed. Eriks hoped that if Zalaman stayed past the month he might assist in some Yiddish translation work he needed some help with, but, for now, there was cleaning, helping organize the professor's work, maybe some cooking?

> <

He left to gather his things from Maskevas and the next morning hauled them into the city in the cart he'd been using to haul rocks and dirt. He had some time to kill before he was expected at Dr. Prokopovics', so he stopped at a coffee shop and read the title piece from *In the Mountains*. He wasn't sure what to make of it, politically or romantically, but she was very good at painting a scene with words that brought back the oaks, meadows, and rivers of his life. He promised himself to read more as soon as he could.

Dr. P's building was a towering, four-story 'Neo Classical'—the largest building on the street. Prokopovics' apartments took up the two bottom floors, with storage space on the third, although the bulk of the third and fourth floors was inhabited by two large Polytechnicum faculty families, which included two nannies and a dozen tightly-controlled children. The 'maid's room,' temporarily Zalaman's, was on the second floor. It was small and low with Erik's extra storage space directly overhead. Zalaman could stand upright on one side when the bed was tucked into the corner under the lowest part of the ceiling. It would not pay to jump out of bed in the morning. But he stood, transfixed with happiness and relief when he saw it. He had a roof. Helping organize Erik's work was another story, requiring some minimal familiarity with the professor's work. Zalaman went about acquiring it. He surprised Eriks with the originality of his suggestions. He looked at the works, mostly political tracts and manifestoes, that the professor thought he might translate into Yiddish. He looked at some of the professor's own translations. He couldn't read the Russian, but he made progress with the Polish and German.

During the day, the professor was frequently out, teaching and meeting with students, and almost every evening, he was out—with colleagues and friends, he told Zalaman. He rarely brought anyone to his apartment. Days when he did not go to the Technicum or meet with students elsewhere, he would sit in his study in front of his massive writing desk with its numerous large and small compartments and partitioned recesses with their own little clasps and locks. He would position himself at that desk—perched on a stool,"to maintain my posture," he said—reading, writing, pacing, walking over to a long table that abutted his desk, covered with piles of velum, consulting some information, then back to his desk again, jotting down notes, then up and more pacing. He reminded Zalaman of the constant pacing of the rebbe in the Lahkvna *shul* he'd so rarely attended.

On the next-to-last day of his trial week, Eriks said he was impressed with Zalaman's work and gave him part of the afternoon off. He wandered the city parks and broad avenues, happy to be outside. He found Rodak and got him to walk with him. They discussed Dr. Prokopovics. Rodak was not surprised the doctor was unwanted in the USA, but thought that could change, comparing President Garfield to Bismarck. But they mostly compared attacking Cossacks and attacking the state—a discussion that involved a comparison of rifles and bombs. They debated and reminisced and the time went so fast, it didn't seem possible that Zalaman's free half-day off was over so soon.

><

He passed the one-week test and as the weeks progressed and turned into months, the more interesting and diverse the work became, the more accustomed he and Eriks became to one another. Eriks' food suggestions broadened Zalaman's diet and cooking skills like the translation work was broadening other horizons. Eriks had theories about everything, and it was no different with food—from cherries and artichokes to herring and cod. They shared a passion for bread from Nomentu and coffee beans from the Trenci.

The professor was still out most nights, but on the odd nights he stayed home, they shared stories about their lives. Eriks was a good storyteller and Zalaman guessed this talent would make a successful professor. He knew how to be dramatic, how to tell a story, even if the stories were about people Zalaman hadn't heard of before—Eriks' colleagues in Riga and New York. Eriks had no female colleagues. Maria was the only female he ever talked about, and her name came up frequently when they discussed politics and social conditions in Riga.

She came to Riga to work with Eriks and see Zalaman and consummated, so she thought, both projects satisfactorily. Zalaman was relieved to find she didn't prefer women sexually, or, if she did . . . well, it certainly didn't seem to interfere. He was excited by her animal exuberance in bed. The sex compared favorably with what he'd enjoyed with Katya and Lechsi, but with Maria it was more exciting, perhaps because of the way her unrestrained sensuality in bed contrasted with her normally staid, buttoned-up self. He might have worried that Eriks would overhear her cries and his if the professor had been home in the evenings. Fortunately, Eriks was out at night when she was there at his house, practically lodging in Zalaman's room.

After one particularly strenuous and successfully explosive bout with Zalaman, she asked if he ever wondered where Eriks went at night. She said it with an inflection that made him hesitate before answering that Eriks went out to meet with students or other faculty. She asked Zalaman if he'd heard of the *Przyprawa*, a saloon favored by men who like other men. Zalaman laughed because trying to picture Eriks with another man was too ludicrous, but then, it wasn't at all—that's when he laughed at himself as a naive *shtetl* bumpkin. "I didn't say Eriks was at the

Przyprawa," she said. "Someone—a person who was admittedly never a source of reliable information—once told me he saw him there. But you never know. People have accused *me* of having affairs with women." They regarded one another, but Zalaman didn't ask her to reply to those accusations because it didn't seem to matter. The places she was kissing him made it obvious she was ready for more lovemaking. In the daytime, Maria and Eriks compared translation work—politics and social movements—and sometimes enlisted Zalaman's help. He enjoyed this work most of all, learning the nuances of fidelity over beauty when translating and earning extra for his efforts. When Eriks went out in the evening, wherever it was he was going, Maria and Zalaman raced to Zalaman's little bedroom. At the end of her first trip to visit Zalaman, on her last night in Riga, the three of them decided to go to the Trenci where Zalaman was to finally introduce them to Rodak, who had insisted Zalaman do so.

Over the months and the next few years, Zalaman was busy saving his money. He had very few expenses and he was getting better at translation. In the daytime, when Eriks was not away at the Polytechnicum, they often worked together closely. Zalaman saw no indication of Eriks having any romantic feelings toward him so, he dismissed that mystery. His friend and employer seemed interested solely in words, especially those with political, social, or moral intent. Zalaman felt he had saved enough to splurge on two occasions and buy a railroad ticket to Warsaw. Whenever Maria came to Riga, the foursome would reconvene at the Trenci. One of the frequent topics of discussion were the incendiary writings of Johann Most. Eriks and Maria had translated many of Most's manifestos and were naturally interested in Rodak's search for the man, a search which took him twice to England without success. Most was certainly in America, Rodak said, probably New York. He announced more than once that he would be traveling there, inviting them to come along. Maria laughed. She would have loved to join 'Roman' in throwing a bomb or two for Most, but she had her children and other commitments. It was equally out of the question for Eriks, who had his own commitments and was waiting to hear from Columbia College. Zalaman had two commitments: Maria and Eriks, so he would stay put.

The long-awaited letter from Columbia College arrived, confirming what they'd been hearing about political change in America. The Arthur administration had relaxed the political climate and Dr. Prokopovics was no longer *persona non grata*. Columbia was asking him back to teach the next term. He told Zalaman he should consider coming with him. He could use his same talents there, pay for the voyage, provide English lessons. Zalaman was tempted. Rodak threatened to come with them. Maria, reluctantly, thought he owed it to himself to go, to get away from the stench of Lahkvna or, rather, Navharadak. Maria was a philosemite, who, like her friend Nietzsche referred to herself as 'an anti-anti-semite.' The slaughter in the *shtetl* that Zalaman had painted in his own words had made her cry and become a touchstone in her current writing. She told Zalaman that if he went, she hoped he wouldn't stay away forever.

But Zalaman couldn't leave—at least not before he returned to Lahkvna, the short journey he'd constantly put off during his few years in Riga. He owed it not only to his family to visit their graves, but to himself. And then a letter arrived from Odessa addressed to him care of General Mail, Riga. When he opened it he found inside another envelope, unopened, this one addressed to him in Odessa, postmarked Palestine, along with a curt note attached: "for you, Royt." Zalaman ripped it apart, thinking it was a message from Davin. It wasn't—yet it was. Edil had written to him. It was a greeting, a description of the Holy Land and his journey there. But it was chiefly about "*a strange encounter*" when Edil had been visiting a village outside Jerusalem and spoke with a man who claimed to have met a man 'Davin' from the unfortunate *shtetl* of Lahkvna, but who claimed to have been sold by a priest to a shipowner and had subsequently jumped ship and washed up in the Holy Land. Though he couldn't vouch for the man's veracity, Edil felt compelled to try to get this information to Zalaman. He didn't think such a thing was impossible, but he gave it little credence, especially the Lahkvna part, suspecting the man of sinister intent: "Perhaps a person who profits through exploiting the misfortunes of others." Zalaman wondered if he could be guilty of this. At the end of the letter, he wrote that he would look into it for Zalaman, who he hoped was well and prospering in Odessa—where he assumed Zalaman was still residing. Edil wrote that he believed he had done the right thing to move to Jerusalem and that Zalaman should join him there before it was too late. He had grown old and his legs no longer worked as they were supposed to.

Zalaman read the letter twice. All the invitations to travel he was getting these days! Edil's brief history of his journey to the Holy Land spurred his inclination to go somewhere new, while he was still young enough at 33 to do so. For Zalaman, the story about his brother was a very slender thread. America held much more interest and potential than the Holy Land. But he couldn't go anywhere yet.

CHAPTER TWENTY-ONE

Return Again

Sorrow is what is left after the rage has gone. That is what Zalaman felt when he arrived at the Lahkvna *kvadrat*—now a memorial and cemetery.

He'd written in advance to Minya Benowitz to announce his coming, as had Rodak to Elizavetta Bartos. He and Rodak had taken the Kuldiga Express from Riga. On the train, Rodak told Zalaman the story of Ignatz Abramowitz, the Lahkvna shopkeeper who, with encouragement and advice from Rodak, had become an excellent maker of Orsini bombs—"so easy, the small casing, then setting in the pins that detonate the powder when the grenade contacts whatever happens to be the first object in its path"—and was responsible for the death of more than one member of the Easter mob. As they neared Kuldiga, Zalaman, thinking of the ten days this trip had once taken, marveled at the way the railroad was making the world so much smaller. Yet amid all this progress, people—from Serbia to the Ottoman Empire, South Africa to England, Italians, French, Belgians Egyptians . . . —were still slaughtering one another.

For the remainder of the trip, from Kuldiga to Navharadak/ Lahkvna, they hired horses, riding together for the first time in years, Zalaman smoking *khat* and reminiscing with Rodak about Stanko.

They passed the spot where the *Weg Heim* had gotten stuck in the snow when he'd been about ten years old and he and Davin and Keila were returning to Lahkvna with Mama and Papa after a long absence, vowing to settle there permanently—as they had until the world tore them apart. Zalaman slowed his horse so he could gaze at a field where he'd once ridden with Davin, both on Marengo, racing back toward Lahkvna after an aborted running away from home. Then the twin towers of Navharadak where, as children, Rodak and Stanko had battled the opposing little Cossacks for control of their domain. Passing through the Christian town to get to the *shtetl*, Zalaman rode along with Rodak to Pane Bartos' house, where, anxious to get to Lahkvna while there was still light, he said goodbye to Rodak and promised to come by and pay him and Elizavetta a visit the following day.

Once he'd left Rodak, Zalaman continued through the streets of Navharadak. The last time he'd been down the street where the Trade Commissioner's mansion was—red-haired Hadar's house sixteen years ago—he'd been fleeing the loss of everything; his one thought had been, *Get away from here*! He'd experienced the strangest sensations, stumbling away from Lahkvna having lost everything he cared about in his life, because he'd witnessed how, just a stone's throw away in Navharadak, there were people going about their normal lives. It had seemed so grotesque, the feeling returned now as the merchants started setting out their gaily burning kerosene lamps. As he passed Hadar's house, he imagined he saw a flash of red hair in one window and shook his head and smiled, impressed by the power of his imagination.

He'd been driven by one thought: Get away! But even then, some part of him knew he'd be back. The bodies were there. Their bodies. When he rode past the stone wall that demarcated the *shtetl* from Navharadak, Zalaman was glad it would be darker soon. He didn't want to see any people until he was ready to see them. Not that he would be recognized after all these years, but the *shtetl* was small and people were curious about strangers. Even more so these days, or so he thought, but the men and women he passed on the street kept their heads down. He saw no children.

The old *kvadrat* was surrounded by a ring of vibrant young trees, soaring birch, and spruce, throwing long shadows over the memorial gravestones. Since Zalaman had left some of these had been improved upon with cement markers, some were unchiseled stone, like his family's. He'd heard about this forest of the dead from Rodak, but it was still a shock to Zalaman for whom it seemed such an abrupt transformation. The young trees were thriving in their bloody soil. Judging from the height and the spread of their branches and the way their roots had already cobbled up the *kvadrat*'s surface, the trees had been planted soon after the massacre. Some of the gravesites were well-tended, remembrance pebbles piled on top of gravestones by whoever remained. But Zalaman found it disorienting with the trees hiding the buildings that he was accustomed to seeing around the square, like the Benowitz' butcher shop. The *kvadrat* itself had become more like a wood, the natural world having moved back into the heart of Lahkvna. There was certainly a new *kvadrat* somewhere, offering space for the peddling of vegetables and spreading of gossip.

He tied his horse to a birch and walked over to the gravesite. He passed the graves of his friends Ev and Aron, their gravesites especially well-tended. He read their names out loud—"Mama, Papa, Keila"—out loud, as he'd scratched them into the stone.

"It's me. Zalaman," he said, wiping away a few tears but then broke down and sobbed unreservedly. He would never stay away so long again. But he also told them that despite having left he'd often felt very near to them, sometimes like they were inside his head. He hoped they weren't aware of everything he'd done.

That thought made him smile despite himself, and he lay down on his back beside the graves and looked up. The new trees were rustling, flailing silver-green leaves in the fading light. On that long ago Easter, after the killing, he'd awakened right around here after being hit on his head and had mistaken the limbs of the dead for broken tree branches. The leaves' susurrus was like whispers from the dead.

He stood, brushed off the soil, and took out his pocketknife then knelt and etched in the dates of birth, as he could remember them, under JOSSEL, LAEL, KEILA ASZER. There was only one date of death. He let the breeze wash over him.

He left the graveyard and untied his horse and walked with it through dark streets lit here and there by kerosene lanterns. It was getting harder to see, but there was his old house. A bit more slant to it, but he couldn't tell which direction it was sinking because the dimming light was playing tricks. But the house still stood. There was a flickering light coming from inside, exposing the tenants as they moved about. Was he watching the shadows of housebreakers? Opportunists in need of shelter? Perhaps they were worthy inheritors. He imagined knocking on the door and introducing himself but couldn't bring himself to do it.

He turned and walked his horse back to the Benowitz' butcher shop where a desecrated Doozy Kurtsak guarded the door. She'd been reduced from the giant chicken, who in better times had welcomed guests, advertised specials, and frightened small children, to a post with a chicken head, her red- and gold-painted body the victim of either anti-Jewish or anti-poultry sentiments. But she was still there. Like the butcher shop itself and the Benowitzes. He banged on the heavy wooden door. An upstairs curtain parted and Minya Benowitz' face appeared in the second-floor window. She smiled down at him and then disappeared to open the door.

JERUSALEM

Edil needed no other reassurances. He immediately saw the family resemblance and so the considerable lengths he'd gone to—traversing the streets of Jerusalem on his failing legs, searching for his brother as he'd promised Zalaman he would—had all been worth it. Davin had explained to Edil how he'd been chappered by two false monks, the same who had distracted his father, allowing Georg to snatch Zalaman. The monks had eventually reasoned that selling Davin to the Russian army might be risky, so they sold him to a wealthy peasant instead. The peasant next sold him to a ship owner. After years aboard various ships, the ship's master relaxed his vigilance and Davin jumped ship when it docked at Haifa. In doing so, he fulfilled a lifelong dream to see the Holy Land where he'd since made a life for himself. Edil, in turn, told Davin about his life with Zalaman, the brother Davin had at first assumed was as good as dead, the result of serving in the Tsar's army, but he'd also seen the half-buried body of Zalaman's captor and couldn't stop wondering. Then, years after the fact, he'd heard about the massacre in Lahkvna. He was still grieving but he'd given up hope. Edil and Davin decided right then, they would write to Zalaman, how they would look forward to seeing him in Jerusalem. Surely, they agreed, he'd come to see his only remaining family.

Acknowledgements

This book was a labor of several years. The work was frequently enhanced by the criticism and encouragement of others. I wish to acknowledge their efforts over the course of many drafts.

Thank you:

Alice Rose George, an early reader, a creative editor, as well as life partner and Muse;

Peter Clothier, a mentor, a friend, my authority on character and story—always with his close reading but his eye on the big picture;

Rick Friedberg, a friend and writer with wise advice;

Moira Hodgson, writer, essayist, critic and comfort;

David Belson, my brother, ally, and persevering reader of multiple drafts;

Katherine Kreilkamp, a generous though meticulous but tolerant copy editor who didn't have to do it, but did;

Cora Spencer, as well, a generous and meticulous copy editor who went far beyond that role;

Bill Jersey, a master documentarian and dear friend whose belief in me encouraged the completion of this project;

Jeff Schlesinger and his team at Barringer Publishing for their insights and guidance in shaping this novel and, above all;

Johanna Belson, my daughter, for her insight and inspiration—a promotor who read every draft (God forgive me).

Printed in the USA
CPSIA information can be obtained
at www.ICGtesting.com
LVHW041202310124
770460LV00065B/1495

9 781954 396524